ANNIHILATION

Alien Invasion Book Four

—————————————————

AVERY BLAKE
JOHNNY B. TRUANT

STERLING & STONE

To YOU, the reader.
Thank you for taking a chance on us.
Thank you for your support.
Thank you for the emails.
Thank you for the reviews.
Thank you for reading and joining us on this road.

ANNIHILATION

ANNIHILATION

Chapter One

PIPER DEMPSEY WATCHED Cameron step out from behind the rock outcropping, unsure of why exactly his body language made her certain he wanted to die.

"Stay low, Cameron," Andreus whispered.

Instead of ducking like the others, Cameron moved forward. Into the gap between rocks, in full view of the massive silver sphere. He may as well have been hands to hips like a gunslinger.

"Cameron," Charlie said.

"It knows we're here either way," Cameron replied without turning. "What's the point in hiding, Charlie?"

As if the words were his cue, Cameron climbed to the rock's top. Piper, not trusting herself to speak, could only watch him do it. She watched him clamber. She watched his feet miss and drag dry lines along the rock's side. She listened, wincing, as a scree of loose stone fell to the ground with a clatter.

She thought Cameron might stand. Instead, he sat on the rock as if watching a sunset, in full view of the mothership.

Piper finally found her voice. She reached up and took his wrist, tugging. But really, what did she think she would do? Drag him off, give him a concussion against the hot, baked ground?

"It's going to see us."

"It can already see us."

Jeanine piped up. "We haven't seen any shuttles since leaving the Mormon archive."

Instead of striking Cameron as a sensible rebuttal, it must have hit him as fighting words. He'd been eerily silent through the trip. She wasn't sure if the hard look in his eyes, on his usually boyish, recently older face, was an improvement or something worse.

"You're right," he snapped. "We *haven't* seen any shuttles. No motherships. No Reptars slinking around the rocks after us … or maybe they'd put their safeties back on, and we'd get to watch a bunch of smiling Titans following like drones? They could get on tiny motorcycles then follow the RV. That'd be funny, wouldn't it? They'd look like those famous fat twins on their bikes. Alien comedy at its best."

Now Andreus looked angry. He'd been wearing a damp rag on his head since they'd left the RV in one of the few places with overhead cover a few miles back. Piper kept wanting to make babushka jokes, but she couldn't quite manage. The man might be firmly on their side now, but he was still terrifying.

It would probably get worse. Piper was sure the warlord's daughter was as dead as Cameron's father and her own stepson, but right now his anger seemed blunted by hope. He'd be terrible once that was gone.

"Get the fuck off that rock," Andreus said. "You'll blow our cover."

Cameron looked at Andreus with a fight in his eyes.

The look, from the once-thoughtful and always-smiling man she'd loved, was awful.

Cameron's jaw worked. He glanced toward the mothership parked over the Moab ranch. The ground was scorched and seemed to have taken at least one blast from an energy weapon, but much of what was once there seemed to be standing. Why, Piper had no idea.

Cameron backed up, stood, and raised his arms overhead, facing the ship.

"Hey, you!" he shouted in the thin desert air. "Hey! We're over here, you motherfuckers!"

Piper was sure Andreus would tackle him, but Coffey acted first. She was simple but effective. She grabbed both ankles and pulled. Cameron fell on his ass, his body bending him in the middle to keep his head from striking the rock. Coffey couldn't have known for certain it would work. She might've figured he'd end up quiet or dead, and either would be an improvement.

With Cameron unbalanced, Coffey dragged him down. A second later, he was in a jumble against the rock's foot, his face full of frustration and stewing emotion. To Piper, it all seemed to be on one end of the spectrum: anger, desperation, maybe self-destruction. He'd done selfless, but he was through. And he'd done surviving, but it seemed like Cameron was finished with that, too.

Andreus and Coffey stood over him. Charlie came to Piper's side and, shocking her, took hold of her arm in a way that was almost comforting, almost human.

Piper thought a fight might erupt, but Cameron only shook his head, looking at the dust, clearly sad. They'd all shed their tears in the three days it had taken to find a way back here — on foot, then right out in the goddamned open in the solar RV that the Astrals had conveniently left behind. Cameron — and unbelievably, even Charlie —

had come from moments of privacy with red eyes. Piper had cried the most, and openly. But it wasn't loss she saw on Cameron's face now. It was something worse.

"They let us go," he said. "They almost killed us back at Little Cottonwood, but then they had their time to cool off, and now they're just watching again. They won't hurt us. No matter what we do, we're free to be slaves."

"We don't know that," Andreus said.

Cameron's eyes went to the warlord then to Charlie before they settled on Piper. When he spoke, Piper assumed his words were meant for Andreus. But he stared right at her, eye to eye.

"We know," he said, "and now we're in hell."

Chapter Two

NATHAN ANDREUS WANTED to punch Cameron in the face. Not just to shut him up, either, though there was that. Mostly, he needed someone to hurt, and this group of five was all he had. Because about that, Cameron was right: There had been no Astrals since they'd left Cottonwood. Their absence had seemed lucky. But now, looking at Cameron, Andreus had to admit he'd always seen it as convenient as well.

"We stop whining," Andreus said, "and we start finding solutions."

"Just walk up there," Cameron said, standing, seeming to make an effort to pull his little tantrum together. He tossed his chin toward the half-destroyed cliffside lab, the ranch house remains sticking their burned members into the sky like black bones. "That's your solution. Just walk right on up."

"There's no cover," said Charlie.

Andreus winced. He was trying to defuse Cameron rather than fuel him. But Charlie had teed him up.

"We don't need cover, Charlie. They want us to go in there."

"We've already done this," Andreus said. "The part where we pretend they can see us and act accordingly."

"We weren't pretending then, and we're not pretending now."

"You saw how they came after us. They wanted your satchel." He nodded to the bag hanging against Cameron's side, indicating the plate with its keylike ridges inside. The device, if the late Benjamin Bannister had been correct, was a key to the Thor's Hammer weapon.

"Then what?"

Cameron shook his head then turned toward Piper, finding the group's easiest audience. Andreus had been trying to keep his eyes forward since they'd left Cotton-wood, choosing to believe they'd find something in Moab worth saving. That Grace was still alive out there some-where, against all odds, and that he was still a father despite his recent role as widower. But Nathan had to admit that Piper, at times, had been one of the group's most determined. They were a pair, same as he and Jeanine. Charlie was the odd man out, and sometimes it felt like they were two teams fighting for the man like a swing vote.

"Then what were they supposed to do?" Cameron repeated, facing Piper, eyeing the others. "If they'd taken the plate from my satchel, what would they have done next?"

"Used it," Coffey said.

"Where?" Cameron met Nathan's eyes, challenging him in a way nobody challenged Nathan Fucking Andreus. "Where would they go to use it? Dad says the Templars took Thor's Hammer and hid it. They took this key," he slapped the satchel, "and hid *it*, too, like removing the core

6

from a nuke. So let's say they caught us back there. What would they have done with the key? Thor's Hammer is still lost." His jaw shifted to the side, biting crosswise, eyes half-lidded. "I just keep coming back to the fact that once upon a time, someone pulled a fast one on the Astrals. And that all we're doing, by keeping up this chase, is helping them find it."

"We're finding it to deactivate it," Charlie said, his tone still neutral, drier than toast.

Cameron leaned against the rock, his eyes wanting to close. When he spoke again, he sounded as spent as they all felt.

"We should just give up."

Nathan's eyes flicked to Piper, expecting her to protest, to feed into his self-pity. But she stayed put, newly hardened by Trevor's death, along with all the others.

"It's lost," Cameron continued. "They don't know where to find it. If my father was still alive, it might make sense to go after it. Maybe we could have pulled another switcharoo and reached the thing with enough time to destroy it, but all we'll do now is lead them right to it. We'll see where they've been hiding, then we can stop pretending we're alone, or ever have been."

Cameron shook his head, finally addressing Andreus with more logic than emotion.

"Nathan. You sent Tarantula into Heaven's Veil to pick us up after watching me walk through the gates on satellite." He looked at Coffey, knowing she'd have seen the same. "You're a communications guy. I know you're smart. But are you really that sure you ever outsmarted them? We made that mistake once, and what happened? It turned out that what we were *getting away with* was something they wanted all along."

Cameron's head bent skyward. At the right angles, they

couldn't see the mothership above the Moab facility, and might have believed they were alone.

"The network is down. But maybe it's only for us. You know what our satellites can see from space. So what do you think *they* can see?"

Nathan looked into the endless Utah sky. He could almost feel alien eyes upon him. He resisted the urge to pull his signal detector from its pouch. He knew it was on and that if there'd been an Astral BB following them through this part of the trip, he'd have heard the detector alarm. But they didn't necessarily need BBs to see what needed seeing. Not when the dumb humans crossed open land. Not when they circled to recover recreational vehicles they'd left behind before a raid, trying to fool themselves into believing they were fortunate to find them.

"So what should we do, Cameron?" Nathan said, not really asking for an answer. "If you've got it all figured out, what's our next move?"

"Partner up," said a voice.

Andreus knew it was Charlie, Benjamin's longtime right hand, before turning to look, but hearing him now seemed so out of place. While Piper and Cameron had dealt grimly with their losses, Charlie had taken his like a mannequin. He'd known Benjamin almost as long as Cameron had — or maybe, Nathan now thought, longer. But the way Charlie acted, his best friend might merely be behind a bush, taking a piss, soon to return.

"They think we'll find Thor's Hammer," Charlie said. "So let's stop playing games and do it."

Chapter Three

THIS WAS A TERRIBLE IDEA.

Behind Cameron, Piper's presence was more assuring than it should be. They were both bent around a rock, hiding in what seemed to be plain sight.

On one hand, the idea of walking right up to the lab as Charlie had suggested was appealing. Either he was right and the mothership would let them go, or Charlie was wrong and they'd be incinerated. Either way was honestly fine with Cameron. He'd been hiding for over two years now, awaiting death for most of them. Certainty would be a blessing.

On the other hand, doing so felt like a betrayal of Benjamin's life. All of those years spent wandering, the broken marriage to Cameron's mother at the hands of obsession, all that time spent researching, analyzing, hoping — it would all be wasted if Cameron made the wrong choice now. And walking right out under a mothership, appealing as it was, felt like the wrong choice no matter how much logic Charlie applied. It was spitting in

Benjamin's eye, tossing out the single advantage Benjamin had earned them at the cost of one human lifetime.

"They're not all powerful," Piper said behind him. "They can't look everywhere at once."

She'd told him about her chats with the Rational Monks during their long, slow, disconnected trip back to Moab, hoping to scavenge whatever evidence might remain. Cameron believed it all: not just the fidelity of Piper as a source, but the monks' words as well. Humanity really had stymied their overlords this time around. The Internet really had confused them; Cameron had seen as much in the way the shuttles and BBs had puzzled over the fiber cables and the infectious curiosity he'd felt from them over Terrence's Canned Heat virus. They really had tricked the tiny surveillance droid that had nearly blown the group's Cottonwood plan before they did it themselves. They really had forced the Astrals' hands in the end; allowing human eyes to see them shift shapes struck Cameron as a move of desperation, not something planned or thought out logically. They *could* be fooled. As Piper said, the aliens weren't all powerful. They were advanced, of course, but not the gods that Earth's ancients had believed them to be.

"So you want to do this," Cameron said, looking at the wide-open pan between them and the lab's remains. "You really want to run over there and trust that they won't destroy us."

"They haven't destroyed us yet."

Cameron turned. Piper was dressed like the no-bullshit Jeanine Coffey, in beat-up men's jeans and an old faded tee. Her hair was in a black ponytail, but coming loose and shining with sweat. She still had her sharp bangs and those huge blue eyes. But something had changed in the woman, scraping her two years at Heaven's Veil away like dead skin to reveal what she'd become after killing Garth outside Meyer's Axis Mundi. Watching Trevor die to save her had slashed an invisible scar across Piper's pretty features that would never vanish. It made her harder than she'd been. Bolder. Bolder, in fact, than Cameron felt now.

Piper went on without waiting for Cameron to speak.

"Maybe you're right. Maybe they're watching us. Maybe it's stupid to consider that we might have gotten here unseen. But that doesn't mean we should just give up."

"If they're watching us," Cameron said, "we're making things worse. We'll show them to Thor's Hammer and sign humanity's death warrant."

Piper shrugged. "Is this so much better?"

Cameron supposed she had a point. Colonization was complete. Thor's Hammer might kill off the entire population before it could stand. But it was either that or continue to live on their knees. It made sense, but it was a dark thought coming from Piper. He'd met her as the kind of woman who'd take a spider outside her home rather than swat it. Now she was the kind who could contemplate mass extinction as a sensible option, all things considered.

Cameron glanced at the trio preparing to try for the ranch house, maybe for the money pit that had so fascinated Benjamin.

He felt the hand return to his back. He turned.

"There's something you're forgetting," she said.

"What's that?"

"They can travel through space, maybe time. They can read humanity's minds with rows of rocks. They can fly faster than the eye can see, and they can level cities."

"I'm not forgetting any of that," Cameron said grimly, knowing a punch line was coming.

"They have everything under control," she said. "But they can lose it, too."

Cameron looked at Piper, unsure how to respond, feeling a scintilla of hope for a reason he could barely understand. He'd expected a platitude that meant nothing. And this, too, *seemed* to mean nothing. But it mattered. For all the world, *it mattered.*

Cameron opened his mouth to reply. But then he saw movement in the corner of his eye and knew their time was up.

Andreus was giving the sign: *now or never.*

Chapter Four

LILA STARED OUT THE WINDOW, watching the city attempt to settle. It didn't seem to want to.

She could sympathize. Lila wasn't sure if she was angry, afraid, or some third terrible emotion. There had been a time when she'd been happy, a time when she'd been innocent, looking forward to little things like movies and time spent with friends. But those days were so far gone as to feel like another person's memories. These days, Lila was a mother whose child was closer to a sister, with a family that had been shattered like glass on tile. People kept coming and going. She'd grown used to Piper in their strange new digs (also more like a sister than a stepmother), but now she was gone, too. So was Trevor. And not long ago she'd seen her mother run across the lawn with her father, sure in a bizarre way that they were leaving as well.

Leaving her trapped with Raj.

Lila wanted to shiver. The thought made her glance at Clara, who was now sleeping peacefully. She'd been restless a while ago, following her return to the room after … after *whatever that was* up in the network center. After Raj had trussed Lila's mother and Terrence, who were supposed to be friends but seemed to have become enemies. After Dad had turned on Raj and shot him with darts to knock the asshole flat.

Then the shuttle out front. Terrence being taken away under Titan and Reptar guard. The shuttle flying high, disappearing somehow through the mothership's titanic silver belly above the Apex. Terrence maybe gone forever, just a shade from family himself.

The door opened without a knock. Lila turned to see Christopher, his dark eyes worried.

"Where's your father?"

Lila shook her head.

"When did you see him last?"

"He was running off with Mom."

"With *Heather?*"

Lila nodded. The tension in Christopher's voice was unnerving. Lila wondered if she'd been rationalizing all she'd seen and realized with horror that she probably had been. Not long after Terrence had been taken away, guards had begun to mill about, alerted but unclear on their orders. She'd seen shuttles buzz by like agitated wasps. Meyer's leaving the grounds on foot was, as Christopher seemed to imply, a bit unusual, and leaving with his ex-wife not long after his current wife had turned traitor was stranger still. Maybe they were leaving too. Soon, Lila, Clara, Raj, and Christopher would be the only people left. They could become the new viceroys, with Mo Weir as an assistant and a direct line to Divinity in the mothership overhead.

Christopher went to the window, where Lila had been a moment earlier.

"What is it, Christopher?"

"We're not being told."

"By who?"

Christopher opened the sash without answering. Lila realized how odd the city sounded. Everything was still, but the silence felt pregnant — the kind of quiet where agitation pauses in its tracks, freezing in unnatural positions. Sometime after Lila's mom and dad had left the grounds, buzz from the Astrals — both inside the house and outside in the streets — had become ... *uneasy*. There was no other word for it. They weren't precisely nervous, because they didn't seem to *get* nervous. But Lila, with echoes of the old psychic intuition she'd felt before Clara's birth and occasionally thereafter as her mother, could sense that unease coming from them all.

Something had gone wrong, and Lila hadn't wanted to ask what it was. The last time the city had seemed this unsettled, it turned out an armored tank had crashed the walls and taken Trevor and Piper away. Lila had thought them dead, and believed her mother dead as well. This felt worse. Like the city itself had taken a stake through the heart.

"Who's not talking, Christopher?" Lila repeated.

Christopher returned to full height shaking his head, sighing, frustrated.

"Take your pick. The Astrals. Captain Jons, who's now sending orders through the house like a dictator."

"How can the *human police captain* send orders through the house?"

"I don't know. Ask Mo Weir." He made a little gesture of fake recognition. "Oh, wait, no, you can't. Because Mo isn't talking either. Only Raj is talking."

"Raj!"

"Oh yes. Raj has lots to say. He's giving orders like the viceroy himself. Stuff your dad wouldn't let him do if he knew. That's why I need to find him. To shut that little motherfucker up." He looked at Clara, still sleeping, and Lila. His eyes almost seemed to apologize. Raj was Lila's husband and Clara's father, but nobody, here and now, was ready to fault Christopher for speaking his mind.

"It's fine. He *is* a little motherfucker."

Lila told Christopher the story of what she'd seen earlier, how Raj had been lording over her mother like a dictator on the prowl, and about her father's change of heart.

"Your dad shot Raj?"

"With a dart gun."

Christopher went back to the window then the door, unsettled like the falsely calm city. "That might explain it."

"What?"

"He's claiming the viceroyship, if you can believe it. As interim head, anyway. Says Meyer is *compromised*."

"Nobody will believe that." Lila almost laughed.

"The Astrals are scattered, Li. My people don't know who to listen to. Remember, Raj outranks me. Doesn't seem to matter that his position is symbolic; there's nobody around to contradict him, and everyone knows he's listed as commander, even though that's not a thing in our hierarchy. So he's taken control of the guard, sending people all over the house and grounds like chess pieces. Telling them to watch out for your father. I heard him say he was taking credit for 'having it handled' when your mom knocked him out or …" Christopher shook his head, half squinting as he continued, "or something. I don't know. I just need to find your father."

Christopher's urgency was making a nervous bubble rise inside her. It was strong intuition, bordering on foreknowledge. But Clara was the clairvoyant, not her. Her creeping sense of unease wasn't a real thing. It was Lila jumping at shadows like always.

Outside the door, down the hallway, she heard the rushing of feet. A moment later, Lila's mother burst into the room, her front dark with a thick, brick-red stain, her hair a halo of black loose ends, her makeup smeared, her face a mess. Her usual arrogance was gone. Her confidence — fake or put on — was missing. Her self-importance and sarcasm had fled. She simply spilled into the room, running on bare feet, ramming into the door frame as she turned, striking the wall, rebounding, facing her daughter with a countenance full of fear and sorrow and tears and snot.

"Mom?"

Lila's stomach dropped like an elevator. Her skin prickled with gooseflesh in an instant, her internal temperature dropping to zero.

"Lila!" She grabbed her by both upper arms, marking them with filth as if she'd spent the last hour running, crawling through the streets on hands and knees.

The room's complement doubled then tripled as uniformed men and women poured into the hallway. Their feet ceased as they saw Christopher, as their quarry stopped running and stopped in front of Lila. A few had their guns out, some raised, some still pointing. Christopher could hear high-pitched shouts from behind: Raj, seeing the chase, coming to shout his orders.

"Mom, what is it?"

Heather watched Lila for a long moment before practically crumpling — from fear, from exhaustion, from lack of breath and an overload of adrenaline. And from sadness judging by the tears streaking her face.

"It's your father," she said, too low, fighting to speak, to form coherent words with the guards settling into place behind her.

"What about Dad?"

Lila could already see what was coming. Heather began to sob, alarming her daughter, who'd never seen her mother so ruined.

"He's dead." Her eyes came up, somewhat harder. "Raj killed him."

Chapter Five

ANDREUS AND COFFEY WENT FIRST. Piper watched them go, feeling the warm presence of Cameron's back beneath her hand. His body shielded hers. From the rear, she supposed Charlie guarded them both. But to Charlie, this all seemed academic. Either the Astrals knew they were here, or they didn't. If they did, they were either letting them reach the lab, or they would soon raise a clawed (or powder-white) hand to stop them. Their course of action was the same regardless.

There would be no surrender. Not now. Not after Trevor. If they stopped now, they might keep living, whereas if they forged on, they might die — and really, hell, all of humanity might perish alongside them. Maybe it was selfish, but for Piper, that right there made the chance worth taking. Because she couldn't return to a life of ease now. The minute she sat with peace of mind, content with the Astrals in charge, Trevor's death would no longer matter. He'd have died for nothing. She'd rather go herself than let that happen. As horrible as it sounded fully articulated, she'd rather the *entire species* die than let that happen.

The bald warlord and his lieutenant crossed the space to the destroyed ranch house. Piper felt a twinge of loss; she'd learned to love Cameron inside that house. That was before she'd boarded the mothership and ridden it to Vail, back when it had still *been* Vail. Before she'd met Meyer again aboard that ship (though exactly when or how that had happened she couldn't recall through the fugue that had found her) then traveled with him to their new homes as god-king and queen. Before that sense of conflict that had lasted for two years, loving her husband as much as she feared him.

"It's insulting," Charlie said behind Piper.

"I'm not going to just walk up there, Charlie," Cameron said.

"This is like playing peekaboo with the mothership. Do you really think they can't see us when we hide behind our hands?"

Cameron looked like he might reply, but it was like dealing with a robot. To Charlie, this was all odds and binary decisions, as it had been the entire trip. When they'd decided to recover the RV from Cottonwood's front (mainly to recover the remote cell phone and check the network, Piper suspected), Charlie's opinion had been fatalistic: They'd survived on foot, so they might as well flaunt it in an RV. And if they died, they died.

Piper had found it hard to be so sanguine after escaping the archive. She'd been terrified. But now, mainly by thinking back to Meyer, she was more on Charlie's side than Cameron's. Maybe the Astrals *were* letting them go like they'd let them before. But now there was a splinter under their shape-shifting skin. On the way to Cotton-wood, the Astrals had felt they were abiding a plan. Now the same was true, but the human group, reduced in number though it was, had introduced an element of doubt.

We made them show their cards, Piper kept reminding herself to steel her resolve. Then, perhaps more to the point and telling in a way she knew was important, again by thinking back to Meyer: *we made them angry.*

They were no longer playing chess with computers. This wasn't about human guile versus Astral omniscience. Now it was about ancestors and progeny, universal parents and Earthbound children. Emotion could unseat them all, it seemed — and if the stunt in the Mormon archive had pissed the aliens off, that was as encouraging to Piper as it was discouraging to everyone else.

Andreus and Coffey sprinted from cover to the home's remains, keeping pointlessly low, looking senselessly upward.

Nothing happened. They made the house without incident then scampered down the stairs into its low-beam basement and were gone.

"How long must we wait," Charlie said, standing tall, not bothering with the pretense of hiding, "before we pretend they've been sufficiently distracted enough so that we can go too?"

"Shh," Cameron said.

"You're insulting yourself. We all are. If they didn't want us here, they wouldn't have let us come."

"Maybe we evaded them, Charlie. The network is out. Maybe they can't access our satellites to see us."

Charlie pointed at the mothership. "I don't think it needs satellites to see us. Ask yourself a simple question, Cameron. Why did it come back?"

Back. Piper knew that was wrong. "Back" implied this was the same mothership that had been over the ranch before, but that ship had moved to Heaven's Veil. And everyone knew capital motherships never left their posts. They were somehow bound to the Apex pyramids. This one was bonded to …

"The money pit," she said.

Both men turned to look at Piper. The pan was open ahead. They should already be crossing it, making for what was left of the lab. It had been built mostly into a cliff, and from what they could see, that cliff had been mostly reduced to rubble. But the place had a lower level as well — and if Charlie was right, the Astrals wouldn't have hit it too hard and wouldn't hit it again. They'd needed Benjamin to read the tablet left by the Templars when they'd moved the Hammer from under Vail, and if there was any hope to find the weapon again, it was here.

The damage the ship — or possibly shuttles — had done to this place matched Piper's feeling of their lost control.

It had been a tantrum. A petulant child destroying a house of blocks for spite; a man breaking a mirror with his fist to teach his reflection a lesson.

Charlie had it all figured out, because he was rational.

But when the Astrals had discovered their ruse in the canyon, they'd struck Piper as less than logical.

The way Meyer, increasingly, had been both more and less reasoned at once.

"What about the money pit?"

This time, Piper pointed.

"You don't see it?"

The men squinted. To Piper, the warbling of hot air was clear as day. There was a long, narrow, perfectly straight mirage between ship and stone arch. Between the floating sphere and the place Benjamin had never been able to leave alone, sure that the fathoms-deep pit, like the one below Meyer's Axis Mundi, held a secret. Or a port. Or a source of power.

"The arch?"

"The beam."

Charlie had already lost interest. Cameron was staring, squinting. "I don't see anything."

"We're wasting time," Charlie said, looking at the lab, perhaps eager to see what Benjamin had left behind. He was the scientist; Benjamin was the archeologist and ancient aliens theorist. Right now, Charlie knew less than Cameron, who had more history traveling the world with his father. But if there were still records inside, Charlie's computer brain was dying to parse them … and, he'd made clear, was positive they'd been spared on purpose.

Cameron seemed about to object, still looking for the energy beam from the pit he couldn't see, still sure the ship would incinerate them the minute they broke cover.

But Charlie followed Andreus's plan. Not ducking. Not running. Simply marching in the open, obeying either faith or a certainty that the Astrals wanted them here as badly as they'd wanted Benjamin to decode the tablet for them.

Cameron followed with a shrug. Piper took the rear.

But there was a flicker of something unseen behind her. The movement of shadow.

Cameron allowed her to pass, but Piper could see the truth: *whatever invisible thing was behind them, he'd seen it too.*

Chapter Six

RAJ WATCHED Heather crumble into Lila's arms, satisfied. The guards had let her enter the grounds because she'd barged through; they'd failed to shoot her despite his orders. But now their incompetence felt like a good thing because Heather was delivering Raj's promotion for him. Announcing the big man's death, and the logical ascension of his next in command.

Not Trevor. He'd left, declaring himself a traitor in the process.

Not Piper, who had no official title and who'd proved herself to be a turncoat as well.

Not Lila. She was weak and clearly unfit to lead. Lila was blood but wouldn't take the position if offered.

Definitely not Heather. Heather wasn't just a traitor; she was more honorary on capital grounds than anything else. Nobody liked Heather except for her family — because they had to.

Not Christopher.

Not Terrence.

And not Mo Weir, of course, considering Mo was only an aide.

No, the only logical person to step into Heaven's Veil command was Raj.

Raj, who'd handled the traitors time and time again.

Raj, who'd always had the city's best interests in mind.

Raj, who'd served the viceroy more faithfully than any of his family, and who'd turned on Meyer when the big man had betrayed the Astrals to help unleash the virus that had killed the network and stabbed his overlords in the back.

There'd still been a chance that Meyer would return and take the reins. He'd turned out to be a shit but had managed to talk his way past Mo and the Astrals once already. He was slippery enough to do it again.

But if Meyer had died some time after Heather had knocked Raj out with that brick? Well, it was surprisingly excellent news. He hadn't known. He'd woken up woozy under the ministrations of maddeningly smiling Titans, unsure what had come of Heather and Meyer. He'd shouted commands to apprehend them since, but of course they'd already wrangled control.

With Meyer dead and Heather finally in custody (or soon to be; there were a dozen guns on her, waiting for her tearful reunion to end), everything had turned out tidy. If Titans had brought Raj back to the mansion, it meant he wasn't in some kind of misguided trouble. Mo would listen to him now. The Astrals would make him.

A flurry of fists came at Raj. He honestly didn't see it coming and had no time to block. Lila didn't bother with slaps. She punched him in the neck and gut then landed a kick to his balls before the guards finally pulled her away. A bit reluctantly and without hurry, Raj thought, wincing while catching his breath.

"You son of a bitch!" Lila blared, her eyes furiously wet, her face ugly with anger. "You miserable, murdering son of a *bitch!*"

"Keep hold of her," Raj managed to say, trying not to betray how much that had hurt.

"You fucking coward!"

"Stop it, Lila. Stop it, or I'll have them cuff you."

"I'm your *wife!*"

Raj ran his thumb along his lip, then looked down to see that it had come away wet. She hadn't hit him high enough to break it, so he must have bitten himself when she'd landed her dirty shots. He licked his thumb and raised his attention to see all eyes on him, watching, waiting.

Lila's eyes, livid, murderous.

Heather's eyes, finally humbled, defeated.

Christopher's eyes, wary. Reasonably so, because this was far from the first time Raj had found Christopher coincidentally in his suite, with his wife, alone. Christopher looked eager to obey, which was good. He was thinking of his own neck now that he saw who was in charge of Heaven's Veil — unofficially now, officially soon. *Rightly* thinking of his neck. Because as soon as Raj felt sure the Astrals wouldn't object, Raj thought he might have Christopher hanged by that neck, for trying to cuckold an entire power structure sure as he was cuckolding Raj.

And the eyes of every guard in the room, respectful and maybe afraid, waiting for orders.

Lila's hard stare broke, her head tipping down then finding her mother.

"You're just messing with me," she said to Heather. Even though Raj could tell Lila had already known, maybe from watching the house activity or perhaps from their

spooky daughter, that something big had gone wrong. Or
— from where Raj was standing — *right*.

Heather was quiet, her piece said. The first time
anyone had ever seen Heather Hawthorne shut her cease-
lessly yapping mouth.

Lila looked at Raj, now more pleading than angry.

He felt less vindictive than he had a right to be, so he
answered with a justification: "He turned on them. He was
endangering the city."

"He was standing up for my mom."

"After you *left*," Raj said, trying to tap his earlier indig-
nation, "after he *tied me up*, Meyer helped Terrence put
some sort of a virus onto the Heaven's Veil network."

As if on cue, the lights flickered, the virus in the power
station trying the home's connections. Power was failing
across Heaven's Veil, and if the human cops didn't get the
city generators running as dutifully as Raj had the mansion
generators, the place would be blacked out come
sundown.

"Try your phone, Lila. Try to sync your juke or
Vellum. We have lights because *I did my job* — after your
mother knocked me cold with a motherfucking rock, no
less — but the network is dead. We're cut off. Thanks to
Meyer."

Lila sniffed, trying to hold herself together as the truth
sank in. "So you ... *murdered* him."

Heather, completely broken, hitched with sobs.

"I did my job." Raj didn't like the way Lila's hurt
expression made him unsure, or the guilt creeping up his
neck like icy fingers. He'd ended a life. He'd ended his
father-in-law's life. He'd ended the life of the father of the
woman he'd once been so innocently, so childishly in love
with. He fought a lump inside, looking to the guards for
confirmation that this had all been necessary.

A tear streaked Lila's cheek. Another spilled, from the other eye.

"He … he was … I had to, Lila." Raj looked at Christopher, at the others with their guns. "He was begging the Astrals to …"

There was a small noise. Before turning, Raj knew exactly what it was.

"Daddy?"

Lila shook the guards away and stood, crossing to Clara's crib. The crib that, according to Raj's two-year-old daughter, was an "embarrassment."

"Shh," Lila said, wiping at a tear.

"I miss Grandpa."

Heather, now half kneeling on the floor, sobbed harder.

"Honey," Lila said, "come here."

"I dreamed that Grandma thought Grandpa left," Clara said as Lila moved to pick her up.

Lila's outstretched arms paused.

"'Thought'?" Lila repeated, her own grief paused, sent back to committee.

"Let's go find him," Clara said, smiling.

Chapter Seven

INTO THE CLIFF'S FACE, looking up.

Beneath a fall of rubble, where an energy beam seemed to have struck nearby.

Charlie gave Piper a look that Cameron found he could read as plainly as if the man had held up a sign: *Does this look like it was done by someone who meant to cause actual damage?*

And Cameron had to admit that the answer was no, it absolutely didn't. There was a mammoth scorch mark in the space between house and cliff — exactly where, Cameron realized with amusement, he'd tripped and fallen on his face while sprinting to grab Piper before the ship could take her into its belly. Assuming the scorch had been made the day they'd outwitted the Astrals in Little Cotton-wood Canyon, it was three days old. But to Cameron it looked like a shot across the bow, nothing meant to obliterate Moab. It was the swing of a bat taken by an angry man who realizes at the final second that he'd better not smash the windshield.

They'd destroyed the area *around* the ranch. But they'd

no more obliterated the actual lab than they had their five-person troupe during the trip here.

Cameron wanted to nod, to mouth something to Charlie and Piper about those who'd stayed behind. Had the few lab techs and others who'd remained been abducted into the mothership? Had they been killed to prove a point? Cameron had been assuming they'd arrive to find nothing, despite his insistence on coming here — because, honestly, it was this or wander forever. Their only hope of finding Thor's Hammer was at Moab if it hadn't died with his father, but Cameron was realizing now that he'd been certain they'd find only ash and ruin.

And yet if the lab was standing, there was a chance people had been left alive.

Charlie didn't see what Cameron was trying to say. He was already ducking though the entrance. And Andreus, whose daughter had been among those remaining (killed, abducted, or run away) was nowhere close enough to catch Cameron's eye.

He looked at the only person left: Piper. But she was already following Charlie, ducking inside, shifting the fallen beam that had done little more than block the entrance.

The lights were off, all of the old power sources either destroyed or shut down by Terrence's virus. Charlie might know where to check a generator, but ahead of Cameron in the gloom, the tall scientist simply lit his flashlight. The thing had a wide beam, more like a camping lantern. Charlie made its glow as broad as it went and shone it around in the eerie silence.

"Ransacked," he said.

Piper seemed to feel none of Cameron's in-the-dark trepidation. Their roles had almost reversed: She was the brave one, and he seemed to have grown a timid heart. Cameron had become the group's most tentative. Mile by mile, Benjamin's death had settled on his shoulders like a heavy cloak. It made him hesitate. He'd lost enough, and couldn't bear to lose more.

But Piper had gone ahead with Charlie, flicking on her own flashlight. She was moving ahead, going farther. From where Cameron was standing, he could see that Charlie's one-word assessment had it pretty much covered. The place had been tossed, every neat pile of research sifted and thrown aside as if by impatient hands.

"Why is the building still here?" Piper asked, fingering a stack of papers. Then, as if remembering, her head moved toward the ceiling as if she could see the mothership through the rock. Wondering, perhaps, if the Astrals had merely been waiting for the mice to come home before closing the trap.

"They need to know where the Hammer is," Charlie said. "We're on the same quest. They want to turn it on, and we want to turn it off, but that doesn't change the fact that finding it benefits us both. They wouldn't destroy the place any more than I would."

Cameron had been scanning the space, his eyes absorbing disorder. The entrance was behind them, outside light already feeling feebly distant. He had his own flashlight but hadn't lit it. Now, in the rocking shadows made by Piper's and Charlie's lights, something struck Cameron as wrong. A shadow that moved the wrong way. An echo, perhaps, of what he'd seen outside before they'd entered.

His hand came up. His light clicked on. Cameron speared the spot where he'd seen the disobedient shadow but saw only the coffee room's open door. For some reason, seeing it gave him a pang of sadness. Ivan had called that plain old coffee room the communications room, and Cameron had sat in there for hours beside his father, holding vigil, waiting to hear from Terrence or Franklin — whom Piper had met before his irrational end.

"What?" Piper asked, noting his urgent gesture.

"I thought I saw something."

Piper turned, her body language changing. Something had been in here, not from this planet. They'd recently left a cave in the rock filled with alien predators. The feeling of being trapped in another with something similar was clear on her face.

Piper shone her light next to Cameron's but saw nothing.

"Over here," Charlie called.

After a lingering moment, Charlie and Piper turned.

Again, something shifted at the edge of Cameron's peripheral vision, just out of sight.

"Look."

Cameron did. Benjamin's keyboard was in front of his old office terminal. Many of the lab units didn't even have keyboards, but Benjamin had always liked taking notes and preferred typing to dictation.

Now the keyboard was a twisted mass of plastic. It had been torqued as if twisted like taffy, snapped in the middle. The two halves were destroyed, keys popped loose and scattered across the floor like knocked-out teeth.

"What do you make of this?" Charlie asked.

"Someone doesn't like lab work."

Piper turned to Cameron. He thought she'd roll her eyes, given the mood. Instead, she gave him a tiny smile. Her warmth barely helped. Cameron still felt a chill at his rear, and no matter which way he turned it felt like there was something beyond his vision, just out of sight.

Charlie picked up half of the keyboard. He set it back down then shone his light around the workstation with fresh interest. The floor was littered with pens and other miscellany. Beyond, one of the thin monitors had been smashed.

"I don't get it. This looks like it was done by people."

Cameron picked up the keyboard. "I don't know. I'd swear this was bitten. Like by a Reptar."

"It's pointless. If they wanted the place gone, they could have just blasted it. If they wanted to get information, tossing it like this would be counterproductive."

"They're not good with our computers," Piper said. "And they don't understand the way we *share our consciousness* over the Internet."

"Then why try? Why walk in here?" Charlie kicked at a wheeled chair lying sideways on the ground beside a shattered water glass. "They've been siphoning the Heaven's Veil network from the start. Not by coming down and hacking, just by using the air. They could have tried that. Maybe already did."

"Terrence's virus," Cameron said. "Maybe it cut all of the connections, and coming in here was the only possible way to get what they needed."

Charlie shrugged. "Maybe. But still ..." He kicked through more debris, the answer apparently too elusive.

There was new movement to the rear. Cameron heard what sounded like a sniff before spinning, sure that the shadow had come to claim them at last.

But his flashlight lanced the face of a teenage girl instead, her blonde hair a mess, her clothing filthy.

Cameron didn't know the girl well, but he knew her, all right: Nathan's daughter, Grace.

"We thought they were looking for something," she said in a broken whisper. "But mostly, they were angry."

Chapter Eight

PIPER LISTENED to the girl for as long as she could.

Charlie had offered to calm her nerves with a cup of tea. When he remembered that the lab didn't have power, he offered to hike back to the RV to boil the water. Cameron looked at Piper when Charlie said that, and they exchanged an amused glance. Charlie barely acted human most of the time, and here he was offering to be this young girl's hero. Grace declined with thanks, and Charlie looked at both of the others as if he'd just realized his fly was open, daring them to call out his tenderness.

There was still bottled iced tea in the refrigerator. It had warmed, but tea was still tea. Grace accepted it even though the lab seemed to have been her home all along and she clearly could have drunk the tea at anytime. When Piper led to her the couch, she'd gone willingly.

Then she unspooled her tale.

Not long into it, Andreus and Coffey entered, their pointless distraction having come full circle in its futility. Of course there was nothing in the obliterated basement.

And of course the Astrals hadn't been fooled, if they'd been watching.

Every card was on the table. The ship above must know they were here; it was too much to hope that they simply looked skyward and never down. The humans knew the ship knew, and the ship knew *they* knew. It was, in a strange way, as Charlie had said: They were twisted partners, each in pursuit of the same thing. The only questions were how long each party would let the other tag along … and who would attempt to knife whom in the back.

Andreus saw his daughter and finally lost his cool. It touched Piper just as Charlie's kindness had, and she fought, strangely, not to cry. The big bald man embraced the girl, holding her tight for too long while she squeezed him back. Then their former awkwardness seemed to recur, and they separated: Grace moving back to the couch, and Andreus to the small group's outer halo to listen.

And then Grace talked.

About the attack, which Piper guessed had timed perfectly with their own escape into the tunnels. The shuttles that had come here first must have arrived seconds after Trevor's death. After he'd kicked Piper away and shut the door, saving her while feeding himself to the wolves.

Trevor had been seventeen. So was Grace. They might have been friends. Or maybe something more. But Trevor would never see another birthday. Or a proper burial.

The ships came. Shuttles first then the mothership. The lab's skeleton crew had hidden with nowhere to go, slipping under desks like a 1950s duck-and-cover drill. There had been a volley of shots from outside. Grace said she'd heard the ranch house break apart and burn, "like someone kicking down a house of sticks." Another energy shot close to the door filled the room like a live wire.

Then the Reptars had come, tall white Titans beside them like escorts. They'd riffled through the papers, to poke impotently around the computer monitors. Either the network had managed to survive that long, or the mothership had somehow held Terrence's virus temporarily at bay because the screens had remained lit; the lights had stayed on.

Unable to access whatever they were trying to retrieve, the smashing and killing started.

The first to go had been a tech whose name Grace didn't know. She'd spent her ranch time mostly in the house out back, and had only run to the cliff after the tumult had started. Telling the story, Grace teared up — not over the tech's life, but over not knowing his name. As if she hadn't cared enough to learn it and had somehow caused his death by her own hands.

"That thing they do," Grace said. "Do you know the thing they do, with your mind?"

Heads shook. Cameron almost spoke, but Grace had moved on by the time he thought to. He knew *a* thing they did, if not *the* thing. He and Piper had shared a strange mental bond once upon a time, but this sounded different as Grace described it. Like an intrusion. Like a rape of the mind, pinning the nameless tech to the wall with Reptar claws, alien eyes meeting his while the thing pillaged his brain like a hacked data bank. Listening, Piper couldn't help but recall the monks telling her how the Astrals understood human minds as they should have developed, even if they didn't understand the Internet.

The others had watched. Literally *watched*. They saw the tech's thoughts as the Reptars searched them. They saw the intrusive images the Reptars inserted to apply leverage. Then they saw the kid die from the inside, and then the outside as claws ripped him to shreds.

Then the next person in the lab.

Then the next. Furious. Smashing things along the way. Kicking like a tantrum. The Titans' big white hands pinning each victim against an outside wall so the Reptars could do their job, the dark-think inside the Titans percolating through to the survivors, indistinguishable in image and tone from that of the Reptars.

Maybe Titans couldn't fight. Maybe they really couldn't hurt a fly. But they could make it easy for Reptars to hurt plenty, and the lines between Astrals, in all of their minds, had grown so thin as to no longer matter.

When Piper could no longer take the story — when Grace neared her climax, the part of the story where she alone survived, possibly specifically to report this grisly tale — she walked away. She didn't make excuses. She simply turned into the deeper part of the lab, searching for all the Astrals couldn't find.

They were so angry. They just smashed and destroyed. Titans and Reptars both. Such … impotent rage.

It hit Piper all at once. All she'd been keeping inside since their trip through the guts of Cottonwood's mountain. Through the dust and bugs and fetid-water sumps that washed her bloodstained clothes partially clean. She'd been strong. She'd even felt strong — for once and for all, no longer the old Piper Dempsey. This woman would never again be a passive city's queen. The new Piper was an insurgent, a troublemaker, an incurable fly in the ointment.

But for the moment, she felt broken. For now, she needed to be alone, to let it settle. To get it out, like infection.

She sat in the back room, in a lonely upright chair. She turned off the flashlight, comforted by the darkness and discussion — more sounds than decipherable words — in the other room. This was a human place. They hadn't cracked it. They'd been so, so angry when Cameron and Nathan had fooled them long enough to grab their ceramic key. But that anger, according to Grace's story, had earned them nothing but a uniquely human emotion: *frustration*.

Piper let the tears come: for Trevor, for Benjamin, for her life with Lila, the changed Meyer, and perhaps mostly for herself.

When she was finished, Piper looked up in the dark, feeling clean.

And saw the thing across the room ... watching.

Chapter Nine

HEATHER COULDN'T TAKE IT. Listening to Clara talk about her grandfather was too sad. She'd tried to spare Lila the uncomfortable duty of responding, stepping in to do so herself, explaining that Grandpa had gone away and wouldn't be coming back. That had confused the girl, so Heather had, despite her disbelief in God, told Clara that Grandpa had taken a permanent vacation to a beautiful place that was better than this one. That last wasn't even much of a lie, despite her atheism. Because really, what wasn't better than Heaven's Veil?

But Clara wouldn't listen. Didn't get it. She kept saying that they could just follow Grandpa — a request that made Lila visibly pale and Raj uncomfortable. The girl kept saying that she really wanted to find him, especially if he was on his way to somewhere idyllic. And, because she was Clara, she used that word, too: *idyllic*. A freaky child prodigy who spoke like a college student but still didn't understand death. It was like a cartoon evil genius who happens to be a cat … and who, accordingly, can't resist playing with a ball of yarn.

Heather left. Raj hadn't ordered anyone to stop her, perhaps rightly deciding she was defeated enough to not be a flight risk. She'd left Lila and Raj's apartment — the uncomfortable trio of confused child, distressed mother and daughter, and the murderer who'd caused all the trouble. The murderer was now in charge, and Heather found herself for once empty of insults. Apparently, she could only mock Raj when he'd done nothing to earn it. It was almost ironic.

On the way down the wide main hallway, Heather heard hard-soled footsteps rushing up behind her. She didn't bother to turn. It could only be one person, and she didn't particularly feel like talking to him. Details were Mo's job, not Heather's. He could arrange the funeral. She was beat and wanted to bunker in until the weight of Meyer's death left her.

Which, right now, she didn't think it ever would.

"Ms. Hawthorne?"

Without turning, Heather said, "Go away, Mo."

"Have you seen Terrence?"

Heather stopped. Turned. Stared directly at Mo with all the irritation and condescension she could muster, which was admittedly little. She didn't feel up to her usual sarcasm. Her middle felt scooped out, and now her top half was wobbling without support.

"*Terrence?* You're asking me about Terrence?"

"Systems specialist. Tall black guy, with—"

"Holy shit, Mo. I know who Terrence is. He lives next to me. I was shut into an apocalypse bunker with him. Maybe you remember the last hour or so, when Meyer sent him to go with the Astrals, and you sat here as arbiter?"

Mo looked almost defensive. He was good at his job and took pride in doing it well — and offense at any implication that he wasn't.

"I know you know. Maybe if you'd just answered the question instead of preparing a witty rejoinder for once—"

Heather resumed walking, ignoring Mo. He trotted beside her.

"Don't walk away from me. Your position here is honorary. Let's not pretend that you hold any authority in this house when we're facing a matter of Astral security and a threat to—"

"Oh, shut the hell up, Mo."

The hallway lights went out. There was only one window in this stretch, and the change made it surprisingly dark. To Heather, with her morose thoughts, the stone palace in darkness felt like a mausoleum. She stopped, feeling blind for the second it took for her brain to catch on.

Then the lights returned. Mo was staring at her, his face smug.

"Nothing but sass with you, huh? Maybe you don't get what's happening here. The entire Heaven's Veil network is down, but it's wider than we thought. The problem has wormed its way out onto the Internet. Not sure how. We think it might be repeating through the mothership. But of course *they* can't tell me because they don't talk, and the only way for an Astral feeb like me and the rest of humanity to get messages is the old-fashioned way, through the computer, which is down because the whole goddamned network is—"

"Is that what's happening with the lights?"

"The house has a generator, but the virus is in the home's systems too. Which is why, until Meyer comes back, I need *Terrence.*" Moe said the last word as if he were teaching someone slow.

Heather blinked, her mind working to understand what he'd said.

"Terrence went with the Astrals."

"He did?"

"You were here, Mo! We all came running down the stairs. Raj was yelling and shouting about conspiracy. Meyer—" Heather swallowed past his name, "told you that Terrence had done something in the network center. You sent him off with the Titans!"

Or maybe not, Heather thought. Too much had happened since that long-ago time. Had Mo gone with Raj, Terrence, and the Astral guards? Or had he simply given clearance and walked away?

"I know what I did," Mo snapped, his patience clearly thin. "But now I'm getting strange texts on Meyer's phone. It was buzzing so much I heard it all the way down the hall."

"I thought the network was dead."

"They're Astral messages. They sort of take over the phone, not like normal texts. They're not good at messaging, either, and I don't think the right hand knows what the left is doing. I can't talk to them, and nobody with a brain — if they *have* brains — is talking to me. I just keep getting messages that say illuminating things like, 'Terrence.'"

"What about Terrence?"

Mo held up a phone, apparently Meyer's. Heather saw nothing on its screen, but Mo said, "I assume they're asking where he is. I need Meyer to interpret, but ..." Mo rolled his eyes.

"Oh."

"So you haven't seen Terrence? The way these are coming through, it's like he's escaped."

"No."

"What about Raj? He'll know."

Heather tried to remember if Raj had said anything about Terrence. She didn't think so. She'd been too busy being crushed by the thing nobody had told Mo Weir, obvious as it was.

"Raj is upstairs."

"Fucking Meyer," Mo muttered. "Now of all times to dip into one of his long Divinity sessions."

Mo walked away, frustrated, having no clue he was now right hand to a dead man.

Meyer wasn't in a session. Meyer was on a slab somewhere, taken away by the shuttle Heather had run from after clocking Raj and watching him die. She hadn't wanted to stick around and Meyer no longer needed her, so she'd put feet to brick, having no idea at the time that she'd steer herself to Lila, right back into the hornet's nest.

They'd taken him away. Maybe to dissect their erstwhile viceroy, like a science experiment. And the humans? Well, Heather would inform them.

She watched Mo reach the stairway. Meyer didn't need a right-hand man anymore.

Meyer didn't need breath or food or air.

Heather blinked. In the split second, behind her closed eyelids, she saw him die on her lap, his lips forming those confusing final words. Words that did nothing to comfort her, though they certainly should have.

Love you.

Heather had thought she was empty. But no one was in the hallway to witness her shame, so she let the tears claim her.

Chapter Ten

CAMERON LOOKED up from the laptop when Piper screamed.

The external drive's cord still protruded from the computer's side, its safety still undecided. Cameron hadn't been foolhardy; he'd asked Andreus and Charlie if cabling the lab's drive to a laptop from the RV would just allow Canned Heat to destroy another machine. No one knew the answer, so Cameron had flipped a coin. So far, so good … though picking through Benjamin's research for an ill-defined answer was like trying to find a hymen in a whorehouse.

Cameron half stood, almost dropping the machine to the floor. But at the last second he pinned it to his legs just as Piper emerged from the back section into the lantern's glow, rushing, glancing back, her eyes wide and frightened.

"There's something here," she said.

Andreus stood from beside his daughter. He was carrying a rather large and intimidating-looking weapon Cameron had never seen. He pointed it after Piper, already taking tiny steps to protect what he'd found.

"Reptars?"

Piper shook her head, her breath heavy.

"Titans." Andreus said it like a lukewarm warning. Just a few days ago, Titans had seemed like powerful pets. They were nothing to be feared because they could only hold you tight. That opinion had changed since Cottonwood. If Titans could become Reptars, then no Astrals were safe. They might all start life as the unseen shape some called Divinity then become one Earthbound form or the other, free to switch behind the curtain as required. And there might be more. There might be other forms. Other talents. Other dangers.

"I didn't see what it was."

"You heard something," Andreus said, his barrel still raised.

"No. I saw it. It didn't make noise."

"No purr. No footsteps."

"Nothing."

"What did it look like?"

Piper paused. To Cameron's eyes, she looked almost caught. "I ... I didn't really see what it looked like."

"What did you see?"

"It's hard to describe."

"Try."

Piper shook her head. Her chest rose and fell in rhythm, eyes flicking around like a nervous bird's. She looked more afraid of the dark than scared of Astrals. The lab's atmosphere was getting to her — or, more practically, the fact that Astrals were closer than comfortable, floating overhead.

"I don't know. I didn't really see it ... directly, I guess. Just out of the corner of my eye."

Andreus looked like he was about to ask more, but Cameron stepped in.

"I saw something outside."

"Okay. What was it?"

"It's like she said. Corner of the eye."

"'Corner of the eye' isn't a shape. It's how she saw it. So, what? You saw it exactly the same way?"

It sounded strange, said that way. Cameron didn't answer. He looked at Charlie for help, knowing there wasn't any point. But Charlie surprised him again, as he'd done when they'd come inside and when he'd offered to run back to the RV for hot tea.

"I've seen it too."

"Okay. Then what does it look like, Charlie?" Andreus sounded annoyed. He and Coffey were practically shaking their heads, irritated by the flighty civilians losing their shit on his precision operation.

"I haven't seen the thing. Just its shadow."

Piper's head flicked toward Charlie. "Yes. It was like a shadow."

"Jesus," said Coffey. "You're literally afraid of your own shadows."

"It wasn't *my* shadow," Piper said, her voice suddenly anything but timid. "It moved when nothing else was moving, including me. And I could feel it ..." she swallowed, "*Watching* me."

"Pull yourselves together. We have a job here." Andreus lowered his weapon. "Holy shit. You people."

Cameron wasn't having it. "Stop being an asshole. You were the one who discovered them watching us last time."

Andreus yanked his signal tracker from his pocket. "With this! Which shows *no* signals, *no* presence at all! And we detected a *thing*, not a ghost!"

"I can feel it watching us," Piper said.

Andreus rolled his eyes, turning, flopping onto the couch.

She looked into the lab's darkest end. Cameron followed her gaze. Of course, there was nothing. Until there was: a fold of shadow making a shape, with pits for eyes. But it was like trying to see a hidden picture in a jumble of shapes, and when he blinked, he lost it.

"There." The moment he pointed, the thing was gone.

"I don't see it," Piper said.

"It's not there anymore." Cameron shook his head, blinking forcibly, trying to see what had gone missing. Piper was right: He could *feel* its eyes on him. If it had eyes. If it even existed.

Andreus stood. With the mothership making no moves overhead, he'd run back to the RV for supplies. He'd returned with a backpack, and in that pack had been a heavy four-cell Maglite. He speared the darkness, the beam landing exactly where Cameron thought he'd seen the shadow thing reform. Nothing moved, but there was nothing in the beam, either.

Andreus stood, keeping his eyes on Cameron. Coffey stood with him, pulling a slightly smaller Maglite from her pack on the floor.

"This is me being a martyr for you all," Andreus said. "We'll look for your spook. And in the meantime, you're going to pull as many drives as you can fit into that over-sized pack I saw in the storage room. You think something's after us? Fine. We'll leave, analyze what we get somewhere that gives you fewer scares. This place is a graveyard anyway." He must have thought back to Grace's story because then, quieter, he muttered, "Literally."

Cameron looked down at his own laptop. At the drive cabled to it — arguably the only one they'd need: a 100TB drive filled with Benjamin's hodgepodge, disorganized research. Charlie's records were definitely neater, but Cameron couldn't shake the feeling that grabbing as much information as possible was overthinking the issue. Benjamin had seemed sure on the drive over that he knew where Thor's Hammer was hidden — and perhaps more importantly, he'd implied it should be obvious to his son. That told Cameron he either knew or he didn't. The rest was details.

"Five minutes," Andreus announced.

He and Coffey headed into the darkness, guns and flashlights ready.

Chapter Eleven

PIPER DIDN'T WANT to look at Nathan or Jeanine. A schism was forming, with Andreus and Coffey on one side and Cameron, Charlie, and herself on the other. Grace was something else — somewhere in between. Or perhaps more accurately, something like a suitcase. Belongings that one side held close, away from the other.

Piper desperately missed Trevor, enough that the thought was an arrow. She missed Lila and Clara. She missed Meyer, as he'd once been. She understood the desire to protect her own, and if she had those precious last seconds with Trevor back, she'd grab his weapon and yank him into the tunnel even if keeping him inside meant barring the door with her body. But what she saw with Andreus was different. Grace had run from him, and now he seemed unwilling to let her do it again. He'd hold her close, not with love, but with force if necessary. For her own protection. Because, in the big picture, of love.

But the roundabout nature of his affection was twisted, damaged, wrong. Piper didn't like it. She didn't like the way Andreus seemed to be wrestling for control of their group, the same way he'd recently commanded his Republic. She didn't like the way Coffey, who was always armed, stood by his side like a good lieutenant. And she didn't like the way her girlish fears had handed Andreus and Coffey more ammunition — more proof that the kid, the scientist, and the arm candy woman were unstable, and probably silly. Fools who needed protection, even if they didn't want it.

Once in the sunlight, the feeling of being watched by the shadow felt far less pressing than it had in the lab. But Cameron had already told Piper that he'd seen something before they'd gone inside. It wasn't just her. Or the dark that had got to her.

They were being tailed. Somehow. By something they couldn't see — or, more accurately, couldn't see directly. It was almost there but not quite, always present but somehow absent.

Once away from Moab with their horde, Piper found Cameron sitting on a rock while Charlie culled Benjamin's data. Cameron was approaching this far more metaphysically than even Piper would have. He seemed sure that the data mattered, but not in finding Thor's Hammer. It would help them reach the weapon, but *finding* was already within him. Benjamin had told him as much before dying, laughing at his son's lack of vision.

Piper looked at Cameron's profile. His stubble was almost a beard — but not really because Cameron's face still belonged to a teenager. His perpetually young look made the stubble more odd than rugged.

She followed his eyes to the mothership above the ranch, now in the distance. Even from here, it was massive. A silver moon that had grown full too near the ground, its swelling metal belly seeming to hang like something pregnant.

Piper said, "If you stare at the ship long enough, the answer will come."

Without moving his head, Cameron replied, "I'm not staring at the ship."

She sat beside him. He was, indeed, looking directly at the ship.

"What's it doing here, Cam?"

"Suckling. Recharging. I don't know. Can you see the beam coming from the stone arch my dad was always checking out?"

In the bright sun, the beam was hard to see. But then it became easier.

"Yes. From the money pit."

"Maybe it's trying to reconnect to the network. Maybe soon, they'll lay more stones and start again."

"You think Canned Heat affected them, too?"

Cameron chewed his cheek, his gaze still unblinking. After a thoughtful pause, he said, "I get this feeling that what affects us affects them automatically."

"Why?"

"It's just a feeling."

Piper understood, in a way. She'd had a feeling earlier, having to do with the vengeance at Little Cottonwood Canyon as somehow related to Meyer, his connection to Divinity, and the way it had changed him. And, perhaps most importantly, the way he'd stayed the same.

"How long are you going to stare at that ship?"

"I told you. I'm not staring at the ship."

Again, Piper compared Cameron's profile to his line of sight.

"Have a seat," he said.

Piper did.

"Look at the ship."

Piper did that, too.

"Now let your eyes settle. Don't focus. Just let the muscles relax. Look *through* the ship more than at it."

"Okay."

"Now without looking away, see if you can check your peripheral vision. To the right. At the base of that big outcropping. And tell me I'm not crazy."

Piper followed Cameron's directions. The first few times she tried, her eyes wanted to look at the outcropping full on, and she had to start again. Then she got the trick of seeing into the corners without actually looking, and —

Piper jumped, breath catching in her throat.

"So you see it."

Piper took a calming breath and gazed back at the ship. She let her eyes defocus. It was still there, right where Cameron had said: a shape like a large dog, an ink-black shadow with nothing to cast it. When she turned to look directly at it, the shadow was gone, but when she merely caught it sidelong, the shape was clear as day. The kind of thing that couldn't be unseen. The kind of thing that would, she felt sure, visit her nightmares.

"I see it."

"Is that what was inside the lab?"

"I think so. What is it?"

Cameron gave a tiny shake of his head. "I don't know. But I think I saw it outside, when we first got near the mothership, before we went in. You saw it inside, and now it's out here."

"It's following us."

"Grace didn't react when we mentioned it. She's been hiding in that lab for days. If it had been there, you'd think she'd have seen it. That makes me think we brought it with us."

Piper found the shape again. She didn't like seeing the

thing, so she blinked away, looking at the formation's base directly. And of course there was nothing there.

"Is it like the BB?"

"Maybe. But my gut says no."

"What do we do? Try tricking it like before?"

"You know what they say about fool me once, fool me twice," Cameron said.

"I don't think we can. I think this is something else. Not a drone. Whatever that is, it's alive. It's awake. And even when we forget to look, it's paying attention."

Piper's eyes strayed to the ship. The giant sphere that had once been elsewhere before returning to Moab for reasons unknown. It must have dropped the troops that destroyed the lab, just enough to let the humans do their jobs as unwitting translators.

The Astrals had played the humans once, too. And just as the aliens wouldn't be fooled twice, Piper didn't particularly want to be played again, either.

"It left the lab so we'd be able to figure out where the Templars put Thor's Hammer and how to get at it," Cameron said.

"I assumed. So what do we do?"

"We solve the puzzle," Cameron said. "Then lead them to it."

Chapter Twelve

CHRISTOPHER DID a double take while passing the network center, on his way to check the roof's dish. He saw a big black circle with eyes in its middle, like a black Pac-Man, then realized he was seeing Terrence's hair, after having made peace with the idea that it was gone forever.

"Terrence?"

There were two Titans, two humans, and two Reptars watching Terrence work. The guards were arranged in a semicircle, paired like a Noah's Ark of security personnel.

"Oh. Hey, Christopher."

The lack of recognition was disarming. Last Christopher heard, Terrence had been sent up to the mothership on something dire enough to raise Raj's dander. But now that Terrence was free and working on computers under the literal gun, Raj was nowhere to be seen, and Meyer's orders meant nothing. Christopher had no idea what side he was supposed to be on, where everyone's allegiances lay, and whether he himself was in trouble. When the bad guys became the good guys and the bad guys' allies made the good guys work while the bad guys vanished …

Well, Christopher was confused enough.

"You're ... *here,*" he said, giving the most neutral, noncommittal answer.

"Yes." Terrence looked at Christopher, seeming to wonder if he could trust him. "I'm here."

"It's good to see you."

This was stupid. Christopher felt like a person talking on a tapped phone line. The Reptars were standing down but glaring with their yellow eyes. Meyer would shit when he saw *that*; Reptars were strictly outside-the-home security. The Titans were watching the men with bland interest, and the house guards were eyeing Christopher with a mix of respect and skepticism. Christopher was second in command only to Raj, and first in command until recently because Raj never used his authority. Still, Terrence was a prisoner, and Christopher knew him from way back. The guards might be for Christopher or against him. It was a knot with too many loose ends.

"Good to see you too, Chris."

"Maybe you can take a break. From ..." He looked at Terrence's position: kneeling on the network center floor, doors propped open, a cowling of some sort removed from one of the large machines, his tattooed arms up to the wrists in jumbled wires.

"From what the Commander of the Guard told me to do, of course."

"Of course."

Christopher looked at the humans. "Take five."

"Sorry, Captain," said Francis, one of the humans. "We're under orders to stay by his side."

"Francis, it's me."

"Sorry, sir."

Before Christopher could protest more, a voice came from behind. Overhead lights flickered, and this time they stayed dead for a full beat. It was as if the voice, at Christopher's rear, had turned the lights on and off to keep everyone quiet, like in kindergarten.

"Christopher."

Christopher turned. "Raj."

"Maybe it's time you started calling me by my title."

"Raj," Christopher repeated.

Raj regarded Christopher, apparently wondering if the fight was worth it. It must not have been because instead of insisting, he wandered away, farther down the hallway. When he looked back, Christopher intuited he was supposed to follow. It was his turn to decide if it was a power play worth resisting.

It wasn't. Not with all the thin ice.

"He's fixing what he broke," Raj said, answering Christopher's unasked question.

"Can he do that? Mo says it's everywhere. Out on the Internet, even."

"With help, he can."

"I came to adjust the dish. Thought that might help."

Raj rolled his eyes with pure drama. Apparently, that had been the stupidest thing Christopher could have said.

"They don't need the dish. Are you kidding me?"

"I didn't know the Astrals were helping."

"Of course they're helping, Christopher. Contrary to what some seem to feel lately, we're in this together."

"Jons is asking for Viceroy Dempsey."

"Did anyone bother to tell him that the viceroy is dead?"

"We didn't have a conversation. It was a request, for the guards. I'll tell him when I get there, but no, it didn't seem necessary to send someone on an extra trip by foot, with the network out."

"Police Captain Jons sent word through *you?*"

"Me and Trevor. But Trevor isn't around, so yes, through me." Something in Raj's face bothered Christopher. He wanted to punch it more than usual. He fought the urge to add, *Is that a problem for you?* But something in that cocky bearing made him hold it in.

"Okay. Run to Jons."

"Not just me, Raj." He was struck by sudden inspiration, eyes flicking to Terrence, who could use a bit of time without the asshole on his back. "He wants to talk to you, too."

"Why?"

"You're commander, aren't you?"

"For now. You can handle it, *Captain.*"

"There's a grid issue. The Apex is drawing a bunch of power. With the network out, it's sucking from the lines, like charging a phone by plugging it into a computer."

"So?"

"I don't know this shit … *sir*. Maybe you'd better come to explain why a glass pyramid is pulling power the city needs, now especially."

"What makes this my problem? The Astrals can draw whatever power they want. This is their city."

"Did you know the Apex even *uses* power?"

Raj looked like he was deciding whether or not he should admit to something. He glanced back at Terrence, maybe realizing that the man, who was trying to clean his own mess, must already know. It was hard to tell in the sunlight, but after getting the message, Christopher had looked at the Apex to see if he could see what Jons had reported. Sure enough, the thing was pulsing like a power indicator. It wasn't normally lit, yet now it was alight as if struggling to get what it needed. Something wired below the city in ways no one had noticed before.

"Yes. I helped design the network," Raj said. "Our part anyway."

"What power does it need?"

"I don't see how that's your concern."

Christopher shrugged. "I just want to know what I should tell Jons."

"Tell him to mind his own fucking business."

"Sure. But hey, you're the one who said we should all work together — us and the Astrals. Jons has his geeks working from the city side. You're on the hub here. But the Apex? If we keep treating it like an unknown …"

"It's an antenna of some sort," Raj blurted.

"They told you that."

"It's obvious. It's also the reason you adjusting dishes is pointless. You can see it in the logs and usage. They're connected to it some other way, but it's fed into the grid, too. With our power off, it's probably acting as a sink."

"Can we just cut it off then, if it has its own power?"

"I …" He looked at Terrence. "I don't know."

"Really. Okay. I'll tell Jons you don't know anything."

Raj's jaw set. "I'm staying here. Tell Jons to leave the Apex connection alone until he hears otherwise. I'm watching what Terrence is doing, and he won't try anything funny unless he wants summary execution. Until then, if the Apex is pulling power from what Jons is supervising, tough shit."

"If that's what you want."

"It's what I want."

Christopher turned, feeling himself dismissed, and walked back toward the stairs.

"Oh, and Captain?" Raj said from behind him.

Christopher turned.

"I know that you and Terrence are good friends."

Christopher considered denying. Instead, meeting Raj's greedy little eyes, he nodded.

"If he can't fix this, I just want you to know that I'm holding you responsible as well."

Christopher felt his patience snap. "How the hell can you—"

"And Captain?"

Christopher held his tongue, his internal temperature rising.

"I suggest you don't stop by to see Lila on the way to Jons."

Christopher bit his lip. With Meyer gone, the Astrals mum, and the city going dark, there was no way to know who'd end up as the new man on top. Raj thought it'd be him, by rook if not by right. If that happened, given what Raj seemed to have done to Meyer, Terrence's work might as well include digging his own grave. And he'd be digging one for Christopher, too.

Instead of replying, Christopher turned and left without a word.

He passed the big window to the Apex on his way, stopping a moment to watch it pulse, wondering what possible signals the big blue antenna might be sending.

Chapter Thirteen

THE TRICK of seeing the shadow was like rolling a quarter across the knuckles for show. Once Piper had it figured out, she couldn't stop trying while Cameron puzzled over their retrieved drives. The difference was that this particular trick chilled her, and distracting Cameron to point out its movements (closer, farther, circling around as if trying to get a better angle on what they were doing) felt like an awful idea. They'd come to dig into Benjamin's research. Nathan wanted to move on now that they'd left the labs — perhaps to study the data away from the mothership's eye — but Cameron was more practical: They didn't know if they had the information required to find Thor's Hammer. As long as the lab was still standing with potential evidence inside, they should keep it close. They might need to go back … but *for what* was a constant question below the group's skin, with everyone afraid to ask.

Piper blinked in the sun, telling herself that her eyes were on the ship and lab, not the shadow with no substance. Not the thing she felt compelled to watch even though it made her flesh crawl, because not knowing where it might be was so much worse.

Piper jumped when Charlie came up behind her.

"Charlie!" A few breaths. "I didn't see you there."

"It occurs to me that the situation may be different than we imagine."

Piper waited for more. There was none.

"Why's that, Charlie?"

"Benjamin said that the Templars left clues like a scavenger hunt. I can't read runes and I don't have his history background, so I tended to take his word."

Again, Piper waited. Then she said, "Okay."

"But the photo you saw, which we assume was taken in a buried temple below the Heaven's Veil pyramid, said, 'Device missing.' Meaning it was taken away, again supposedly by the Templars. There were instructions, written by humans and meant to be read by other humans of the same mindset, leading to a location inside Cottonwood Canyon. But the instructions were to the plate in Cameron's satchel, not the missing device itself. The key to start it up rather than the thing that needed starting."

"Charlie said that Benjamin knew where Thor's Hammer was. He didn't actually say, though. The way Cameron tells it, he thought it was a big joke."

"That's what I've been thinking. That it *would* be a joke. The Templars took the key. They hid the key. So where is the Hammer? Why split them up?"

"Maybe it's like hiding the gun in one place and the bullets in another."

Charlie was looking at the ship. Maybe at the shadow, too.

"There's more missing here than their device," he said after a long moment.

"Hey, you two," Cameron said, beckoning. He'd raised

an awning on the RV's side and had been sitting in the shade, a long power cord running from the vehicle's interior to a folding metal chair Cameron had fashioned into his outdoor office. The setup made Piper uneasy. They were taking the ship far, *far* too much for granted. Charlie could talk all day about how this was all a shell game with each side trying to outwit the other without actually hiding, but to Piper it was more like tumbling dice. Driving away from the mothership might keep them safer or it might not, but sitting so close was spitting in fate's eye … like Benjamin beneath it all those years ago.

Piper came forward, flanked by Charlie. Andreus and Coffey, watching them gather from a distance, came into the shade to see what was going on.

A collage of photos showing the blue pyramid being built in the middle of Heaven's Veil lit Cameron's screen.

"I didn't know where to start," he said. "Dad knew a lot about many things, and he'd spread his interests across the globe. I tried searching this drive for Thor's Hammer, and found a lot of results. A *lot* of results. He's been fiddling with the theory forever. But I don't see anything concrete — just mentions of ancient doomsday weapons from religious texts, rumors, stories of vengeful gods who came from the sky. There's so little in common between the stories — other than weapon or plague or *reset* itself — that nothing stuck out. So I set them aside. Anything before Astral Day is suspect. Too much has changed. So I started looking only at documents that mention Thor's Hammer since that time, in the last two-plus years."

Nathan looked at Charlie. "Shouldn't you be doing this rather than Cameron?"

"He said I knew where it was," Cameron said, a trifle shortly. "On the ride to Cottonwood." He looked at Piper and related what she'd just told Charlie. *As far as historical jokes go, it's a doozy.*

"So where is it, Professor?"

Cameron shook his head. "Somewhere we went together, I guess. But we went so many places. We went to Giza. We went to Aztec and Mayan settlements, to Turkey, to the Painted Desert. We saw the Olmec heads, all over Europe, the Rose Stone. I was like luggage to my father. He had places to go, so my mom and I went too. After a while, she stopped going and stayed home. That was the beginning of the end, and I'd chosen my father by default because he kept dragging me along. When she finally left him, I was in the middle. So I spent a long time turning my back on what now, I'm supposed to see as obvious."

"Egypt," said Andreus. "That seems logical."

"I guess we'll hop on a plane," Charlie said.

"There are ways."

"Especially when there's so much evidence to support such a long, dangerous trip."

"Hey," Andreus said, his brow pinching, "you were the one who said they want us to find it."

Cameron raised a hand for calm. "When we were at Cottonwood, their little spy device went inside my satchel. It saw our key." He nodded toward the mothership. "So what's stopping them from taking it?"

"They tried to take it from you plenty in the mountain," Andreus said.

"I think they were angry in the mountain." Behind Andreus, Grace had emerged from the RV. He nodded toward her. "And what Grace said about their behavior in the lab proves it. In two years, we've never seen them react impulsively ... until then. Reptars will rip people apart, but they do it efficiently, like duty. Titans smile. Everything is always precise and intentional. But we surprised them in there. We caught them with their intergalactic pants down — surprised them enough that they broke from what was precise and intentional and showed us their shape-shifting trick. But where's that anger now?"

He looked at the mothership.

"Back to sensible. Back to waiting and watching. Seeing what we'll do next, because they have all the time in the world."

Cameron gestured to the laptop screen.

"I know how my dad was. He got excited, and he wasn't good at containing his enthusiasm. Or at sitting on problems while dying to solve them."

Piper looked at the images, not understanding.

"How often, once we discovered that little BB watching everything we did, did Benjamin ask to borrow your signal detector, Nathan?"

Nathan blinked as all eyes turned to him. Whatever he'd been expecting Cameron to say, that wasn't it.

"A few times. How did you know?"

"I sorted everything on this drive by file modification date and began at the end, just to see what he'd been working on most recently. Say, after reading that Templar tablet. With your detector at his side, doing his thing whenever it told him he wasn't being watched."

Charlie crossed his arms beside Piper. He looked at the ship, and there was a small nod, as if something had suddenly made sense.

"The Apex," Cameron said, still pointing at the screen. "The last subject of my father's obsession was the blue pyramid in Heaven's Veil. And seeing all these images and soundings and schematics makes me wonder: Why would the Templars hide the key in Little Cottonwood Canyon rather than Thor's Hammer itself … unless they never intended to hide the Hammer at all?"

"You're kidding," said Andreus, realization dawning.

"What better *grand historical joke* could the Templars have pulled," Cameron asked, "than to conceal the thing the Astrals lost — in the exact place they left it?"

Charlie was still staring at the mothership. At the energy beam connecting it to the money pit. He gave another small nod. "Vail," he said. "Again."

Piper followed Charlie's gaze and saw the shadow.

It had come closer, as if to listen.

Chapter Fourteen

CHRISTOPHER DIDN'T LISTEN. He went to see Lila first. Because, of course, that had been the whole idea.

Now that Meyer was gone — away in a trance with Divinity, according to Mo Weir, who hadn't been given the memo — Raj was nominally in charge. It made sense. Who in the house outranked him? Who in the house (or, really, in Heaven's Veil) could challenge him? Captain Jons, maybe. But Jons had his hands full with Reptar peacekeepers, and now this bullshit with the Apex's power. Raj would be running the place before Jons knew what hit him.

For now, everyone was toeing the line. Christopher would do as ordered where his dick wasn't concerned while the other guards licked Raj's boots.

If Raj wanted snooping devices installed, he could do that kind of thing now. Meyer already had. That's how he found out about the virus Terrence had unleashed onto the network, when it had been changing hands with ... well, with Christopher. Raj had seen the recordings — right there on the house server, accessible with his plain old sysadmin access.

Raj went to the office down the hall. The last time he'd been in here, Heather had come in with some sort of vampy comedian routine to insult and distract him from what Terrence was up to — from what Meyer (and everyone kept forgetting this) had *let* him do. Meyer got what he had coming. Traitors got the broadsword. So it had always been; so it would always be.

Raj closed the door. Pulled out a tablet. And, of course, watched from the far end of Lila's room as Christopher entered. The little bastard didn't leave the doorway and kept checking the hallway, probably sure that the minute he unzipped, Raj would be there to cut something off.

Which was accurate.

But the door stayed open. Christopher stayed professional, save one telling, too-deep kiss. Clara was in the room while Lila and Christopher betrayed her daddy, back turned, her spooky internal eye surely wide open. She'd been withholding, too. She knew what the others were up to yet failed to tell her father.

Why was everyone against Raj? He was a good guy. Smart. Great at solving problems. He'd always tried to do the right thing. He'd stuck by Lila's side, tried to keep her safe. But he just wasn't goddamn good enough.

"Terrence is back," Christopher told Lila on-screen.

Lila's eyes, from what Raj could see, looked red. That bit of information cleared them enough to snap around, stare Christopher in the face.

"Back?"

"Upstairs."

"Did he escape?"

"No. Raj has him. He's under guard. Trying to undo what he did."

"Mom made it sound like it wasn't un-doable."

"Who knows." Christopher shrugged. "This is Raj we're talking about."

His skin prickled. Raj wanted to head down there, punch Christopher in the throat. He could do it, too. Get a few guards to hold him down then beat Christopher's face off with his knuckles while his lover watched.

"How are you doing?" Christopher asked.

"I don't know."

"I haven't heard anything. I ran into your mother. She said Mo is looking for him."

"For Raj?"

"For your dad."

Lila sniffed. The idea of an aide searching for his dead master seemed to strike her as especially sad. She sighed.

"What about Clara?"

"I can't tell her. I just can't, Chris. She's adamant. Wants to go find him." She sniffed again. "Wants to play."

Lights flickered around Raj but also around Christopher and Lila. The tablet stayed on, as both it and the spy device ran on internal power. The signal was over the air, not the net.

"Terrence?" Lila said.

"The house has its own power. But it's … infected somehow. The rest of the city is another problem. I'm headed to Captain Jons."

That must have rung a bell for Lila because she sort of blinked then stepped past Christopher to peek into the hall. Like Christopher, she didn't feel confident enough to close the door but did lower her voice and pull them deeper into the suite. Toward Raj's listening device, as luck would have it.

"Do the police watch city security? Is that something Jons handles?"

"Some. Well … mostly?"

"You're not sure?"

"It's the outage. Terrence might be able to shunt some stuff around, but I doubt he's trying. Or if he is, he's hoping to reestablish a line to the others."

Raj sat up straighter. *Line to the others?* This just got juicy.

"Can he talk to them? Can he get them a message?"

"Raj is an idiot, but he's not stupid enough to let that happen," Christopher said.

Raj's fists clenched on the tablet. There was a tiny cracking sound, and he forced his hands to unclench.

"Besides, I doubt it. I'm not a tech guy, but from what Jons says, there's a steep slope the farther you go from the mansion. There's some power, some scant communication inside the walls. But nothing outside. It's a dead zone out there. There was something happening out in the desert. Something Terrence knew about, something to do with Cameron's crew. It just got cut off. Like there's nothing there."

Lila's voice inched upward. "Cut off?"

"Just the communication."

"Have you heard anything about Trevor?"

"Li. I told you, I haven't heard anything. I'm sure he's okay."

Lila relaxed. "Jons then."

"What about him?"

"Could he get a message out?"

"Not without smoke signals. What's going on?"

Lila exhaled then chewed her lip.

"Lila, *what?*"

"Something Clara said after I brushed her off enough about … about Dad. I think they're coming back."

"Who?"

"Cameron. Piper. That soldier guy."

"Andreus?"

"Maybe."

"Back where?" He sort of flinched, and Raj, watching, set the tablet down to keep from dropping it. "Not here. Not to Heaven's Veil."

"I think so."

"Why? They barely escaped last time."

"Maybe they want to rescue us."

Christopher laughed. When Lila didn't join him, he composed himself and said, "Lila."

"What?"

"Why would they do that? We're safe here, and—"

She laughed. Raj could almost hear his name in that cynical bark, reading a thousand words in its single syllable. *Poor little Lila, kept captive by her strong, providing husband while she sucks the subordinate's dick. Boo-fucking-hoo.*

"Safe *enough*," Christopher amended. "They're the wanted ones, by both humans and Astrals, I think. We're in a big house with lots of protection."

Protection that might turn on you soon.

"Besides, there's no way to get in here."

"Cameron got in," Lila said.

"They *let* him in. They wanted the virus."

"You fooled them then. We need to fool them again."

"Lila, they won't come back. This is the lion's den. We can't know what they're doing because Terrence had the line outside, and now both he and the line are out of service. I'll keep checking in with him when I can, and maybe he'll open something back up and let me know how to use it. But I wouldn't count on it. Not to be dramatic, but this is kind of a *save the world* situation. Whether they have a chance or not, they'll definitely try. And coming here instead of doing what they need to do, even for you and Clara and Heather, when you're fine where you are? That'd be stupid."

Lila shook her head. She looked off frame — toward Clara, Raj assumed. The girl must have gone into the other room when they'd been talking because they wouldn't be discussing her otherwise. Not that Clara, who had a way of knowing everything, would ever stay in the dark.

"She said they were coming. 'Grandma Piper, Mr. Cameron, and their three friends.'" Again Lila sighed, her worried eyes on the tablet's screen. "She didn't mention Trevor."

"Did you ask?"

"I was afraid to."

"And you believe her?"

Lila gave him a look. *"Chris.* When has she ever been wrong?"

"Then Trevor is in the group that's not doing something dumb. The group that's doing what they all should be doing."

"We need to send them a message, let them know the network is out here, too. Maybe they can sneak in. Past the usual security systems. Your monitors must be going too, right?"

Christopher nodded.

"Tell them how to find their way in. Or meet them at the gate, if they're here for us. They need to come around. The cameras by the fences at the rear, near the church? They'll be out. But not the guards in front."

Raj had a chance to level up. To be a next-level hero, by bringing some intruders to justice.

"We can't send a message. There's just no way." Christopher seemed to think. "But I can talk to Jons. If you really think they're coming, maybe he'll help make them a hole."

Lila seemed uncertain. "He's the chief of police."

Christopher gave a little smile. "And he's also one testy, irritated fucker. Let me feel him out. Jons doesn't always play well with others."

"And Trevor?" Lila asked, her eyes getting freshly wet. "You really think he's okay?"

Christopher pulled her into a hug. "I'm sure," he said.

Raj made notes on a pad.

Maybe Trevor was safe.

But whoever had plans to sneak up on Heaven's Veil? They weren't safe at all.

Chapter Fifteen

NATHAN FOUND Charlie Cook's long and lanky form around the RV's side while the others were loading up. They were about to do something that felt — even in Nathan's mind, now — necessary. He wasn't convinced that Benjamin Bannister's doomsday weapon was hidden in plain sight beneath the Apex, but he hated the thought of running or hiding. He'd always been in charge, and when someone fucked him, he fucked them back harder. The Andreus Republic, which didn't have the same importance to the Astrals as the Moab facility, had probably been obliterated. Nathan didn't like the idea of lying down and taking it. Heading to Vail — to die in a blaze of glory, perhaps — felt like a fitting response from a warlord scorned.

Charlie was standing under the far side awning, alone. He was still staring at the mothership. Now that the light had shifted, Nathan could see what the others had pointed out: the thin, perfectly straight line of light stretched, like a tether, between the ship's belly and the stone arch.

"We've got a problem, Charlie," Nathan said.

Charlie turned. Despite the world's end, the man still looked like he belonged in an office, poring over actuarial tables. He had his glasses, his bug eyes, his short-sleeve, business-casual shirt, and his mismatched brown tie. His hair was a mess but managed to be unstylish at the same time — cut wrong in a new world where there was no such thing as *cut right*.

Cook didn't reply other than to stare. So Nathan continued.

"I think this is the Salt Lake mothership. There's really no way to be positive, but I'd bet my life that it's not the one from Heaven's Veil — the one that was here before."

"And?" Charlie asked.

Nathan pointed. "I see an animal at a watering hole. It's fueling up. For what?"

"We assume they're powered with fusion reactors. They probably scoop hydrogen from the atmosphere."

"I'm not talking about what makes them fly."

Charlie looked for a second like he might argue because trying to seem superior during a dispute is what he did. "I'm not either," he finally said.

"How many of these money pit things are there around the world, do you think?"

"There's no way to be sure. We know of eleven. This one, the one under Dempsey's old place in Vail, pits at the other eight capitals, and the original on Oak Island. When the Internet was up, some of the people Benjamin talked to claimed they had satellite feeds capable of seeing blooms like that one there." He nodded toward the ship. "But we've only ever seen them suckling power from this one."

"We saw the same," Nathan said. "I had this theory for a while that the motherships would all visit something like that to charge up, like rubbing your feet across a rug to make static electricity. There's not a lot to do out there, and our access, thanks to our partnership, was mostly unrestricted. So I believe what I saw. And it never happened. The motherships don't seem to draw power from the pits below them. They're just docked. Oak Island hasn't, as far as I've seen, even been visited. It's just this one. This one ranch, where all sorts of weird shit has happened over the years, mecca to paranormal investigators."

"What's your point?"

"Why is this ship here now? Why is it charging up?" He nodded toward the ship's silver belly. "This is exactly what we were watching for."

"It's one ship."

"Why now?"

"I don't know."

Andreus moved around Charlie then met his eye.

"You're sure watching it a lot for someone who doesn't think it's any big deal."

Charlie turned, meeting Nathan's eye.

"Do you know SETI?"

"The people who used to spend every day listening to space for alien radio."

"Correct," said Charlie. "After Black Monday, the air went out of a lot of the world's governments. I'd guess they're still out there, hiding, planning ways to rattle their sabers. But programs like NASA and SETI fell apart too. Except that they didn't. Not really. Benjamin used to talk to a group who was working rogue on some of the SETI equipment — remotely, I'm sure."

"And?"

"Before the Astrals censored the net, near the beginning, those people told us they were finding new signals. From the moon."

"So now there really *are* little green men on the

moon?"

"These people weren't official SETI. They didn't understand the data at first. Turns out, they were hearing an echo. Something not *from* the moon, but *bouncing off* the moon."

"From where?" Nathan asked.

"Earth."

Nathan's tongue found the corner of his cheek. He'd come out here to tell Charlie about an unpleasant itch that he knew Cameron and Piper wouldn't be able to hear, as keyed up and jumping at literal shadows as they were. Now there was this plan to head into the throat of Heaven's Veil, which Nathan was okay with ... though for very different reasons. He respected Cameron, but since the beginning they'd never truly seen eye to eye. Now his father's loss had damaged the kid. Made his decisions stupid and in need of a guiding hand — with rational assistance like Charlie's, if he could get it.

Nathan thought he'd come out here with a warning worth heeding: After two years of dormancy, their little Cottonwood stunt seemed to have prompted the Astrals into action. But as it turned out, Charlie held the trump card.

"The message obviously wasn't something we could interpret, but it seemed too unchanging to act as more than a beacon," Charlie continued. "That bugged me. Because if the Astral fleet was already here, what was the purpose of sending a signal?"

"You think they were calling home."

Charlie shrugged. "The archaeological records say they've come, taught us, then destroyed humanity. Over and over. But what's the point? My theory at the time —

and the beacon fit right into this — stated it was research of some sort. And that they wouldn't move on until their fieldwork for any given round was done."

"You're saying that Earth is an ant farm."

"Maybe. And if so, they'd want to communicate their findings. They'd *need* to *call home*, if they didn't want to wait until the planet was cleaned up before working on what they'd found. But it was only a beacon. A repeating signal. They'd only need to send a real signal after they had enough information." Charlie's eyebrows twitched. "Once they were done with us."

Nathan looked back at the ship. Charlie's theory fit in with his and Coffey's discussion. Charlie was a scientist. Neither Nathan nor Jeanine had been before the Astrals turned them all into astronomers. But he knew how to fight, and how he'd proceed were he in the aliens' shoes.

"When was this?" Nathan asked. "When you noticed the 'beacon'?"

"Before the net was censored. But after they began building the Apex in Vail. And, presumably, around the world."

"I heard Benjamin theorize that the Apex was like an antenna," Nathan said.

"There are *nine* capitals, each with an Apex pyramid. So no, it's not just an antenna. It's an *array.*"

"If your guess is right," Nathan said, "what would that 'array' need before it could send a data-rich signal through space — once they had reason to relay information for real?"

Charlie nodded toward the ship, apparently gathering a charge from the underground pit. "Power."

Nathan's head turned as well. In the corner of his eye, something seemed to move. But it was just a trick of light.

The hardpan between their position and the ranch's remains was empty.

"Let's head to Vail regardless," Nathan said. "Whether Cameron is right about Thor's Hammer or not."

"I don't want to go at all." Charlie bit his lip. "But I will."

Chapter Sixteen

By the time Christopher arrived at the police station, the sun was halfway down and the Veil's north-south streets were rich with shadow. Reptar patrols surprised him no fewer than five times, and Christopher found himself staring down the blue-glowing maw of one of the beasts, hearing its gut-deep purr. Each time, he pointed to his uniform, implying his right to be exactly where he was unless the Astrals planned to drop the facade and take over for real. And each time, the thing let him pass — leaving the distinct impression that a clock, inside Heaven's Veil, was ticking on the human/Astral alliance.

The station had begun preparations for nightfall. The lights, once away from the viceroy mansion, were entirely out. Generators could be heard running behind several of the businesses, giving the air a vague tang of gasoline. Where lights ran, they were too bright and scattered — positioned like shop bulbs, meant more for utility than decorum.

Christopher fought his way through workmen in blue who were setting up large tripods with big lights up top, like something on a back lot. He stepped through a snake's nest of black cables, minding his footwork. In the middle, surrounded by milling Titans whose presence was clearly unwelcome, was the big form of Malcolm Jons.

"Christopher," he said, less authoritatively than Chris had come to expect from the big man, who was usually shouting. He beckoned with a frying pan-sized hand. "Get over here. I don't know that I've ever been more glad to see someone in my life, except my family or my god."

Christopher resisted the urge to ask if Jons had actually seen God. Stranger things had happened.

The big hand settled on Christopher's shoulder. Jons looked up a short set of stone steps into the HVPD station. Inside were more Titans — a stray Reptar purred as it scuttled behind on insect legs. That was something Christopher never thought he'd see. But then again, he never thought he'd see Reptars in the viceroy's mansion, either.

Jons's face twisted in disgust as he looked through the station's door. He moved his hand to Christopher's back, turned him around, and said, "Walk with me."

Once away from the door and alien ears, Christopher found himself facing Jons in a loose knot of roving policeman. Some were helping with the street lighting, apparently deciding that the lights would still be off come nightfall. Most were simply pretending to help, not wanting to enter the Astral-infested station any more than Jons had. Watching them, Christopher had the strangest feeling: the streets weren't lit to prevent crime, but to make sure a night patrolled by Astral peacekeepers wouldn't be entirely dark, for the officers' sake.

"Did you ask about the Apex?"

"I asked Raj. He said ..." Christopher paused, unsure whether Jons would be offended. Christopher decided he would be. But Jons was strong, and his offense would be in the right direction. "He basically said to tell you to fuck off." Another pause. "Sir."

Jons looked for a second like he might scowl. He laughed instead.

"That kid might as well have scales and eyes that change color. I expected as much."

"He said it'll pull the amperage it's supposed to. I don't want to ask any of *them* to dim their lights." Christopher's eyes strayed to the Apex. Now that the light was lower and the nearly finished pyramid was in shadow, he could see its slow pulse plainly. Had it always done that? Christopher didn't think so.

"Doesn't matter anyway. Our old trickle seems to be off for good anyway."

Christopher looked around. The square around the station was fully lit, as was the station itself. Generators hummed around the buildings.

"Even in there," Jons said, following Christopher's glance. "So we've got lights and copiers. No Internet, or way of reaching the other capitals. My phone's stopped working. Yours?"

Christopher nodded.

"Same for the hard lines. The Astrals may have a way to communicate, but they're not sharing. Tell the truth, I think they're deaf, too. They can fly fast, and talk like that, going from here to there. It's been shuttles in and out for an hour now, much more than usual. We're just being handed commands from the Titans, but I don't think they're talking over the air. I think it's all Alien Pony Express." Again, he made finger gestures in the air, indicating the ships that ran hither and yon to talk in person.

"Look. I know you're house guard, but I'm getting a strong vibe of *every man and alien for himself* as shit falls apart around here. They're keeping cool now, but you should have *seen* them a while ago. There were all these shuttles buzzing around, and when they came out — Reptars *and Titans* — they were *pissed*. Tell the truth, it scares me. Frightens a lot of my people. So we're in this together, you and me. All us humans."

Jons looked around, scoping for Astrals. The knot around them remained human.

"City's on lockdown, Chris. High fucking alert. They're buzzing the place like a battle zone, and it'll only get worse. More peacekeepers coming in, offloaded by the dozens. There's nothing official yet, but I expect that to change. Heaven's Veil is about to become a police state."

"Because of the blackout?"

Jons shook his head. "Something happened in the desert. They won't give us details. And you know how they are with communication. They either mind-rape images at you or talk on the computers. Without the network, the last is shit. Right now, in the station, there are Titans trying to figure out our keyboards so they can type shit at us. It's embarrassing. For them more than us."

Christopher craned his neck, newly interested in the station's interior. Now that he had some context, Chris could see some of what Jons had mentioned: Astrals talking to humans, the humans not comprehending, ranting, annoyed. Titans patiently trying again, like big, ironically dumb, superior animals.

"I just know that some of the rebels out there tried something. Something that actually *worked* judging by the Astral response. It's like they realized bees have stingers. They've even tried to take our guns. This partnership has a half-life, Chris. Shit's about to get bad."

"Lila's brother is with the rebels." Christopher paused, feeling like he must look caught. But not only did the entire city know that Trevor and Piper had hopped into that armored car to flee the city; Jons himself had smiled as if in on the secret. As if he didn't only *know* about Trevor and Piper's rebellious acts, but applauded them.

"Like I said, no details. We heard some shit. Saw a lot of shuttles run off, headed southwest, like their alien asses were on fire. They all got real agitated. Restless. Then the shuttles came back, and all the *we're in this together* kind of fell apart at once. One of my men pulled his weapon when he was surprised by a Reptar, and the thing just ripped him apart. When other cops crowded around, I thought there'd be more blood. But it stopped there, and we cleaned up his pieces."

"What happened?"

"Don't know. Something they didn't like. We know they were hit back, and hard. But we also know that some were allowed to live, for reasons unknown or at least unspoken. But they don't seem to trust any of us. So I need your help, Chris. Whatever manpower you can give me."

Christopher sighed. "I'll try. But Raj—"

He was cut off by a tall man who'd entered their loose knot mostly unseen, waiting his turn to speak.

"I'll handle Raj," said the deep voice.

Jons nodded a welcome to the newcomer, seemingly relieved, maybe grateful for the help.

Christopher's reaction, on the other hand, was more on the spectrum of shock.

Viceroy Dempsey wasn't dead.

Chapter Seventeen

HEATHER HEARD the commotion as Christopher returned, as Raj ran downstairs to meet and berate him while being a loudmouth little bitch, then again as Mo Weir beat his saffron ass with a flurry of words.

Heather had to see.

She ran down the hallway barefoot, her utilitarian clothing unchanged since she'd run off with Meyer, since he'd died in her arms. She was covered in blood, but so far she'd ignored it — somewhere between denial and its opposite. She didn't want to consider what had happened or what might happen next. She wanted everyone to know that her granddaughter's daddy was a monster, and that proof was splashed all over her.

Whatever had been happening in the foyer broke up before Heather could reach it. Then Raj rounded the corner and came at her, stalking, his eyes unreadable.

Heather flinched, sure he was after her despite Mo's reprimand. But Raj bolted by without eye contact, his posture defeated, bent at the upper back as if he'd been swatted with a newspaper.

Heather turned to watch him go, walking almost sideways. She didn't see Mo round the same corner behind her and struck him full on in his dark-suited chest.

Except that Mo didn't wear dark suits, and wasn't this tall.

Come to think of it, the voice she'd heard beating Raj had been much deeper than Mo's.

Heather looked up. Met green eyes. And would have fallen to the floor if strong arms hadn't caught her.

"Meyer?"

He was smiling. When was the last time she'd seen Meyer smile? He hadn't done it often in his old life, and definitely hadn't smiled much since ET had shoved his hand up Meyer's ass to use him like a puppet. Pre-abduction Meyer had been stoic and hard. Post-abduction Meyer had been kind of a dick, if she could get past thinking ill of the dead enough to say so.

"Hey, Heather."

"You're ..."

She stopped herself. Something descended inside her mind like a steel blast door. She flinched away from him, pushing off, staggering backward. He continued to smile, enjoying her reaction. She considered running from ... well, from whatever the hell this was. Except that it was her ex-husband, who, it seemed, had never quite stopped loving her.

"Surprise," he said.

"You're dead."

"Funny, I feel alive."

Heather shook her head. "I watched you die. I could feel your breath against my lap. I was watching your wound, where Raj shot you, and it stopped pulsing blood. I stayed, Meyer. I stayed with your body for minutes afterward."

"I remember."

"You remember *dying?*"

"Heather, calm down." He raised his arms and took two steps forward. She took three steps back, rapping a door frame. The room behind it was empty. She could dart inside. Slam and lock the door. Then crawl out a window, or shout for help.

But she stayed rooted, meeting Meyer's pleasant gaze — the kind of a look a man might give you if he hadn't bled out all over your pants.

"No, I don't remember *dying*. But I remember everything before you *think* I died." He looked both ways down the hall, possibly because this dead man's final actions had been distinctly anti-Astral, and because the town's chaos, thick with the Canned Heat virus, was at least half his fault.

"I remember running."

He took a step.

"I remember meeting Raj, on the motorcycle."

He took another step. Heather stayed frozen. The door frame pressed into her back. Her heartbeat throbbed in her temples, breath shallow.

"I remember being shot." He laughed — as strange to Heather's ears as his smile. He rubbed his chest where the bullet had ended him. "I don't recommend it."

He took the last step. He could reach her now. She should have run, but didn't. *Couldn't.*

"You're smiling. Why are you smiling?"

"I guess I remember the last bit, too."

Love you.

Words he'd seldom said in his old life. Words he shouldn't have said to Heather at all these days, dead or alive.

"What last bit?" She wanted to hear him say it. Not

because she believed him or felt the same. She very much did not. If he touched her, she'd scream. Because he was dead. Because she'd begun making her peace. She'd felt the energy leave him, as he'd slumped like meat on her body. Heather had stayed with him longer than she should have. Until she heard the ruckus and an overhead shuttle shocked her into motion. She'd started running, leaping over Raj's knocked-out body before he stirred. She hadn't known where to go, and through her sobs, which she'd fought to keep quiet, she'd heard him calling — a second bullet, with her name on it.

She wanted Meyer to tell her now what he'd told her then. Not because she needed the sentiment, but because it was the only way to pop this impossible bubble.

She'd heard blood gurgle down in his throat.

She'd seen the life leave his unclosing eyes.

She'd felt his chest fall still.

He'd pissed himself when everything went black, for Christ's sake.

He was dead, dead, dead.

Except that here he was, alive and well.

"There will be time to talk about that," he said. "Later."

"Say it."

Instead of saying anything, he closed the remaining distance. Heather slid to the side, into the room, practically falling over a low table in her rush to shamble away.

Meyer calmly entered and closed the door behind him.

"Get away from me."

"They got there in time, Heather."

"There was no time. You were gone. *Meyer* was gone."

"People can be revived. You know they can."

"Not you."

He spread his arms slightly, giving her an almost humorous expression. *And yet here I am.*

"A shuttle picked me up. They're *aliens*, Heather. When we were in Vail, they picked me up in a beam of light. They read the population's minds. They crossed time and space. Why is it so hard to believe they can fix a bullet wound?"

"Show me." She nodded at his chest.

"There's no scar, if that's what you're asking." He gave a tight-lipped, shrugging sort of smile. "Alien technology."

"I don't believe it."

"I don't know why. Come on, Heather." His voice had slightly changed. Now he wasn't quite as friendly. Now he was Meyer Dempsey in his prime — the man who won every argument and dominated every room. The Meyer who didn't just defeat his opponents but made them feel stupid for ever having disagreed.

Heather edged the room, unwilling to get close. She thought he might grab her. She'd scream if he did.

They circled like gunfighters, his arms slightly forward as if searching for embrace. For reconciliation. But Heather kept back, her heels striking furniture.

"It's okay now. It's all over. Meyer is back, and all is well."

Heather reached the door. Her hand found the knob, somehow expecting it to be locked. But it wasn't, and of course she stepped out easily, and of course he didn't try to chase her. They'd shared their lives, including the years after his second marriage. He'd never tried to eat her before, and wouldn't now.

"Stay away from me," Heather said.

And then she ran.

Chapter Eighteen

"I've lost it."

Piper looked at Cameron. He was still staring straight ahead as the RV sped down the road, hands on the wheel. The thing's autodrive still worked, but it didn't have satellite guidance or any other connectivity with the network outage. Cameron said that the idea of a vehicle that drove itself without being able to gather more than strictly visual information from its surroundings was terrible. Piper had told him that was exactly what any human driver would do, and Cameron had agreed. But he still drove, Piper in the right seat, the three others somewhere in back.

"Because you're watching the road," she told him. "You'd better stay focused if you want to drive this thing on manual."

"Do *you* see it?"

Piper eyed the horizon, where road met sky. The trick was easy, now that she'd done it a few times. She blurred her eyes and immediately saw the dark shadow where she'd seen it last, running down the road beside them like a spectral cheetah with an endless supply of energy.

"Yes."

"Where is it?"

Piper pointed. Then she relaxed her attention, and the thing seemed to vanish. She kept thinking of something her mother had told her: *Keep making that expression, and your face will freeze that way*. Maybe the same was true for defocusing your eyes. She didn't want to see the shadow on their heels — and whatever else might be out there at the limits of her vision — forever and ever.

"It's keeping up?" Cameron asked.

Piper nodded.

"I wondered. I thought we might leave it behind."

But that's not the way the strange shadow-shape struck Piper. Cameron had said the thing had been following them since before their return to Moab. But she felt different. *It* seemed to be doing the leading, and if they risked falling behind, it would slow enough to let them catch it again.

"I don't like this," Piper said.

"Which part?"

She made an all-encompassing gesture. As she did, Piper's surroundings struck her with an intense sense of *déjà vu*. She'd ridden shotgun with Meyer at the wheel in their Jetvan, with three kids in back. Reduce ages by a few decades and subtract a person, and they'd be more or less the same now.

But then again, maybe they hadn't been running away back then, either.

"All of it."

"Be more specific."

"Okay," Piper said. "Driving right down the middle of the road instead of keeping a low profile."

"The Astrals know we know. They still need us, same as

before, only closer to the bone on both sides. We're playing chicken."

"I also don't like the shadow thing. It's leading us around by the collar, and we're letting it."

"*We* decided to go to Vail, not it."

"The feeling we're being used. Again. The fact that people keep dying. The fact that we're headed to the same place we ran from not long ago. Both of us, Cam."

"We know something now that we didn't know then."

Piper nodded. "Yes. And yet we don't know all we need to know. You don't know you're right about Thor's Hammer. You don't know how to use that plate thing, or even for sure that it's really a key. You don't know how we'll get into the city."

"I didn't know how I'd get in last time, and I managed to find a way."

"Because they opened the door, needing you to take me to Benjamin to decipher that stupid stone tablet!"

Cameron apparently didn't know how to respond. He remained mute. After a few seconds, Piper went on.

"You can't just waltz into the Apex. You don't know what it is, what it does, or what might protect it. The place is probably surrounded by guards. Reptars." Piper looked out the window, their shadow long on the road as the sun set behind them. "And even if we find Thor's Hammer, *if it even exists*, we have no idea if it *can* be deactivated. You might wind it up and set it off early."

"All I can do is try, Piper."

"We can't call anyone. Can't look at the satellites. Can't—"

"Okay, stop. *Mercy.* I see your objections."

Piper watched Cameron drive. She hadn't expected him to turn the RV around after she'd aired her grievances, but the entire conversation's point seemed flagrantly moot. Why had he wanted her objections if it was all just FYI?

"What makes you so sure you can do any of what you think you can?" she asked, unwilling to drop the issue. She would have, in the past. She'd never put her foot down even halfway with Meyer (in New York, on the road, or in Heaven's Veil), and for some reason at least attempting to now mattered. Not because she was sure of anything, or because she was afraid. Just because, like humanity, Piper didn't intend to end her life on her knees.

Cameron sighed. He looked at her as if asking a question he couldn't quite vocalize then followed with one he could.

"Remember how when you and I went to Moab the first time, we walked through a line of monoliths and could suddenly hear thoughts?"

"Sure."

"And how we seemed to know things? Like how we almost walked into the Andreus group once, but we saw the path and suddenly knew that going ahead was wrong … and so we went down into the ravine?"

"I remember."

"Does that feeling ever — you know — return a little? Do you ever get flashbacks?"

Those were two separate questions. For Piper, their psychic interlude had ended by the time they hit Utah and never recurred. But she still heard things in the dead of night while sleeping. She still saw things. They might be dreams, and Piper had always dismissed them accordingly. But seeing the ship above the ranch had stirred something inside her. Memories of being taken as Meyer had. Memories of minds that weren't hers. Memories that she'd lost and that had only resumed their continuity once she'd disembarked in Vail. It had never seemed strange. But now it felt like a conspicuous omission — a jump cut in her mind, with a whole world missing. Except in half-seen phantasms, like the shadow pacing them on the berm.

"No," she said, not wanting to delve. Not here. Not now.

"I wonder if it was the same for them in Vail — what you told me about Heather seeming to communicate with Meyer, and about Lila seeming to hear Clara inside her before she was born."

"I have no idea."

Cameron's head bobbed. She could tell he wasn't done, or didn't want to be.

"Why?"

"Nothing."

Piper felt a chill. He'd raised the issue after she'd asked what made him believe he was right about heading to Vail now.

"Why are we really heading to Vail, Cameron?"

"Because my dad said I knew where it was. Because he made it sound like it was all so obvious. We'd get the key from our supposed cake walk to Cottonwood Canyon, then we'd head back to where Thor's Hammer was buried. A thing that was big enough not to move ... so maybe it didn't move far at all. Dad said the plate confirmed what he'd already suspected. Something obvious."

That was Benjamin Bannister, all right. He acted like everyone should know what he knew — especially his estranged son, who'd combed the world alongside him in youth.

But the answer struck Piper as complete. Yes, Benjamin had been researching the Apex when he'd died, and yes, the Hammer's location, if it was right where it should have been all along, would be amusingly obvious. But it wouldn't just be an obvious joke to Cameron, who had much of Benjamin's context. It'd be an obvious jest to everyone — the Astrals included.

"There are other obvious places than Vail."

"It's there, Piper. It's under the Apex. I'm sure of it."

Sure of it? On a *hunch?*

Piper watched Cameron, knowing he wasn't telling her the whole truth. He was hiding a secret. But she'd have to let it go, at least for now. He had a reason, even if he wouldn't say it. He'd tell her eventually.

Until then, they could drive.

They could ride the wide-open road straight down the throat of those they hoped to choke, clinging to slivers of hope that they wouldn't be eaten after reaching Vail's borders.

Chapter Nineteen

CAMERON FELT ANOTHER PRESS COMING. So he peeked at Piper, touched the button on the wheel with his thumb, and engaged the dumb but relatively still reliable autodrive.

He waited for it, arms braced, secure at least that the coming shock wouldn't steer them into a ditch.

Then he saw a sequence of images, somehow superimposed over his natural vision. It wasn't like a movie, or a projection. It wasn't even precisely sight. He could see the images; he could describe the colors and what he watched happen within them. But there was more. The experience was closer to memory, like an intrusion of something he couldn't forget if he'd tried.

The Apex, now almost complete.

An ornate chest, like something drawn by ancient artisans in his father's old books.

Hands — Cameron's own; he could read their scars like a map — setting the ornate plate with the spiral pattern into a flat circle on the chest.

The Apex somehow shifting. *Changing*. The image dug

its claws into Cameron, tightening his grip on the wheel. He could feel the blue pyramid's energy in his bones. He wanted to clench as if receiving a long, hot electric shock.

He saw a house. His own feet walking the hallways.

A tall man. The viceroy. But in the vision he wore a mask, like something from a Day of the Dead parade.

A flash of light. Maybe an explosion. In the vision, Cameron felt something break. Something come undone, become nothing at all.

He saw a small girl, a few years old but with wisdom in her deep, fathomless blue eyes. She had a single finger pressed to her lips, telling Cameron to keep the secret.

Then someone was snapping in his ear, over and over. At first, he thought it was part of the vision — something he felt sure was being sent to him deliberately like a siren song. Then he realized it was Charlie, displaying his usual lack of tact.

Cameron blinked up. It was dark. The passenger seat, where Piper had been sitting three seconds earlier, was empty. Charlie sat in it. Cameron pushed away a strange sense of unreality, sure that Charlie was about to sit on her.

But then the tall man was in the seat, staring blankly at him. The world beyond was dark except for twin cones of light from the RV's front.

"I thought you didn't trust the autodrive," Charlie said like a challenge.

"I only turned it on for a second."

But that second had lasted longer than Cameron thought.

"Where is Piper?"

"Asleep."

"But she was just ..." He let the sentence hang, knowing Charlie wasn't socially adept enough to care.

Obviously Piper wasn't "just" anything. It had been light outside when he'd last seen her. Which had been less than ten seconds ago.

"There's a problem," Charlie said.

"Okay. What's the problem?"

"Andreus sent out a drone. I wouldn't have allowed it if I'd known."

Cameron almost laughed. The idea of Charlie forbidding Nathan Andreus from doing anything was ridiculous.

"It works off a stored map, independent of satellite guidance. But without GPS, he says it could only ballpark, based on our believed position. So he programmed it to go high, spot from a distance, then zero in on the Heaven's Veil lights. It was then supposed to fly lower, make a sweep, and return. There's a homing signal it finds on this end when it gets close."

"Okay," Cameron said, still trying to shake the cobwebs from his vision — his strange certainty that he could do what he was proposing, based on intel from a little girl he'd never met and wasn't entirely sure even existed. The dreamlike state was hard to shed. He'd apparently been steeping in it for much longer than the few seconds he'd imagined.

"So what was the problem?" Cameron asked.

"There *were* no lights at Heaven's Veil."

Cameron took his hands from the wheel, surrendering the farce of driving. If they took a wayward road to the wrong place, armageddon's edge would have to wait for them elsewhere.

"The network failure?"

Charlie gave a small nod. "And perhaps I'm overstating. There were some lights, but it's clear they're conserving power. I can see some small dots of civilization on the footage. But it's just a few floods. Most of the city is black. Except for the Apex."

"What about the Apex?"

"We've never seen it at night. There was never a reason to. But with the rest of the city's lights off, it's clear that something is happening inside. And outside."

"Outside?"

Charlie fished a tablet from his shoulder bag. Cameron hadn't noticed the bag, despite Charlie's carrying it inside. Testament to how odd Charlie could be.

Charlie glanced at the wheel, saw it making minute steering adjustments on its own, then held the tablet so Cameron could see it. He started an already paused video and saw a shaky, green-tinted overhead shot of a city in the dark, most of its buildings unlit. The camera swooped higher, and Cameron could see the Apex, not just glowing blue but *pulsing* azure. There was a line protruding from the Apex's top, like a string hooked high in the sky above.

"What's this?"

"That's what bothers me. This is an infrared shot, so I doubt this is visible to the naked eye — or it's very faint if it is. But that's not all of it. Look."

Charlie skipped ahead. The drone was now flying over the area beyond the fence, where the artists had created their enormous stone carvings of Divinity's various forms. Hulks of rock in the desert were difficult to see in the dark, but Cameron made them out with effort simply because of their size. They were *so* huge that the Astrals had clearly placed the source stones in place for the artists to carve. There were no high-rise cranes in Heaven's Veil, as far as satellite footage had shown. Just buildings and fence and monoliths connected by narrow bands of light like the one streaming from the Apex's top.

"Are those the statues outside the city?" Cameron asked.

"Yes."

"What are these lines between them?"

"Either they're being projected by the carvings themselves, or the Apex is projecting them. I think it's the latter. See how this line, between this statue and this one, is broken? There's a church steeple here—" Charlie paused and scrolled the shot back to show what he meant, "that would, if it's projected from the Apex, be in the way. But again, all infrared. People probably don't know it's there because they don't see the city from above, in the dark, at night."

Cameron felt a chill. Seen from far enough back, the pattern was obvious. The sculptures, with dull-green lines between them, formed an enormous spiral.

"What do you think it is?"

"It's a Fibonacci spiral. Like the one in a nautilus. Or the spiral of a galaxy."

"But why?"

"I don't know. It might be a landing pad, like a runway. It might be a marker. Or it might be a call for help."

"Help?"

"Not as in *Save us*. But it might mean Give us a hand. *Assist* us.'"

"Why would they need assistance?"

"Because they've encountered a problem they can't solve. It's the same thing we'd do. We'd call someone who would know better."

Cameron touched the tablet's screen then the line at the top of the Apex. Like something coming into it. Or something going out.

"There's no way to be sure when this happened. Not

without my equipment, and not without talking to others around the world."

"Why would you need to talk to others?"

"This might be happening at the other capitals, too."

Cameron thought of the visions he'd been receiving — that he'd been *given*, more accurately. The missives that felt half like informational bulletins and half like calls from a little girl asking him to come and play. They were new, too. Just another thing that seemed to have changed since Cottonwood, since they'd kicked the hornet's nest.

"If you had to guess, Charlie," Cameron said, "what do you think this means?"

"That I hope you're right. And that either way, the clock is ticking."

Chapter Twenty

LILA CROSSED the dark lawn to Heather's house, feeling unsure. Clara's hand was in hers. It was late for the girl, but not too late. She slept erratically, in fits. Sometimes, she was down for fifteen hours out of twenty-four. Sometimes, she barely slept at all. She wasn't tired now. And there was no way, with six playmates on the way, that she could calm herself to sleep a wink.

"Mommy," she said. "Look."

Lila looked toward the Apex, where Clara was pointing. The thing was making its eerie blue pulse, though the tempo seemed faster. With city power off, the thing seemed ominous.

"It's like a flashlight beam," Clara said.

Lila looked over again. It wasn't like a flashlight at all. It was like a nightlight, making sure that no one in the city could sleep.

"You're sure she's in here?" Lila said instead of answering.

"Not there." Clara pointed at Heather's small house, then her finger swung toward Terrence's. His place was dark. Terrence was back, all right, but Raj was keeping him under lock and key and on a rather tight leash. "There," Clara finished.

"That's Mr. Terrence's house, Sweetie."

Clara broke Lila's grip, skipping across the partially lit lawn toward the tiny home. The house had lights, but they were only as needed, giving the place a spooky, half-dead feel. The grounds were worse. There were outward-facing security lights, but in here, between main building and the row of guest houses, it was mostly long shadow. The air was warm. Watching Clara skip between long shafts of dark and light gave Lila a chill she couldn't articulate.

Clara climbed the porch steps. Then, without knocking, she went inside. The place was nothing but darkness. She tried to cut into the gloom with the small flashlight she'd found on Raj's nightstand, but the thing was barely fit for a keychain, too dim to reveal more than the doorknob.

Lila stood on the lawn, feeling the silence before crossing to the porch herself.

"Clara? Come on out, honey."

But there was no answer.

"Clara?"

The door was still open. Lila entered, fighting dread, and batted at the wall for a switch. She flicked it, but nothing happened.

Too close, someone said, "Power's out."

Lila jumped. She turned her light and found herself feet from her mother, with Clara perched happily on her lap.

"Mom! What are you doing in here!?" *In the dark. Alone. Sitting in Terrence's chair, saying nothing even when I shouted.* The hairs on the back of Lila's neck rippled in a wave.

"I thought he might go to visit me in my place. So I came here instead."

"Who?"

"Your father."

"That's not funny."

The flashlight's beam lit Heather's face. Clara, on her lap, seemed overly content, but Heather was neither welcoming the girl nor pushing her away. It was as if she had yet to notice her.

"Seriously, Mom."

"I didn't know where else to go. I didn't know where we were going when your dad and I ran away, but he always had a way of knowing what to do and where to go. I trusted him. Believed him. Without him, I'm a loose end."

"You're just sitting in the dark."

"The power is out."

"There's power in the house, and plenty of extra bedrooms."

"But he's there."

"Who?"

"Meyer."

Lila wanted to shout. This wasn't fair. She shouldn't have to deal with her father's death and her mom's mockery in the same day. Or with her losing her shit. Again.

She met Heather's eyes, unsure how to respond. They were here because Clara insisted: If she wasn't allowed to see Grandpa anymore, she wanted to see Grandma. Why not? Lila wouldn't be getting any sleep tonight anyway. It seemed that Heather wouldn't, either.

"I don't like you joking about it," Lila said.

"I'm not joking."

"*Stop it,* Mom." Lila pressed her lips together, fighting

something that might, left unchecked, turn into tears. Anger and loss in a horrible flurry. She wanted to cry. She wanted to shout. But most of all she wanted to take Clara by the arm, drag the girl out of the house, and tell her to keep her goddamn scary powers to herself. Tell her to stuff those things down and be normal, for once.

"Go inside, and ask for the viceroy, Lila," Heather said, her usually nasal, usually sarcastic voice deeply changed. This voice was more mature — the kind of maturity forced on a person through trauma. "Go in, and ask for him if you don't believe me."

"This isn't fair."

"It definitely isn't."

Lila pulled Clara from her mother's lap, turning on the ball of her foot. The yard seemed bright — albeit a frightening kind of illumination made of hard shadows and sharp angles — compared to the house. She wanted to be out there. She wanted to cross back to the mansion, to her room, to her bed. Raj would probably work all night, hoping to become the big man in charge. She'd have the place to herself, and maybe overnight, it would all go away.

"Goodbye, Mom. Enjoy your insanity."

"But *Mom,*" Clara said.

"It's bedtime, Clara. Come on. We're up too late. We need to get to bed. Nighty night."

"But Mom, I want to see it! I want to see it happen!" And with that, she sprinted outside. Lila followed, giving Heather a final, loathsome look. She found Clara on the porch's edge, sitting cross-legged, elbows to knees and chin on palms, facing away from the mansion, toward the Apex.

Lila didn't feel like asking. Didn't feel like indulging. Didn't feel like playing stupid games perpetrated from women either above or below her by a generation. She grabbed Clara, perhaps too roughly, and marched. Away from Heather and her unfair, cruel jokes. Away from whatever waited in the shadows, and whoever, if Clara was right, might be approaching from beyond the city wall.

They were halfway across the lawn when a flash lit the sky from behind. By the time Lila turned to look, everything was back to being perfectly normal, leaving no clue as to what had just happened.

Clara kicked the dirt with her bare feet.

"Aww, we missed it!"

Chapter Twenty-One

Jons looked up from his desk. To Christopher, he seemed like a parody of an ancient officer — possibly something out of a gumshoe movie set before the electrical age. The shop next door happened to sell oil lanterns, so Jons had bought a dozen. Now the place was filled with flickering wick lights, cops still on duty scribbling on paper with pens. A few tablets still had juice, and there were a handful of external batteries. There was also a generator, but Jons wanted to save it all. He knew Terrence. And whether Terrence's virus intended to kill the network or not, one truth remained: what Terrence did, he did thoroughly.

"What the shit was that?"

Christopher shook his head. He, like Jons, had been looking down when the flash had lit the windows. One hit then gone, like an old-time flashbulb to match the antique mood.

Jons rose and crossed to the window. Christopher followed. A few of the other cops went to other windows, but most seemed to have decided that whatever it was had ended and that they might as well return to work. Few were in the building to shuffle papers. Most were here to suit up, now that the order had come down from the mansion ... where the viceroy, it seemed, wasn't dead after all.

"Was it a searchlight?" Jons asked.

"I don't see a searchlight," Christopher answered.

"It looked like an explosion."

"It didn't *sound* like one." The flash had been silent, like something on a muted TV.

Jons was scanning the city, seeing more of the earlier nothing. The Apex was visible, looking mostly (but not entirely) the same as always. It might be cycling faster, but that was probably the greedy thing gobbling power, heedless of the city's needs.

Jons rushed past Christopher, headed for the door. A moment later, Christopher found himself outside, following the chief like a puppy at his heels.

Jons looked around again, still seeing nothing.

He looked right at Christopher. Then, as something seemed to click, he dragged him down the stairs and around a corner.

"Is it your buddies? Is this some kind of an attack?"

"What are you talking about?"

Jon's eyes, in the shadow, were almost like pits. He was boring right into Christopher, the chief's giant fist still gripping the front of Christopher's guard uniform. But despite the situation, he didn't feel menace from Jons. It was something different, but no less urgent.

He let go, looked around, then spoke more quietly. "The Astrals let your people go."

"What people?"

"Don't act like I'm stupid, Chris. I know Terrence, too. He's my boy. I know all about you two being in with Bannister. Not Benjamin. His kid."

Christopher considered playing dumb, but Jons was right. He wasn't stupid, and Terrence did talk. But Terrence was a good judge of character and always had been. He only talked — in the way Jons surely meant — to people he trusted. Terrence was a rock. An anchor. And those he took into confidence, Christopher took into confidence, too.

"I know Cameron, yes."

"And that thing with the tank that crashed in here. We know that was Andreus Republic. Terrence thinks the Astrals are leaving them alone, too. Maybe even working with them. That tank that took Piper and Trevor away." He looked around again then spoke even lower. "When Bannister gave Terrence the Canned Heat."

Christopher exhaled. Jons must know it all. But he hadn't said a word, even after Terrence had been caught.

"Tell me the truth, Chris. They coming in?"

"I don't know."

"They pulled some shit. They're in with the rebels we keep hearing about, am I right?"

"I assume. But I don't know what they pulled."

Jons paced a small strip of pavement, eyes peeled for patrolling peacekeepers. When he saw one, and saw the station's door still unattended at his back, he turned back to Christopher.

"Okay. Let's talk for real, you and me. Know that if you fuck me, you fuck friends. You hear me, Chris? You and Terrence, I'm on your side. And I don't think Terrence would be in with someone who'd fuck friends."

Christopher nodded. Jons was a giant, and his voice was timpani deep. It was hard not to be intimidated.

"They don't tell us much, so it's always possible we're being played, but I'm told more than anyone still alive is supposed to be. Why, I don't know. Something that serves the Astrals. I don't know for sure that they're expected here, but my gut says they are. Not called. Just expected."

"Why would Cameron come here?"

"I don't know. But the Astrals are letting it happen."

"But why?"

"Terrence said they were trying to get something. My guess is they got it, and that's what made the Astrals so pissed. Now I'm thinking they want to get whatever that thing is. So they can't just kill your buddies. They have to trap them. Pin them down. Then carefully take it away."

Jons looked toward the Apex.

"If I were them, I'd have my guard way the hell up. Especially coming here. I'd have an ace. So you've gotta tell me, Chris. You heard anything from them? Because if they plan to nuke their way in, a lot of people are going to pay. If they got artillery, I'd rather know it's coming."

"How would they get artillery or a nuke?"

"Nukes weren't all spent on Black Monday. And they got fighters. A bomber that one time. And latest, a tank."

"I don't know."

Jons's expression turned assessing. He shook his head, again turning toward the Apex.

"I hate being in the dark." The police captain wasn't talking about the blackout. He was talking about being totally cut off, having to operate in isolation. Unlike he'd grown up thinking, before the Astrals, before the network had failed. Unlike the aliens, who seemed to have many bodies and one shared mind.

Across the small yard, two Reptars emerged from the shadows. They passed each other, one headed in each direction. One seemed to snarl and growl at the other. Its purr grew louder. Two heads thrashed, as if trying to bite. Then it was over, and the aliens moved on, out of sight.

"Seems like they do too," Christopher said.

Chapter Twenty-Two

TERRENCE LEANED back in his chair and stretched. He looked at Raj. The little bastard had been holding a gun on him the entire time, practically twirling it on his finger for show. Now, as Terrence stretched, his gaze leveled. His grip tightened.

"Get back to work."

"I'm just stretching." He gave Raj a look. "Raj. Brother. What say you put the gun down?"

"What say you fix what you broke?"

"Are you going to shoot me if I don't debug fast enough?"

"I shot Meyer."

Terrence considered saying, *Yeah, you did a great job killing him*, but it was a bit too far over the line. Raj had probably realized his failed plot during his earlier absence because that was when he'd become so suddenly strange, distant, and sulky. Meyer had put an exclamation point on his resurrection by showing up in person, tipping Terrence a look that Raj hadn't seen. The rapport between the two seemed unchanged. Usually, when one person tried to kill another (and came damn close, according to what Terrence had gathered), there was bad blood between them afterward. But to Meyer, Raj still seemed unworthy of mention. And Raj, because he was a spineless shitheel, just went right back to licking boots.

"We don't have to be like this. I'm doing all I can. I couldn't escape if I tried, and you know it. We have history. How about we act like men?"

It was all half truths. If Terrance tried to escape, he could probably ignore the human guards as obstacles. Christopher was definitely on his side, and the guards had always liked Chris and Terrence more than Raj, whom they openly despised. Loyalty was a funny thing. It had to be earned, and was never conferred by promotion.

And as far as Raj and Terrence having history? They did. But Raj had always been aloof. He'd never trusted the newcomers to the bunker, even and especially in the end.

Surprisingly, Raj holstered his weapon. He sat forward, hands on thighs.

"Okay."

Terrence fought back his surprise.

"Thanks."

"No problem."

"In fact, why don't you take a break?"

Terrence blinked. "Really?"

"It's late. Go ahead. There's water in my office refrigerator."

Terrence half stood. Raj being civil, after his wounded pride and all that had happened, was odd. But Raj being obliging? Accepting requests and making offers? Terrence had no idea what to make of it.

When he saw that Raj wasn't going to shoot him or take it cruelly back, he stood all the way up. His spine cracked. He'd been working too long in one position, his eyes fatigued from staring at a screen. The work was difficult. Considering that Canned Heat wasn't something that could simply be removed but had actually caused irreparable damage, it was impossibly hard. Futile. The kind of work that one person made another do only because he didn't understand it was pointless, or understood fine and was enjoying the torture.

"There's some snack bars in there, too. Not good ones. Ones Lila made. You can't get the good kinds anymore." And then Raj, impossibly, smiled.

"Okay," Terrence said, puzzled. He looked at the door, but Raj didn't move.

Halfway to the door, Terrence stopped. He shouldn't rock the boat, but he couldn't help it. "Why are you being cool to me?"

"Hey," Raj said. "We have history."

Terrence left, sure that at any minute, he'd get a bullet in the back.

But Raj didn't shoot.

He just picked up a tablet and turned it on.

Chapter Twenty-Three

RAJ FLIPPED to his office camera feed.

Too much had changed in the last several hours. Raj felt beaten, humiliated — exactly the way, in fact, that he always felt around Meyer Dempsey. And was any of it fair? Of course not. Not at all. Everyone was either incompetent or deliberately subversive. Everyone except Raj, who did his job and nothing else. Raj, who'd come so close to having the big chair — but had it snatched away when the two-faced son of a bitch he'd tried to kill popped back up like a jack-in-the-box.

Meyer hadn't mentioned it. He hadn't even spoken. Ironically, it seemed that Raj had blown the lid on himself. Who'd taken credit when Heather quite unnecessarily began to blab. Raj killed the viceroy? *Fuck yes*, he did. The viceroy had stabbed his keepers in the back, helping Terrence and Heather, loosing that virus on the city. Anyone could see he was telling the truth. Raj didn't lie, and he helped the Astrals at every step.

He'd helped them find Piper.

He'd helped them tighten the hatches following her escape, when the city had been in turmoil.

Now that the city was again in distress, Raj had been heading up repairs, not so much as leaving his post for dinner.

And Raj already had a rather juicy bomb, about who might be returning to the city, who knew about it in advance and was turning traitor, and how those intruders might be intercepted before they could do any more damage.

Yes, Raj had been an ideal soldier.

But did anyone believe him about Meyer? Nope. Not even after Raj had commandeered the Titans and Reptars himself, all of them catching Meyer red-handed together. Raj didn't buy that crap about the Astrals not understanding the Internet. You could have read Meyer's guilt right from his face.

But who was let free to resume his post, and who was reprimanded?

And now that Meyer was back, somehow miraculously unharmed despite Raj being quite sure he'd landed a fatal shot? Whom did the Astrals and Mo defer to now? Was it Raj, who'd been a hero? Or was it the traitor?

Well. There was only one sensible path between the fourth-floor network center and Raj's office, and it led right by the library where Raj had spied Meyer searching for something not five minutes earlier, on a trip back from the bathroom, while other guards held their eyes on Terrence.

Meyer was in the library with a pair of Titans.

But Terrence was alone.

With any luck, what Raj suspected would happen was about to … and this time, he'd finally have proof.

Raj watched the feed from his office.

Waiting for the viceroy to hang himself.

Chapter Twenty-Four

NATHAN WAS ON HIS BELLY, flat on the ground, binoculars to his eyes. He handed them to Coffey, who took a look.

"Just like with Bannister," Coffey said. "There's nobody there."

"The drone showed police and peacekeepers shuffling. When Cameron went through the gates, they were all lined up waiting. It'll be the same this time. They'll be hiding. Waiting inside."

He looked over at Coffey. Piper, Cameron, and Grace were back at the RV, hidden behind a clutch of trees past the scorched, barren apron. Preparing, supposedly. But they weren't soldiers. That's why true warriors had to step up.

"They want the key," Nathan said. "That's why they let us come. They'll pin us down so they can take it without damaging it." He corrected himself, tipping his head toward the RV. "Or rather, they'll pin *them* down."

"They know we're here too, Nathan. It's naive to think they haven't seen us."

Nathan nodded. "Of course. But we're not going in. Not yet anyway."

"Yet?"

"We'll go in when we're invited."

Coffey stared at him.

"The drone dropped a message. It's not reliant on the network."

"Who was the message for?"

"The viceroy. I dropped it on the doorstep."

Coffey was almost shaking her head. She probably wondered why he was only telling her now, as if he'd broken their bond of trust. The *why* was simple: Nathan had betrayed their mission. Coffey might disagree with his decision, but now it was too late to make a difference.

"What did it say?"

"It told them where we are and what we have. It offered to give them up."

"Why would you do that?"

"Amnesty for the Republic. We helped them. We harbored Bannister's cohorts. At the time, we didn't know the Astrals wanted them taken in, so it was an act of betrayal: the Andreus Republic breaking our arrangement. Then we pulled Cottonwood, and that was a *definite* act of betrayal — one that kicked them in their probably dickless crotches. They hit us back, hard. So now we're scared. Now we want a summit."

Coffey narrowed her eyes.

"They'll never believe that."

"I think they will. Think about it. This isn't our fight. This is Benjamin Bannister's grudge. I'm just some asshole who built an army in the outlands. Before Bannister stuck his face into our situation with the Astrals by sending Cameron, we were copacetic with ET. We helped in exchange for information. We got burned because of it, an eye for an eye."

Nathan didn't want to elaborate, but Coffey seemed to understand. He'd helped Cameron, but the Astrals had killed his wife and nearly killed his daughter. It wasn't an even trade, but those who commanded the planet made the rules.

"So you're turning on them. That's what your message says."

"'Hey, you guys — there are some rebels out here, and they have what you want,'" Nathan said, quoting his message.

"You said it yourself. They still need Cameron to help find Thor's Hammer."

"Maybe there was more to the message. Detailing the location of Thor's Hammer, somewhere under the Apex."

Jeanine was still studying Nathan, trying to puzzle him out.

"You son of a bitch."

Nathan put the binoculars back to his eyes, now seeing Piper and Cameron enter his view from the side. Walking straight at the front gate, which began to open obligingly.

"They're dead anyway," Nathan said.

Chapter Twenty-Five

TERRENCE WALKED past the library before pausing then took a few steps back. He'd only seen who was inside from the corner of his eye, but it had been enough; the Titans were flashes of white inside their cloaks, and Meyer practically radiated a presence of his own.

Terrence peeked. His angle showed him Meyer but not the Titans. He stopped for a second, wondering if he should try to catch the viceroy's eye. He finally decided to risk it, walking closer, waving a hand.

Meyer looked up. Their eyes met, and again some unspoken message passed between them. The same sort of unspoken message that Meyer had seemed to give Terrence earlier, up in the network center. A look that said, *We should talk.*

Terrence moved out of view, preparing a plausible excuse. He'd just been walking by. Raj had released him for a break, even suggested he head down to his office without guards to get sustenance for the long night ahead. If the Titans emerged first, he could keep walking. If they came out together, he had good reasons for having loitered before moving on. Maybe to pay his well-wishes to Meyer after his near-miss.

But the viceroy emerged alone. He snatched Terrence by the sleeve and dragged him forward. His eyes searched the hall, but the mansion, in the chaos, was busy.

"Raj's office," Terrence said.

They crossed the hall. Went down one corridor then entered the second room on the right. Meyer closed the door. He looked at Terrence, whom he'd practically thrown into the room. Then he just stared, as if made of wood. As if he was confused despite having started this.

"Raj thought he killed you," Terrence said.

"He didn't."

"Do they know?"

Meyer looked around the room, possibly for someone else. "Who?"

"The Astrals."

"Do they know what?"

"That you helped us. That you tried to get away."

"I don't know," Meyer said, a strange look on his face. "Probably. Yes."

Terrence didn't know what to make of the answer. Upstairs, when Raj had been being his asshole self, gloating while Heather and Terrence were trussed and Lila grew angry, Meyer had what Terrence thought was a spontaneous change of heart. There should be more here. More information beyond a pat yes or no. Perhaps the seeds of a plan. An explanation of what had happened when he'd been picked up, for sure.

But Meyer simply stood there.

"I think I was confused," he said.

"Confused about what?"

"Why did I shoot Raj? Why did I go with Heather?"

He pinched the bridge of his nose. "It must have been a mistake. Do you know?"

"What are you talking about?"

"I hate Raj. I've always hated that kid. Heather does, too."

"Yes, but—"

"Have you made any progress on the network issue?"

"The network? You grabbed me."

"I talked to Heather earlier. It made sense when I did. Did she tell you about it?"

"You mean earlier? Before you shot Raj?"

"No. Just recently. She didn't believe me."

Terrence felt like the room was spinning. "What … what didn't she believe you about? Did you find a way to get her and the others out of here?"

"Cameron Bannister and Piper are on their way back," Meyer said. It came out fast, practically blurted.

"Okay. So how do we get to them?"

"You're a prisoner. You have to fix the problem."

This was exasperating. He'd understood when Meyer threw him to the wolves, sending him with the Titans and Reptars up to the mothership before being called back. When they'd been caught by Raj and stood before Mo Weir, the choices were for them all to be caught or for Terrence to take the bullet. It was a choice between bad and worse, so Terrence went willingly. But now there was no threat. The house guards — both human and Astral — were again deferring to the viceroy's authority. If he'd been suspected, he was now in the clear. So why should Terrence fall back on the blade?

"Lila, Clara, and Heather are where they belong."

"You said you were going to send them out with Cameron and Piper."

"No."

"Why not?"

Meyer blinked. He looked lost — the exact opposite of Meyer Dempsey's usual look. "They're going to be caught. They were double-crossed. They have something the Astrals want, and now something the aliens want to know."

Terrence bolted up. "We have to help them!"

"They're enemies of the state."

"Piper is your wife!"

Meyer blinked. "Get back to work, Terrence."

"You pulled me in here!"

"You waved."

"Goddammit, Meyer!" Terrence wanted to grab the viceroy and shake him. "You helped before. What happened? Did they scare you? Turn you chickenshit, only thinking about your own neck?"

"I … I made some kind of a mistake."

"When!" It wasn't a question. It came out of Terrence as an exasperated shout. Meyer seemed to be attempting to explain his actions to himself, and the results weren't gelling.

"Maybe with Heather. Something I said. But Piper …" Again, he pinched his nose, looking for all the world like he might collapse in the grip of a migraine.

"The guards carry walkies," Terrence said, realizing he'd need to take charge if anything was to happen. "They're short-range radio and won't be affected by Canned Heat. Call them. Tell them to let Piper and Cameron through. We can get down there. You can give them a pass. Let them into the house here, anything. The humans aren't a problem. Keep them from the Astrals. That's all."

"They're carrying something."

"Then take it. Keep it. Hand it to the Astrals if they insist. But Piper and Cameron—"

"Are dissidents," Meyer announced suddenly, pulling himself upright. "There are plenty of guards deployed. That part is handled."

"But—"

"Fix the problem," Meyer said.

Then he left, leaving Terrence feeling lost. He stormed between the Titans at the door.

The Titans beckoned.

And Terrence followed.

Chapter Twenty-Six

SPOTS WERE BRIGHT OVERHEAD, pole mounted and solo, too harsh for ordinary lighting. A generator purred in the distance. Gates yawned to the left and right.

Piper was thinking of reaching for Cameron's hand, beside the satchel and key. She flicked her fingers and decided not to take it. She'd leaned on men too much, and there wasn't a time so far it hadn't landed her in trouble. Poor little Piper, capable of shooting a man but unable to keep her shit together without protection. Well, that girl was gone. Dead. She'd been murdered, many times now.

Instead, Cameron's hand reached for hers. Shaking, he took it.

"You don't think this is going to work."

"I've done this before. It's like you said. This was stupid." Cameron looked over his shoulder. "We could run. We're barely through. They'd chase us, but they might not shoot. Probably wouldn't. If they hit me, they hit the key. And they need the key."

Piper repeated Cameron's words back to him. "It's the only chance."

"They opened the doors. They'll be waiting."

Reflexively, Piper's eyes searched the gate area for the shadow creature, but she was too keyed up, too high on adrenaline. She couldn't settle her eyes enough to see it. She was focus personified. Everything seemed interesting. Everything a threat.

"We're handing them the key on a silver platter. We should have left it with Nathan. Maybe he'll be able to sneak in once their eyes are on us; who knows." Cameron's teeth wanted to grind together. He touched the satchel. "I could smash it."

They'd discussed that, too. There were too many unknowns. If smashing the key was the solution to solving Earth's Astral problems, the Templars would have smashed it long ago. But they hadn't. They'd kept it protected and whole, as if it was important to humanity as well.

Instead of giving Cameron the answer he already knew, she squeezed his hand. She kept her feet moving, forcing his to move right beside her.

But Cameron was right. This had been done. Last time, she'd been inside the city walls, wanted and trapped. Cameron's permitted entrance had heralded her exodus. Now she'd returned. There were no Astrals in sight, but she could feel them watching her nonetheless.

But he said what they needed was here, along with what they needed to do.

The gates fell to their rear. The air was still. Lights were bright, like spotlights on their progress. Both sides had their cards on the table. It wasn't a matter of conceal-ment. Or a question of trickery. It was a matter of who would be the first to flinch.

They entered the slow, upward-sloping entrance valley. Their chance to turn and run, if it had ever been a real thing, vanished by the step.

Piper's eyes found the Apex. It was pulsing faster than normal, particularly visible now that most of the city's lights had gone dark. Heaven's Veil's usual sounds were quiet beneath the generator, as if the city was holding its breath.

"Do we just walk right up to it?" she asked.

"I think something's supposed to happen first."

Piper's head ticked toward Cameron. His earlier secrets seemed to rear back up, reminding Piper that he hadn't quite told her the full truth. He was looking mostly forward, his eyes in the distance. Not just watching. But waiting as well.

She looked back. Toward the open pan, where Andreus and Coffey were hiding with Charlie and Andreus's daughter, Grace. They kept trying to take the group's lead. They were the soldiers. But Andreus had seemed to be holding something back as well. Officially, the Astrals wanted the key and knew Cameron had it. Leaving the less-sought-after members of their group behind was supposed to be insurance.

Maybe.

Maybe not.

Up the rise. Between the buildings at the city's main thoroughfare, mostly dark. A few curious faces appeared at windows, watching the newcomers march into their midst.

Piper heard something at the rear. She turned to see the big gates closing. There was an indifferent air to the swinging doors, casual emotion somehow conveyed by the movement of metal and wood. *Now you're inside,* it said. *So let's get comfy.*

Piper heard the grating of grit and rock.

Two large white forms appeared between the buildings to their rear, on the right. Another two Titans emerged on the left.

"Piper."

She turned back to see Cameron's face then turned farther to follow his gaze. Titans were emerging there as well. Percolating between the dark buildings like water gurgling up through the cracks. Forming a long double row with a clear spot through the middle, like a gauntlet.

More Titans.

And more.

Piper's heart slammed into her ribs. She looked around in a circle, seeing Titans lined behind them to the gate, then in front in the long, curving line of buildings ahead.

"What do we do?"

"Keep walking."

The line of bald white heads turned placidly to watch them pass. Piper's mind kept returning to Cottonwood, watching the Titan guards become the prowling black Reptars. Were all masks now off? Would these Titans hesitate to change, having already shown humanity that particular trick?

"Cam …"

Cameron still seemed to be focused somewhere else, walking slowly, at least one trick still seemingly up his sleeve.

"Any time now," he said.

Chapter Twenty-Seven

"Jesus."

Christopher turned. Jons was staring straight ahead, past the station's wall. Uniformed officers were streaming out like water, headed toward the city's front.

The big man pushed past Christopher, grabbing a kid who looked about fifteen by the back of the shirt, stopping him sharp. The kid's hand flinched toward his sidearm, but when his wild eyes saw it was Captain Jons who'd snatched him, they ratcheted down.

"Where are you going?" Jons demanded.

"Word on the walkies," said the kid. "From the house."

"What word?"

"From …" The kid swallowed, eyes flicking to Christopher. "From the viceroy."

"Meyer Dempsey doesn't call the shots here. I do."

"Sir. Sorry. He said the gates are open and undefended. Some sort of mix-up. An oversight at the house because of problems with the grid."

"Dempsey told you this."

"Through Guard Commander, Sir. I'm sorry. Burmeister took the call. When he couldn't find you, he sent everyone out. We're to secure the gate."

"Guard Commander," Christopher said. "Raj."

"They watch the fences, not us," Jons told the kid, giving Christopher a nod of acknowledgement.

"Sorry sir. Burmeister said—"

"Shit. Just go." He released the young cop's shirt, causing him to stumble. The kid looked back then seemed to take Jons's mumbled assent as an order and shambled on, leaving the small plaza around the station with the others.

He turned to Christopher. "I guess this is news to you, too?"

Christopher nodded, confused.

"'The gates are open.' Why would the gates be open?"

"It's Raj. There's no way that came from Dempsey. It might mean nothing. *Probably* means nothing."

"Unless Dempsey knows something. Knows your people are coming."

There was motion overhead. Cameron looked up, saw a trio of shuttles cross the space between the buildings' peaks and the mothership, headed toward the cops.

"Looks like they know, too."

"Level with me, Chris. What the shit are they trying to pull? They've tried to hit the city repeatedly. Tried to crash a plane into the viceroy mansion. Bannister walked right the fuck into the city and was busted out by a goddamned tank from nowhere while the shuttles kept their asses docked and allowed it to happen. I know we're just puppets, but it's goddamn hard to do my job if I don't know what I'm supposed to be protecting, and against what."

"I have no idea. Terrence had no idea. The networks are down."

"But you knew they were coming."

"That's harder to explain," Christopher said, thinking of Clara.

Jons moved. Christopher followed, both men heading in the flow's general direction at a light jog. Shuttles buzzed overhead. A stream of Reptar traffic packed parallel alleys, all attention moving toward the gates. But the Astrals must have suspected something more as well because Christopher could see another group of shuttles making slow laps of the perimeter, swarming the city's other edges like water circling a drain.

"What do they want, Chris? Why would they just walk right the hell into the middle of the city? I'm on your side, you hear me? But I can't help dumb motherfuckers who get themselves surrounded the second they step into enemy territory."

"I don't know."

Christopher stopped when Jons practically clotheslined him with his big arm. In front of them, as they rounded a corner, was a line of cloaks: Titans, in their usual monklike uniforms.

Dozens of them, stone still. Thick in a circle, moving away from the curbs and into the open street ahead, surrounding something.

Jons whispered, "I want to help, but I can't unless you tell me what the hell these dumb assholes think they're doing!"

"I ... I don't know," Christopher stammered.

Then many things happened, all at once.

Chapter Twenty-Eight

CLARA WOULDN'T GO to bed.

She was mad at Lila for not playing along earlier, when she'd wanted to watch the Apex for "something neat" that it was supposed to do. Lila's nagging insistence on storming away from Grandma Heather's place (or, really, Terrence's place, where Grandma Heather was mired in a psychotic episode) had caused Clara to miss the neat thing she'd been hoping to see. That had immediately become a source of friction. She was pouting, excited, angry, manic. A bit psychotic, like Grandma.

Grandma, who kept screwing with Lila in such unfair ways.

When they'd reentered the mansion, Lila had nearly knocked Mo Weir flat. He'd been bustling across the rear hallway, hell bent on getting somewhere fast for something apparently important. Lila thought of stopping him, of asking sideways questions that would tell her just how batshit her own mother was. Seeing Meyer's murder had shattered something inside her. Lila felt it broken inside herself as well, but she was dealing with the tragedy in a normal way. Without changing history. She wasn't trying to take back her earlier assertions that certain people had left the planet — in, Lila thought with black amusement, the old meaning of the phrase rather than the new one.

Mom had seemed so certain. So sure. So serious, without any of her usual jokes.

But something was going on with her and probably had been for years. Since Astral Day. She'd been through as much as the rest of them, maybe more. But she wasn't keeping it together. Heather masked torment with humor. Lila tended to feel the pain, which she supposed was healthy. But now all that bottled emotion must be backing up inside her mom like a clogged toilet trying to clear its throat. And now she'd either broken inside or had leveled up as an asshole.

Still, Clara led Lila angrily up the stairs. The small girl never looked back. If she had, Lila would have realized something she'd been trying in various degrees to ignore: that Clara, not Mo Weir, was the one to ask about any happenings in the house. She could ask Clara directly, without the subterfuge that would be necessary if she asked the aide. Clara wouldn't think her mom was ridiculous to ask if Grandma was telling the truth, when everyone knew she was short a few critical nuts from her snack bowl.

Her father was dead. It was an impossible thing to think, given the mansion's reaction. What she'd overheard from Mo earlier. What Raj had said — his claim like the planting of a flag.

She was being stupid.

Maybe her father was alive after all. Not asking made her the sick one, not Heather.

"Clara ..."

Clara kept moving. Her small legs were, as with the rest of her, oddly certain. It was eerie, watching her climb. She was barely old enough to be clambering up the stone steps hand-and-knee, yet she took them like an adult, holding to the newel posts because the risers were huge relative to her natural gait.

Lila didn't need an answer. She already had it.

Let's go find him, Clara had said earlier. About Meyer. About Grandpa, while everyone else was saying he'd kicked his final bucket.

But nobody told Lila anything. No one had in forever. Terrence and Heather didn't try to enlist her help to overthrow the Raj regime; she'd had to discover that by chasing her father. And Dad hadn't asked her thoughts; she'd had to guilt him into changing his mind and shooting Raj, right there on the spot.

And Raj? He was so much worse. Normal husbands talked to their wives. He might have said, *Honey, your mom and everyone else in the world seem to be up to something, like trying to overthrow the city.* She might have listened. At least he'd have been sharing his day, discussing his work.

Back upstairs, Clara grew quiet. Suddenly uninterested in the Apex, which had claimed her attention just minutes before, now back to pulsing blue outside the window — albeit brighter with the lights out. Maybe faster.

Clara shuffled blocks. She lined them up in long rows. Two banks with a space in the middle, like a highway. She arranged tiny men and women from a play set no two-year-old should have. But getting them from imported merchandise stockpiles had seemed so natural. Clara didn't play like a toddler. She played like a teenager and swallowed nothing.

"What are you doing, honey?" Lila asked, coming to

her knees, dismissing thoughts of her father — something to deal with later, like her mother's mental collapse.

Clara said, *"Shh."*

Lila shushed for a few seconds, but there was a meticulous feel to Clara's play. The kind of play, she realized, that Lila had come to view like a news report or weather forecast.

Rows of blocks.

Little plastic men and women, lined along the edges.

Two figures in the middle — far too large for the rest, a Barbie and a Ken.

A second line of people and set-aside blocks to one side. If the long row was a highway, the offshoot would be an exit ramp. A second option, smaller than the first.

But most of Clara's attention had, strangely, turned to a dark-purple scarf that one of the other capitals' ambassadors had given to the Heaven's Veil viceroy's family members as a gift. She didn't need a scarf; as New American royalty, Lila had ample closet space, stuffed with all the clothing she'd ever want — not that she ever went anywhere or did anything worthy of her fancy apparel.

Lila had given the scarf to Clara. Somehow, the thing — fine to touch, surely expensive in the old world — had made it to the floor. Now it might as well be a rag. Something Clara was cleaning her play area with, bunched in one childishly pudgy fist.

Except that Clara wasn't cleaning with the scarf. She was playing with it, trotting it along at one end of the line of blocks as if it were a character in her game.

"What is that, Clara?" Lila asked. Not meaning its real-life identity, but its function in her game.

Again Clara said, *"Shh.* It's almost time."

Clara touched Ken's forehead.

She swooshed the scarf, beyond the line of people, as if unseen.

Lila watched a smile form on her daughter's lips.

The scarf unfolded. Clara tossed it lightly. And beneath it, all of the little people vanished.

"Good night," she said.

Chapter Twenty-Nine

Rows of Titans moved closer. First at the front and rear and then from the sides. It happened like squeezing a tube; ahead, the Titans came from right and left to meet in the middle. Then the line pinched down from ahead, closing like an approaching zipper.

Piper stopped. Cameron turned.

It was happening at the rear, too.

Closing around from the sides. Slowly. With smiles. Piper didn't see Reptars. Just Titans, politely choking in.

"What do we do?" she asked Cameron, who seemed to have an answer tucked up his sleeve.

"It's okay. I … I think this is okay."

"What are you expecting to happen?"

"I don't know what it is. Just … *something.*"

"Cam …"

"It's okay. They don't know where the Hammer is. They still think we'll lead them to it."

If the Astrals needed them, Piper wasn't seeing it.

The Titans inched closer. They didn't look menacing or threatening. They almost looked curious. But then again, that's how Titans always looked. It hadn't changed them from becoming beasts, then tearing their friends to shreds.

They didn't need anything. They'd take the key. Then they'd kill them.

Cameron's eyes flicked to the side. Piper turned and saw human officers filling the space behind the Titans. Reinforcements, as if they were needed.

Piper felt a change sweep the air, as if something had flown by unseen. The generator-fueled lights flickered then blinked out. Something seeped from the street itself, filling the air like a fog. Something that filled her ears with sinister-sounding whispers.

In the pulsing blue glow, the Titans looked at each other. They looked at their hands, as if they'd never seen them before.

The pyramid's light came and went. While lit, Piper could barely see with her adjusted eyes. Once it was out, she could only see silhouettes.

A black fog oozed among the Titans. A fog she recognized. And when Piper forced her eyes to defocus, she could see it happen: that one black dog shape she'd seen at the edge of her vision for days was splitting into many pieces, running amid the Titans, becoming mist, sliding into their bodies through their humanlike noses.

Ahead, one Titan looked at the Astral beside him.

The second Titan shoved the first, whose face formed a scowl, some unknown grievance suddenly pressing between the always-placid hulks.

The one who'd done the shoving opened his mouth to a sharp row of Reptar teeth.

The blue light from the Apex departed. The blue light returned.

More shoving from the other side. Grunting shouts. All

around them, Titans began to transform — not morphing as they had in Cottonwood Canyon, but becoming confused hybrid things with parts of each: eyes of a Reptar, throat-deep blue and glowing. Titans grew scales. Fingernails became claws at the end of muscular white arms, ready to slash.

Piper heard human shouts. Somewhere in the dark, a gun went off. She could see its flash in the blackness: a millisecond starburst of white.

Piper looked at Cameron. Cameron looked at Piper. They were afraid to move, still in their capsule with its empty halo around them.

The Titans weren't coming for the intruders. They were too preoccupied, all of a sudden, with fighting each other.

"What the hell is going on?" Cameron shouted.

But he'd known something was coming. Piper could only watch it happen. Struggling to maintain her lack of focus in the flickering gloom, she watched the dark shape change again, moving from mist to something larger, collecting to the right. Forming a partition, prying Titans apart, making those it touched all the more furious.

Piper watched one's entire arm become that of a Reptar. The Titan slashed another's throat, spilling blood that, in the dark, looked all too human.

The wedge between dark shapes opened. And at the end of the newly opened way, Piper saw Christopher.

They didn't hesitate.

Piper and Cameron ran, leaving the alien bloodbath behind.

Chapter Thirty

ONE MINUTE, Raj was looking down at Terrence, watching his progress without knowing what he was doing. In that minute, all was well with the world. He'd learned something the Astrals couldn't know, and he'd sent the cops out to handle it. He hadn't quite unearthed the dirt on Meyer he wanted given the strange way he'd freaked out while speaking to Terrence, but he was on his way. With a victory in the streets under his belt and forthcoming evidence of the viceroy's duplicity, it was beginning to feel like Raj might ascend in the Heaven's Veil power structure after all.

But the next minute, the lights flicked away. Raj saw something approaching, big, and fast. The room's single battery-powered security light flickered on, and Raj saw that the big thing was the viceroy. Meyer grabbed his shirt with both fists, not bothering to yell before hurling him backward.

Raj spilled from his chair, the seat wheeling out from under him. His head rapped the ground. The chair struck one of the server racks and rebounded, rolling to Meyer's feet as he continued to come, murder still burning bright in his eyes. He grabbed the chair without seeming to think, raised it over his head, and threw it hard at Raj as he lay sprawled on the floor. Raj managed to roll to the side but not far enough; the chair hit his leg sideways, its metal frame tearing a gash on his leg.

Raj looked up. There were guards in the room as before, but they were just watching. Letting the man in charge do whatever he chose.

"WAIT!" Raj yelled, on his back like a beetle, hands up toward Meyer, legs held off the floor to deflect further attacks.

But Meyer didn't wait. He came hard, grabbing Raj by one upper arm and a fistful of canvas undershirt, dragging him to his feet far too easily. The man's strength was insane; he always looked fit, but now he lifted Raj like a strongman, slamming him into one of the racks, making it clang. Hardware dropped to the floor. The viceroy's fist returned. Raj tried to hold up a hand, but the knuckles came anyway, and Raj could only duck away.

Fist met metal, hard enough to dent it. Tiny electronics tapped onto the surrounding surfaces like blown shrapnel. Terrence yelled out, raising his hands, standing, concerned more for the machines than for the human combatants.

Raj slid to the ground. When Meyer picked him up again, Raj's eyes rolled to his fist — a red, shredded mess. Bone was visible at his knuckles, blood running down his punching hand to stain his white cuffs.

A rocket detonated in Raj's left cheek, shooting all the way up into his brain. He'd never before understood *seeing stars*, but he got it now, his vision blackening, white pinpoints of light dancing around him like fireflies. Then he was limp, trying to stand, able to think bizarrely only that the fist Meyer had hit him with had been macerated.

A blow to his stomach. A guttural roar, like an animal's. Lights strobed, turning the room into a disco.

Something crashed. Raj could barely pay attention. Terrence was somewhere above, now trying to hold Meyer despite being, Raj thought, firmly on Meyer's side. He tried to sit up and say something, but his body wasn't working. Something erupted in his side, and Raj rolled away, coming back to see the viceroy's polished black shoe recoil, preparing for another kick.

Then the lights came on.

And Meyer, with his foot back, slowly lowered it.

"I didn't have a choice," Raj croaked, looking up at Meyer, meaning his assassination attempt, meaning the way he'd only been doing his duty while everyone else stood back and let Rome die in fire around them.

But Meyer didn't look down with anger. His eyes clouded, and the expression crossing his features seemed confused, almost lost.

Then Meyer left the room, his fist dripping, without saying a word.

Chapter Thirty-One

THE GENERATOR SEEMED to kick on, purring without anyone bothering to start it. Coughing back from nothing, returning the newly mounted floods to life around them.

"Get down," said Malcolm Jons.

Cameron looked up at the man, now kneeling behind a wheeled refuse bin beside Piper. Jons had his arm out, his uniform sleeve straining against his massive diameter. Jons clearly trained, but he also struck Cameron as a natural giant. He probably looked at iron and grew muscle — as opposed to Cameron, who'd experimented with weight lifting in his twenties, only to give up in abject frustration.

He didn't know if he could trust Captain Jons. But at this point, it hardly mattered.

"They were going to take us," Piper said. "They weren't going to let us near the pyramid. They were just going to take us in, maybe kill us outright."

Cameron could only shake his head. That was only one of several things that had gone horribly awry in the last ten minutes.

"I thought they needed us to find Thor's Hammer," Piper said.

Cameron was still shaking his head, out of breath, adrenaline filled, and shocked. "Apparently, they decided they don't need us after all."

"Shh," said Jons, warning arm still out, searching the street for signs of pursuit. Cameron thought they'd got away clean while the lights had been out, but there was no way to be sure. This hadn't been like last time, when the Astrals had let Cameron believe he might be alone, that there'd been a huge oversight in security and intruders were free to wander the streets at will. This time, they hadn't been as subtle. Piper was right; they weren't planning merely to shadow them to the Apex, leaving them alone until they revealed what they knew in the quest for Thor's Hammer. That had been a mob, closing around them like a noose.

It had always been a possibility, of course, and Cameron might never have gone if not for the visions — if not for the certainty that when they entered Heaven's Veil, something unexpected would intervene to help them. And when the Titans closed around them in the knot, that had felt dream familiar too, as if he'd known it was coming. He could only see a few seconds ahead, but he'd believed those visions.

But that didn't mean he had any idea what had just happened.

"They'll be looking everywhere," said Christopher, speaking to Jons. And as if to underscore his point, there was a purr one street over as a Reptar (or perhaps a contingent) ran past. Cameron could hear their claws scraping on concrete, the rattle of indrawn breath.

"Surveillance," Christopher said when Jons didn't respond.

"The networks are down. Surveillance is down."

"The Astrals have their own devices."

Cameron was about to speak up from their hidden position, adding his two cents about the tiny silver BBs. But Jons seemed to know about that, too.

"Based on what I got from those bald white fuckers earlier, most of *their* shit isn't working, either. At least as far as prying eyes. If it was, they wouldn't have been licking our balls to help out."

"We can't take them to the station."

"We'll take them to Grandma Mary."

"Who's that?"

But Piper seemed somehow, impossibly, to know. She raised her voice to Jons.

"They know about Mary. The church by the wall was an underground camp. I was with them a while ago. The church was raided, and we escaped through a tunnel that came up in Mary's basement."

"They don't know about Mary," Jons said.

"How can you be sure?"

"Because she's my grandmama. And she said they didn't follow you through the tunnels."

"I heard a shotgun behind us," Piper protested.

"She shot a few through her window."

"They'd come after her for that."

"They *did* come after her for that. But Grandmama shot them, too."

He lowered his arm then waved for them to follow.

"Let's go. Her place isn't far. If your asses are lucky, she'll have a pie on."

Chapter Thirty-Two

SHE COULDN'T JUST SIT HERE.

Heather stood from her chair. Dusted herself off, even though Terrence's old house (presumably *old*; he'd probably be cut into pieces and sent to the mothership as lunch after he was done) wasn't especially dusty. She took a few deep breaths, looking out across the lawn between here and the main house.

Security lights had come back on a few minutes ago. City lights were still stubbornly dead. Neither had affected Heather as she sat in the dark. But now with the lights on, she could see the line Lila and Clara had tromped through the evening dew, straight as an arrow slicing the grass between here and the mansion's side door. Even the line of footprints managed to look angry, as if Lila had left all her frustration behind.

Well, fuck her. She was Heather's daughter, but if Lila didn't believe, *fuck her.* This wasn't a joke, and nobody — even the Queen of Mean, hiding from Meyer's creepy doppelgänger in one of the small houses — thought it was funny. If she'd been trying to have a laugh, then okay, Heather could see Lila's point. But she wasn't.

Meyer was dead.

And now he wasn't.

Not only was it crap to blame Heather for simply stating facts; it was dismissive of all that she'd suffered. Was it Lila who'd had to watch her father die — to let *Raj* kill Meyer, to add insult to mortality? Nope, that had been Heather. And was it Lila who had to face off against ... against *whatever the shit that was* in there? Nope. Again, that honor had fallen to her.

And now she was being *blamed* for her horrid experiences? For her trauma? For being forced to endure so much terrible, gut-wrenching crap in one day?

Yeah. Lila was Heather's blood and the apple of her eye, but right now: *Fuck. That. Bitch.*

The jolt of righteous anger made her feel better.

Heather stepped out onto the porch. She still felt nervous, still unsure. Not long after Lila had stormed off with Clara (who'd wanted to stay; that was another reason for *FUCK LILA* right now), the security lights had buried the lawn in darkness.

Then there'd been some sort of enormous commotion from the home's front, from past it. Like out near the gate.

Not long after that, there'd been a ruckus in the house itself. Heather looked up now, seeing a window open and a light way up on the fourth floor. She knew *that* place well. That's where she'd gone with Terrence then been trapped and tied up by Lila's cunt of a husband. That's where Meyer had done the thing that had — and she was sticking to this version of the story, though it hurt more — got him killed.

Again, by Lila's cunt of a husband.

Maybe he was a cuckold. The odd, irreverent, irrelevant thought gave Heather a jolt of glee. Clara didn't look like Raj at all. Usually, those foreigner genes were dominant as hell, but Lila had squeezed out a blonde with blue eyes. It would point to Heather's failure as a mother if Lila had been playing the field of dicks and only *telling* Raj this kid was his, but it would also strike Heather as more awesome than disappointing if true.

The fourth-floor window was quiet. That must have been where the crashing had come from, though; the noise had been sharp, and no other windows were open. No other lights on this side (notably: Trevor's, which also hurt) were lit. Terrence was burning the midnight oil, with Raj whipping him to undo what he couldn't — what he probably *wouldn't* undo if he could.

Yes. Well, it didn't matter. What mattered was that she couldn't just sit around and let ... well, *whatever it was* ... happen. Throughout her life, Heather had always faced adversity in one of two ways: Either she'd run and pretend she didn't care or face it the way someone would fight while a camera was on her. Heather had a reputation as "feisty" in Hollywood before Astral Day, but really it was all a performance. When her adversaries got reasonable and discussed resolution, she always folded. Without a fight worthy of the front page, Heather's soft center just wasn't strong enough.

No more.

Some weird crap was happening here, and for once, she wouldn't be the wiseass who made jokes and did nothing.

Meyer Dempsey had, it seemed, never stopped loving her.

Whatever it was inside the house wasn't the man she once adored.

She owed it to him. To Meyer. To his memory. Heather crossed the grass, her fists clenched.

Chapter Thirty-Three

WHEN THE LIGHTS came back on and the tumult from above finally settled, Lila let Clara go. Her daughter hadn't wanted to be held in the first place. Lila told herself she was protecting her child. But really, she was looking for a teddy bear to squeeze.

With the lights on and Clara gone from her arms, Lila walked to the window.

Grid power was still off. She plucked her phone from the end table and verified that there still wasn't service. Outside, she could tell that the less superficial networks — used by the city's bones and even the Astrals, she suspected — were probably still out as well. From her room, she couldn't see much more than she'd managed on the ground, except a scattering of cops running hither and yon, not at their proper posts inside the house grounds, not coordinated at all. She could see the Astral shuttles patrolling like people would without leadership: more or less randomly — every man (or alien) for himself.

But the generator lights were back, just like in the

house. Even the lights not connected to the grid had winked out, before returning.

"You feeling okay, Clara?" Lila said.

Clara was curled up on the floor with the blocks and toys that had so recently and so intensely interested her. The purple scarf, which had seemed to play an important role in the game, was lying discarded to the side. Clara's power was like the city's, it seemed. Bright one moment and dead the next.

There was a small baby blanket, too small for her daughter last year, on a low shelf. Lila grabbed it and draped it over what little of Clara it managed to cover.

"Yes, Mommy, you should go."

Lila realized she'd been thinking about her father. It wasn't surprising, given what had happened or what she'd been recently mulling — not even including the face-off with her mom across the lawn. But still she hadn't noticed until Clara spoke, and she couldn't help hearing those words as a suggestion about Dad. Or maybe permission.

"Go where, Clara?"

Her daughter was already sleeping, looking for all the world like an ordinary two-year-old.

Chapter Thirty-Four

HEATHER EXPECTED to find Meyer in his office. His life had been defined by work. That was who he had been. It was, until he'd died, who Meyer was even today.

So it surprised Heather when she walked through the big dining room's east doorway and saw him bleeding all over the formal table, wrapping his hand in gauze and tape.

He looked up. He seemed to smile, feel the grin on his lips, then consciously fight to keep it down. It was a confusing sequence of actions, and seeing it unnerved her.

"Heather," he said.

Lila entered the dining room from the other end, through the west doorway, before Heather could respond. Her mouth hung open. She looked at her father then her mother. Heather saw remonstration. Of annoyance. Maybe of hatred.

That was a cruel, sick joke to tell me he'd died, she seemed to say.

Heather opened her mouth to reply, but then Lila rushed forward and hugged Meyer around the middle.

His hands went up. His destroyed, dripping right hand brushed Lila's side, painting her with a broad stroke of crimson. She hugged him while he waited, holding up gauze and disinfectant, dark blood trickling down his arm. A wad of paper towels was on the table with the rest, soaked.

Lila released him, her eyes wet.

"Hey," he said, forming a smile. "What was that about?"

Instead of replying, she hugged him in an encore. Then she released him again and said, "I love you, Daddy."

A strange, defenseless look crossed his features. "Thanks, sweetheart."

"Mom said you were dead." She looked hard at Heather then back at her father. She seemed to realize what a strange thing that was to say to someone who seemed so healthy (other than one smashed hand), but she forced her next words behind it. "She said Raj killed you."

Meyer gave a dismissive little laugh. "Well, he didn't."

Heather came forward, skirting the table. She looked at Lila.

"Don't look at me like that, Lila. You heard Raj. You saw how bloody I was. Don't act like this was all a big joke. And don't you dare act like you were right, seeing as I told you he was alive again." She paused. "Except that like I said, he's dead."

Heather could hear herself, knew how ridiculous she must sound. *Alive again.* And *Like I said, he's dead.* Yeah. Those weren't things a crazy person said. It was positively shocking that Lila didn't believe her every word.

It was impossible to talk with Meyer between them, with him dressing his wound in the middle of the formal dining room instead of somewhere logical, like a bathroom. How had this little display even happened? They didn't store gauze in the dining room. He must have run somewhere for it then brought it here. Or he'd started to clean this strange new wound (and forget *that* mystery for a second) before getting suddenly hungry.

Heather grabbed Lila's arm and dragged her aside, to the room's end, as if Meyer might not notice them standing there talking about him.

"I wasn't lying to you, Lila."

"Mom …"

"I told you he died. He did. I saw it happen. He wasn't breathing. His eyes were open. It was over." She blinked back tears, realizing how strange it would be to cry over the death of a man who was, in most people's opinions, standing five feet from her now.

"I know you thought that, but—"

"And then I told you he was back. I told you to go in and find him. I was telling you the truth then, too."

"Mom, I know how you are, and I just—"

"This isn't funny to me, Lila. I haven't been screwing with you. You need to believe me. That's not …" Heather stopped, hearing herself. She was about to say, *That's not your father.* And when it had been just Heather and Meyer in the room, that had been easy to believe. But now she wasn't just seeing Meyer through her own eyes. She was seeing him through Lila's, too.

What, did she think he'd been body snatched?

Was it really that hard to believe what he'd said earlier, now that she really thought about it? After knocking Raj out cold, she'd seen a shuttle coming. She sat on the stones, sobbing over what she'd thought (perhaps erroneously) were Meyer's final breaths. The shuttle's approach was the reason she'd run, fleeing in futile circles before realizing Dorothy was right, and that in an alien-colonized city, there really was no place like home. She'd assumed the shuttle would arrive, see what had happened, and cart him away. Maybe finish Raj off for her. Or perhaps give pursuit, knowing Heather was a saboteur, and a potential murderer.

But maybe that's not what the shuttle had done.

Maybe it had fixed him, even though he'd been technically dead.

After all, when people drowned, CPR could revive them minutes later. When they flatlined in ambulances and emergency rooms, countless TV shows had proved that a crash cart could bring those people back.

Yes, he'd been dead. Shot through the heart or lungs or God knew what else. Diced inside. But maybe the aliens had been able to fix the damage and re-fire his system.

"That's not what?" Meyer said, looking right at her.

Heather said nothing. Lila's hard eyes softened. Heather exhaled, her shoulders dropping, defensive tension draining from her frame.

Heather thought Lila might cry, for reasons unknown — for the stress if nothing else.

Or maybe she'd walk out, still annoyed by her jackass mother's antics.

But instead, Lila hugged Heather, too.

Behind her, Meyer smiled.

He continued to wrap his damaged hand.

Because even though Astral technology had healed a bullet through the chest, it somehow wasn't available to fix a tenderized fist.

Chapter Thirty-Five

WHEN CHARLIE CAME around the RV, Nathan had parked himself in a folding lawn chair at the vehicle's front, kicked back with a beer that had to be at least three years old. The moon had emerged and Nathan had no idea what time it was, but in this shitty folding chair he'd enjoyed the feeling of sitting under the sun on a summer day. Possibly while swatting flies and bitching about welfare.

"Send your drone," Charlie said. There was no hello. There was only a command.

Nathan looked to Coffey for support, but she must have gone inside. The lawn chair next to him was empty, its garishly colored straps of woven plastic fiber exposed to the cool nighttime air instead of safely concealed by her ass.

"It's malfunctioning," Nathan answered.

"Let me look at it."

"It's so malfunctioned, you can't even look at it."

Charlie stood still, staring at Nathan through his thick glasses, his bushy brown-and-gray beard doing nothing to make him look softer or less angular. Charlie didn't have particularly large eyes, but they always seemed to be sticking out, accusing the person they were watching of idiocy.

"The lights have been on for a while now," Charlie announced. "Still just the generators. The drone might be able to spot them and go unseen if you got it close before. We need to know if they went toward the Apex. If they're on target."

"I don't think they are," Nathan stared.

Charlie stared.

"Are you going to ask *why* I think they're not on target?"

"Why?"

"Because the Astrals probably chose to arrest them instead. It was inevitable."

"We decided that the chances of arrest were low. That's why we did this."

Nathan swigged his beer. "Ah. Yes. But that was back when we thought the Astrals would need our friends to show them to Thor's Hammer because they themselves didn't know where it was."

Charlie's stare faltered. So he was human after all. "What are you talking about?"

"I dropped a message to Meyer Dempsey. Told him that two people were entering the city and that they were carrying the key to something the Astrals were very interested in, inside Cameron's satchel." Another sip. The beer tasted like gasoline.

Nathan tipped his beer at Charlie. "Oh. And that that what the Astrals were searching for was almost for-sure under the Apex after all, just in a different chamber, and that if they scanned down there for stone matching the unique kind used in the key, they'd probably have no trouble fi—"

Nathan stopped talking when Charlie, showing agility

never before seen in a scientist, leaped forward and rolled them both over the chair, onto the ground.

Nathan had thought Charlie might try to hit him, but he hadn't expected his fervor. The quickest and easiest way to let Charlie in on the situation was this ripping off of the Band-Aid, so Nathan had come ready to parry. But Charlie was stronger and more lithe than he appeared to be, and Coffey wasn't around. Nathan was pinned in seconds.

"You turned them in?"

Nathan raised his leg, fast and hard. The knee struck Charlie in the balls, and he rolled away, moaning. Then, as Nathan righted the chair and brushed himself off to stand, Charlie hobbled over and tried to hit him. This time, Nathan was ready. But still, Charlie's effort — stepping up with his boys crushed — was admirable.

The fight was over in less than thirty seconds. The scuffle pulled Coffey from the RV, but there was no longer a need. Nathan and Charlie were both leaning against opposite awning supports, panting. Two men past their youth, scrapping like teenagers.

"What's going on here?" Coffey demanded, eyeing them both.

"I don't think he likes my plan," Nathan said.

Charlie lunged again. This time, Coffey was in the middle. She did little other than extend an arm but must have hit Charlie because he staggered and again found his place in the corner.

"You sold them out to save yourself," Charlie said.

"Sit down, Charlie."

"You're a selfless, brutal—"

"Sit *down*, Charlie," Coffey repeated, pushing her chair toward him. "Let him explain."

Charlie seemed both shocked and darkly satisfied by

Coffey's lack of surprise over the duplicity. His eyes were wary as he slowly sat, his body tense.

"We've been through this song and dance before," Andreus said. "Man walks to gate. Man is allowed to enter. Then man does what the Astrals expect, hoping he'll somehow be allowed to leave when he's done, and of course that's not how it happens. Last time, the Republic managed to get in there and take them out, but even that shouldn't have worked. If they hadn't specifically wanted us to get away so we'd get to take Piper to Moab, my people would have been fried as they'd rolled across the land between here and there. Think about it. Why has your lab been permitted to survive, even today? Because they needed Benjamin. After his death, they needed Cameron to go through his father's research, and of course they need that power outlet on the property. Our truce is the only reason my camps haven't been destroyed."

He paused. Chances were extraordinarily slim that the Republic, which didn't have the strategic significance to the Astrals of a Moab laboratory, was still in existence.

"Or *had* a truce, anyway," Nathan finished. There should probably be emotion there, but he didn't want to go looking. He'd managed to find Grace. That was enough. "We only truly fooled the Astrals once. Don't tell me you can't see the difference."

Charlie was still watching Nathan with his big bug eyes.

"Cameron's plan wouldn't have worked. Somehow, he was supposed to do the exact same switcharoo we did in Cottonwood? It was absurd. Maybe the standoff would have held until they'd entered the Apex, which the Astrals would likely have allowed them to do. But they'd have been watched. By Reptars, if it's true those little BB things don't work with the network out. He'd basically have had a guard on his tail the entire time. They'd have taken him the minute he reached the Hammer. Maybe Benjamin figured out what the Templars pulled off better than the Astrals, but I'll bet they know how to use their own doomsday weapon just fine. There'd be no more need for Cameron or Piper. They'd have taken the key and turned it on. Then we'd all be fucked."

"So you turned them in to save your skin," Charlie said.

There was a low whistling noise in the sky above. Charlie looked up nervously, searching for a shuttle or perhaps the dark specter the others said they kept seeing like kids afraid of the boogeyman. But Nathan knew what it was, and it was right on time.

The black drone glided by, rolling to a stop on the flat land just beyond them.

"Malfunctioning," Charlie said.

Nathan and Charlie stared at each other while Coffey trotted over. She returned with nothing more elegant or spectacular than a slip of paper that must have been banded to the drone's belly.

She handed the paper to Nathan. He read it and smiled.

"What?" Charlie asked.

"Looks like Dempsey got my message turning them in to save my skin," he said, "and has requested my presence in Heaven's Veil."

"Why?"

"To make peace," Nathan said. "To discuss resuming my duties, controlling the outlands for our alien overlords."

Chapter Thirty-Six

CAMERON KEPT LOOKING UP, reminding himself that nobody was all knowing or all powerful, and that the Astrals weren't an exception.

There were no shuttles directly overhead, following them. There were no Reptars on the streets ... on their paths. Without the reminder, Cameron couldn't help wondering what game was being played against them — why the Astrals were letting them go free. But there was another possibility, if Cameron could let himself believe it: that the Astrals weren't letting them go at all, and that for a change, they had actually managed evasion.

He thought of the Titans — the way they'd turned on each other like common thugs.

He thought of what Piper kept asking herself, and Cameron: what the black shadow had done back there, when it had diffused and surrounded them all. Was it responsible for what had happened? It sure seemed that way. But why? What was it? And what, precisely, had it done?

And again: Was the shadow — or the Astrals as a

whole — playing them like the BB had been playing them before they'd discovered its presence? Was this another game? Another ruse designed to ease the fugitives into a false sense of security, as they'd been lulled before? Were the Astrals still watching ... and were Cameron, Piper, Christopher, and Captain Jons now doing exactly what the Astrals wanted them to do, for reasons unknown?

Piper watched Cameron's face as they half ran, half stalked the Heaven's Veil streets. She seemed to be wondering the same things. Piper had run this same basic route before ending up at the church. Now they were headed almost all the way back, hoping for different results: a genuine escape rather than one they were coached to make. But Jons had sworn that Grandma Mary was still safe, that she hadn't been discovered.

Unless, of course, Jons was against them, too. Playing them as one escape within another, either as part of the Astral cause or because he planned to turn them in for alien favor.

"Don't do that," Piper told Cameron, whispering when they stopped to scan an intersection so that the others wouldn't hear.

"What?"

"Don't look at Christopher and the captain like that. I know what you're thinking."

Despite the tension, Cameron couldn't help a small smile. The last time he'd been running for his life, Piper had been tortured and weak. This time, she was the stronger between them.

"How do you know what I'm thinking?"

"Because I'm thinking it too."

Cameron caught a flash of her big blue eyes. There was something there below the surface, and for a second he sensed more than what her face was saying, as if he could again peer inside her mind. The shared bond that had struck them while traveling from Vail to Moab had dissipated years ago, but its ghost, Cameron thought, still lingered.

"You said Reptars followed you. To this woman's house."

Piper shook her head. "They followed us. But I don't know where. And if they never made it to Mary's ..."

"Shh!" Jons held up an arm and gave them a warning look that said, *You two want to yammer on and get your asses caught, do it when I'm not risking my balls to be here with you.*

But still, Cameron looked up. Waiting for shuttles to spot them. Thinking, *If they're looking, why can't they find us?*

He could sense Piper as she watched him. Her head slowly shook. There was something about what had happened in the melee near the gate that Piper understood even though Cameron didn't. Something she seemed to have fathomed at Moab, before they'd sneaked —Cameron wanted to add mental air quotes: "sneaked" — in to find research that the Astrals wanted them to find. And Andreus's daughter, whom they'd left to deliver a message.

They have everything under control, Piper had said, *but they can lose control, too.*

"This is it." Jons pointed to a small house on the corner.

Cameron watched the skies, desperately hoping that Piper was right, and that even aliens might only be human.

Chapter Thirty-Seven

THE FIRST THING that assailed Piper when they entered Grandma Mary's home through the concealed back door was, shockingly, the yeasty scent of baked dough blending with cinnamon and apples. She'd baked a pie, just as Jons had said.

The second thing that greeted Piper was more familiar: the muzzle of Mary's shotgun.

"Malcolm," the old woman said, lowering her weapon and sliding it into the wheelchair's holster. "It's good ta see ya."

The enormous cop bent to wrap the woman in a hug. For one strange moment, Piper half expected him to pick her up, to hug her upright with dangling legs. But he merely straightened while the old woman's hands stayed high, seeming to seek a final second of contact. Then the limbs lowered, and Mary met each of their eyes. It was neither a good nor bad look — the assessing glance of a person who's lived enough life to know that what would be would be, and that she merely wanted to assess its shape in the meantime.

"Brought me visitors."

"Yeah, Grandmama. This is Cameron. Piper, you've met."

The small black woman tipped Piper a nod. They hadn't met so much as Piper had run past her with Gloria, Franklin, and the other monks. There had been a muttering of thanks and a few words from the abbess, but Piper only remembered Mary as she'd remember a nightmare's oasis. Despite the circumstances of their previous encounter, Piper felt comfort in her gut. This woman had been willing to hold off Reptars for them.

Then Piper saw Cameron's look and knew exactly what he was thinking — exactly the same thing she was thinking in the cynical half of her brain: If she'd survived Piper's last trip through this house, was it because she'd been lucky and the Reptars hadn't found the exact passage? Or was Mary — and Jons — in on all of this?

Stop thinking crazy.

She forced herself to breathe. Forced herself to trust, and believe. She'd come. Now she was here. If this was all another part of an elaborate snare, it was too late to do anything about it now.

"Din't catch ya name last time. But good to see ya got away, and good to have ya back." Mary turned to Jons. "You ain't stayin'." It was a statement, not a question.

"No." Jons clapped Christopher on the back. "Me and Chris got stations to man."

"You think they fooled?"

"Nobody saw us."

"They see a shit more than ya think, Malcolm."

Jons shook his head. In Piper's mind, she saw the shadow. She saw it spread out and become mist. She saw Titan turn on Titan, tempers erupting as if from a long-held grudge. That part of Meyer, at least, hadn't changed post-abduction. He'd always had a child's patience with those who annoyed him. He had a biting tongue and a tendency to snipe before thinking. He was cool in the negotiating room but petulant in the privacy of his home. Short on patience. Infuriating to live with, in the few instances where his will didn't force his way.

"This time it was different, Grandmama."

The woman had a face that seemed to have been wrinkled by the press of years. She looked like a person who'd had a hard life and emerged its humble champion, but who wore those old stories' scars in folds of skin. Piper thought she'd protest. Perhaps point out that those in charge had their ways, that Grandboy Malcolm would be a durn fool to believe what he did.

Instead, she unlocked the wheelchair brakes and turned, making for the kitchen.

"Keep your bags and guns close 'case you gotta run," Mary said, "but bring y'selves inta the front. I ain't gonna give this pie to Donna an' her kids when I got hungry mouths in my own home."

Chapter Thirty-Eight

RAJ LIMPED into the network center with a look that said, *Don't you say a fucking word*.

Terrence averted his gaze immediately. There were times to trifle with Raj, but they'd been diminishing in recent weeks. Back in Meyer Dempsey's Vail bunker, he'd been the group's punching bag. Heather had hit his pride with a vengeance, Lila had cheated on him, and together she and Christopher had played him for a fool. Meyer, both before and after the bunker, had supposedly walked across his back like a welcome mat. Even Terrence had taken his shots when he could.

But then Raj had decided to start taking his job seriously. At first, it had been pathetically funny, before it became something darker. Something dangerous.

With a bruised and cut mouth, Raj said, "Tell me you're almost done."

Terrence shook his head. He found himself answering Raj straight, without any rancor. When Meyer had left the room, he'd honestly thought Raj was dead. Two of the human guards had pulled him up, dragged him out, and apparently taken him somewhere for first aid. The whole process had been done aseptically, as if the guards' cargo was a sack of inert matter instead of a human. Now Raj was back: cut, bruised, able to walk but clearly with pain. It was hard to be cruel to Raj when life already had been.

"It's not something that can be fixed," Terrence answered.

"You started it."

"Raj." He inhaled then exhaled, trying to make his voice eminently reasonable. "I could start a fire, too, but I couldn't unburn a home from ash."

"Then rebuild it."

"Every machine connected," Terrence said. "Not just the servers here, but anything pulling data from the polluted streams."

"You must have had a way to undo it so your friends could get help when they needed it," Raj said, sitting with obvious pain.

"It wasn't supposed to do this. It went wrong. It was always 50/50."

"Just fix it," Raj said.

Terrence felt his shoulders rise and fall in a halfway shrug. Why not? It was better than the mothership. He wasn't doing more here than pushing code around, and deep down Raj had to know it was pointless. But he didn't seem to know what to do or where he stood. For a while, everyone had thought he'd managed a coup, killing Meyer. But now Meyer was back. Raj didn't know his place any more than Terrence. And nobody knew where the viceroy stood, except *back in charge*.

After another few minutes, a curious voice asked a question at Terrence's side. It took him a second to place it, simply because the tone seemed wrong. Raj was always arrogant, hectoring, a total asshole. This was almost amicable.

"What's wrong with him, do you think?"

Terrence turned.

"I know you talked to him. I saw it all."

"How—"

"And I know you talked to Christopher. I have proof. I'd have shown it to Meyer already, but …" He trailed off, again indicating the problem that was Meyer Dempsey.

"By now the Astrals should have Cameron Bannister in custody. Probably up where you were, on the mothership. Applying probes and whatnot. Did you get probed, Terrence? Did it hurt?"

He didn't know how to respond. The sadistic glint had reentered his eyes. Raj was a man with nothing to lose, it seemed. Even his allies had turned traitor.

"I killed him. Chased him and Heather off the grounds after they took you away. Shot him right in the chest. Heather hit me with something after, but I *saw* him hit. And when I came to, I was right there on the street because nobody bothered to help *me*." His lips twisted with bitterness. "Meyer was gone, but the street was stained red. And yet now he's back."

Terrence's eyes went to the door, as if expecting Meyer to return and finish what he started.

"The question," Raj said, "is why I'm not on your side."

Terrence's head perked up.

"I tried to please him. I did my job. And when he betrayed everyone, I did my job then, too. Did what nobody else would. What nobody else had the guts to do. And what happened? Did anyone listen? Or did they patch him back up and send that traitor out to do the same job as if he wasn't as responsible for this as you are?"

Terrence watched, seeing something in Raj come slowly undone. He seemed to be warring with competing emotions. With something unsolvable.

"If Meyer is on your side, am I on your side? Whose side am I on, Terrence?"

Terrence looked down at the monitor filled with senseless characters, at the house he was trying futilely to recover from cinders. Then he looked up at Raj. Security, both Astral and human, was near the door. Too far back to be hearing any of this.

"You could help," Terrence said. "It's not too late to do the right thing."

Raj seemed to consider. Then he leaned forward and, with his uninjured fist, hit Terrence hard in the gut.

"I know whose side I'm on," he whispered, still leaning forward. "Not on Dempsey's. Not on yours. Not on Cameron's. And, it seems, not even on the Astrals'."

Terrence, even as he fought to regain his breath, wanted to ask which side was left.

"I'm on *my* side," Raj said, his voice close to Terrence's ear. "Now fix what you broke, if you don't want to become disposable."

Chapter Thirty-Nine

HEATHER STOOD ACROSS THE OFFICE, watching the man who might or might not be Meyer Dempsey shuffling papers. She was leaning against the door frame. Meyer wasn't paying attention. He seemed to be searching for something, unable to find it.

"What are you looking for?" Heather asked.

"My cufflinks."

"Why?"

"For the formal dinner."

Heather bit her lip. The dinner had been days ago. She said so.

"Not that dinner," he said, though he clearly seemed flustered. "A new one."

"Hmm. And I'm supposed to go?"

"Of course. You, Lila, and Trevor."

"Trevor left the city, Meyer."

Meyer seemed to reset. Heather saw him pause, blink, and resume searching. Then he stood erect, snapped the drawer he'd been pawing through closed, and looked up.

"Just me," he said. "I got it mixed up."

"Just you for what?"

"We have a visitor coming."

"To a formal dinner?"

"Just a sit-down."

"So you don't need your cufflinks."

"I guess not."

Heather shifted her weight to her other leg, very aware of her body. She'd spent too much of her adult life willfully blind. She'd looked away from so much that she should have stared in the eye. Heather felt like she'd gained a new sense of vision in the past half day, a new way of seeing the world around her. With half of her mind, she felt defenseless, as if facing an attacker without armor even without anyone physically present. But with her other half, she felt a fresh curiosity. A new level of no-bullshit, and this one without all the biting sarcasm.

"When Raj killed you," Heather said, "did you see the light?"

"What light?"

"The light people see when they die."

Meyer still seemed distracted. He didn't look up. "I didn't see any light."

"What was it like, dying?"

"I didn't die, Heather."

"You definitely died. If you want me to believe that you're you, then don't insult me by saying you didn't die."

"Maybe medically," he said. "I don't really remember."

"But you remember what you said."

"Of course."

"What did you say, Meyer? Just so I believe you."

Like a robot, Meyer said, "Love you."

"Do you?"

"Do I what?"

"Do you love me?"

"I don't know, Heather. I'm busy here."

Heather's jaw moved side to side. She wasn't precisely wary of Meyer anymore. She was more curious than anything.

"Why did you attack Raj?"

"He was insubordinate."

"I'm insubordinate all the time, and you've never attacked me."

"That's different."

Heather nodded, but of course Meyer didn't see it. "Because I'm a woman."

"That's right."

"And you don't hit women."

"No."

"And Raj tried to kill you."

Meyer stopped with his hands mid-rummage. Heather didn't know what he was doing and wondered if he did. He'd already said he didn't need his cufflinks for … for *whoever* was coming to visit. So what was he trying to find? He struck her as an animal pacing its cage, unsure what else to do with his time.

"He did."

"So that's why you beat him up. That's how 'insubordinate' he was."

"Right."

"Terrence said you nearly killed him. An eye for an eye."

Meyer paused, looked up, then resumed his pointless rummaging. That should maybe ring some bells that, for whatever reason, weren't ringing. What had changed for Meyer? Her question about seeing the light wasn't a joke; Heather didn't believe in afterlife but did believe in how people always seemed to change after near-death experiences. That's how Meyer was now. Before he'd been shot, he'd almost become the man he hadn't been for years: the strong, independent, bullheaded man she'd fallen in love with more than two decades ago. He'd finally stopped toeing the line to do what was right. He'd fixed things with his ex-wife (whom he seemed still to love) and his daughter, before turning against the force occupying the planet after years of working on its behalf. That had seemed to make sense.

But this? This blank return to business as usual? This didn't.

"Maybe. I don't know, Heather. Why don't you head back to your house for a bit? I need to get ready."

"For what?"

"I'm meeting someone. Someone from outside the city."

"On behalf of the Astrals, I assume. Like a stand-in for them, since they don't talk."

"Divinity says they may use me as what they call a surrogate. Them talking through me."

"And this makes sense to them. Using *you*, who turned on them."

Again, Meyer looked up. "That was a mistake. I wasn't thinking straight."

"They must know. Raj told them, and they're not stupid."

"They know it was a mistake. They know I understand."

"Enough to trust you completely?"

"Yes."

"How can they trust you when you turned on them before? They must have their doubts, right?"

Meyer looked up again. This time, his jaw seemed restless, chewing on something that wasn't there. Shifting side to side. Annoyed and tired of the discussion.

"You should go back to your house," he repeated.

"There's no power in my house."

Meyer grunted, still staring at her.

"Because of the virus you released."

"We need to focus on the solution, not the problem," Meyer said.

A hunch told Heather to move forward. She kept her usual sarcastic vampiness out of her walk, and the annoying lilt from her voice. She tried to act normal, straight. It was possible, with effort, even for Heather Hawthorne.

Six steps closer to her ex-husband, she asked, "Why did you do it, Meyer? Right or wrong, why did you help us, if you now realize it was a mistake? Why the *temporary insanity?*"

"It was just that, Heather. A lapse of judgment."

"But you remember it."

"Of course I remember."

"It was Lila, wasn't it?"

"I was weak. I forgot my responsibilities."

"Because you saw that your daughter hated you. Because you thought you were going to lose her."

"The best way to 'lose' anything is to keep doing the stupid things I did then."

Heather wasn't buying it. Meyer sounded brainwashed.

She paced closer.

"What if it happened again, Meyer? What if you had to face the same thing again, and on one hand you could make your daughter keep loving you … but on the other hand, you could *do your duty* and she'd think you were a son of a bitch?"

"I wouldn't be that stupid again, Heather."

"Why were you stupid that time?"

"I'm tired of answering your questions. Go. I have a visitor."

"A visitor. Is there a chance to redeem yourself here? To do something at your 'meeting' to stop being a son of a bitch in your daughter's eyes?"

"I'm not," he said, an irritated look in his eyes. "You saw what happened in the dining room."

"Lila is happy because she thought you were dead." Heather took another step, confidence growing. "And because the last time she saw you make a choice, you chose to be noble."

"She'll respect a father who does what's right."

"But what if you had to choose? Duty on one hand, her respect on the other."

"I won't govern one-ninth of the planet based on the opinion of a twenty-year-old."

"And yet," Heather said, pointing toward the ceiling, toward the network center where he so recently made his act of sabotage, "the last chance you had, that's *exactly* what you did."

"Get out of here, Heather." Now he was coming forward, his pointless business in the office concluded.

Heather didn't back up. "I'm not saying you should do it. I just want to know why."

"That's immaterial."

"And I want to know why, when you were dying, the last thing you thought to say was that you loved me."

"It doesn't matter, Heather."

"Just tell me. Tell me why you chose to do either of those things, even if you now think they were stupid and a *dereliction of responsibility*. Just tell me, Meyer."

"I don't need to explain myself to you."

Again, he took a step. Again, Heather refused to back away.

"Just tell me," she said, "and I'll leave you alone."

Something seemed to war beneath Meyer's skin. His eyes shifted. He bit his lip. He looked away then back to meet Heather's eyes.

Then he pushed past her and walked out.

But at least he seemed angry, Heather thought. And that was a start.

Chapter Forty

CHRISTOPHER LOOKED up to see something hobble through the police station's door that almost made him want to laugh. But then he got one look at the thing's face and pressed his lips shut.

It was Raj. He looked like he'd been dragged behind a squad car for blocks then stepped on by something enormous. His face was bruised and starting to puff, tinged a black and blue that showed even through his dark coloring. Beneath his nose was a crust of blood. It seemed to still be seeping. One of his eyes was swollen half-shut. He had a severe limp, as if one leg was broken and he was insisting on walking atop it anyway. There was blood all over his uniform in the most random spots. Observing the pattern, Chris couldn't tell whether Raj had been repeatedly stabbed or if he'd just gushed blood like a geyser to land in many small pools.

Christopher drew to half attention, more acknowledging Raj's pathetic presence than deferring to his authority.

But Raj didn't go to Christopher. Instead, he detoured

once through the door, drawing looks from humans and Titans alike in the generator-lit atmosphere of bright lights and knife-edged shadows.

Christopher followed.

"What happened to you?"

"Fuck off, Christopher."

"I'm just asking."

"I slipped in the shower."

"Was there a fight?"

"That's none of your concern."

"Who did you fight with? Was it … is Terrence still at the house?"

Christopher tried to cover the awkward, telling fumble, but Raj spun to meet his eyes. One of Raj's whites had a spot of blood in its corner, as if the eye itself had been punched.

"I know about you," he said.

Christopher tried to play the accusation off but couldn't quite manage. There had always been something comical about Raj's anger and pointed fingers. He'd been given his honorary position because it was befitting the father of Heaven's Veil's princess, and none of the many tasks the household had given him meant a thing.

Usually, his tirades were met with an eye roll and a silent chorus of, *Oh, Raj. Nobody would ever take him seriously.* But this was different.

"I was just asking if—"

"No, Terrence didn't fight me. Yes, he's still up there. Still being watched. Not escaping. Everything he's doing with the computers is being sandboxed. Once he claims to have a solution, I will inspect it personally. He will not be able to get you a message under my nose."

"Not for me," Christopher stammered. "Why would he need to get in touch with—"

"Save it," Raj snapped. "I know about your talk with my wife, on top of your *fucking* her. You knew they were coming. I know you've been with Terrence all along. You might have fooled Meyer, but you can't fool me." Raj's head cocked. "Or maybe you didn't need to fool Meyer. Maybe he was with you from the beginning."

"I don't know what you're—"

"Where is Jons?"

Christopher said nothing. He felt too gobsmacked. He wasn't sure if he was frightened or not. Raj's threats had always amounted to nothing, dating all the way back to the bunker under Meyer's old house. Nobody took him seriously, but now Christopher couldn't help but feel a target on his back — possibly because they'd left Mary's house not a half hour ago, and he'd thereby painted it himself.

They may have been followed. Tracked by the mothership or shuttles despite their care at staying low and keeping the open sky eclipsed. Raj might be bringing the first drop of a flood. He'd had viceroy access for a few minutes there, before Meyer had shown up. He might have received a message directly from the Astrals, and the weapon on his belt might even have an Astral-ordered bullet inside it, meant for him.

"Where is Jons, Christopher?" Raj repeated.

"In his office." Christopher didn't point, but his gaze did.

Raj turned and headed for the open door. When he arrived, Christopher tried to shoot Jons a warning: *Treat this one differently. Something has changed.* But the chief saw Raj before he saw Christopher, and where Chris had contained himself, Jons openly laughed. The big man's cavernous chest made a booming sort of guffaw, rich and dark like a thunderhead.

"You finally say the wrong thing to Ms. Hawthorne?"

Christopher turned to watch Raj's profile, sweat threatening to form on his scalp. He saw Raj scrunch his lips. He didn't retort, or answer, issuing a demand without pause.

"Where are they?"

Jons's face became serious. This was his castle, and he wasn't used to being pushed about by skinny little assholes.

"Who?" Jons replied.

"Cameron Bannister's group."

Jons finally noticed Christopher beside Raj. A telltale look passed between them and, it seemed, wasn't lost on Raj. Jons, like Christopher, was probably trying to remember what he was officially supposed to know. They'd been sent to the gate, and then all hell had broken loose once the Titans started throwing uncharacteristic punches.

"I have no idea," Jons said.

"No idea what I'm talking about?"

"I know what you're talking about. The people come into the city. Don't puff up your chest to me, little man."

Christopher hoped that was right. Officially, without information they weren't supposed to have, did they know people were supposed to be coming in? That they were dissidents? That the group was supposed to include Cameron?

"So where are they?"

"I told you. I have no idea."

"You're the chief of police."

Jons stood in one heavy motion. His giant black hands clapped the desk's surface. Satisfyingly, Raj flinched like a man afraid of being hit — probably because he so recently had been.

"And you're the grand poobah of the motherfucking mansion guard! So why don't *you* tell *me*? Maybe you can let us know what happened out there. Why those Titans lost their shit. Why—"

Raj looked blindsided. "What happened with the Titans?"

But Jons was on the offensive, coming around the desk now, not slowing.

"They just *let the rebels go* instead of picking them up. You want to tell me *that*, you've got the viceroy's ear? Takes one or two peacekeepers to catch anyone they want to grab in the open. Maybe a few more Titans. But this time—" Something furrowed Jons's brow as if he'd just recalled it. He looked at Christopher, asking an unspoken question. "And what the shit was happening to those Titans, anyway? To their skin and bodies?"

Christopher felt himself blink in shock. He'd pushed that away, losing it in the frenzy of shuttling their wards away and fearing capture themselves. By the time he'd thought back to events in the square, he'd convinced himself that hadn't happened — especially given how blocked their view had been from the group's rear. He hadn't really seen Titans seem to form scales, their eyes to change color, their hands to grow claws and their mouths to bloom needle-like teeth and begin to glow. It felt too surreal, except that now it seemed Jons had seen it too.

"You're saying they *escaped?*" Raj's voice was thick with unbelieving accusation.

"Of course they escaped! Where the hell have you been?"

Raj looked caught between righteousness and supplication. Should he be angry at being excluded or timid because he was so far out of the loop that he was embarrassing himself?

Raj looked hard at Jons, who stared just as hard back. He seemed to be weighing a decision. Finally, he reached it, grabbed Christopher by the arm, and shoved him into the room. Given Raj's own precarious state, Christopher was amazed he'd been able to manage.

"Christopher is a dissident," Raj said. "You don't have *them?* Arrest *him.* Then make him talk."

"What the fuck are you jawing about, Gupta?"

"I have proof."

"Show me," Jons challenged.

Christopher could see doubt in the big man's eyes. Doubt in himself, in the ability to hold his own farce, maybe in his ability to shuttle off another via the Underground Railroad when he'd already let two escape.

Raj hesitated. Christopher wanted to exhale, but Raj's eyes flicked directly at him. Jons had called his bluff. Either there wasn't proof after all, or there was a problem with what he had.

"Come back to the house. It's on the CC system. On my tablet."

"I got more shit to do right now than going to your place for home movies. You got something to say, you bring it to me." Jons saw the opportunity to twist the knife deeper and did. "Come to think about it, you got something to prove, why didn't you bring this *evidence bomb* with you?"

"I didn't think of it," Raj said, his voice turning slightly pouty.

"Who beat you up, Gupta?" Jons demanded, moving in for the kill.

"That's not your concern."

"Was it Dempsey?"

Raj said nothing.

"Mmm-hmm. I heard about that. You turn on the big man then try to kill him. Somehow, someone takes pity on you instead of tossing your ass into one of my cells, and you keep running around trying to cause trouble instead of quitting while you're miraculously ahead." Jons nodded. "Yeah. I think in the viceroy's shoes, I'd have kicked your ass, too."

"I have proof against Meyer Dempsey, too."

"Great," Jons said. "So you just take that 'proof' against Meyer and your 'proof' against Chris, and you show it to Meyer. Try to convince *him* that he and his guard captain are a problem, because I sure as fuck don't want to be the daddy you run to on this one."

Raj looked like he might want to spar but seemed to realize that quitting was his only option. He made a face, threw hard eyes at Christopher and Jons, then gave his head a disbelieving, petulant little shake.

"You're up to something here. And you won't get away with it."

Then he left without waiting for a response.

"Jesus," Christopher said, "that was close."

"Closer than you know," Jons said. "He ain't gonna give up. And judging by the fact that Dempsey seems to be back on his alien throne instead of supposedly helping out like Terrence said, he might be looking for someone to blame for this clusterfuck."

"So what now?" Christopher asked.

"Now," Jons said, "we hurry."

Chapter Forty-One

PIPER PEERED out Grandma Mary's window, keeping the slit between the drapes thin. The fabric was decorated with pictures of fruit. Piper wondered at that, as she wondered at so much of the house. There wasn't a structure in Heaven's Veil that was more than two years old, and construction had been managed with the scraps of humanity's manufacturing sector. Where had these old lady drapes come from? And how had Mary achieved so much old lady ambiance, right down to the house that wasn't as new as it should be?

But as interesting as the drapes were, it was the Apex behind them that drew Piper's attention, pulsing like a beating heart.

Cameron spoke from behind, making her jump.

"Why is it doing that, do you think?"

"It always does that. But it's faster now."

"And the flash we saw?"

Piper shook her head.

Cameron sighed. He moved away from the drapes and into the kitchen beyond. Mary was elsewhere in the house.

Piper didn't know where. She'd been blasé when Jons and Christopher had shown up to hide them, and she was blasé now that they'd gone. Just two more houseguests that could get the home's entire occupancy cut to shreds. No big deal.

Cameron sat in one of the kitchen chairs — classic old lady vintage, like everything else. Maybe a raiding party had gone to the homes that were here from before the occupation and stripped them clean. Some of those homes must have had old people.

Piper sat opposite him, their hands up on the small table, not quite touching each other.

"Do you trust them?" Hearing Cameron's low voice, Piper throttled surprise. He was actually asking. Not discussing: *asking*. There was a difference. He was deferring to her, as one who knew more than him. When had their relationship changed? Had it been Cottonwood? After Benjamin's death?

"Captain Jons and Grandma Mary?"

"Yeah."

Piper thought before answering. She'd trusted in the past. But this felt more certain. She wasn't sure what was different, but something definitely was.

The changed Apex.

The fight among Titans.

The grid Andreus had mentioned, projected as if beckoning for alien backup to arrive.

The changed game, from end to end.

"I trust them."

She thought Cameron might ask further — perhaps inquiring as to *why* she trusted them and asking her to detail evidence of their honor when they'd been so thoroughly manipulated before — but he merely sat back, eyes straying toward the window and the pulsing blue pyramid beyond.

"How are we going to get in there?" he asked.

"I don't know. Maybe we can't, now."

"If we can't …"

"I know," she said. If they couldn't get into the Apex, they were right back at the same old stalemate. The best guess put Thor's Hammer below it, hidden more or less in plain sight, its activating core safely (for now) nestled in Cameron's padded satchel. Benjamin had seemed to feel that they had to find the Hammer first and use the key to somehow turn it off, or put it to another use which, hopefully, would become apparent.

They couldn't smash the key.

They couldn't just walk away.

And even if they knew how to get out of Heaven's Veil now that their mission had become harder, they couldn't do that, either. Because Thor's Hammer was here, in the throat of the lion trying to devour them.

"It's so close," Cameron said, again gazing.

"Maybe we can sneak."

"They'll be watching." He shook his head, exhaling. "They were tipped off, Piper."

"You can't know that."

"They were. They wanted to take us in. Maybe kill us. They wouldn't have done that if they didn't know where the Hammer was, and only wanted us to *think* they needed our help to find it."

"Maybe they wanted to catch us, take the key, then force us to show them."

"It's too unsure. We could refuse."

"Then maybe they figured that if we came back here to Heaven's Veil, we'd only have done it *because* the Hammer was here."

"Too unsure," Cameron repeated. "Think about it. They hadn't touched us before. They let us enter Moab then let us come all the way here. What's the advantage in not letting us go until we couldn't go anymore? Keep their distance, let us lead them right to it. *Then* grab us, take the key, and fire it up."

Piper opened her mouth, but she had nothing to say. He was right, and she hated the implications. The Astrals had already shown they didn't know how to find Thor's Hammer. So unless they'd stumbled upon it by accident and assumed Cameron would be dumb enough to walk right into Heaven's Veil with the key he'd been trying to conceal, the only other possibility was that someone had tipped them off.

Andreus.

Coffey.

Andreus's daughter, Grace, somehow.

Or Charlie.

"Maybe it was the shadow," Cameron said. "Maybe it's like we thought at first. Maybe that thing really was Astral, like a spy. Just like the BB. It heard us talking, only this time we didn't try to fool it. So the thing ran and told."

Piper had considered that, but it didn't merit much consideration. The aliens had already shown them a sensible spy device: tiny spheres that echoed both mothership and shuttle, small enough in most cases to dart about unseen. Sure, Andreus had his signal detector, and sure, the network was out. But couldn't it record now then zip off and play it for its owners in person? What were the odds that the Astrals had an entirely *different* means of surveillance — one *so* different as to be unreal — and had only loosed it now?

Piper wasn't buying it. But there was more to it. More reason to disbelieve that the shadow had ratted them out.

"I don't think it's against us," Piper said. "I think it's *for* us."

"Why?" Cameron asked.

While they sat in Grandma Mary's kitchen, Piper told him.

Chapter Forty-Two

As PIPER TALKED, Cameron's mind wandered to recent images and thoughts that didn't seem to be his. Thoughts and images nobody else seemed to be experiencing. He wanted to dismiss them, but he'd had this experience before and knew to take them seriously. The Astrals had once lined the planet with monoliths to harvest humanity's thoughts. Those monoliths were gone, but the feeling was similar. And yet the source — Cameron had no more idea how he knew this than Piper seemed to know what she knew — was different.

He'd been down this road. So had Piper, in the past.

But this was new.

Still, as Piper spoke, Cameron felt the unknown finger beckoning, drawing him toward something he couldn't reach. Some unknown intelligence seemed to spot the obstructions and encourage him anyway.

Yes, I see the wall as well. So what? Just walk through it.

But strangely, not to the Apex. At least not to Thor's Hammer, sitting in its glass belly.

This was something else.

"When you came out and saw me?" Piper asked.

Cameron shook his head. For a moment, he hadn't heard her. Piper's voice hadn't existed. He hadn't been in Grandma Mary's kitchen with only a small lantern and the glowing blue Apex for illumination. He hadn't even been in Heaven's Veil.

A giant hill, like a mountain.

A dark place.

And a misconception. Something Cameron already knew, but a small, female voice was only reminding him to consider. Something he was doing wrong, though not terribly so. Something he'd realize because he'd known it long ago but had buried it like …

Well, like Thor's Hammer.

Broken. Sifted. Contained. Handed down and obeyed then stored like a book on a shelf.

Cameron blinked up at Piper.

"I'm sorry?"

"I said, what did it look like to you when you came out and saw me?"

"In Moab?"

Piper nodded. "When the ship took me. When it flew me to Vail."

The strange new images fled Cameron's mind. All at once, he was back in that dark night, two years ago, on the evening the Vail mothership first became *Vail's* rather than Moab's. He remembered running, breath ripped from his lungs. He remembered tripping. Falling. Feeling helpless, impotent. Watching the ship snatch Piper away when he could only watch.

"It looked like you were in a trance. Like it had you hypnotized."

"I thought I didn't remember any of it," Piper said, her eyes straying to the blue-lit window. "I just remembered going to sleep, dreaming of Meyer, and coming back to reality in Vail. Trevor and the others came and drew them out of the bunker." She sniffed, pushing past thoughts of her stepson. "But over the past few days, I've started to remember more."

Cameron turned to face her. Piper's face was lit by the lantern, arced with shadow, eyes mostly black pits, her hair a curtain of ebony.

"I don't know how to describe it. It must be how it is for people who've repressed something. I know these things happened two years ago, and now that they're coming back, it's all obvious. But they're new, too. Do you know what that's like? To experience something old yet feel astonished as if you were looking at something new?"

Cameron gave a noncommittal nod. The answer was maybe. What he'd been sensing lately (small female voice notwithstanding) felt a lot like what Piper was describing. Maybe it was. Some of the images and thoughts were yet unseen. But some — deeper back, as if prompted by new thoughts rather than being those thoughts themselves — contained Benjamin. Tours through ruins that Cameron had bottled as parts of his old life, back when his father had been his hero. Childhood memories of ancient alien exploration that had been repressed, ironically, because the times portrayed were too happy for Cameron's often-jaded adult mind — at least, where his father was concerned.

"If I think back on that night now," Piper said, "I get two sets of memories. The first is the one I've been telling myself all along: that I went to sleep in the house, dreamed of Meyer, and woke in Veil. But now there's another set. In this one, I wake up and see a light through the window. I decide to get up and check it out. I'm not afraid, even though I should have been. I remember feeling almost giddy, but not stupid. I could see Meyer. I wanted to go to him. I was aware with most of me that it couldn't really be him, just hanging out outside. I knew it had to be an illusion — something put on for my benefit. But I knew it didn't matter anyway, and that it was safe to go. That I *should* go. Maybe even that I was *meant* to go. Does that make any sense?"

"Not really," said Cameron, wearing a smile he didn't feel, encouraging her to continue.

"I remember a feeling of every part of me being lifted when the ship took me. It wasn't like being raised on a hoist, where a strap or restraint is digging into your skin. Or where there's an elevator under your feet, with the rest of your weight pressing down. Or like being pulled up by your hands. This was like floating. Being raised by my every square inch at once. Then I was inside. And if I really focus and go quiet now, I can remember pieces of it. I remember a smooth surface. A sound I can't quite put my finger on, running from me now like a dream in the morning." Piper shook her head. "There's not much more I remember about what I saw. At least not yet."

Cameron sat back. It felt like a secret responsibly kept. Why hadn't she said more? Why had she kept it all to herself when it suddenly felt so pressingly important?

And why does *it feel so important?* asked a voice inside Cameron. Maybe his own. Maybe another's.

"What does this have to do with the shadow and what happened when we entered the city?"

Piper shook her head. It was a frustrated little motion, accompanied by slightly pursed lips. "I don't know. But I feel like I should, or like I *almost* know. It has something to do with my time on the mothership. Not the shadow, necessarily, but the reason I feel ... connected? ... to it. Or like I might understand it, or once did." She exhaled heavily. "It just feels so familiar. I don't really know how or why.

I only know the second-degree things. Not how I know it, I mean … but that I do, somehow, and that *knowing* is enough that I trust it."

"I'm not sure what you mean."

Piper sighed, calibrated, then touched Cameron as she found a new tack.

"Do you remember when we were … mentally connected?"

Cameron remembered it well, the most interesting form of intimacy. This wasn't the first time she'd asked. He nodded.

"I felt that return once I was on the ship, I think. Not with you, but with—"

"With Meyer?"

He'd answered too quickly. Piper gave him a semi-pleased, semi-awkward look. The issue of Meyer versus Cameron might one day be faced, but so far they'd belonged to separate parts of her life and it had always been one or the other.

"Maybe with Meyer. But more with *all of them.* I don't think it was something they were trying to bring me into; it was just something *there.* The way lights are shining overhead in a store whether you care to partake or not in their light when you enter."

Cameron looked up at the dark ceiling. Piper chuckled.

"It's all still fuzzy, and I can only remember it the way I'd remember a memory from when I was just a few years old. There are shapes and feelings, nothing specific."

"And?" Cameron prompted. Piper was steering. She wouldn't have brought it up if, in all this indistinctness, there wasn't meaning.

"It was so calm. Pacifying, really. Not in a quelling sense, like they were giving me opiates to keep me quiet.

There was just this abiding, genuine sense of peace. And a feeling of *time*. I've thought of some of the questions Benjamin and Charlie asked since — how they wondered why the Astrals were going about things the way they were. Why not just blast through the mountain to find Thor's Hammer? Why painstakingly construct all of their monoliths and the Apexes around the world when there must be faster ways for an advanced species to work? I think it's because they simply don't feel the pressure of time."

"So they're timeless? They're not in a hurry because they live to be a billion years old?"

"I think it's bigger than that. Do you remember what I told you about what the monks told me?"

"Sure."

"Franklin said that they were surprised and confused by the way we've 'externalized' our collective in the form of a computer network rather than connecting our minds directly, which is what he thought happened with the old civilizations, like the Egyptians and Mayans. I got the feeling that the Astrals are like that. Individuals — who knows how long they live? We know they die as easily as we do. But above that, I felt a kind of collective. It gives them an enduring identity. And that collective *is* ancient. It's not even that they're not in a hurry. It's more that 'hurry' has virtually no meaning to them." She bit her lip.

"What?" He could tell there was more, and didn't like it.

"I think it might also make them sort of *accidentally merciless*, by our definition. Why would they think it was cruel to kill a single person if they're used to seeing their entire species as one giant organism? It'd be like shedding a skin cell or a strand of hair, not ending anything with meaning in itself."

Cameron watched the window and the Apex beyond, unsure what to say.

Piper went on.

"But again, what hit me most was the way they seemed so calm. It was like entering a room full of people who were all meditating, even though I'm sure I remember them moving around and being active. They were cool and collected. And I could feel them pinching me off — not because I was human and wasn't supposed to be there, but because I wasn't as cool and collected as they were."

"You were a prisoner."

Piper's head tipped. "Maybe. But at the time, I don't know. It felt like I'd be welcomed if I'd been ... *cleaner*, maybe."

"So ..."

"It took me a while to understand the reason I felt like I did about the shadow, that it's more friend than foe. It scared the hell out of me when I saw it for the first time. And when it followed us or we followed it, the thing reminded me of the BB that followed us before, and I didn't like how it seemed to be watching. But after what happened at the gate ..."

She trailed off, seeming to think. But the silence stretched and stretched. In the interim, Cameron realized he couldn't hear Mary. They might be alone. Not just in the house, but in the entire city, state, and world.

"Piper?"

"The more I think back on it, Cam, the more I realize it feels familiar to me in the exact same way that sense of *wholeness* felt familiar to me on the ship. Just as indistinct, of course. It all feels so disconnected and without basis, like a dream from long ago. But ... I don't know."

Cameron waited. Piper continued to arrange her thoughts, trying to make sense of what seemed so senseless.

Cameron could relate. So much, even within the walls of his own skull, worked on faith these days.

"The Astrals are strong because they're 'one,'" she said. "That's how it felt on the ship. Looking back, that made me feel like all of this was futile. How could we ever pull one over on them if they were so eminently logical and worked so smoothly as a unit? They couldn't be scared like we could because their perspective was so different. They couldn't be provoked or made to feel pity for disconnected, *incomplete* beings like us. And they couldn't be angered." She said the last with a knowing glance.

"Like they got angry at Little Cottonwood Canyon."

"And like they got angry at the gate. Like that shadow … Cam, I'd swear it somehow *made* them angry. It made them disagree. It made their perfect culture of harmony want to fight itself."

Cameron looked down. Away. Back at Piper. They had to make it to the Apex. There was no way. Unless there somehow was.

"So what is it? What can get inside their heads like that, Piper?"

"I keep coming back to the question of whether it's *already* inside their heads," Piper said. "And if that's the case, we don't need to decide if it's good or bad for us as much as finding the truth of something else."

"What's that?"

"Whether it's the chicken," Piper said, "or the egg."

Chapter Forty-Three

MEYER FOUND his cufflinks in the bedroom. He didn't need them for his meeting with Nathan Andreus, but he put them on anyway. A professional front was never a bad idea. He was humanity's spokesman — a bridge between the Astrals and people like Andreus. A way to show those who wanted to play along that they were all, ultimately, sharing the same side.

There would always be dissenters. People who thought they knew best, despite abundant evidence to the contrary. Meyer's old life had been filled with them: those in charge of companies that had stood in his way, even dissenting opinions at Fable Studios, whose salaries Meyer paid. Healthy debate was acceptable. A good idea even. But once objections were addressed, people had to understand where certain slices of bread were buttered.

Meyer supposed he'd forgotten that the other day. He was only human. But after the Astrals had patched him up, he'd made sure to get his shit straight.

But even thinking back on those incidents was uncomfortable. It made Meyer want to fidget. It made him want to check the length of his cuffs. It made him want to cross his legs right over left after they'd been perfectly content left over right. It made him want to pace, the way he used to while sorting things out.

Why had he done it? It bothered him that Heather's questions had no acceptable answers. He'd given her responses that made sense ... but they weren't precisely accurate. Or at least not the whole truth. He'd been irrational to the point of insanity. He'd upended sense for no reason and couldn't replicate the moment of stupidity, even as a hypothetical, inside his mind. It was a bit like calling someone for a faulty appliance, only the technician arrives to find the appliance working just fine. You can't fix a problem that refuses to appear.

Meyer closed his eyes in the bedroom, fingers trailing across the viceroy cufflinks. With his lantern off, the backs of his eyelids were black, not even noticing the Apex's cycles as it powered up and prepared to broadcast in concert with its worldwide brothers.

He conjured the memory, which still felt fresh like dripping blood. He remembered running upstairs. He remembered seeing Raj sitting on Heather's back with that dumb look on his face. That had seemed wrong; he'd told him to get off. Then Lila had appeared, and Meyer had ...

He had ...

He squeezed his eyelids tighter, trying to step into the memory. He knew what came next; the recollection was whole and easy. He'd taken the gun full of Terrence's tranquilizer darts, and he'd fired them into Raj's chest. Into Raj's tough canvas shirt that had blunted all but the tips from scratching him.

But *why?* It was so irrational. So stupid. So contrary to what was obviously the best course of action. Look how things had turned out: He'd run; he'd allied with those who were now bound in captivity and likely meant for execution; he'd attempted in vain to betray a force that held the planet quite firmly and couldn't, in any meaningful way, be subverted; he'd nearly got himself killed. He hadn't saved Heather, Lila, or Clara so much as thrown them in danger. It was as dumb and ill-thought-out an action as whatever Piper had done (though for that, the Astrals were to blame) and what Trevor had done, in running with her.

Meyer thought of Lila, who'd caused all of this. She'd stared at him. She'd said words meant to cut him. But he was smarter than to fall for them, wasn't he?

There was nothing. No understanding. No light on his own actions, as if they'd been perpetrated by someone else. Someone stupid.

Meyer opened his eyes. Clara was sitting on his bed.

"Hi, Grandpa."

"Hello, Clara," Meyer said, feeling an involuntary smile touch his lips. "Shouldn't you be in bed?"

"I got out of bed. Mom was scared."

There was a twitch of something inside Meyer. Something that felt like it had meaning, but then it was gone.

"Why was she scared, Sweet Pea?"

"Grandma is acting funny. The lights are off." Clara shrugged. "She's just ... scared."

Meyer watched the girl. He should be astonished by everything about her, but he'd grown used to it all. She walked and held herself like a five-year-old and spoke better than half of the city's human leaders. She had, it sometimes seemed, more insight into the Astrals than Meyer himself. It was how she was, and nobody questioned it anymore.

"I'm sorry to hear that, honey."

Clara shifted on the bed. "I don't want to leave our house, Mister."

"'Mister'?"

"'Grandpa,'" Clara corrected.

Meyer scrunched his brow. He decided to let it pass. It was hardly the strangest thing the girl had ever said.

"You don't have to leave."

"I think we will. I've already packed." She indicated a small teddy bear backpack Meyer hadn't noticed. It was on the floor beside her. He hadn't seen her put it there — but then again, he hadn't seen or heard her enter the room, either, and it wasn't like his eyes had been closed long. His ears, in fact, hadn't been closed at all.

"Who said you had to leave?"

"Grandma Piper." Clara made a small wave, correcting herself. "Not that she knows it yet."

"'Yet'? Clara, who have you been talking to? Did you overhear something Mo said? Because whatever he might have said wasn't for your ea—"

"I haven't seen Mr. Weir," Clara interrupted.

"Then—"

"I'm bored. Do you want to play a game?"

Meyer watched the girl's eyes. They were shockingly blue, like Piper's. Like those of the stepgrandmother who'd told Clara that she'd need to leave home, even though Piper herself apparently didn't know it. Yet.

"I can't. I have a guest coming." He forced a patronizing smile, but it didn't come easy.

"Who?" And Meyer thought, *What, you don't know?*

"Someone who helps me protect the city."

"Like Captain Jons?"

"Sort of. Except that he protects the area outside the fence. The Astrals can't do it all. They need human partners to help out. Like me, and like Mr. Andreus."

"Oh, okay."

"And you should be in bed anyway. It's late, Clara."

She hopped down from the bed. The sound of her slippers against the floor made a noise like a clap. She picked up the small backpack, letting it dangle from a hand. Meyer thought she might repeat her question about moving, but Clara said nothing.

"Okay. I guess."

"G'night, Clara."

"Good night, Mister."

Meyer felt the same strange expression form on his face, accompanied by an unknown sensation in his gut. He hugged her, scared to ask what he wanted to.

"Have fun talking to your friend who's coming," Clara said, turning toward the door.

"I will. Don't let the bedbugs bite."

Clara yawned. When her plodding feet reached the door, she turned halfway.

"Ask him about Uncle Trevor," she said.

Chapter Forty-Four

CHRISTOPHER FOUND Terrence alone with his guards in the network center. The guard unit was composed of five humans and two Titans — not a Reptar in sight. That must be Meyer reasserting his command, pushing the Raj regime right out the window ... while, apparently, punching it repeatedly in the face.

Passing them with a nod of acknowledgement, it occurred to Christopher that the guards — the human ones, anyway — might have been poisoned against him. Raj had been mouthing off everywhere all night long, it seemed, and he might have blabbed. The guards might have heard stories of Christopher's disloyalty. But even though Raj seemed to have attained a new, listen-to-me edge, Christopher doubted the guards had accepted it. Their necks weren't nearly as much on the line.

The looks Christopher got seemed to confirm it. Guards allowed him entry with respect, giving him distance. The Titans stayed far back, respectful and deferential as always.

He gave them all one final glance then sat beside

Terrence in a way that hopefully seemed appropriately suspicious. The man was a prisoner and traitor, after all.

"I haven't seen him in a while," Terrence said. "Raj, I mean."

"How's the network fix going?" Christopher asked. He made his voice artificially loud so the guards would hear then raised one eyebrow, hoping Terrence would get his meaning.

Terrence seemed to. "I've been waiting for Raj to come back. I can't do more until I get access to the network spindle," he answered, also in full voice.

"I'll take you to it. It's in the annex. Don't try anything." Then Christopher rose, taking Terrence by the arm in a way that was perhaps a bit too rough — but better to put on a decent show rather than anything unconvincing. Then he half dragged Terrence through the door, into a smaller room next door. Beating the guards to the punch, he ordered them to line up outside the door, looking in, keeping their guns ready just in case.

Once they were pushed back into the annex, Christopher lowered his voice and said, "What's a network spindle?"

"I made it up."

"Here." Christopher handed Terrence a tiny screwdriver from his clutch of tools. "Open this panel, and try to look busy."

"What if Raj comes back? You try to feed him 'network spindle', and he'll arrest you, too."

Christopher frowned. "He's down at the police station, trying to dig up dirt. I radio'd up myself before he came back last time, had some of my men confiscate the commander's tablet before he got back because he was *under suspicion*. But it's only temporary, until Raj shakes enough cages and gets it back. I'm afraid the ship's sailed on my innocence. Raj says he has evidence against me. Both of us together, it sounds like. I think he has cameras. That's why I dragged you in here. Maybe we can actually talk without making things worse."

Terrence's gaze flicked to the guards.

"I can't spring you, T. The guards like me a lot better than Raj, but the Titans won't let it happen. They're not that stupid."

"I can't do what Raj wants. He won't listen. Canned Heat isn't like a normal virus. It *consumes*. It was supposed to do it selectively, eating through what they've firewalled. I figured they'd cut off the new connections, but we'd get our chance. Instead, it spread. There's no undoing this, but he refuses to buy it."

Christopher nodded. "He's desperate. Dangerous. Did Meyer really beat him up?"

"Jesus, Chris, did he. You should have seen it."

"Why? What happened?"

"He just stormed in. But you know he supposedly shot Meyer. I'd want to beat up the shooter, too." There was more, but Terrence didn't continue. As with Christopher, the perfectly logical "he tried to kill me" excuse wasn't ringing true as Meyer's motive.

"Look. Cameron's in the city. Cameron and Piper."

"Like Lila said?" Terrence looked surprised.

"*Clara* said," Christopher corrected, nodding.

"Where are they?"

"A safe place." Christopher looked around the room, trying to help Terrence's hands look busy to the guards. Raj had hooks in him. He probably would have explained further, but if he did and Raj was listening, axes would fall.

"They weren't picked up by the Astrals?"

"Something happened out there. Have you seen what's going on with the Apex?"

"I saw a flash."

"Well, something's going on with *them*, too. They … hell, they started to *change* somehow, T. Fought like a bunch of football hooligans." He shook his head. "I don't like it."

"Sounds like it's working out, if they're safe."

"But why?" Again, Christopher looked at the guards. "Terrence, your Canned Heat … could it affect them, too? Whatever shit connects their ships to each other?"

"I don't see how. I mean, it looks like they've piggy-backed off our ground- and satellite-based networks, but they communicate all through space without our help."

"But … could it infect them? It's a virus."

"No. It only destroys, and they still have plenty of power." Terrence's eyes went to the window. "*More* power, maybe. Tell you the truth: Since that flash, it's occurred to me that I might have *helped them* as much as *hurting us*. I don't think their shuttles can talk to each other right now, same for the little surveillance droids the others mentioned before the network blacked out. They're fast enough that they don't need to — they can fly wherever in no time and *talk* in person, if that's a thing for them. If they're drawing more power into the Apex, that gives them an advantage. Especially if they're planning …" Terrence trailed off, aborting his ominous what-if.

"Cameron said there's a mothership over Utah again. Where his dad was."

"Did the mothership destroy the lab?"

"I don't know."

Terrence looked up. "Because you said 'was.' 'Where his dad *was*,' past tense."

"He's dead." Christopher sighed. "Benjamin is dead."

"Shit."

"A lot of their people. The rebel thing I mentioned, that Jons told me about? It was them. They got a thing." Christopher paused again before describing the key and the idea of the weapon, wary of revealing too much for ears in the walls. But then he added, "Trevor too."

Terrence closed his eyes and shook his head. "Hell. I liked Trevor."

Christopher bobbed his head grimly. He'd liked Trevor too. A lot. But there wasn't time to mourn with so much still in the balance.

"But the mothership. Cameron said it's … I don't know … leeching power from this underground plug. Like it's charging up, back in Moab."

"Why?"

"That was what I was hoping you'd have thoughts on, Terrence."

Terrence shook it off. "Same question. They're probably planning something if they're powering up."

"Look, they need to get …" Christopher paused, but there was no way to convey the information without simply saying it. "They need to get into it. Into the Apex. Is there any way to clear a path from where you're—"

"Forget it," Terrence said. "First, I'd have no way to affect that. *Any* of that, and certainly not with Raj's oversight. But there's a bigger problem."

"What?"

Terrence pulled something from his tool bag. It looked like a 1990s-era phone — something with alligator clips on one end, old like a repairman might have carried before Christopher was born.

"I can hear your radio transmissions," he said.

"Okay."

"Well, haven't you been listening?"

"I've had it off."

"Turn it on when you get out of here. You'll see. It sounds like *they're* swarming the Apex. Forget about being kept out. Cameron and Piper would be mobbed. Like fighting through a crowd, from the sounds of it."

"Why?"

"I'm hearing human talk, not Astrals. So you tell me; you're the one in uniform."

"Something to do with the 'powering up?'"

"No idea. But it's occurred to me that—"

A voice from the doorway: "Well, isn't this a nice little reunion?"

It was Raj, with a tablet in his hand.

Chapter Forty-Five

THE VICEROY WAS TALLER than Nathan expected.

Usually, people who appeared to be larger than life — and Dempsey was certainly one of those, both before and after Astral Day — earned their size through the media's flattering eye. There had always been tall actors, politicians, and leaders, but more often than not, anecdotes said that meeting them in person was disappointing.

Not so for Meyer Dempsey. He was several inches taller than Nathan, firm in bearing, and with a strange look in his eye that Nathan, who was used to intimidating his way through negotiations, felt himself wanting to flinch from.

No wonder some people said that Dempsey was a god. He'd been scooped up by aliens and returned like Lazarus. He'd risen to power in an obvious fashion, as if he'd always intended to be and everyone had expected it of him. His presence was unflinching. And, if the murmurs he'd heard on his way in were true, the man might have been shot, before emerging from death unscathed.

"Come in, Mr. Andreus." Meyer nodded to the man who'd led Andreus in. Then the man left, and he gestured at the seats. Nathan took one, careful to select the highest and largest. That was how you took command of a discussion: by sitting in the room's obvious throne.

But Dempsey effortlessly trumped him. Only once seated did Nathan look up and realize Dempsey meant to stay standing.

"I received your message," he said.

"And?"

The viceroy nodded. "I believe it. The Astrals believe it."

"Why do you need to *believe* it? Couldn't you see it for yourself?"

"It's none of your concern."

But watching him, Nathan realized he'd scored an early — if accidental — hit. They'd escaped. The son of a bitches had somehow slipped away, despite the Astrals' force and might. That could be good, or bad. It certainly weakened Nathan's bargaining position. If they'd captured Cameron, they'd have recovered the key Nathan had told Dempsey he was carrying. They'd know that Nathan was telling the truth. Now, he had to take at least half of his informant's information on faith.

"Have the Astrals found the item they were looking for? Under the Apex?"

"A search is underway. But unfortunately," Meyer gave Nathan a sidelong look, as if reminding him who was skeptical of whom, "your suggestion to scan the chambers for stone of the same composition as the key has run into trouble."

Meaning: Without capturing Cameron and getting the key, the Astrals couldn't yet verify that Nathan had been telling the truth about *that*, either. Stupid fucking ETs. It wasn't Nathan's fault they couldn't get their big white heads out of their muscular white asses for long enough to catch one man and one woman walking directly into the city, unarmed and without backup.

Maybe he shouldn't have done this. Yes, ratting out Cameron had gained Nathan entry into the city and earned him the viceroy's presence, but he hardly had all the chips in his corner. He was sitting like a supplicant while god-king Dempsey stalked around him, large and in charge.

Maybe it was all for nothing.

"Well …" The single word made Nathan sound weak, further backed into a corner.

"I'll be blunt. Word from Divinity on the mothership is that the Astrals don't like you. They also don't trust you."

Nathan felt his chest constrict. He wanted to stand and act like a man instead of a mouse, but it was hard. The room's oppression, even for Nathan Andreus, was too strong.

"But they need you. And while they don't trust you, they believe you in this case. At least they buy your sense of self-preservation." A smile ticked up the corner of Dempsey's mouth. Nathan felt him shift off the official script, now speaking as himself rather than as the Astrals' mouthpiece. "A trait we share, as selfish sons of bitches," he added.

Nathan shifted. Tried to sit taller. Tried to make his face impassive, as if none of this mattered.

"I've been asked to act as a surrogate for Divinity. Are you familiar with the process?"

"No. I was contacted by people like you when we made our first arrangement." Nathan tried to add a sneer to his voice. "Like you" was supposed to be an insult: meaning puppets, meaning those who got down on their knees whenever the aliens asked. But judging the lack of change in the viceroy's expression, he seemed to take it as a straightforward phrase: "like you" meaning an authority, a person in charge.

"Divinity does not leave the mothership. It will speak through me. As far as you are concerned, you will keep speaking with me. But it will be them."

"Like a puppet with a hand up your ass," Nathan said, finally standing to match Dempsey.

The knock registered this time; there was a flicker of annoyance before the viceroy's face went placid and blank. So unlike the intimidating presence he'd just portrayed. Still in charge. Now more quietly so.

"Nathan Andreus," Divinity said using Meyer Dempsey's mouth.

"You got 'im."

"You entered Heaven's Veil, domain of human viceroy Meyer Dempsey, dominion of the prime North American mothership, in an armored vehicle. Since that time, we have considered you a threat worthy of eradication. The matter has been given serious consideration."

Nathan watched Meyer's face. It wore a totally banal, matter-of-fact expression.

"As we know you have surmised, extracting the fugitive Piper Dempsey was exactly what we wished for you to do."

"You're welcome."

"It was, however, unexpected. The plan was to ferry Dempsey out of the city. Your intervention was helpful, though not anticipated. But you did not know of our plan. You believed you were acting against, not for us."

"I heard you didn't speak," Nathan said.

"Viceroy Dempsey speaks."

"Is he still in there, or have you completely taken him over?"

"Details of the surrogate process are irrelevant. How do you answer the charge?"

Jesus. It was such a formal, stilted way of speaking. Nathan found himself fascinated. Dempsey knew English, so apparently that allowed Divinity to speak the language through him. But the syntax and diction was nothing like it had been a moment ago.

"I was provoked. You struck first."

"There was no strike against the Andreus Republic," said Puppet Dempsey.

"Against the rebel camp outside of Moab."

"That did not concern you."

"My wife was there. My daughter was there."

"This was not known to us."

Andreus felt his jaw work. "I don't believe you."

"Belief is irrelevant. It was a counterstrike meant to eradicate a threat."

"A threat you allowed to survive for two years."

"It became a threat."

"And that just so happened to occur after I helped Cameron Bannister cross to Heaven's Veil."

"Also our intention. And also, a betrayal you made of us, without knowing it was our intention."

Dempsey stood still, waiting, accusation in those not-quite-his eyes.

"My wife was killed. By you."

"We have come to comprehend human attachment. There was one surviving member of your party. She was watched by one of our droids, and when the Moab facility was destroyed, she was spared as a gesture."

For some reason, that made Nathan's blood want to boil. Grace was safe. But what? Was she a cookie earned for a job well done?

"What do you want me to do?" Nathan asked. Not as a

request for command, but as an expression of futility. Dempsey — or Divinity — seemed nevertheless to take it as the former.

"Command the outlands. They are your domain. The only way for us to truly control your population is to enslave it, as we may soon need to rule Heaven's Veil if the fugitives are not found. We do not wish this. You must be controlled for your own good. But it should be by your own, as your society understands."

"You're saying you need me."

"We do not wish to patrol the outlands. Our domain comprises the capitals and select cities. We do not wish to destroy human command structures."

"You don't want to micromanage us," Nathan said.

"If you wish."

"Why me then? Why the traitor?" Part of Nathan wanted to rebel, to take it back and play nice. The whole reason he'd done this was to get his audience, then lie down and roll over. But now that he was here, being pandered to, being commanded, being treated like a child, his instinct rebelled.

Remember what you came for.

"You have an established power structure. If we must replace you, we will, but we believe you want what we are not equipped to desire."

"What is that?"

"Power."

Nathan stopped. He felt the need to sit, and did. Something Dempsey had just said was clanging in his head, refusing to settle.

"I have an established power structure."

"Yes."

"The Republic. You didn't destroy it."

"Your actions at the Cottonwood outpost were not anticipated. An error was made."

"Oh, it wasn't an error," Nathan said. But something about the surrogate's voice told Nathan that the error referred to wasn't the rebels' mistake.

"Harm was caused. We do not wish to continue along this path. It is not ideal. You can be controlled, and—"

"I can 'be controlled,' huh?"

"Your position harmonizes with checks we are easily able to make."

"Which controls?"

"If you do not wish to comply, your outposts may yet be destroyed. Easily. And your daughter's position is still known to us."

Nathan bolted to his feet. He almost punched Dempsey out before realizing it would solve nothing.

"I knew it. You kept following us. You kept watch. Because that's how you treat your 'human partners.' And that shadow thing. So that was real. You sent it to watch us."

A strange thing happened. Dempsey's brow wrinkled. Nathan again found himself fascinated. It was somehow working through Dempsey's actual person, not just moving him as if on strings. How would Divinity wrinkle a brow when confused? It was a human reaction, known only by a human body.

"You were watched from above."

Nathan let it go.

Apparently, you don't know everything after all.

Chapter Forty-Six

DEMPSEY/DIVINITY laid out the proposal. It was simple: Nathan would resume his duties as warlord of the roads and lands surrounding Heaven's Veil. He was in charge of Salt Lake City and dozens of smaller outposts. He would, as before, be considered autonomous. He wouldn't need to check in. He would be supplied with fuel, and the Astrals would stay out of his way. He would maintain order, exactly as he'd always done, with his past transgressions forgiven so long as everyone agreed that getting back onto the same old rails was a good idea.

And really, it *was* a good deal. Nathan would be entirely absolved of any responsibility for his previous actions. No harm, no foul. All had worked out as it should, and Nathan Andreus was still the best choice for the job. It was the epitome of a logical, non-emotional decision. A human would have wanted to punish Nathan. But the Astrals, who saw larger and further, knew it was cutting off the nose to spite the face.

It was a good deal right up to the point where Nathan considered the "check" the surrogate had mentioned.

Of course Nathan would do the job. He'd requested this audience, and he'd betrayed his supposed cohorts to do it. He'd helped the Astrals, even though they'd botched the handoff by allowing Bannister's escape. He still wanted the same things, and it was always — even now — better to live atop the hill rather than under another's heel.

But (and this was irrelevant, considering that Nathan wanted to comply for other reasons) there was the small matter of the check.

The small matter of the gun that would perpetually be held to the back of Nathan's head to ensure that he'd be good, just in case.

If he didn't do as he was asked, it was simple to kill his daughter.

As much as Nathan wanted to blame the Astrals for Julie's death, he believed what Divinity had said. It was an accident. But either way, the aliens had killed her. And that death had given them an important piece of information to consume and assimilate: that for Nathan Andreus, the most effective lever was his family's blood.

"Is that all?" he asked, his hands wanting to form fists.

"Do you agree to retake your post?"

"Yes."

"We have sent a shuttle to face your people outside the city. No harm befell them. Pattern matching has shown that one is your lieutenant, as known, Jeanine Coffey. The other, also as known, is your daughter. The third is Benjamin Bannister's partner, Charles Cook. They will be allowed to live. As will all Andreus outposts."

"What about Cameron and Piper?"

"Not relevant to your concerns."

"And the Apex? If you find what you want in the Apex?"

"Not relevant to your concerns."

"Benjamin Bannister believed it was a weapon."

"Not relevant."

"Bullshit!" Nathan felt his blood chilling, his voice rising, knowing he'd trapped himself in a snare. "If you set off a weapon, the whole, *you won't kill me and my people* agreement falls apart."

"No harm will befall you."

"And my people?"

"The agreement will be honored."

Nathan's jaw worked, sliding side to side. He watched the surrogate through slits. He still wanted to punch it. To cause harm. But there was nothing to do. Nothing to do but ...

Something popped to mind.

"You're honorable beings, aren't you?" Nathan said.

"We do not have that concept."

"But you do as you say."

"Yes."

"Including your *agreements* with Dempsey. To protect his people, too."

"Yes."

Again, Nathan's jaw slid to the side, as if searching for his tongue.

"Does he know about his son?"

Something in the surrogate's face changed instantly. No delay. For a moment, Meyer Dempsey was back, and Divinity was gone. Then it changed again, and Andreus found himself facing the surrogate.

But something must have remained because the surrogate's fist clenched once, twice, three times. In Meyer Dempsey's voice — not the identical but tonally distinct voice of Divinity — the man in front of Nathan said, "I'm supposed to ask you about Trevor."

Chapter Forty-Seven

JEANINE COFFEY WOKE and saw that the sun wasn't yet over the horizon. The networks still seemed to be entirely down, but there was a small clock on the RV's dashboard that, she guessed, was keeping approximately correct time.

Not that the time of day mattered much anymore, but it appeared to be 6:13 a.m.

She yawned then poured some of the water Nathan had packed into a coffeemaker and set a pot to brewing. It was using water and power from the batteries. That power, courtesy of the sun, was plentiful and free. As to the water? Fuck it. There were so many more interesting ways to die than thirst, and last night necessitated a strong wake-up this morning.

She peeked in on Grace — a bundle of blankets at the rear. Her own bunk was at the front, and (obvious jokes aside) she'd been sharing it with Nathan, keeping two separate sets of sheets. But last night, she'd had it all to herself.

It wasn't until the coffee was halfway brewed when Jeanine realized the final member of their party was missing. Charlie had been on the fold-out couch in the RV's middle, but now it was tidily away, sheets folded into neat squares and sitting on a small shelf along the window.

The window.

She looked through the glass. They were behind some trees, but their hiding place was fooling no one. The way Nathan figured, the Astrals knew exactly where they were and had from the start. It wasn't line-of-sight cover keeping them alive.

"It's not in there."

Jeanine jumped. If she'd been holding a knife, she'd have stabbed someone with it purely out of shock. And if she'd been holding a gun, Charlie Cook would probably have been turned to paste.

Instead, he remained where he'd greeted her: in an alcove near the bathroom. Just standing there. Possibly, he'd recently emerged after having washed his hands, or maybe he'd stood there all night waiting to scare the shit out of her.

"Don't you ever say good morning?"

"Good morning," Charlie said. "It's not there."

"Care to give me some context?"

"I've been looking through Benjamin's research. The longer I piece it together, the more obvious the conclusion: Thor's Hammer, at least according to Benjamin, is not in Vail."

Jeanine let her shoulders relax. She turned away and watched the coffee brew. Looking into Charlie's eyes was creepy; so was looking in his general direction. He wasn't lecherous; she was reasonably sure he wouldn't know what to do with a woman if she wrapped herself around him naked. He was just ... *there*.

But the coffee wasn't finished. She resisted the urge to flick the pot, hurrying it up.

"Did you hear me?"

"I heard you."

"Are you going to do anything about it?"

Jeanine sighed. She turned, steeling herself for his gaze. Charlie had a way of making her (and, surely, everyone) feel stupid for not knowing things they had no way of knowing and never would.

"First of all, what makes you so sure?"

"Benjamin."

Jeanine put her tongue under her lip, assessing him.

"Go on."

"Benjamin makes me sure," Charlie repeated.

"Let's play a game, Charlie."

"No."

"Let's pretend you're a normal human being, on the same side as me. And as part of that game, let's suppose you *want* me to understand what you're saying rather than this intellectual one-upmanship wherein you get to win the knowledge war but nothing is learned or accomplished."

"I do want you to understand."

"Okay. Then just tell me. No one-word answers. No assumptions of things I should know, followed by eye rolls when I don't. Just fucking tell me, okay?"

Now it was Charlie's turn to look pensive. This had to be hard for him. And, she thought, he must have barely slept. The bed had been out last night; he'd definitely used it. But it was early, and he'd clearly been up for hours. His collared shirt, buttoned to the top, looked almost pressed, as if he'd decided it was worth ironing.

"Cameron didn't know where to begin when he was looking through Benjamin's files. He didn't understand Benjamin's organizational system."

"But you do," Jeanine said.

"Yes. In that he didn't have one. He saved anything he was working on to his desktop, and then when it got too cluttered, he made a folder and dumped everything into it. Some of the techs who worked with his stuff tried to get him to make bookmarks lists, to put things in logical places so they could make sense of it. He'd try for an hour then go back to his old way."

"So?"

"Cameron was just searching. First, he tried looking for words in documents, and what led us here was sorting by file dates, to see what Benjamin was working on last. We can't ask him why he was so interested in the Apex near the end, but seeing as we were all focused on finding the key and Thor's Hammer, it seemed a safe bet. Ditto that there are some Thor's Hammer notes in that chain, but that was just Benjamin hopping around."

"Do you miss him, Charlie?"

"Do you miss Nathan?"

"Nathan isn't dead."

Charlie's lips formed an ultra-rare, slightly bitter smile. "Next time I see him, maybe he will be."

Jeanine decided to let it go. She'd started the diversion; maybe she could bring it back on track. Nathan wasn't around right now. She thought she knew where his motives lay, but the man wasn't always an open book and resented explaining himself.

"I still don't see what makes you so sure Thor's Hammer isn't at Vail."

"Because I find it unlikely that it would be so coincidental. The Hammer mentions in Benjamin's file history lift right out. They don't overlap with the Apex research at all."

Jeanine shook her head. "I feel like I'm missing something."

"He was researching the Apex for a totally different

reason. So if Thor's Hammer is there too, it would be a coincidence."

"What makes you so sure he wasn't—"

Charlie's voice slipped into its usual impatience. "We've already seen that things are changing out there. There was a surge of some sort last night, and its pulse rate, at least according to Piper, has increased. Benjamin seemed to think it was pushing out some sort of a beacon, or at least preparing to do so. We saw that grid it's projecting among the monoliths — another tidy coincidence. Between what I'm seeing here," he pointed toward the small built-in table, where Jeanine now saw Charlie's laptop, "and what *we've* seen, it's clear that they're 'powering up' in some way, and it has something to do with the Apex. So you tell me. As a matter of deduction, does it seem coincidental that Benjamin would have been spending all his time investigating power use in these Apex structures for its own right … and *just so happen* to also have been thinking that the Vail Apex is the resting place of Thor's Hammer?"

"But Cameron—"

"Cameron isn't a scientist."

"He said Benjamin told him where it was."

"He said Benjamin told Cameron that *he, Cameron*, already knew where it was," Charlie corrected.

"But if he assumed Cameron would know—"

"Benjamin was a good man but an idiot as a scientist. He didn't organize his research. He didn't document his findings properly. He didn't take enough notes. Half of the notes he did take were dictated emails sent to himself. But he never went through them to clean the dictation. A lot are undecipherable. He dragged Cameron all over the world. I was there for some of it. The kid was fascinated 10 percent of the time, bored to death the other 90. To Benjamin, those trips were the ultimate bonding experience because he assumed Cameron shared his interests, even when he clearly didn't. He was always quizzing him. When Cameron didn't know the answers to the obscure archaeology or ancient aliens theories Benjamin asked about, he rolled his eyes and goaded him. The man was a good friend, but a total narcissist in his own way. If he'd been sensible, he'd have talked to Cameron. It would have been simple. But instead, it was a game to him. Something obvious."

"So you're saying—"

"Benjamin clearly assumed the Hammer's location should be obvious to Cameron. And in retrospect, it might turn out to be, but for now it clearly wasn't as important a memory to Cameron as it was to Benjamin. But it's not in Vail. That's not enough of a hilarious 'obvious joke' to be the answer. I'm sure he was quizzing Cameron all over. Recalling some 'joke' Benjamin assumed was between them. But until Astral Day, our lab had no interest in Vail. The only way Benjamin took Cameron there in the past was to ski."

Jeanine watched Charlie, wanting to disagree on principle. There was no upside to what he was saying: They'd sent Cameron and Piper in with the key, and Nathan (whose allegiance Jeanine still wasn't sure of) was in the city now. They were vested in Vail, and she wanted to argue and make him wrong. But his words rang true, and he'd known Benjamin best.

"Are you sure?" she asked, already knowing the answer.

"Yes."

"So why all the interest in Vail?"

"I think he must have seen this coming yet didn't discuss it with us because he didn't want to be overheard by that little thing that was watching."

"See *what* coming?" Jeanine asked. There was still an assumption being made. Charlie, always with an arrogant ace up his sleeve.

Charlie's face registered surprise. "You haven't seen."

"Seen what?"

Charlie was looking at the door to the outside, which he seemed to have left ajar.

Jeanine walked forward. Stepped into the cool morning air.

And saw the second mothership docked beside the first, a beam of energy pouring from its underside into some unknown alien machinery.

Chapter Forty-Eight

Lila awoke to shaking. When she saw that the perpetrator was Raj, she nearly socked him and screamed, given how much had changed in the past few days. Then the sensible part of Lila remembered that he was her husband and the father of her child, and that this was still where he slept, too — albeit lately on the couch.

"Get up," he said.

"Lemme sleep."

"Believe me, I'd love to leave you out of this. But I need your help."

Lila rolled over, now fully awake. She propped herself up on her elbows and looked up at him with disbelief.

"You're kidding."

"There's something going on with your father."

"Why don't you just shoot him again?" The sentence simply came out. But despite Lila's foggy morning brain, she'd managed to infuse it with the perfect amount of reproach and scorn. It made Raj pause.

"Get up."

"What's 'going on' with him?" But something else was

itching at Lila. The room was different, as if spun end for end. She couldn't see why at first, but then it hit her: the light was all wrong. The morning seemed dim, as if it were overcast outside. But still Lila could see a few sharp edges here and there, as if the sun were blazing despite the gloom.

"He's locked himself in his office."

"That's his business, not yours."

"He really did help Terrence and your mother, Lila," Raj said, his tone shifting.

"Good for him."

"He let them release the virus. He's the reason the power is out and there's no prediction of when it might come back on. Even the Astral ships seem to be affected. There's been more shuttle activity, but they're all docking on the mothership rather than circling and circling like they do on patrol. Terrence thinks they're having to check in manually because they can't do it over the air."

"Good for Terrence," Lila said, flopping back down and turning away.

"*Lila.*"

"Where is Terrence, anyway? Did you even let him sleep?"

"He's upstairs." Raj didn't answer the second question.

"With Christopher?"

Lila couldn't see Raj but thought she could hear the change in his voice like a snarl. "Your lover? He's been arrested."

That got Lila's attention. She sat up all at once, all thoughts of sleep gone.

"Who arrested him? The Astrals?"

"Me."

"Why?"

"For the same reason I should have you arrested."

"I don't know what you're—"

"I'm not stupid, Lila. Everyone acts like I am, but I've known for a long time that you, your mother, Terrence, and Christopher have been playing for the other side. Talking behind my back, making me look like an asshole. I have proof. I showed it to Captain Jons then to the Titans down at the station for good measure. Now you can either pull your ass out of bed and help me, or I can haul you down there, too, so you can live your little princess life in a cell."

Lila felt acid pulse through her veins. "You wouldn't dare. My father would—"

"Your father's objections are a quality problem. He has to come the hell out of his office if he wants to protect you. As things stand, I could tie you over a table and whip you to death. Believe me, Daddy wouldn't come your rescue."

Feeling bile rise in her throat, Lila said, "What do you want me to do?"

"Get him to open up."

"Why?"

"The grid is still down, but Terrence says there's tons of new power pumping into the Apex. 'Charging up' is the way he said it. And with the second ship feeding it—"

"What second ship?"

"But the Astrals won't talk. Shit, *don't* talk, maybe *can't* talk. Except to your father, or through your father, or through his computer — hell, I don't know. But nobody here knows what's happening. There are Reptars everywhere out there — searching, prowling, fucking slaughtering people, I have no idea. The Apex has a goddamned line out front, all Titans, like a nightclub. You can see it flashing and strobing even with the sun up. It seems to be projecting something into the desert; that's new. It's like they're gearing up for something. Shuttles are buzzing all over the place, and nobody is even showing us what we're maybe supposed to be doing. They don't care about us, Lila; they *let* us run this city, but they don't need us. Now they're not even pretending. Even Jons says he's not sure what he should do because the Titans all just gesture and point, like a giant game of charades."

Lila's anger melted into fear. She was back in the bunker again, with menace above, helpless and waiting. Maybe Raj wasn't the enemy here, for once.

"I know he's in his office," Raj went on. "I can hear him in there, maybe with someone who came in last night; I'm not sure. But he won't open for me or for Mo, and I'm not about to ask your mother. That leaves you. And maybe Clara."

Lila's eyes went to the crib, where her too-old-for-cribs daughter was sleeping through her parents' argument. That had been a step too far.

"You just want me to talk to him," Lila said.

Raj nodded.

"Get him to talk," he said, "and find out what's going on."

Chapter Forty-Nine

CHRISTOPHER WAS SITTING in his cell, exhausted, unable to sleep on his shitty cot. Jons had tried to help. He'd given Christopher additional blankets and pillows, and he'd slipped him some extra food. But he could only do so much. The human police station was overrun with Titans — more proof that Heaven's Veil had, for reasons unknown, become a police state.

There was a shuffling from the front room, where Jons had stationed a skinny cop named Mallory. At first, Christopher thought the girl must have stumbled and fallen, but then the last person Christopher expected burst through the door and came running forward.

"Lila?"

Mallory was behind Lila, her hands up as if making a gesture of trying to stop her without actually intending to. But then her hands just sort of fell and she walked out without a word. Christopher was human. Lila was human. And so Officer Mallory, who was human as well, seemed not to give a shit what they got up to so long as it was for humanity's general advancement.

Lila rushed to Christopher and tried to embrace him through the bars. They clanged their heads. When she pulled back, Christopher saw what a mess she was: sweaty, dark hair askew, big brown eyes wild. She had wet patches under both arms and a mist of perspiration in her cleavage. It might have been a turn-on if not for certain obvious buzzkills.

"What the hell are you doing here?"

Before responding, Lila took several deep, heaving breaths. She was completely winded, as if she'd taken the station at a sprint.

"I have to … be quick. Raj—"

"Is he bothering you? That motherfucker tossed me—"

She shook her head vigorously enough to make her hair fly. "No. Listen. He … thinks I'm … with Dad."

"So you ran down here?"

"Raj …" deep breath, " … knows."

"I know he knows. That's why I'm here."

"No. About Cameron … and Piper. About—"

"They're safe. I know where they are."

She shook her head again, frustrated. "The Apex."

"What about it?"

"Raj knows they're … in the city. And the Apex is … something's changing."

Christopher didn't like the sound of that. He straightened, his skin prickling.

"What do you mean?"

"They can't … try for the Apex." Finally, she sat on a bench, forcing her breath back to normal. "The Astrals are swarming it. They'll … be caught. You need to get them a message."

Christopher looked around the cell. "I can't."

"Then I have to," she said. "Where are they?"

"You can't. Raj will have you arrested."

Lila's frustration was boiling over. Her big eyes looked bloodshot. Her breath was calming but still not even. She was beaten, tired, emotionally wrecked. Terrence had told him that Meyer was acting strange, Heather was always strange, and Clara was strange with an exponent. Lila had married an asswipe, and now her lover was in jail. His simple statement seemed to be the breaking straw, and her eyes began to mist, threatening to spill.

"I have to! You have to tell me! The whole Astral army is on the Apex! Raj makes it sound like … they've pulled out all the stops to … find them! If they don't stay put—"

Christopher cut her off. An idea was forming. One that would keep Lila safe, protect Cameron and Piper, and maybe earn humanity a few disarming brownie points with the Astrals — all while getting their scattered eggs closer to sharing a basket, back where they belonged.

"Jons," he said. "Go out into the other room, and ask Captain Jons to come in here. But first, tell him to call the house and ask for Raj. Tell him to have Raj haul his ass down here, post haste."

Exasperated, near panic: *"Why?"*

"I want the two of them to go get Cameron and Piper then arrest them."

Chapter Fifty

LILA BREATHED.

She went to one of the hallway mirrors and tried to fluff her hair. With Raj called to the station, there was no rush. He wouldn't have the mental bandwidth to think of Lila, and any possible delays she might have committed on her way to her assigned errand. Not with Cameron and Piper in his greedy little sights. She simply didn't want to look like a pig — or to give her father, if he'd talk to her, reason to wonder why she looked so harried.

But when Lila was sufficiently composed and turned from the mirror to the office hallway, she heard the sounds of activity ahead. And when she arrived at Meyer's office door, it was as her gut had promised: the door was open as usual, her father puttering around as if nothing was amiss.

Hearing her approach, he turned and said, "Hey, Pumpkin."

Pumpkin? When had he last called her that? The pet name felt a thousand years old. From a simpler time, before alien motherships hung from the sky like poisonous fruit.

"Dad?"

Meyer smiled. Seeing that felt strange, too.

"Do you need something?"

"I …" She stopped. This was clearly a mistake. The house, being stone, was quiet even with all the Astral activity outside. The home was typically filled with Titans, but Raj had been right: They seemed to be massing on the Apex, bleeding them from their normal positions in the corridors. The way Lila and Meyer were now, they might have been any father and daughter, anywhere, any time other than here and now.

"You what?"

"Raj asked me to come see you."

"Oh yeah?" He set down a stack of papers he'd been carrying. "About what?"

Lila almost said *It's nothing* and left, but the abject normality of the situation was, in itself, unusual. Raj was right: The viceroy alone talked to Divinity and might have some clue as to what was happening outside — and having gone outside herself, Lila could say for sure that something was definitely afoot. Beyond the mansion grounds, Heaven's Veil seemed under siege. And yet here was Meyer, all but holding a placid cup of morning coffee as he went about his paperwork.

"He said you had a visitor." Lila looked around the room, seeing that they were alone.

"I did. He's gone."

"Who was it?"

"A friend."

Lila wanted to ask but knew it would be prying. It could have been anyone. Viceroy business had never been her business and likely never would be. And besides, that wasn't what mattered now.

"Raj thought you were still down here with him."

"No. He's gone."

"Where?"

"Where he needs to be."

"Dad, are you okay?" It was an absurd question. Of course he was.

"I'm great."

"Have you seen what's happening outside?"

"I have."

"And?"

"What's on your mind, Lila?"

"The second mothership," she said, forcing the sentence out. The foreign words felt strange. How could she be talking about motherships and little green men who, it turned out, weren't little or green? This was only an office. Just another day in logical paradise.

"What about it?"

"Why is it here?"

"It's feeding us power. Because the network is out."

Lila flicked the wall switch. Nothing happened.

"Not the house," Meyer said.

"So, the city."

"No. The power is for them."

"Why?"

"Because they need power."

"*Why*, Dad?"

"Why do you want to know?"

Lila paused, resetting, wondering if she should try again from a new angle.

"I heard you and Raj got into a fight."

He nodded, his lips pressed. "We did. That was unfortunate."

"Why?"

"I'm not sure."

"And Mom. Mom said you were all worked up over something."

"Did she? Well, I'm not anymore."

"Dad, I—"

Meyer came forward, cutting her off. He took her by both shoulders. She wasn't tall, and her father was. His large form eclipsed the window's light, draping Lila in shadow. Without warning, he wrapped his arms around her and squeezed.

"Dad?"

"I haven't told you lately how proud I am of you."

Lila felt her brow crease.

"You should tell people things. There have been times, when I've been busy in the past, that I've forgotten that." He half laughed. "It's funny. This shouldn't be a revelation, but it feels like one. Like I'm just figuring it out, though I know I've figured it out before. Ever since the Astrals came, it was rush-rush-rush. Even after we got to the Axis Mundi, I couldn't relax because I kept waiting for the next thing. I was always *Dad the protector*, not *Dad the dad*. Then they sent me back, and it seemed I knew what to do as viceroy, and the whole world felt like a startup. Well, North America, anyway. So I worked it. And again, I forgot."

He was still close. Lila could still only see his suit. She looked up to see his face. With this new demeanor, she could almost see Trevor in him, or vice-versa.

"But now you've remembered?"

"Seems so."

"Did you … was it like a near-death experience?"

"Sometimes, we just need distance, Pumpkin. Maybe I just needed sleep."

"Okay," Lila said, unsure of her reply. After a quiet moment, she added, "Dad?"

"Yes, Li."

"What are the Astrals doing? What's going on outside?"

"It's hard to say."

"You have a line to Divinity. They talk right to you, don't they?"

"They have, yes, in the past."

In the corner, something seemed to move. An end table jostled as if something had run by its legs, but she saw nothing. At first, Lila thought she'd imagined it — spied something from the corner of her eye that wasn't there because she was tired, or emotionally spent — but then Lila realized she could still see the minute movements of a vase as it wobbled side to side on the table.

"Dad?"

"Yes."

"What's going on with you?"

"Have I ever told you, Delilah," Meyer said, embracing her anew, "that you were named after a song?"

Chapter Fifty-One

HEATHER'S HEAD spun like a top. This time, she felt sure she wasn't imagining things. There was nobody in her small house but Heather herself, and yet the shadows cast through the windows kept changing as if someone was passing on the grass. But the lawn was empty. The city beyond was another story. But royalty, in Heaven's Veil, got its own slice of tranquility.

She moved to the window and looked up. But no, there were still two giant ships in the sky, their silver sides almost kissing, dangling above the city like almighty balls. They hadn't moved. Hadn't shifted the light. And the shuttles, which buzzed like a swarm of wasps between the pair and the city at large, were still avoiding mansion airspace. The angle was wrong. Whatever she'd seen, it hadn't been shuttles.

A ticking, metronome-like noise from behind her. Heather turned to see a tiny figurine rocking back and forth. As if someone had brushed the table as they'd clumsily passed.

The figurine settled.

"Now, you're finally losing your shit," Heather told the room.

It had only been a matter of time. There was only so much a human brain could take — particularly if it was already damaged like Heather's. She'd thought she was getting better. The last time she'd spoken with Meyer, she'd felt less her usual wiseass, walls-up self, and that had seemed like a good thing. Like she was finally facing issues and emotions rather than sarcastically deflecting. But maybe that wasn't it at all. Maybe she was just losing her fucking gourd.

The door, which was ajar, squeaked slightly farther open. Because of a draft. Not because of some weird shit in Heather's little house.

The widened door allowed a thicker sunbeam. It swallowed a lamp, which threw a shadow on the floor in the slanting morning light.

Except that on further inspection, the lamp wasn't in the light at all.

On further inspection, the shadow was casting itself.

Heather blinked. Turned her head, explaining it away, refusing to look. But the strategy backfired; with her head turned, in her peripheral vision, she could see the enormous thing in her doorway plain as day.

Her breath caught. Heather's hand jumped to her chest like a scared animal seeking solace. A half second later, she was staring at the doorway again, her pulse beating three times per second at her temples, her breath coming in a shambling intake of breath.

The doorway was empty. The shadow remained, but whatever had cast it was nowhere to be seen.

It was nothing. A trick of the eye. A strange slanting of light, bouncing off objects unseen, screwing with her already fragile mind. Her disbelieving, saw-her-husband-die-and-come-back-to-life mind.

Because of the breeze and nothing else, a tall vase filled with decorative rocks and sand tipped on its delicate end, fell to the floor, and shattered.

Heather stood, backing away.

An unseen hand wrote in the sand, slowly.

The message read, *Follow.*

The shadow on the floor vanished, but if Heather turned her head to the side and watched the doorway from the corner of her eye, she realized she could see the huge black shape farther up, waiting for her like an oversized dog seeking its handler.

While Heather watched, the shadow moved to the left, out of her line of sight.

Heather, wondering what the hell was wrong with her, followed.

Chapter Fifty-Two

MEYER CLOSED HIS EYES, obeying the summons. But this time, Divinity's presence was further away, not as intimate. He doubted it knew the difference; the collective, as he was starting to suspect, was mostly one way. He could hear it when it let him, but it pulled back from fully touching him. There was something about humanity that confounded the Astrals. Or — and this, Meyer was beginning to feel like a truth — perhaps humanity revolted them. Not in an overt way or in a way that was *truly* disgusting. Just in the way Meyer had never really cared to touch his food with his hands. Food was delicious, but gross to the touch.

That's how Divinity seemed to feel about Meyer. He was part of their organization and was, in whatever way the Astrals understood such things, like a partner. But they wouldn't let him fully in. They wouldn't wrap him with their minds as they wrapped each other because that would be like taking a delicious but reeking piece of limburger and rubbing it all over his face.

Yes, they were keeping him out. It was fine. Meyer knew he was being excluded — that, frankly, he was being *commanded* to do things without the Astrals bothering to ask for his input. It rankled him. It made him question his decision to be here at all, to do the things he was doing.

But then, wasn't this how a man kept his family safe? Yes, he'd made hard decisions, but it was all in the interests of those he loved.

Loved.

It made him think of what had happened on the Heaven's Veil streets. His words to Heather.

Why had he said that? For one, if he loved anyone, Meyer loved Piper. Piper was his wife, not Heather. And also, regardless of whether it was true or not, *why had he said it?* He'd just made a point to express himself to Lila, but that was mainly a counterreaction having to do with unexpressed regrets, about not saying things when one should say them, before it was too late. That was mainly because of what Andreus had told him about …

But Meyer didn't want to go there. Not yet. Not with Divinity in his internal ear, maybe listening.

He'd been contemplating all night. Meyer barely remembered Andreus leaving or where he — or Divinity, back when Meyer had been allowing *that* particular violation — had sent him. After that, he'd been in his own head, searching old memories like a historian sifting through records. And oh, the things he'd found! Things he'd known but allowed himself to forget. Things that were once important, that he'd shoved aside to make room for the present.

Why had he spoken that way to Heather? It was hard to say. The kind of thing a man says when dying, to make amends. Looking back, Meyer supposed he *had* thought he'd been dying, before the Astral ship arrived to revive him.

But that memory — far more recent than others, and

hence supposedly more durable — was most fractured of all.

For illogical reasons, he'd led Heather off the grounds, meaning to flee.

For illogical reasons, when Raj had confronted them, Meyer had decided to attack rather than be led back to his duties.

The memory was oddly devoid of color. He could see *what* had happened, but not *why*. As if he'd forgotten the reasons, or forced himself to shove them down.

In the memory, there was a jump cut, like an effect in one of Fable's movies.

Here, the timeline became confused. There was something just out of sight. Something that hadn't appeared in his mind until recently. *After* his talk with Andreus, when he'd *wanted* to spend the night poring over old memories. He'd wanted to delve, to appreciate what had been set behind. But at the same time — again, after Andreus — his memories began to feel distant. Far off, as if seen through foggy glass.

The jump cut had become obvious. Evident. There was a splice. And between the stitches of that splice, there was a voice he couldn't quite make sense of because he hadn't heard it in life, although part of Meyer felt certain he had.

There was an imperfection. A chain of events.

A room full of light. A dancing of specters. Not Meyer's memory, but Meyer's memory nonetheless.

In the forebear, there was an unspooling. Regrettable but now rectified.

A flash of thought. A spark of emotions, new though they couldn't be new at all: fear. Loneliness. Panic, both existential and local. A feeling of falling. The loss of closely held control.

We have taken care in this iteration to remove discursive stimuli from the stream before passing the donor's essence into you.

It made no sense. And yet that memory and those that came after it were somehow more real. And beyond the splice, memories had color. Rich with discursive stimuli.

Inside Meyer's mind, Divinity listed shuttle positions. Requirements of human police, which he was requested and required to hand down. Detailed deployments of peacekeepers. Gave instructions and orders, as if Meyer were only a go-between.

There was an unspooling.

Meyer opened his eyes in the office. Blinked. Focused on Divinity's words, which weren't really words at all.

Groupthink. It's called groupthink. And there is no need for a surrogate when we talk one to the other.

Meyer kept his wall up. Kept Divinity at arm's length, speaking in human terms as it issued commands. As it told him what the fuck to do as if he were a slave. As if Meyer was only a pawn. As if nothing in him mattered, as if he had no fucking say in those things that concerned him.

The importance of the Apex. The grid. The network. A pulse must be sent. It was the only way because with a strong enough beacon, anyone, from any distance, could be drawn to any thing.

Do this. Do that. Go here. Dance and sing because it is commanded.

Something boiled inside him. Red. Barely contained. Something that made Meyer's human skin form gooseflesh and got his human temples throbbing. Something shoved down that felt like an explosion. Something he was supposed to repress because it didn't concern him. Because it was discursive. Because to indulge such base ideas, which had no relevance, might cause an unspooling. Something,

Meyer felt sure, that the donor might feel differently about, whatever that meant.

Something about Trevor. About what Andreus had told him. Something bottled because it couldn't be true. And something Meyer, in turn, had told Andreus.

The communication with Divinity ended. Meyer found himself alone. He stopped for a second, blinking in the still air of the office, which he'd closed for privacy after Lila's departure. She'd left after he'd taken his hours, combing his memories. The ones that felt distant, unlike those that came after the splice and the curiously flat memories immediately before — flat because the stimuli had been purged. Pushed out. Sent from the groupthink because *we are pure, we are above, we are not base.*

But he was alone. Horribly, hideously, painfully alone. Cut off. Discarded. Chattel, meant for spending and sacrifice. As Meyer Dempsey, but also as ...

But there was nothing there.

The wall fell. What he'd pushed down came flooding back up.

It could not be expunged. It could not be eradicated. In the human mind, hate and loss and grief were like viruses. There was no vaccine. Like Canned Heat, it turned out that what had burned could not recover from ash.

He recalled holding Lila. How that had felt. How it had been necessary.

He recalled Heather holding him, only *not* him, exposed as truth now that the internal schism was forced asunder.

Meyer was an evolved man. An evolved being. He understood sacrifice. He was strong enough to accept, even in his current polluted state, that what must be done had to be done.

He grabbed the computer screen, held it high, and shattered it on the floor. He put his foot through the desk, finding that even though its wood was solid, he was far stronger than he should have been. The discursive stimuli flashed. The memory of groupthink resurged.

Fury rose inside him like a gusher.

Trevor was my son. My son! MY SON!

Meyer's fist had begun to heal, but as he let the rage fill and become him, he opened it again, and again, and again.

Chapter Fifty-Three

CAMERON WAS DREAMING about his father. They were in the desert somewhere because other than the Central American ruins, everything seemed for some damned reason to be in the desert. Sand, sand, and more sand — that had been Cameron's childhood. His first friend had been an obelisk. His most constant playmates had been the specters running through ancient crypts.

But it wasn't just Benjamin with him. There was someone else. A little girl whose growth must have been stunted, because she was tiny. She had a toddler's body yet held herself with an adult's confidence and pride. Her eyes were deep blue and her bearing crisp. Precise.

Benjamin looked from Cameron to the girl.

Oh, her? he said. *She's our guide.*

Cameron looked around. They'd found Thor's Hammer. He couldn't see it, but the sense was strong. With the below-the-skin knowledge common to dreams, Cameron could feel victory as if it were in his past. As if the moment of discovery had come and gone and he'd missed it, but it remained a memory nonetheless.

At the top of a very tall hill. Like a mountain. Granite and volcanic rocks. A chapel.

Where are we? Cameron asked. *Did we find it?*

Not where you thought, Cameron, Benjamin said. Beside him, the little girl nodded her head in agreement.

Then where, if not the Apex?

Benjamin smiled. *I know exactly where Thor's Hammer is, Cam. You do too. That's what kills me. As far as historical jokes go, it's a doozy.*

The words were familiar. Cameron squinted into the dream sun.

But where, Dad?

Benjamin laughed. *Think about it, Cam. A weapon from the ancient aliens theorist texts. Where would it go?*

The girl held her hand in a thumbs-up, smiling. As she did, Cameron's inner vision turned to something large and glittering. Maybe gold. Shining as with an inner light. Held aloft by a team of people. A huge thing, like a chest. Something inside, broken, crumbled, from the last time around, someone's ancient decision cast.

Where is it? Cameron asked as something sounded from outside his awareness — the dream crumbling as it became self-aware, as Cameron's mind pulled him from the fathoms of its false reality.

I know exactly where Thor's Hammer is. You do too.

But —

As far as historical jokes go, it's a doozy.

The dream was cracking like ancient ruins baking beneath a millennium of sun.

A weapon from the ancient aliens theorist texts. Where would it go?

Where? Just tell me how to find it!

Benjamin touched the girl's shoulder.

You don't need to find it, he said as the dream's underpinnings gave way and Cameron slowly woke. *Just find her.*

Chapter Fifty-Four

CAMERON AWOKE to the sound of breaking glass.

A rock crashed through Grandma Mary's window. It rolled to sit across the room, at the base of a dresser that was fifty years too old to be in a house so new.

Piper sat up. She crossed to the rock while Cameron, fighting a chill, raised his hand to send her back, as if it were a bomb.

But it was only a rock. They'd made a mistake entering the city, had been given a distraction by the strange shadow thing before getting hidden by the police captain, and they'd somehow need to be extracted ... or, Cameron supposed, ride out the coming turbulence with Captain Jons's grandmama. All were fine. He was with Piper, and they weren't running. Things could be worse. They were safe.

Piper held it up for Cameron to see.

"Kids, acting out, breaking shit," he said.

"No, Cam." She looked suddenly pale.

Cameron looked more closely as Piper extended the rock.

On its flat side was the message, *DON'T RESIST.*

Cameron looked from the rock to Piper, into her petrified eyes.

"What does it—"

There was a shotgun blast from below. The sounds of struggle. Cameron heard Grandma Mary shout, then crashing amid the tromping of boots.

Piper went for the window. Cameron stayed on the bed where he was, and Piper looked back at him as if he were stubborn or stupid or an idiot.

"Let's go! There's a trellis!" Cameron could see beyond her. The streets were clear, at least as far as he could see. No visible Reptars, Titans, or shuttles. No purrs. Only the sounds of cracking and breaking below, of hard soles on hard wood.

"Wait." He crossed the room. Picked up the rock.

"Cameron! We have to go! Now!"

"Where?"

"To the Apex!"

That was a joke. They'd been watching the Apex. Something had definitely leaked because everyone in Heaven's Veil was suddenly interested in the usually silent Apex. But her eyes said that this was no joke; people were coming, and they needed to run.

He shook his head.

"Cameron!"

He held up the rock then turned it to show her the words in big, bold letters. Overly done, really, practically with serifs on the tops and bottoms of each stroke.

"Close the window."

She stared, one leg already out below the shattered pane.

"Piper," he said, again displaying the rock. "It's Christopher's handwriting."

Piper didn't come fully back into the room, but she stopped moving out of it. She looked at the rock. Cameron watched her think, her expression halfway between terrified and brave.

There was nothing to do. Staying was the wrong answer given their reason for coming, but Cameron trusted Christopher. He had no choice but to trust Captain Jons, who'd been with Chris the last time they'd seen him, who'd ferried them to safety at his grandmother's house. And Grandma Mary, if she was as involved in any of this as she was in the underground movement, had already helped save Piper once.

Cameron felt heavy breath in his chest. Boots tromped up the stairs. Among the coming voices, he could hear Raj.

Two breaths. Three.

The door burst open — more kicked than opened. That was Raj for you; he hadn't even bothered to try the knob. And yet it had been open, and now Mary's door frame was kindling.

Raj came forward. He tossed a glance at Cameron but detoured to the more apparently immediate flight risk, taking Piper roughly by the wrist. Guns filled the room, but there were no Titans or purring Reptars with their needle-like teeth. Not that there was any longer a difference between them in Cameron's mind.

Christopher, despite seeming to have authored the rock through the window, was missing.

Raj yanked Piper away from the broken window. He turned her around, placing her in unnecessary cuffs. Piper kept her eyes on Cameron. Raj looked at Jons, who was sliding restraints onto Cameron's wrists, behind his back.

"He wasn't lying," Raj said. "I guess I owe you a Coke."

Cameron felt the band on his wrists tighten. He looked up at Jons but saw only a grim little frown. It could mean anything.

But when Raj moved far enough toward the door with Piper, Jons chanced a whisper.

"You and Chris owe my grandmama a new door," he said.

Chapter Fifty-Five

HEART BEATING HARD, Lila climbed the steps to the fourth floor. She felt disoriented and out of time. She might have been speaking with her father for two minutes, but it seemed equally possible that she'd been in his office for a half hour. Or an hour. Or for her entire life.

Something about his demeanor unnerved her. To put things simply, he was too nice. Too calm. The city was still eating itself; she could see it through the windows along the main staircase. The Apex's pulsing had brightened. Now, she could see it in the daytime. It had flashed again a time or two, and all of that oddity didn't even consider the second mothership that had established some sort of energy beam between itself and the ground.

Beyond the mansion, Heaven's Veil looked like the kind of place where citizens never came outside, preferring to huddle indoors lest the police carry them away for existing. There were human cops, all kinds of Astrals and their spherical vehicles, and even house guard who'd stopped tending the estate to knock heads in the streets.

And just a minute ago, Lila thought she'd seen her

mother leaving the grounds, headed out into the thick of it. Again. Why did nobody put a leash on the woman? Last time, she'd nearly got herself and Dad killed.

Lila made the third floor. With a guilty glance around, she climbed toward the fourth.

There was no reason she couldn't go where she was headed. No reason at all. She couldn't be *caught* because she wasn't doing anything wrong. It was her damned house. Never mind that there was nothing of interest to her on the fourth floor. Never mind that the last time she'd gone up here, she'd walked in on a standoff — then watched her father shoot her husband in the chest, heralding the start of this seemingly in-progress end.

Was Meyer better now? Or was he worse? He'd been acting like people do just before they kill themselves. Or, in Lila's mind, when they're about to do something rash or regrettable. Lila believed people could and did change, but these things were supposed to be gradual. She loved her father dearly, but he'd been such a hardass lately. Even before Vail became Heaven's Veil, he'd been a hardass. For most of her life, he'd been a hardass. You didn't precisely live with Meyer Dempsey. Life was more like one long audition.

His kindness, simply because it was so out of character, was frightening. It made Lila wonder what had happened to change him. Made her wonder what might be coming. Somehow added troubling context to the changes in the city, the sky, and the big blue pyramid — or somehow drew context from it.

She reached the fourth floor, again looking around. Raj should still be out there somewhere; that had been Christopher's point. The only person Raj would delight in bringing to justice more than Cameron Bannister and Piper Dempsey was Christopher himself. But Chris was protected from Raj, safe in his cell. Cameron and Piper would be soon. Which was also the point.

It's the only way to protect them, Lila.

As usual, there was too much unsaid. And as usual, no one told Lila more than what she strictly needed to know. She didn't understand why Piper and Cameron had returned given their narrow escape or why, now, that they had returned and found a hiding place — granted in part by Chris, no less — it suddenly made sense to protect them behind bars. So they wanted the Apex. Could they leave without accessing it, if it was so damn important?

Maybe Dad could get them into the Apex, Lila thought.

The idea lasted only a second. Lila was reaching. Ever since this had all began — way back to the day she'd skipped school to join Raj in the park, discussing the little problem that grew into Clara — Lila had been one step above luggage. Dragged here and there — first by her father, then by Raj. She wanted to *do something,* not have it all *done to her* for a change. But trying to get favors from her father, the way he'd seemed just now, was a giant mistake.

Dad shot Raj. He's on their side.

But the reminder that there were sides only made her trepidation worse. She'd played right into her role as luggage, because dammit if she hadn't simply accepted it all. She'd been barefoot and pregnant when her father had told her that the Dempseys would be treated special, and despite their firm establishment in the bad guys' camp, she'd gone along with it because it meant safety for her baby. It was understandable. But it sure made the notion of revolt hard to stomach now.

Because even if there was a way to help the rebel cause, she'd be shooting herself in the foot. And really … what would happen with Clara? Lila wasn't just responsible for herself. She had a daughter to think about, too.

And yet here she was, crossing to the network center.

There were only three guards: one Titan and a pair of humans. Even the two humans looked exhausted and exasperated. They seemed tired, likely because Raj didn't think of simple things like letting his people sleep and eat. And judging by their glance at Lila and the working form of Terrence's back as she approached, they clearly thought this was a fool's job anyway. Terrence was one guy, unarmed. And from all Lila had heard, he was twiddling his thumbs up here anyway. The damage was done. The network couldn't be debugged. It would need to be rebuilt, at least inside the city.

But that was Raj: beating a dead horse because his fragile pride insisted he not appear weak.

Which, in Lila's disgusted opinion, made him look weaker than ever.

Lila nodded to the Titan, who, true to protocol, nodded politely back. Then she did the same to the human guards, whose body language all but declared, *Do whatever the fuck you want; we couldn't care less.*

She crossed to Terrence.

"Christopher told me to suggest that you—" Lila began, keeping her voice low.

"I don't need Chris's suggestions to look for shit like encoded RF signals," Terrence cut her off, as if he'd been waiting to deliver a line.

Lila sat beside him. Again, she chanced a look at the exhausted-looking guards. You couldn't stay vigilant forever without anything happening. The way Christopher had described the situation on the fourth floor, it was more like an endurance contest than a repair job. The only question was whose will would break first: Terrence's, or Raj's?

"That what he told you, Lila?" Terrence asked.

Lila nodded.

Terrence sneaked a peek. When it seemed that the guards wouldn't flinch, he whispered, "There's a small stealth drone overhead. It keeps circling and circling. That mean anything to you?"

Lila shook her head. It only raised more questions.

"Near as I can tell without better equipment, there's a group outside the fence in the east quarter. I doubt the shuttles have seen them because for some reason all of their activity has moved to the Apex."

"Who's the group?"

"No way to tell. But they're not smashing in. So either it's someone who *can't* smash in or someone who means to get in quietly to establish positions without being noticed, like arranging pieces on a chess board."

Lila turned the revelation over in her mind. Christopher had told her to ask Terrence about this specifically, before Raj returned from his fruitful arrest. Now, Terrence had found something. But she couldn't see what help any of it was, for any of them. The group, whoever they were and whatever their intentions, would only be useful inside. But they hadn't entered. Maybe they couldn't.

"What do you want me to tell Christopher?"

Terrence exhaled then rubbed his eyes. "I have no idea. Tell them they're there, I guess, if you can. But I have no idea what good that will do. If they don't have enough force to gate crash, they're irrelevant. And if they have the force but haven't done it, that either means they're waiting for the right moment (which I doubt, seeing as the streets are getting *more* overrun with Astrals every hour now that the second mothership seems to be sending its own shuttles down) or they need a helping hand to get inside without attracting attention."

Lila swallowed, finding a decision.

"I'll do it."

"You'll do what?"

"I'll help them."

Terrence laughed then put a hand on Lila's back. It was affectionate, not patronizing — the tired touch of a man who sees his own inevitable end yet still wants to comfort the silly girl who yearns to do the impossible and save them all.

"It's noble, Lila, but look out the window. It's a police state out there. Sure, that's a low-priority section of the fence, but there are sensors around it, with battery power and none needing the network to sound their alarm. Even if you could open the fence, which you can't, how the hell you gonna get there unseen with all the new patrols?"

Lila slumped.

"Chris says Jons can be trusted. So there's something else important you can do: Get him a message for me. About the Apex."

"What about it?"

"Did Chris tell you it's like a big antenna?"

Lila nodded.

"From what I see here," Terrence said, indicating his monitor, "it's cycling up to broadcast."

"Broadcast what?"

Terrence's face formed a grim line.

"Something big," he said.

Chapter Fifty-Six

MEYER STOPPED.

His fists, newly bloodied, dripped on the floor. In the quiet corridor, he could actually hear each droplet striking the sealed stone.

There was a voice behind him. It was Beta. But then it wasn't because Meyer didn't know anyone named Beta. He only knew four white walls, a floor, a ceiling, and an immersion to keep him busy. The voice was Mo Weir.

"Meyer?"

Meyer turned and gave Mo his patient face. But Mo's attention was drawn to his fists.

"Jesus. What was it this time? Raj again?" Then quieter, with a sideways smile that had no real warmth: "Did you kill him?"

"It wasn't Raj."

"Then how did you do this?" Mo picked up Meyer's left hand at the forearm, keeping his hands away from all the blood as if it was infected. Which, Meyer was beginning to suspect, it might be, in its own way.

"I had an accident in my office."

"What kind of accident?"

"It will need to be cleaned up."

Mo looked at Meyer with an unreadable expression. "What's going on with you, Meyer?"

"Trevor is dead."

Mo's mouth fell open. There was a long moment where the aide didn't seem to have any idea what to say. Sympathy was the predictable response, but Meyer had just beaten Mo over the head with surprising information. There was no decorum. No slow reveal. No tears, nothing at all. Just a bland face that barely felt like more than a prop, put on for show.

"What ... how? What are you talking about?"

"Nathan Andreus told me."

"Andreus?" Then: "Did he do it? Was that what he came here to tell you?"

"It was the Astrals. Trevor was with the rebel group that caught them with their pants down."

"He could be lying, Meyer. Trying to twist you into—"

"He was telling the truth."

About Trevor.

About the fact that the Astrals did it.

And, perhaps most importantly, that Andreus was sorry. Meyer didn't know why that was important, but it was. Meyer was definitely sorry — a hollow feeling that left him feeling like a shell. He could feel the Astral reaction by contrast; its bland lack of emotion was comparatively stark. Sensing it, Meyer felt a strange duality: He almost wanted to join the Astral perception, to see it as they did. He'd known the truth as Andreus had said it because something had unhitched and in a way, Meyer could see Trevor die through Divinity's eye. He'd been split down the middle. Part of him saw it as information. The other half had caused what he'd done to his own fists, as if that had made sense.

"Wh …" Mo stuttered, seeming to know he should ask more but unsure which W word to begin with. Finally, he settled on, "Was it an accident?" Then, after a small pause: "When were they going to tell you?"

No, it wasn't an accident. In fact, the Reptars responsible, Meyer could sense, had felt a rather inappropriate sense of delighted anger. They weren't supposed to relish their kills. It was all business, another rebel necessarily eradicated. But they had. Just as the Titans, when they'd discovered the rebels had played them for fools, had taken it personally.

Meyer's fist clenched. The pain was a pleasant distraction. That's why he'd kept going, alone in his office. The more it hurt, the less he had to focus inward. Pain was the ultimate bright and shiny object. Keep your eye on the agony, and you wouldn't have to experience anything else. God knew the Astrals weren't sharing more than the tip of their collective mind with him, like they used to in a long-ago time that Meyer Dempsey had no business remembering.

"Not an accident. And they—"

(Red-hot fury, roiling like a storm; Meyer wanted to hit Mo too, just to break his clotted fingers open)

"*Weren't* going to tell me."

"Why the hell not?" Mo looked indignant. *Good.* Angry on Meyer's behalf. He knew how the Astrals thought, as one giant hive mind. A mind that didn't include Meyer because he was human. Because he'd been pinched out. Because he'd stopped mattering the moment he'd been … Well, what *had* he *been*? It was all so unclear, so distant.

Humans could be a hive mind, too. Here he was, with Mo angry for Meyer, claiming his rage as if it were his.

Meyer said nothing.

"Does Heather know? Does Lila?"

"No."

"Are you …" Mo paused, seeming to sense something dire and unpleasant in the works. "Were you on your way to tell them?"

"No. I don't want them to know."

"What? Meyer, they have to know."

"It will hurt them."

"But Meyer, seriously, they have to—"

Meyer resumed walking. Where had he been going? It was irrelevant. He'd been in his office. Now he was in this hallway. And yet somehow, he'd also always been in that white place. Four walls. A ceiling and a floor. And an immersion like TV that kept him alive. Healthy and strong, but hollow inside.

"Meyer!"

"Please have someone mop up the blood in the hallway."

"Where the hell are you going?"

"And my office. If you could have it tidied."

"Meyer, shit! Stop, will you?" Mo had his hands on Meyer's jacket, on his lapels, gripping his arm. Mo's emotions now worse than Meyer's. He'd always been able to mute or kill them. Part of being in a group. Nothing was wholly anyone's, same for responsibility. He'd had that once, but now he'd lost it. Because he'd been forced out. Like the essence he could still feel, more homeless even than himself.

Mo turned him around. Looked into his eyes. This solid, serious, obnoxiously responsible man, coming undone over news that wasn't even his own. It made Meyer falter. It made him see himself in Mo, knowing how he was supposed to react. Seeing how he, too, was pushing something out, shoving it down. Building more discursive stimuli. Unspooling.

But what the other had done, Meyer could do, too.

Something snapped. Meyer remembered all at once. And he knew how he could fulfill his bargain with Andreus, before he'd sent the man on his way.

"Just breathe," Mo said, and Meyer thought the man should take his own advice.

"My hands," Meyer said, feeling a firmly held wall starting to falter. "I think something is broken. I need medical treatment."

"I'll send one of the guards for Dr. Olivier."

But Meyer shook his head. "*Astral* medical treatment," he said. "Send for a shuttle instead."

Chapter Fifty-Seven

HEATHER WATCHED the thing from the corner of her eye, sure she was being a complete fucking idiot. This was how people got themselves killed in horror movies. There was always a clear exit or an obvious way to lie low, but then some dumbass would follow the man with the axe, walk into a dark basement for no reason, or do ...

Well, do something like this. Like following a shadow monster just because it suggested she do so.

I don't want to live in a world where a girl can't trust shadow monsters, Heather told herself. But even in the privacy of her mind, as she avoided her terror, the one-liner wasn't funny. Without sarcasm as a weapon, Heather felt like Superman robbed of his powers. Or Wonder Woman minus her lasso.

She'd crossed street after street. It was hard to focus on the thing, given that seeing it seemed to require a *lack* of focus — a certain laziness of the eye muscles to spy it in her peripheral vision — but each time she crossed an intersection, Heather caught her breath and paused until she could see it again. It always waited. And now that she was getting better at looking-without-looking-at-it, she could *almost* make out features. Eyes, perhaps, as it watched her.

Why am I doing this? she asked herself.

But the answer — as unilluminating as it was honest and true — came back immediately: *Why the hell not?*

Heather Hawthorne had once lived in a world of stringent plans. A world where she had to schedule visits with her lover around her manager's calendar. You never forgot where you were when the biggest moments hit, and Heather could still feel every ripple and contour from the day when she'd learned the ships were coming.

On the phone with Meyer, suddenly catching sight of the TV.

The clothes she'd been wearing. The position of the phone in her hand. The feel of carpet underfoot at her (formerly *their)* home in LA, the minute ticking of a clock that she'd somehow heard despite the television.

She'd been trying to find a time to meet him. Around a schedule that was so rigid, she refused to bend it even as Meyer reminded her that she could.

But things had changed, and the Heather who lived by plans and schedules was dead. She was still famous, but now she was the Queen Mum of Heaven's Veil rather than the Queen of Mean on HBO comedy specials. Now she could do what she wanted, when she wanted. And increasingly, as shit had flown in steady streams toward life's largest fan, she'd found herself caring less and less for what was sensible.

Being quiet and playing by the rules hadn't worked.

Joining Meyer in a defiant *run for ze hills* after sabotaging the Internet hadn't worked.

So now, Heather was phlegmatic. The world was ending again. Meyer was dead, but not gone — something new, yet clearly still Meyer Dempsey. The goddamned

Apple Store pyramid in the city was flashing like a bomb, Trevor and Piper had run off to fight with the Contras, Lila had given her a spooky grandkid, and maybe, shit, the entire city was going to eat itself in search of two people whom the Astrals had fucking let into the city on purpose. Why *not* follow a big giant imaginary wolf made of smoke? How much worse was it than anything else, past history considered?

A large patrol — five or six Reptars, plus Titan guards — rounded the corner. Heather ducked back. Her heart skipped, but not as much this time. If she'd obeyed her gut instead of the insistent shadow thing in front of her, she'd have walked right into that patrol. But she'd been following the shadow for a while and had grown used to close calls. Five or six times now, it had miraculously guided her around the perfect corner at just the right time. It was like having an escort with intimate knowledge of everything in the area, including the exact time to move and where to go. Like playing Frogger with a savant.

In the corner of Heather's eye, a column of darkness seemed to protrude from the monster's body. It beckoned like a big hand, urging her to cross the street.

"Yeah, yeah," Heather muttered.

Five blocks and two near-misses later, Heather defocused to see the shadow leading her into a building. It was a store of some kind, but it had either been raided or closed. The door was ajar, and opened easily when Heather pushed it.

Inside, she found herself staring down the barrel of a gun. A bald man with a black goatee was holding the weapon, but he lowered it after a surprised second of staring.

"You're Heather Hawthorne," he said.

Heather skipped the obvious counter-question, opting

for something more self-promotional — there was some of the old, arrogant Heather left inside her after all.

"I guess you know me as the poor girl's Piper Dempsey," she said, taking the lowered weapon as a good sign — and, now that she thought about it, glancing around for the shadow that had, for reasons unknown, led her to this strange man.

"No. I know you from *Good Girls Don't Have Wet Panties.*"

A small smile formed on Heather's lips before she could stop it.

"Who are you, and why are you in here?" *And why,* she wanted to add, *did my big bad wolf of a companion bring me here?*

He told her his name, his mission, and what he might be able to do if he hadn't found himself pinned by patrols, unable to leave the building.

Then Heather, who found herself (maybe not so) coincidentally able to make a difference after all, told him how she might be able to help.

Chapter Fifty-Eight

To PIPER, Raj's gloating outside the cell bars felt a bit like Rumpelstiltskin, except that instead of raging at story's end, he'd done a happy dance. Raj hadn't actually danced, of course, but his body language had been buoyant, boyish, very *I told you so.* Piper was almost glad for him. Everybody won here, and if Raj wanted to believe they hadn't gone willingly, then let him.

Jons entered the holding area after Raj left. He waited longer than Piper would have thought, but she assumed that was Raj's doing, too, or at least in deference to the supposed man in charge. This was kabuki, in part. If Raj didn't leave feeling that Jons was uninterested in speaking to his prisoners alone, it could fall apart. He might have watched Raj victory-dance back to the mansion through a window. He might have followed him for a few blocks, returning to the station only once it was obvious that Raj wouldn't be doing the same.

He didn't immediately speak. Jons looked from Piper and Cameron in one cell to Christopher in the other then said, "I hope you bitches are happy."

Piper blinked. Christopher, who seemed to know the chief well, took the bait — not quite asking for clarification but making vague hand gestures indicating the man should continue.

"Grandmama Mary gets Miss Dempsey out once. Right through her motherfucking basement. Nobody even knows she's involved, and why should they? Old black lady in a wheelchair. So now I put her ass on the line again, not actin' like a proper grandson at all, and what happens? 'Oh, Malcolm, go arrest them from your grandmama's house. Bring trouble down on your grandmama, Captain Jons.'"

"You could have moved them before doing what I told Lila to—"

"Shut your fucking mouth, Christopher. I'm not finished."

Christopher held up his hands. Jons turned to Piper and Cameron.

"'Course I can't move you. 'Cause how would that look? Can't call Grandmama on the phone, can I? Can't go running over, 'cause Big Chris says it has to happen *right fucking now*, isn't that right?" His gaze flicked to Chris.

"If we'd waited, it only would have—"

"Thought I told you to keep your mouth shut?"

Again, Christopher raised his hands.

"Not so much I mind helping out. I didn't become a cop to help ET take over the planet. Ain't what I signed up for. I gotta choose a side, I guess it's my species. And okay, Grandmama's house is good cover. And if that cover's gotta blow, so be it; at least it served its purpose. But you send *me* in there? *I* gotta do it?"

"You could've sent—"

"I meant in the big picture, Chris! Ratting on ourselves." He turned again to Piper and Cameron. "Why didn't we just bring you two here to start, save the poor old lady?"

Piper wanted to point out that the decision to hide them had been Jons's, not her request. But she didn't like being told to shut up.

"Did ... is she okay?" Cameron asked.

"Oh, sure, if you count havin' to pay for a new door out of Astral Social Security okay. If you count Raj *taking a fucking pie* okay. Since when is it okay to walk into some old lady's house and take her pies?"

"But is she ..."

Jons waved a mammoth hand — perhaps, Piper thought, realizing how ridiculous his rant might sound. "Oh, like I'm gonna tell Raj who she was, and like he's gonna figure it out without a computer. She puts on a good act. He buys they forced their way in and scared her, poor confused lady, can't find her pills in the morning. Whatever. But now what? Chris, you're such a smart guy, what you gonna do now, with all three of you in here? Raj has his way, he'll ask for your heads. It's all I could do to get there as humans before the Astrals caught you. You're *lucky* the network is down. I'd have had to enter you. They'd probably be all over this place right now because of it. Clock's ticking, kids, and here we are with our fists up our own asses. How we gonna get those fists out our asses before someone makes the connection between Mary and me or Raj comes back with Reptars wanting to eat you?"

"We could run," Cameron said.

"Oh, that's fucking *brilliant.*"

"Why not?"

"That's how this started! You're in *Heaven's Veil,* son! I don't mean to insult you, but the two times you *busted your way in here*? They opened the door. And from what I hear, about the one time you *excaped*?" (Jons said the word with an X: *excaped*.) "Sounds like they let you go because they needed you to do shit for them. So now I'm supposed to just let all three of you go? And hell, don't tell me I guess I go, too, because now I've got an expiration date, thanks to you. All four of us, just march up to the gate. 'Hey, Mr. Alien, you mind if we run out for some bread and milk? There's a Quickie Mart just down the road — we promise to come right back.'"

"We can't just sit here," Cameron said, weaker than Piper would have hoped.

To the ceiling, Jons said, "Jesus, my man, look at this white boy." Then to Cameron: "Maybe I can draw you a picture. You are in the safest place you can be. This is *the best you can do* right now. You hear? That's why Chris sent me. Now Raj is off your ass, and Chris looks a little bit better. The Astrals won't look for you in custody if I don't tell them you're here and the network stays down. But this ain't Candy Land, neither. You're in a box, and there's nowhere — and no way — to run."

"The Apex …" Piper began.

"Is a dead end," Cameron finished.

Piper looked back. "What?"

"Thor's Hammer isn't there."

Piper felt the floor fall from under her. She should feel disoriented. Instead, she felt anger.

"*Excuse* me?"

"I was wrong. I was wrong about my dad's research."

"When did you have this grand epiphany that sent us into the city, where I never wanted to go in the first place? When were you going to tell me that we'd come for nothing and that I was right all along?"

She thought Cameron might fight back, but he looked stepped on. Piper wanted to hit him, to tell him to stand up straight and be a man.

"I'm sorry," he said.

"Sorry?"

"I told them. I told Charlie and Nathan that I didn't know where it was. How could I? I'm a guitar player. I was traveling, playing dive bars and hooking up with groupies." He glanced at Piper, maybe wondering if he shouldn't have said the last thing. "My father was the scientist. I thought he was crazy. For years, I wanted nothing to do with him. Fucked up his marriage, fucked up with me. A nut job crawling through caves, looking for giant rocks, dragging his kid to Egypt to dig through pyramids and climb Mount Sinai looking for shards of stone tablets. But I was a punk kid back then. I didn't care about any of it. Mayan temples, Olmec heads, who gives a shit? I certainly wasn't taking notes."

"But his files …"

"I was guessing, Piper." He sighed, his head practically hanging. She wanted to shake him. She wanted to fight, and he wanted to surrender. He slumped back, finding the wall. Finding the bunk, wasted.

"I don't know what to tell you, Bannister. You say you shouldn't'a come? I've got to agree. Now there's a second mothership. Lots more shuttles, more Titans, more Reptars. I can barely keep them out of the station." Jons huffed a small laugh. "Hell, I *can't* keep them out of the station. Now that the chips are down and they've got something brewing at that big blue pyramid, it's become apparent just where we stand in the natural order. Maybe they mean to kill us all or make us slaves — either way, this playing house we've been doing for two years isn't how it's gonna be for long. We're still around, pretending to be civilized, because they *let* us. Now it seems they've got other plans. There are Titans in and out of here all day long now." Jons pointed at the door out of the holding area.

"That door right there? That's the only thing between the three of you and a laser beam execution. But now it's not just a Titan deciding to walk through that you have to worry about. Raj will gloat for a while because he wants to savor his shit. But then he's gonna tell Dempsey. And if he doesn't trust the viceroy, he'll start talking to Astrals, looking for a promotion. We four got days left, maybe hours."

There was a knock at the holding area door. Jons called for entry, and a bland-looking policewoman opened the door, with two people in tow.

"Captain Jons?" the woman said. "This lady needs to talk to you."

Piper was surprised to see the station's visitors and wanted to call out, to cry — *something*.

But her own emotion fled almost as it came. Because how she felt seeing the new arrivals was nothing compared to the shock that had claimed Cameron's face.

Chapter Fifty-Nine

MEYER WATCHED THE PILOT, trying to get inside its head. It was impossible. He could feel something coming off the Titan, like heat. He could sense chatter with the collective in the way Divinity had always ...

(Since before? Since years and years past?)

... spoken inside his mind, but it was third party, from a distance.

Meyer focused. Watched the Titan's hands move. He found he could almost participate, in some odd way, in the process of flight. The large white female in her robe was in the middle of a brightly lit circle, pan-sized hands out like someone searching for balance.

But Meyer could see more than most humans would be able to. To most, it would look as if she was steering the shuttle with her hands, even though they were touching nothing. Moving through some sort of force field or aether. But it wasn't quite that. The hands were moved by the mind, much like the ship. After all, how *could* a ship be moved by hands? The hands were only an intermediary. Only mentality allowed the ship to move from here to there without spending more time than necessary in between. Only mentality allowed the micro-distortion inside the ship's belly that kept the occupants from being liquified by what would appear, from the outside, to be instant accelerations and decelerations.

"Are we going to the primary mothership?" Meyer asked.

The pilot gave a placid smile.

"I've only been to the primary mothership."

The pilot's hands moved. The trip was taking most of a minute. Straight flight was easy, but there was a human aboard. He might not understand — at least that's what the pilot probably thought. What the *collective* probably thought, through the pilot's single instance. And humans (so Astrals seemed to think) couldn't grasp the idea of believing a thing into truth. They'd think it was magic. Humans thought that the world occurred and observation followed, despite their scientists demonstrating otherwise.

Stubborn.

Impatient.

Chaotic.

Cruel.

Pitiable.

Redeemable.

The adjectives flew through Meyer's mind along with ten thousand others. His brain only caught those that sped by in his language, although he couldn't help feeling that once upon a time he'd have heard and understood them all. Not because Divinity spoke to him, but because his was a mind Divinity was *able* to speak to.

Because how he was right now, Meyer was becoming increasingly sure, wasn't the way he'd always been.

He thought of Trevor. The pilot's flat, bold features flicked toward him, eyes assessing. Meyer pushed it down and away. Just another datum buried in the dark, muddled depths of a human mind, unworthy of chasing into the muck.

The pilot looked away then up. Watching the bottom of the approaching mothership, clearly visible through the one-way silver skin like a giant overhead window. He'd been resisting the urge to look down, but casting his eyes up and seeing only the slight sliver haze to remind Meyer that he was in a supposedly opaque craft made him do it now. Below the pilot's feet was the lighted flight circle, and below Meyer's nothing but a light gray fog.

He felt nerves, decided they'd serve him. Part of Meyer's mind made the adjustment perfectly because he'd been in shuttles and motherships untold thousands of times, but the more pressing part insisted he'd flown a scant few. He was Meyer Dempsey, wasn't he? Meyer had grown up on Earth with his feet on terra firma. He'd flown in hulking metal beasts with floors that mimicked ground.

He allowed himself to feel jitters. Allowed himself to sweat. He looked up and watched the hole form in the mothership, watched the area darken from the top in a spreading circle as they eased up inside it. But before the mothership's floor irised closed below the shuttle, Meyer looked down and let the fear of falling surround him. Let it radiate from him so the pilot could feel it.

The pilot gave Meyer an easy smile. Pacifying.

"I don't love heights," Meyer said.

The pilot held the same smile. Lowered her hands. The circle of light below her bare feet dimmed, and the shuttle's outer hull reappeared, now solid from the inside. This was all for his benefit, Meyer could sense. In order to see a door form, the human would need to first see the wall in which it would appear.

He exited. Below him was a gantry, smooth and gray,

without any features. If he was barefoot — Meyer knew from experience he shouldn't have been — the surface would feel soft and gently yielding as if walking on firm rubber. Below the gantry, there appeared to be nothing but Heaven's Veil. But if he fell — which, of course he wouldn't thanks to correction fields he knew were around him without being told — he'd strike the ship's one-way transparent hull rather than plummeting to his death.

The Titan, now a guide instead of a pilot, gestured for Meyer to proceed. It was unnecessary on two levels, but Meyer pretended it wasn't.

He could hear the groupspeak urging him forward, as if he'd still be able to hear it — which, he felt quite sure, he wouldn't.

And secondly, he knew the way. *Of course* he knew the way.

Meyer looked down at the long white arm, draped with its robe, and walked in the indicated direction. He took a wrong turn deliberately then allowed himself to be gently corrected. The Titan remained a silent presence beside him, shepherding Meyer toward the medic able to easily heal the viceroy's very important hands.

There had been no questions about his injury. Why would he *not* smash his hands? Humans were irrational. That's why the Astrals were necessary. Humans had done many, many, *many* irrational things in the past two years, and well beyond that according to their history texts. Surely, there were many other irrational things (and surely some wonderful ones; humans were their children, after all, and not beyond goodness by any stretch) done in the last epoch.

They couldn't verify any of it yet thanks to the delay. But that would be over soon. Now that the Apex was charging and prepared, that would change.

Meyer sensed great conflict on that last point — both native and exacerbated by the aberrations within the collective that hadn't, it turned out, been fully purged. It was unfortunate, what would need to be done. But there was no progressing without it. The end, *in* the end, was always the ultimate decider. And in that end, the humans had made it necessary by their own shortsighted hands.

Not their first time, of course.

Meyer saw it all as he walked. As the Titan led him to the medic. He must be generating feedback — more of those troublesome outputs that would, to anyone with a bit of groupsense in their groupthink — indicate that the viceroy heard more from the Astral collective than he was strictly supposed to be feeling.

But Meyer had figured *that* out, as well. Astral minds could (via certain tools or when a mind was half-connected like Meyer's) hear human emotion when it was *loud*. Like his almost-slip, thinking about Trevor on the ride up. But they didn't usually hear quieter emotions, as Meyer's were now.

Not because they *couldn't* hear those emotions and thoughts from halfway-connected minds. It was more that they *wouldn't*. They refused, closing their collective minds to human pollution, like that coming off Meyer. If they didn't, the collective might become infected, then a Gathering would happen, discursive thoughts expelled in a Pall, purged like pus from a wound.

They stopped at a door. Meyer knew he could open it with what felt like an *Astral half* to his mind, but he held back, knowing that would be showing too much. So he waited and watched as his guide projected. He heard the groupthought then watched the door dissolve and bead into the edges like liquid racing from the center. He entered alone, leaving his guide outside, and found himself facing a medic.

The medic held a box made of what looked like red glass. He held the box out, and Meyer …

(knew)

… guessed that he was supposed to put his hands inside.

Then the medic looked at Meyer and …

(asked a question)

… said nothing at all.

(Why did you do this?)

Because nothing was asked, Meyer didn't respond. He kept his mouth shut. Pretended this was all strange yet fascinating. Allowed his wound to change, even though he was already suspecting that if he wanted it badly enough and understood his shape for what he wanted it to be, he could probably heal the wound himself.

Meyer withdrew his hands from the box. Held them up and observed them. He pretended to be shocked/surprised that such healing was possible then ran the fingers of each hand over the other for good measure. He smiled at the medic and nodded.

"Thanks."

The medic nodded back. Then the door again melted away, and Meyer exited.

His guide was gone. Possibly because Meyer had already groupthought ahead, explaining to the guide in another's voice that Viceroy Dempsey was gone, that he'd already taken a shuttle back. The Titan who'd flown him here wouldn't wonder at the idea. Why would she? The collective knew. The collective always knew.

Meyer paused on the gantry. Because his human shape seemed to demand the ritual, he closed his eyes and slowly inhaled.

After a few moments, he seemed to remember. He remembered where he'd gone and never left. He remembered where, conflicting realities aside, he still was now.

A white room. Four walls, a floor, and a ceiling. And an immersion to keep him busy, healthy, and strong.

Meyer groupthought ahead, noticing a few others between his position and his destination, and gave them the idea to move elsewhere.

Then he walked along the gantry, recalling the way and seeing it for the first time, following a trod path and having no idea where he was going, seeing new and known in unison.

Eventually, he came to a door.

He knocked because it was polite.

Then Meyer went inside.

Chapter Sixty

NATHAN FOUND Heather Hawthorne to be different in person. That shouldn't have been surprising, but it was. She didn't strut while crossing the floor of the dark, empty store. She didn't insult him with each passing second. She seemed scared yet strangely confident, not merely caustic and sarcastic. It all made sense, but Nathan had formed a mental image of this woman — had, in fact, kept recordings of a few of her specials on the juke at Andreus HQ — and it was so odd to see her here, now, talking about escape and shadows.

"What led you here?" he asked, sure he must have heard wrong.

"Never mind. I found you."

"Were you *looking* for me?"

"I ..." It was as if she'd only now stopped to consider. Strange, the things that made unquestioned sense these days. "I guess not," she finished.

"A dark shape. Like a big dog that seems to be stalking you."

"It didn't stalk me. It ..."

"Oh, forget it."

"Heather." Nathan gave her an even look. "Can I call you Heather?"

"Call me whatever the hell you want."

"Heather, let me tell you a story."

"Great." Now she was rolling her eyes, turning away.

"I talked to your husband."

"*Ex*-husband."

"And he wasn't exactly normal. Set off all my alarms. If I'd been able to sneak a gun into the house, I think I'd have pulled it out and kept it pointed. He didn't come at me. But it's like he's insane. Especially after I told him ..." Andreus trailed off. He needed her focused right now, and she might not yet know. Meyer certainly hadn't, and the results when he'd explained about Trevor had been ... unsettling.

"Told him what?"

"About this," he lied. "When I told him I sent a drone. I did it on a lark, sure I was just wasting the drone's time when I might need it somewhere else. But then he ... well, not *him*, but the aliens, I guess ... told me that they hadn't destroyed my camp after all. If they got the drone, they'll be here. But I can't reach them."

"Reach who?"

"The Andreus Republic. My people. Dempsey got very interested in helping at the end of our conversation. Gave me a code that will open the fence without triggering an alarm. But here's the problem, *Heather*. Would you like to know what it is?"

Heather said nothing, seeming to see the entire conversation as rhetorical.

"The problem is that the Apex is that way—" He pointed to his left. "And for some reason, the Astrals keep putting down from their motherships over there." This time, he pointed right. "Best guess, mainly because I haven't seen death rays and explosions, is that nobody's paying much attention to the perimeter and my people are hiding reasonably well. There's a gully that direction, and they hide for a living, when they're not fighting. Meyer pretty much said this, and I've seen the same: Right now, they only have eyes for the Apex. Which is part of this whole problem, but farther down the chain. Right now, I can open a gate with the viceroy's code. But I've been waiting here for hours. The traffic back and forth out there stops sporadically, and I don't have my drone or a spotter. I go to the gate, I'm just hoping to get lucky."

"There must be—"

"So, Heather, if you tell me that you think your spirit guide will get us to the fence, I'm understandably curious about *what. The fuck. You're talking about.*" He metered the words precisely, tapping a dusty countertop for emphasis. "Does that seem fair?"

"Look, if you don't want—"

She jumped midsentence, as if goosed. Then Heather turned her head to the side, eyes on the window.

Nathan spun, raising a long piece of metal he'd found on the floor. Oh, what he wouldn't give for a proper weapon — one that wouldn't have been confiscated at the gate. Dempsey had sent him out like a pilgrimage, free to go but carrying nothing. That had been strange in itself … but if Dempsey's permission to go was the small act of oddball rebellion it seemed to be, why not give Nathan a gun to defend himself? He'd been lucky so far, but making the gate from here was impossible. Both corners were blind, and there was no way to peek from above: nothing more than a roll of the dice.

He watched the window, trying to see what had made Heather react so violently.

"Did you see something?"

"Hang on." She raised a hand but kept her gaze forward, her manner precise.

"What? Reptars?"

"Hang on." Again with the hand. Then, "Don't move."

The way she said it gave Nathan gooseflesh.

"I'm not looking outside. I'm looking at you in my peripheral vision."

"You were looking at me a second ago," Nathan said.

"It surrounded you."

Nathan looked down, around, behind him. Heather was reminding him of Piper, with her own spectral sightings. Apparently, Meyer had a type: kooks who saw ghosts. But a large part of Nathan didn't buy that. Whatever Heather saw, it was almost as if he could *feel* it.

"Where is it?"

"Behind you. Moving toward the door. Now back to you. It's lost its shape. Like a mist."

"What are you talking about?"

"I think it wants me to help you."

Nathan exhaled. "That's the biggest sack of—"

Without warning, one of the small tables upended, leaving the diner's ground for a second before crashing down and shattering a leftover glass. The sound, in the otherwise silent room, seemed tremendous. Nathan flinched, waiting for patrols to hear it and descend, but nothing happened.

"And I don't think it wants to hear your cynicism," Heather said, still with her head forward, still peering at him from the corner of her eye.

Nathan looked to the table. To Heather, to the mess of glass on the floor. That had grabbed his attention and erased a few doubts. He kept his outward cool, but his heart rate had doubled, slamming against his ribcage.

Why couldn't he see it, if something was there?

"It knows where they are," Heather said. "If that's where it means to go and we follow, it can get us to your people without being seen."

Nathan looked around the room, feeling cold. When his eyes reached the door, he watched it ease slightly open, as if goosed by a draft.

"What is it?" Nathan's tough skepticism was suddenly gone as he deferred to Heather.

"I don't know."

"How do you know you can trust it?"

Heather looked back.

"I don't."

Chapter Sixty-One

CAMERON GASPED. Piper gripped the cell bars beside him.

Two years hadn't changed Lila much. She looked at Cameron while Jons held most of her attention. Their eyes exchanged a silent hello, but he'd only seen the small girl with Lila in dreams.

"Lila!" Piper said.

The girl — now woman, really — pushed past the police chief and away from the skinny cop. Jons dismissed the officer as Lila went to Piper, holding her hands. The girl stayed at the door, holding her eyes on Cameron.

"Why are you here?" Lila's gaze flicked to Jons.

"He's on our side," Piper said.

"Terrence sent me. Told me to tell Captain Jons that something is happening with the Apex."

"We knew that," Christopher said.

Lila released Piper's hand, and inched toward him — a greeting without a proper salutation. She shook her head, unsure of whom she should speak to, then chose a mixture of Piper and Jons, her eyes sliding between the two.

"Something else. Terrence says the Apex is an antenna.

He says to tell you it's preparing to broadcast something. Something big."

"What does he want us to do about it?" Jons said.

The girl was still staring directly at Cameron, still near the now-closed door. She wasn't impatient or eager. She was simply there. Cameron was having the hardest time figuring her out. She had a little girl's pudgy look but held herself like a scholar.

"I don't—" Lila began.

"You have to destroy it," the girl cut her off.

Lila beckoned, then the girl left the door and hugged Lila's leg.

"Clara, why are you here?" Piper asked, looking up at Lila.

"Clara?"

He'd said it too loud. Everyone in the room stopped and turned to look at him.

"She's ..." Cameron squatted, meeting the girl closer, almost eye to eye. "Clara, how old are you, honey?"

"Two."

"You're ... big."

"You act so surprised, Mr. Cameron."

"How do you know who I am?" He looked up — at Lila, at Piper, even at Jons.

"She insisted," Lila said, finally answering Piper. "I didn't want to bring her, but I couldn't find Mom. And Dad ..."

"Meyer?" Piper said.

"He's different now," Lila said.

Clara's eyes stayed fixed on Cameron, patiently waiting for the adults to finish so she could answer. After a moment of quiet, she said, "Because I've seen you before, silly."

"You have?" Cameron looked up, but Lila shook her head: How could Clara have ever met or seen him? She'd been born and raised in Heaven's Veil, and he'd only come once before — to the square, before his rapid, violent extraction.

Cameron looked back at Clara. The girl was still waiting patiently for him to get his head out of his ass. To stop playing this game where they pretended they'd never met.

"What is the Apex doing, do you think?" Slowly, with resistance, Cameron's mind was assembling a familiarity profile of the girl. He wasn't used to including information from his dreams. Had she spoken of the Apex? No. She'd talked about something else that was wide at the base, narrow at the top. Not a pyramid, but a mountain.

"They can't find it, Mr. Cameron. Now that they know you were only playing, they're going to turn on the searchlight. They don't *want* to, but they think they have to."

Cameron looked up at Jons and Christopher. "Searchlight?"

Both men shook their heads. When he turned back to Clara, she looked patient: allowing the silly man to ask people who couldn't possibly know anything when the person who did was right there in front of him.

"What's the 'searchlight,' Clara?"

Again, Cameron looked up at Lila, but this seemed like news to her. Piper had said that Clara was strange and precocious, but he'd had no idea, and apparently her odd knowledge bled out on a need-to-know basis.

"It's how they can find the chest."

"You mean Thor's Hammer?"

"That's not what *they* call it," Clara said, wrinkling her nose — a childlike gesture, reminding Cameron who he was speaking with.

Cameron reached for his satchel. Jons had rushed them into the cells for show. But he hadn't searched them or confiscated belongings, and Raj had been too giddy with victory to notice when Jons had pushed them behind bars unprocessed.

Cameron slid the stone disc out and held it delicately in front of Clara, like a plate.

"This," Cameron said. "Is this a part of the ..." he glanced up at Jons for help then got it himself, "the 'chest'?"

She nodded. "They lost it. They want to find it."

"We lost it too," he said.

Instead of speaking, Clara smiled.

There was a booming outside. The walls shook. Dust sifted down from the ceiling.

"What the fuck was that?" Jons said.

"The spotlight," Clara said. "They're getting ready to turn it on."

Chapter Sixty-Two

HEATHER DIDN'T ASK QUESTIONS. She'd followed a spook out of her house, found a guy whose reputation was that of a barbaric warlord at the end of its pointed finger, then together the two of them had *lucked* past countless Reptar and Titan patrols to reach the fence — this time obviously following something Nathan couldn't even see. So the whys, wheres, and hows of Andreus getting a security code from Meyer were small potatoes by comparison.

When the wave of energy (there was no better way to describe it; it was light and sound but mostly just *force)* rushed from the Apex pyramid, Heather barely cared. Shit might blow up soon. So what?

Andreus wasn't as casual. He stopped with his hand on the small fence gate, his fingers hitting buttons on a touch screen. The code seemed long and complicated — as much pattern as numbers and letters. But Andreus did it easily, his mind having no problem with recall under pressure.

"What was that?"

"The pyramid."

"What's it doing?"

"There's obviously no way I'd know the answer to that, but I could make up some bullshit. Can I interest you in some bullshit?"

Andreus was still frozen, now staring directly at the Apex. Staring *through* the shadow creature, from where Heather was standing. It had been putting out long tendrils, like horizontal columns of smoke. And even now, as if summoned, Heather could see people creeping forward from the distant gully.

When the Apex did nothing further, Andreus's attention fell from it.

He turned to watch the forces approach. Opened the gate. And let the group of around fifty people — along with a few hand-wheeled motorbikes that would make entirely too much noise when started — into the small alcove behind buildings. It was an oasis of relative quiet near the main Astral traffic thoroughfare, protected but surrounded. They'd be safe here, so long as they didn't move. And if this had been a trap from the start (to get Heather and Andreus's soldiers all in one place for a tidy slaughter), then ... well, frankly, they were fucked.

A brunette woman of around Heather's height and build pushed through the crowd. Andreus seemed surprised to see her and embraced the woman before suddenly becoming awkward. Apparently, that wasn't their normal manner of greeting, and Andreus wasn't as imperturbable as he seemed.

He introduced the two women, ignoring the others. They were all settling in, jostling weapons, looking uneasy to be deep in enemy territory — or, if Heather understood Nathan's story of his encounter with Meyer, *friendly* territory. The Astral/Republic arrangement struck Heather as a deal with the devil, and one where the devil never took his knife from your throat. Probably the reason Andreus was double-dealing so readily: if they'd threaten his daughter to gain his allegiance, the man's nature was to bite, not to lie down or roll over.

"Why are you here?" he asked the woman he'd introduced as Jeanine Coffey.

"They got your drone. You told them to come."

"I asked why *you* were here. Where are Charlie and Grace?"

"Same place we were when you left. A mile off the front gate."

Andreus's face changed. "You shouldn't have left them."

"They'll be safe, Nathan. I had to come. I had to tell you something: Charlie says Thor's Hammer isn't under the Apex."

Heather watched a frown form on his face. "I thought that might be the case," he said. "How did you know the Republic was here?"

"I didn't."

"Then how—"

This time, Coffey's face pinched. She looked at Heather, seeming to decide if she wanted to share with an audience.

"The thing Piper saw. The thing she said was following us from Moab. It led me here."

Andreus looked level at Coffey, glancing at Heather. Then he said, "Charlie is sure?"

Coffey nodded. "You know how he is. I was insulting him by even asking."

"Then where is it?"

"He doesn't know. But he says the Apex is important for another reason, and that's why Benjamin was studying it. We assumed he'd be researching Thor's Hammer right before we went *after* it in Little Cottonwood Canyon, but based on what Cameron said, I think Charlie might be right and that there'd be no reason for Benjamin to research the Hammer's location."

"What did Cameron say?"

"That Benjamin already knew where it was. Like it was obvious. He thought Cameron would think it was obvious, too. But the joke was on him, I guess, since the next thing Benjamin did was to die."

Heather felt a chill. She hadn't known Benjamin Bannister. She'd never even met him. But she knew the name, she knew his son, and it seemed too many people were in mortal peril these days.

"And the Apex?"

As if on cue, the big blue pyramid flashed again. The second mothership's energy beam seemed to have finished whatever it was doing — powering the thing up, perhaps — but when Heather looked toward the flash, she saw something on the horizon that chilled her blood: another two spheres approaching: motherships, possibly with their own bellies full of power, like giant batteries.

"It was interesting to Benjamin. That's all Charlie knew." Coffey's gaze ticked up. The second mothership began to move away. The others were already closer.

Changing of the guard.

Nathan looked up, noting the arriving ships with a neutral nod.

"I think we might know more than Benjamin right now," Andreus said, "and what we need to do next, if we won't find the Hammer here, is obvious."

All eyes turned to the Apex.

"The rebels have tried to destroy it a dozen times with no luck," Coffey said.

"We'll try something different," Andreus said.

Heather watched him. In the corner of her eye, the shadow stirred, agitated.

"We'll hit it," he said, "from the inside out."

Chapter Sixty-Three

"WHAT'S THAT?"

Terrence looked up. The drone had stopped circling, called home as if by its mother. The view, such as Terrence had cobbled it with approximately half of his ass, had gone black. Based on what he'd seen last, Terrance guessed someone had stowed the thing — maybe inside the city's fence and maybe outside; he didn't know. But the RF signal was still active. Still right there, for anyone paying attention and knowledgeable about communications to pluck from the air, decode, and watch even without a network in place.

Raj was standing over him. Behind him. Having approached and taken Terrence by surprise, seeing as Terrence thought he was still encumbered at the station with Christopher, Cameron, and Piper. But here he was, staring at something Terrence shouldn't be able to see — and that Raj definitely shouldn't be *allowed* to see.

Terrence quickly recovered his cool. "It's a dead surveillance feed."

Raj said, "Nothing's back up."

"I know. I keep telling you, I can't unburn a—"

Terrence stopped when Raj hit him, hard. His hand went to his chin, moving it to test its integrity, wincing from the dull throb of pain.

"What were you looking at?"

"A dead surveillance feed!"

Raj hit him again.

"Don't bullshit me, Terrence! I'm not my wife! I know this shit as well as you do and I'm not the goddamned joke everyone thinks I am!"

Terrence looked up at Raj. His face was purple everywhere Meyer had struck him. His eyes had swollen slightly, giving him a somewhat squinting appearance. But the bit of his brown irises Terrence could see was ripe with menace. Maybe murder.

But it's not like he could say what he'd really been checking, no matter how much Raj meant business.

"Look. I know the network is down, *obviously*." He held up a warding hand. "I really can't fix any of this, Raj. You can hit me as many times as you want, and that's not going to change. But there are still recordings on the server." He decided to tell a revealing lie, incriminating himself a little so that Raj wouldn't incriminate him all the way. "I know I shouldn't be looking. But I wanted to see the footage of you shooting Meyer."

For a second, Terrence thought Raj believed him. It was just macabre enough to be true, and forbidden enough to be something worth hiding. But Raj snatched the tablet, cabled it to one of the bigger machines, and went to work with grim dedication. He wasn't stupid. Being a fool was something different, separate from intelligence.

"It's an RF feed. Where is there still an RF feed active?"

"I don't know what you're—"

Raj slammed his fist on the table.

"I just saw it was out there. You can see it yourself, Raj. It's black. Nothing to it. Some kid probably has one of those remote-control cars with a camera; remember those? And it's parked under his bed, left on. I just happened to find it."

"And then you hid it from me." He set the tablet down then sat slowly across from Terrence. His manner wasn't Raj at all. Cool and calm. Precise enough to give Terrence a chill. "Why wouldn't you tell me about this when I asked?"

"I didn't think it mattered."

"But I asked you what you were looking at. And not only did you lie; you flash-erased your history. Like you thought I wouldn't know how to check the logs."

"I ..."

"I'll tell you what I think it is," Raj said, meeting his eyes and daring a challenge. "I think this is something from your buddies. Christopher, Cameron, Piper, Heather — maybe Meyer, if he's still allegiant where I think he is, even though he's clearly lost his fucking mind."

Raj shifted. Resumed.

"I think that black feed was showing you something you needed to see. Not just something interesting, but some sort of a communication."

"Raj, you've been watching every type of—"

Raj raised a hand. In a way, it was worse than being hit.

"If that's what it was, then there's someone you need to get that information to. And that means someone is up to something. Something coordinated. So that means someone will eventually check in with you because you know something they need to know. How will they contact you, Terrence?"

He watched Raj, wondering what lies he could get away with and which truths would see him punished.

Raj reached for his side. His right hand came up holding a black handgun. He placed the barrel to Terrence's forehead. Terrence felt his eyes tick toward it, trying to see the barrel. He felt the press of cool metal.

"What happens," Raj said, "when you're unable to deliver whatever you're supposed to?"

"Raj—"

"You know, the viceroy won't talk to me. Me, of all people, who's never turned on this city's leadership. Mo Weir won't talk to me, and the Titans and Reptars don't talk to anyone."

The weapon shifted as Raj moved his thumb. There was a heavy mechanical click from above.

"But I'll bet you know, Terrence. You're a really smart guy. So tell me: What's going on out there? More mother-ships are arriving and pumping beams into the Apex. The thing keeps shaking and flashing. You always had the best theories. What do you think is happening?"

"They're …" It was so hard to speak smoothly with a cocked gun to his head. "It's an antenna. You know the Apexes form an antenna array!"

"Uh-huh. And what are they doing? Calling other Astrals?"

"Maybe! I don't know!"

"If you had to guess."

Terrence swallowed.

"I see. You don't know. I'll bet you wanted help figuring it out. Christopher? No, he's an idiot. But he knows the Astral movements, and he's your pal, right? Or Cameron. I'll bet *he* has thoughts. But you couldn't possibly be talking to them. Not now that they're both in …"

Raj stopped. Terrence went cold, seeing revelation.

Raj stood. He pulled Terrence to standing, the gun still to his head. Raj's hand was suddenly shaking, his finger maybe under the handgun's guard, Terrence's brains kept in his skull only by a few ounces of missing pressure on the trigger.

"They're in jail *together*, aren't they? That's what they wanted, isn't it? Jons knew exactly where they were because Christopher told him. Is Jons in on this, Terrence? Is *everyone* in on it?"

"I—"

"Don't lie to me!"

"Maybe Christopher told him! Maybe Jons beat it out of him!"

Raj's lips firmed. His eyes grew hard. The barrel's pressure against his forehead increased, becoming a knife's dull edge. The weapon shook, and for a long second Terrence was sure it was over. Then Raj snatched the gun back, shoved him away, and took a step back. He became agitated. Fidgeting, pacing, ranting.

"The information about the 'antenna,' Terrence," he said, making a clear effort not to snap as realization dawned. "How did you get it to them?"

"I didn't! I don't even know that—"

"I knew that was too easy. Just me and Jons and his men. No Astrals. Hell, they didn't even try to run. Just let us shove them in right beside Christopher." He was gesturing with the cocked weapon, and with every sweep of his arms Terrence braced for the gun to go off. "But whatever you were watching on that tablet. The RF feed. And maybe the thing about the Apex. Christopher can't come around anymore. Jons stays at the station. And—"

Raj stopped speaking as if interrupted.

"Lila."

"What?"

"It was Lila. She's your go-between, right?"

"No!"

"LILA!" Raj shouted.

"Raj, she's not—"

Raj pointed the gun at Terrence from across the room and yelled again, louder.

"Our apartment is right downstairs. I know she can hear me. She's not in the house, is she? Where is she, Terrence? Is she down at the station?" His temper slipped another notch. "Did she come to visit you while I was out on that little fool's errand?"

"No!"

Raj stalked forward, grabbed Terrence by the shirt, then dragged him from the network center and down the stairs, murder audible in every breath.

Chapter Sixty-Four

PIPER DIDN'T UNDERSTAND how Clara and Cameron seemed to know each other. They'd never met, and it was unlikely that Piper's scattered profile made her seem as familiar to him as she apparently was. There was something going on. Something she couldn't quite …

But maybe she could. Piper looked over at the small girl and the man opposite her, on his knees. They could talk easily enough through the bars, so Jons had vetoed the idea of opening the door. It was unnecessary, and if any of the station's cops (or Titans, though they'd seen almost no Astrals on the trip over) entered to an open cell door, there would be questions.

Watching them, Piper felt an intense sense of déjà vu, as if she'd seen this all before.

A man. A girl. Speaking across symbols of confinement, discussing what needed to be.

Whatever Piper was feeling, it wasn't exact. Close, but not precisely the same. But yes, she remembered this. Not from a dream, but from life.

Jons reentered the room. He looked at Cameron and Clara in their whispered concentration then at Lila, who was watching them both. Christopher was across the room in his cell. So Jons spoke to Piper.

"There are more motherships." Jons was a big man with a booming voice, intimidating simply by his presence. But Piper could tell he was frightened.

"What do you mean?"

"Outside. Near the Apex. *Connected to* the Apex. Two more."

"Two more?"

Across the room, Christopher was gripping the bars, as close to the conversation as the cell allowed. Lila was watching the police captain with big brown eyes. Only Cameron and Clara, still deep in some kind of shared mumbling trance, were oblivious. Or, Piper thought, perhaps unsurprised.

"Three total." Jons said. "The Apex is glowing brighter. I saw another flash, like that one last night. It made a little boom like before. Did you feel it in here?"

Piper nodded.

"Something big is happening. Like she said." He tipped his head toward Lila. "There's no Astrals out there. Not on the streets, anyway."

"Then we can get away!"

Jons shook his head. "There's shuttles. Lots of 'em. Each of the three new motherships seems to have brought its own. But they've cleared the streets. Or gone to the Apex; they seem to have been headed that way earlier."

"Why, do you think?" Piper asked.

Christopher spoke before Jons. "Sounds like an evacuation."

The word prickled Piper's skin. She looked down at

Cameron, but the two were still immersed, doing something odd like meditation, something she couldn't …

You know, Piper. You just don't know you know.

Piper blinked at Cameron and Clara. The voice in her head was nearly audible, almost present. The press of déjà vu deepened as she tried to grab its edge, to catch its ephemeral shape before it could slide away like a dream upon waking.

Meyer. It had been Meyer's voice. But when?

Heather. Lila. You know what they've been hearing. The Astrals say we're different and can't hear minds. But we're still their children. The ability is inside us.

"Piper, what's—" Lila started to say.

Piper shot a hand out, one finger raised, telling her to shut up and wait. She didn't move her head. She couldn't. She almost had it. *Almost* understood why seeing Clara and Cameron now raised such déjà vu. It had something to do with Lila. Heather? And Meyer. He'd been speaking to her. But where? When? And why couldn't she remember?

The others don't matter, came Meyer's voice inside her mind, streaming up from some forgotten past. *They will only compromise for our own because they matter to me. To you. To us. It's just Heather. Lila. Trevor. If others die, they die.*

"Piper …"

The hand with the finger wagged. Jabbed insistently. The memory was wafer-thin crystal. She almost had it. But if her attention flagged, it would shatter.

Something she'd tried to remember before. That had occurred to her when they'd been on their way from Moab, with Andreus and Coffey and Charlie and Grace, crossing land in the solar RV. Something to do with …

(the Pall; they call it a Pall)

… the shadow creature that had been following them. And she'd thought about it because …

(later)

The Titans. Becoming Reptars. And the black fog near the gate. So it wasn't during the RV trip at all. She'd been thinking of it later after she'd seen the …

(Pall)

Shadow thing infuse the Titans, turning them mean, upsetting their equilibrium. Their collective mind. Poison in the system. And …

(when you were on the mothership)

(!!!)

Piper's head ticked up. She looked directly at Lila, locking eyes.

"Piper?" Lila looked like she wanted to take a step back.

"Lila. When you were in the house, at Vail, the day Meyer came back. What made you leave?"

(Trevor. Trevor went out first, and Lila followed.)

"What?"

"Was it Trevor? I barely remember. He came to me, and you followed."

"Of course. Me and Mom and—"

"But you were hearing something. You were hearing …

(Clara)

"A kind of voice, telling you that there was something under the house and that you had to … destroy it?" Piper concentrated. They'd had some of this discussion, but in guarded tones. After that day, most of their history had gone into moratorium. A chill swallowed them all. But Piper knew, just as she knew that —

"And your mother. Heather was hearing something else. Hearing Meyer. Is that right?"

"She wanted to protect it. The pit under the house. She was trying to dig it out. To help him."

Piper blinked. It was all coming back.

Herself on the ship.

Talking to Meyer, before she'd been offloaded as bait. Because Heather wouldn't leave otherwise, and Piper knew it. The Astrals had agreed, with Meyer as their primary interpreter of human emotion.

(Maybe that's when it started.)

"I could hear it all, Lila. I came on the mothership from Moab. With your father. The Astrals wanted to destroy the house to access their power source under it. But he wanted to save the people inside. What happened was the compromise. They wouldn't wait for everyone to come out. Just you, Trevor, and your mom. But I knew what you and your mother were hearing. I didn't remember until now, but I knew it then. Heather was obsessed. The only way to get her out was to get *you* out. So they put me down first. Had me find one of the cameras. We knew Trevor would come when he saw me because—" Piper swallowed past a lump, blinking waiting tears, refusing to betray his shameful but noble secret now that he was gone, "—because that's how he was. And—"

"Was?"

"And once he was out, we knew you'd follow. Then Heather would *have* to come — because you were in danger. Then they could dock, no matter who was still inside. Once you were safe, because your father wanted—"

"What do you mean, Trevor *'was'?*" Lila said, stepping past Jons, who looked dumbfounded, to hold the bars.

But now there was something else. Something she'd just remembered about Meyer.

She looked at Cameron and Clara, both leaving their trance.

The whole room was looking at Piper. Waiting.

The man and the girl, on two sides of captivity, sharing minds.

Piper looked up; she could feel her mouth hanging open. "I didn't realize. I'd completely forgotten."

"Piper, *what?*" Lila demanded.

"Your father—"

The backroom's door banged open, and Raj burst into the room, dragging Terrence and holding a gun.

Chapter Sixty-Five

NATHAN STOPPED, looked at Heather and Coffey, and resisted infusing his voice with sarcasm. "What's it want us to do now?"

They were massed behind a sprawling wall that was probably the side of an apartment building or even an in-city factory; Nathan honestly had no idea. He wasn't used to urban warfare and frankly found all of Heaven's Veil confining and creepy. They hadn't seen many people, which wasn't surprising given the police-state atmosphere perpetrated by the Astrals. Of the visible humans, most had been cops. And If Andreus had to guess, even cops knew the score. They'd avoided them all, but it was hard not to walk up to every scared-looking kid with a uniform and say, *Hey. We're fucking shit up. Want to help us do it?*

"It's gone," Heather said.

"Gone?"

"Yes, *gone,*" Heather repeated then returned her gaze forward, watching the mall's worth of Titans in the Apex courtyard. To Nathan, with his bald head and decent physique, it looked like a semi-nude convention of like-minded individuals.

Nathan said nothing. He didn't like this. These were *his* soldiers, *his* army, *his* equipment. Even the useless motorbikes they were wheeling along with stilled engines were his. At the very least, Coffey should be leading the group, but she couldn't see their scary spirit guide nearly as well as her Queen Bitchiness, so Heather had been in a lead that seemed to have stopped in front of an impassable horde. Nathan liked Heather, in theory. But he didn't want anyone else in charge of his people. Especially not someone who lit up when allowed to boss others around.

"Why is it gone?"

"I don't know, Nathan. Why don't you call it and see if it comes back to you? See if it loves you most of all?"

"I'm not even sure you're not making this up," he said.

Both women turned to stare at him then rotated forward. That had been a dumb thing to say. He couldn't see the specter but was clearly in the minority. Denying its existence — especially after all the impossible corners it had pulled their group from unseen — was pouting.

Coffey peered through tiny binoculars. They were at the top of one of Heaven's Veil's few slight hills, looking down. Most of the land had been flattened, but everyone knew that the Apex was — apparently, among other things — a dig site. Starting lower seemed to make sense, especially since the structure's massive height more than made up for its low base. Nathan didn't even like looking up at it. The pyramid made him feel small. And this mission, looking down at several hundred Titans, already felt impossible.

"Maybe we should just go up there and politely ask to go inside," Heather said. "You know how these guys are."

"Turns out Titans have a dark side," Nathan said.

"Sure," Heather replied. "Sometimes, when we spill something in the house, they hesitate slightly before cleaning it up and … *What?*"

Coffey was watching her. She stopped when Heather paused then resumed spying through the binoculars. "Trust us," she said.

The women retreated. All eyes turned to Nathan as the Republic's rightful leader.

"We have to get in there," he said.

To their credit, both Heather and Coffey nodded. No protest from the ranks, despite what they'd seen. Despite what his drone had conveyed to the Republic about the Titan secret, and the fact that everyone present — except Heather, perhaps — knew that they were looking down on a shallow dish teeming with leagues of potential Reptars.

"You said Charlie's concerned about what's happening with the Apex. That combined with what we're seeing right now is probably enough. But there's also my chat with the viceroy. You ask me, one of two things is happening. Either Charlie is wrong about the Hammer — it really is in there and they're finding a way to power it up, or this is a workaround. Like they're going to call home for help finding the thing. Or maybe they'll have home base send another. Either way, we've got to take it down. Even if it means we die doing it."

Again, no one protested. Members of the Andreus Republic hadn't always been warriors, but they'd *become* warriors through a gauntlet of fire. Two years of fighting and seeing the unrelenting press of the Astral thumb had driven a few home truths into every one of them, included Nathan himself. For one, the fate of humanity might really matter more to brave souls than their own tiny lives. Secondly — and this reason was decidedly darker —

Nathan was starting to wonder if life would be worth living under the Astrals' newest regime.

"We don't even know that it *can* be destroyed," Coffey said.

"Right," Nathan said. There was that. Not only were they carrying pea shooters; they had no explosives or heavy equipment, nothing capable of bringing down a drywall partition in a cruddy human apartment. So how were they supposed to destroy something huge, alien, and maybe indestructible?

"Meyer suggested it could be done."

Heather squinted. *"Meyer* told you that?"

"You said he helped you before."

"Giving you a code is one thing. That sounds like suicide talk."

"What did he say specifically, Nathan?"

"He said to go to the fence then the Apex."

"And?"

"He said we could disrupt it."

"'Disrupt' is different from 'destroy,'" Coffey said.

"How did he say to disrupt it?"

"He ..." But there was nothing. Meyer had become strange. He'd blathered on with his thoughts buried in nonsense after Nathan told the truth about Trevor. Nathan had left through the front doors, Titans already having abandoned their post, apparently on their way here. He'd felt happy to get out alive. He'd expected an escort to the gates, a return to Jeanine and the others with a plan to strike from a few fronts at once.

But about this, there was nothing useful at all.

"He implied it could be done."

Heather shook her head. "There's something wrong with Meyer, I'm telling you."

There was a shout. A loud, annoyed, self-righteous bellow, demanding attention.

Hundreds of Titan heads turned at once, like a flock of birds taking notice.

At the edge, out of sight except from above, where the Andreus army was hiding, one of the Titans ducked until it was on all fours.

It changed.

Seeing the sole newly formed Reptar in the crowd, Heather covered her mouth and stifled a scream. But not quickly enough. Even as she dropped down, Heather could see Titan heads turning toward them.

The demanding, all-too-human, viceroy-like shout continued to trumpet from the other side of the Apex courtyard.

"Who is in charge here?"

Chapter Sixty-Six

RAJ STOWED his gun like a hypocrite. He kept the thing in his pocket, hand on the butt and finger on the trigger. He seemed to somehow imagine that his prophetic, seemingly psychic daughter wouldn't figure out what was going on.

Lila couldn't help but feel insulted on Clara's behalf. She hadn't been fooled by peekaboo back in the day, either. She'd looked at all who tried it with scorn, seeming to say, *So ... when you cover your eyes, I'm supposed to think you've vanished? Yes. I see. Very amusing.*

Clara was looking at Lila like that now. She didn't look 10 percent as afraid as Lila felt but appeared equally insulted. Lila wanted to start a gab session. Could Clara *believe* Daddy was trying to pretend he didn't have murder on his mind? Oh my *gawd*.

But Lila said nothing, and not just because one parent isn't supposed to speak ill of the other in front of their child. She stayed mum because of the way Raj had eyed her on entry. In the past, she'd seen rage directed at others: Christopher, Terrence, occasionally Piper, definitely

Heather, and recently Lila's father, whose boots Raj used to so studiously lick. But now, she was in the out-group. Now, the gun in Raj's pocket was on her, too.

Still, he spoke to Clara as if she had no idea. *Come over by me, sweetheart. Take Daddy's hand.* And Clara, to Lila's immense relief, merely walked alongside him without claiming his offer.

Raj took the party's rear. Thanks to their charade, only Jons had been wearing a sidearm. Raj had demanded and pocketed his weapon immediately. Jons had tried to berate Raj into subservience, but Raj seemed to have it all figured out: Jon's complicity, likely from the start. Christopher and Lila's affair. Their little band of resistance, spanning from Christopher to Terrence to Cameron to Piper to Heather … who, Lila realized, she hadn't seen since that odd exchange with her father.

Dad. Where was he? Raj had already tried to kill him once; he'd damn near succeeded, according to Heather. All bets seemed to be off. Raj was rolling some mighty big dice and going for broke. If right, he'd end the day atop the pile. If he was wrong, he'd pay for subverting Meyer, and the Heaven's Veil chief of police.

Lila watched Raj slip Jons's pistol into his belt then nudge the others ahead with his own. There was no discussion. No decision. No debate. Raj had already hit Christopher twice: once when he'd tried to lie as an explanation and once for no apparent reason. Piper went numbly along with her hand in Cameron's. Lila wanted to bristle at that — she was her father's wife, not Cameron's girlfriend. But it looked as if she might be both. And so much had changed.

"Piper?" Lila tried to ask.

Her stepmother looked lost, eyes like saucers, blue surrounded by a startling white. Cameron wasn't merely comforting her; to Lila, it almost seemed as if he was supporting her. She'd either aged or regressed twenty years; Lila wasn't sure which. Her gaze was wizened, as if she'd witnessed too much. But Piper was docile. Compliant. Whatever she'd realized as Raj had rushed in, it was now trapped inside and eating her like cancer.

Lila could relate.

We knew Trevor would come out because that's how he was.

There was no reason for that simple, by-the-way mention to bother Lila, but it did. Piper was speaking of a time now two years gone. She was nervous; she'd been tossed in prison with no way out and wouldn't be thinking eloquently. She'd clearly been recalling a repressed memory — possibly *supp*ressed by the Astrals. Lila had asked Piper many times about what it had been like to travel on the mothership. Piper's answer had always been the same: *I think I was asleep.* But it turned out she hadn't been. Now, Piper had recalled something that made her pale, that made her shudder in a numb way that had nothing to do with Raj's pointed gun.

Because that's how he was.

Piper and Cameron had returned to Heaven's Veil. Piper had mentioned Charlie Cook and the maniac from the outlands who ran the Andreus Republic. Why hadn't she mentioned Trevor?

Lila didn't want to think about it. She didn't have the mental bandwidth to consider the ramifications of that particular question. Her situation was dire enough. So yes, it must have been a slip. A misspeaking of tense. Trevor *was* that way two years ago merely because it was in the past. That's all she'd meant because if anything had gone wrong, Lila would know by now. Hell, Clara would have told her.

At that, Lila relaxed. Yes, of course. Clara would have told her.

She tried to catch her daughter's eye. Reached for her small hand — backward because Raj took the rear, behind Jons, Christopher, Piper, Terrence, Cameron, and finally Lila. Anyone could run. But right now, given Heaven's Veil's present state — and ultimately, the horrid truth that there was nowhere to go — all would stay put. Follow orders. And wait to see.

But Raj saw her hand move back. He stepped between Lila and Clara, gestured down toward his gun, and tossed his head to indicate that she best know her place.

There were no Titans outside the station. After finding none inside, Raj seemed desperate to reach the next place and see whom he might find to hear his complaint. But the streets were empty except for bemused human cops, clutching their duties by the thinnest of threads.

"Captain?" said one, watching Jons.

Jons could have told the cop to draw his weapon and arrest the Indian kid at the parade's rear. But the captain seemed to see what Lila saw.

The cop didn't know which side he was supposed to be on.

The police force finally had what it always claimed it wanted: dominion over at least this part of Heaven's Veil without any meddling Astrals. But the reality was like a table without legs, and the cop seemed lost. Without Astrals to enforce the rules, who were the police? Familiarity had bred atrophy. If the cop tried to draw on Raj, he'd shoot. Whom he'd shoot (the cop or one of their party) hardly mattered.

Jons said nothing. Tried to give the kid — as that's all he was, to Lila's eye — a knowing glance. But then they were past, into silent streets with one weapon leading.

"Raj?" Lila asked.

"Shut your mouth," came the reply.

"Where is my dad?"

Raj didn't answer.

But when Lila looked over, Piper was staring right at her.

Chapter Sixty-Seven

"Raj, hang on. I need to—"

"Don't try *explaining* anything to me. I understand just fine." He stared at Piper for an elongated moment. Raj knew what he wanted; he knew who were his friends and foes; he knew exactly where he had to go and what he needed to know. About those things, Piper could only guess, but the minute they'd left the station courtyard he'd shouted directions to Jons that had steered them toward the big blue pyramid.

The one place where Raj knew he could find Astrals in the city — because when you meant to complain about one boss, you had to do it to the *bigger* boss.

Toward the single place Piper had decided they absolutely should not go.

"They won't listen to you. You don't know what they're doing."

Raj scoffed. "I suppose you do?"

Piper glanced at Clara. She looked pretty and ordinary, as if this was all very matter of fact and by the book to the little girl.

"They're doing something at the Apex. Cameron and me, we came in here to …" *Oh, what the hell. What could it possibly hurt at this point?* "To find a weapon. Something the Astrals need."

"Really."

"When I was on the mothership, I could sense them. They're like one mind."

"What a great insight, Piper," Raj said.

"But something went wrong. Things are different now. The weapon isn't at the Apex, but it's …" Her eyes went to Cameron, even to Terrence. "The Apex is something else. What they're doing, they weren't supposed to do. It wasn't in the original plan."

"Really?" Raj stopped and turned, hands on hips. "And how do you know that, Piper?"

"I can feel it. I can …" She didn't want to say it. Not now. Not to Raj. "There's something coming from the mothership," she finished, knowing how lame she must sound.

Not something. Someone. A mind that shouldn't be there. Someone I remember from recently, that I may not have actually seen for two years.

"I can *see* what's coming from the motherships." Raj looked up at the energy beams.

Her patience snapped. She grabbed his shoulders — not to attack, but to make him see sense. How was this not obvious to him? Raj was blinded by his own self-pity, unable to see what was right in front of him. Over the past weeks, Raj had become like a dog with a bone. His position as the sole remaining human toady in Piper's circle had become obviously pointless, but he refused to stop and think, to consider things from a new and obvious angle. In his mind, Raj was going to march right up to the nearest Titan and air his grievances then await his reward.

"We can't be here! You don't know what they're feeling, what they might do, what's boiling and about to—"

Raj pushed Piper away. His stowed pistol resurfaced, leveled at her chest. His finger twitched. For a scant second, she imagined she heard a report. Felt the bullet kiss her skin. But he was only pointing, shaking, while the others backed away.

Cameron's hands closed on her shoulders from behind.

"Just walk," Raj said. "You're not getting away this time."

Piper walked.

She looked up.

It was all a lie. Every bit of it.

She remembered the way Meyer had looked, in that all-white room, when she'd spoken with him on the ship. The way her mind had melded into his every bit as easily as it had into Cameron's on their trip from Vail to Moab. The way they'd worked together to find the best way to get the others out of the house before docking.

She remembered leaving him in that all-white room, coming down to the ground, her memories already retreating.

She remembered watching Meyer emerge from the ship with the Titans behind him.

Believing he was himself, when he very much wasn't.

What was supposed to happen had gone awry. Piper could see that now — thanks to Meyer, thanks to all the others. Thanks to what was different this time.

They rounded another corner, and Malcolm Jons practically ran into the back of a big white Titan. One of hundreds, all surrounding the Apex.

Talking to it.

Helping to focus it.

Thor's Hammer didn't need to be at the Apex for them to find it. Not if something in the group mind made an illogical suggestion.

Raj pushed his way forward, through the outer line of Titans, shoving their muscular frames aside. Piper sensed movement from the rear; she turned and saw Clara running away as fast as her small, strangely adept legs would carry her.

"Who is in charge here?" Raj shouted across the group.

When the black smoke returned, Piper felt as if it was welcoming her home.

Chapter Sixty-Eight

HEATHER SQUATTED, her heart hammering, as the self-important shout rang across the gathering of Titans below. She tugged Jeanine Coffey down beside her.

"I just saw—"

"We've seen it before," Coffey said. "Titans can become Reptars. I assume it goes the other way around, too."

Heather clawed herself mostly upright, again peeking out into the gathering. She felt like a woman who'd nearly stepped onto a rattlesnake then pulled her foot away purely by chance a second before it was too late.

But when she looked again at the placid white forms below, watching them turn toward the voice — Raj and others, it looked like — Heather didn't see more becoming the black-scaled monsters as her mind had already imagined.

Instead, she saw the Titans flinching.

Then they started to swat — first at the air, as if bothered by flies, then at each other. The sight was almost comical.

"It's back," Coffey said.

Heather glanced up at Andreus, who looked puzzled, both by her statement and the disconcertingly chaotic scene unfolding before them. There was nothing to cause the commotion.

Then Heather turned her head. Watched from the corner of her eye. And saw it happen.

The shadow thing had spread wide, now slithering beneath the Titan group like fog. It covered their legs. It rose, burying them to the waists. It pulsed and swayed from group to group, inciting unrest. Near Raj, the Titan-turned-Reptar charged, rearing, looking for a beautiful second like it might bite Raj in two. Then one of the Titans tackled it, taking it down, into the black soup.

Fighting began.

When the blindness came, it was total, for Heather as for them all.

Chapter Sixty-Nine

CHRISTOPHER'S HAND found Lila's before the sun died. Then the light was gone, and it was all she could feel.

"Lila!"

"I'm here." She kept her voice calm, but it was as if her eyes had stopped working. She couldn't see a thing. Whatever this was, it had come all at once. She'd thought she'd sensed motion in the corner of her eye, but when she'd looked toward the sparring Titans she'd seen nothing. They were fighting over a thing that didn't exist. Waving phantom insects away.

But then she'd seen it.

Everyone had spied it plain as day, not from the corner of eyes but right in front of them. Lila could tell by the screams.

She looked up. Looked down. There was nothing at all, as if the world had disappeared.

"Can you see?" Christopher asked. He was close. Inches from her face. She could feel his harsh exhales as the tumult ahead, entirely unseen, grew louder. She could hear ... well, not screams, precisely. But grunts. Noises like animals.

"I can't see anything at all," Lila said.

"Where are the others?"

"Lila? Is that you?"

Piper, to her right.

Panic choked Lila's heart like a fist as an unknown dawned: "Where is Clara?"

"I saw her run. She ran." Piper's voice was throaty and rushed. Stronger than she normally seemed.

"Where?"

"Clara is okay."

Lila felt something break inside. "How do you know that? We have to find her!"

A woman's hand touched Lila's — soft, assured, in no way hesitant. As if Piper wasn't blind and could still see the world. "She's okay."

Something in Piper's voice soothed Lila's fear.

"We have to go," Piper said.

"Where?"

"Away."

"I ... I can't see."

"I know," Piper's voice said. "That was his intention."

Lila wanted to ask about that, but Piper's hand tightened and pulled. Lila had already lost her bearings; she only knew that the other hand in hers — mute, waiting to follow — seemed to be Christopher. Who else had been in their party? Cameron, Terrence, and Captain Jons? They were on their own. They had to be.

"Come on," Piper said.

"We have to find Clara."

"Not now. Come on, Lila." Pressure intensified, but Lila's feet were planted. She couldn't see the street. Or the sky. She thought she could hear Raj ahead, and could certainly hear the sounds of thrashing and shredding. Were the others even there? It was only Titans and a single Reptar. What was happening up there? And where was Clara? Piper's hand pulled one direction, but Lila had lost her orientation. Which way was backward? Which was ahead? Was Piper pulling Lila toward her daughter or away?

"Come on. Now."

"No!"

Lila dug in her heels, finding scrabbling purchase on footing she couldn't see. Her hand slipped away; her momentum hurled her forward, and she struck the ground hard. Christopher's hand had stayed where it was, and within seconds Piper was on her again, just as assured, yanking harder.

"Come with me, Lila."

Piper pulled.

Christopher shifted around and tugged as well, now from the same direction. Lila felt betrayal flood her. She couldn't just go. Clara was out there, somewhere, alone.

Lila screamed.

But inch by inch, she went.

There was a heaving, crushing sensation as Christopher seemed to pick her up. To shift his grip to Piper's hand instead of Lila's. She thrashed on his shoulder in a blind fireman's carry.

Piper led.

Christopher followed.

And foot by unseen foot, they fled.

Chapter Seventy

RAJ WAS flat on the ground.

Miraculously, nobody had stepped on him. He couldn't see a thing; it was as if he'd been struck over the head and lost his sense of sight. And that made sense. It even explained why no one had crushed him. There wasn't anything wrong with the air. That was absurd. No, this was only happening to him. Only to Raj, as usual.

But no. That wasn't true. He sat up then voiced a girlish scream as some fool's foot finally trod on his palm. He heard the someone stumble and fall. There had been a clutch of garbage cans beside them when they'd entered the Apex courtyard; maybe the hand stepper had fallen into that.

It wasn't just him.

He could hear Piper and Lila somewhere behind. Possibly Christopher. As he came upright, his hand hit something like a close-cropped hedge: Terrence's giant hair, possibly. But it was on the ground, as Raj had been. Everyone had flinched when the Reptar had come forward then staggered away when the Titan, of all things, had taken it down. Raj hadn't understood that, but he'd been grateful. Then the world's lights had been extinguished.

"Jons!" Raj called out.

Nothing. Just grunting, struggling, and the sounds of thrashing teeth. Claws and feet and things run into, spilled to the ground. Was he in a cloud? How large was it? The darkness was absolute. Everyone close enough to hear sounded uncertain, hard on their feet, vocalizing (Astrals) or yelling (humans) as if trying to find their bearings.

But wait.

Wait.

He could see something after all.

Compared to the black ink Raj saw everywhere else, the dim gray shapes to his left looked almost transparent. In that direction, at least, the fog was thinning. He looked back to verify, judged it to be the way they'd come from. The way, if he'd been hearing right, that Lila and Piper had gone. The clear patch was ahead. Clear*er*, anyway.

Despite the situation, despite the peril, Raj couldn't resist a smile. Fucking Lila had gone the wrong way. She'd gone into the soup, instead of away.

The parted area was narrow. Almost artificial. On both sides was a churning wall of nothingness. Down the center was barely better — gnarled with shadow. But he could almost see, like a person with their eyes adjusted to darkness.

Ahead, at the end of the tunnel, Raj could see the silhouette of someone beckoning.

He moved closer.

And saw Meyer Dempsey, waving him forward like a guide.

Chapter Seventy-One

NATHAN HADN'T MOVED. He couldn't see a thing. He stared into the empty pit of a black hole.

He had no idea if this was what Heather and Jeanine had claimed to see earlier. Regardless, his eyes had learned the trick of seeing it now. The women had reacted. Nathan had kept his eyes forward, held to the Apex, watching the Titan heads turn and doubting they could see him anyway. Then came the cloud, now dark pillars like the arms of a giant black squid. By the time it reached him, he'd decided it was over. They'd die here. And that would be fine.

Then the blindness.

Heather's scream. Coffey's almost-cry and nervous twitters. Shouts and scuffles of the group behind him — steeled less than Nathan might have hoped, for soldiers.

Someone pawed at his side, hands like claws. Grabbing like a drowning person, trying to drag him down, to use Nathan as a life raft. He cuffed the hand away.

"Have some dignity, Heather," he said, fighting his own panic. The world had become a sensory deprivation chamber — a *sight* deprivation chamber, anyway. He was wearing an impossible blindfold, trapped in an old chest freezer that latched from the outside. Buried alive. But he held it all in. He focused ahead, as if there was something to see.

But the grunted response wasn't Heather.

"Coffey. Where are you?"

"I can't—" came her reply.

"I know you can't! Do you have a weapon?"

"Yes …" deep breath, "Yes, sir."

"Where is Heather?"

"I don't know." Then: "It's happening again. They're turning. Can you hear it?"

He could: the soundtrack of Cottonwood Canyon with the lights off.

"This is your shadow," he said.

He thought she might protest. Might say it couldn't be — and if she had, Nathan would almost agree. He hadn't seen the shadow, but he couldn't help but see this.

"I think it is," came Coffey's breathless reply.

"Then we have to go in while they're distracted. You said the shadow was helping us."

"But I can't see anything at—"

Coffey stopped speaking just as Nathan saw the narrow, barely visible passage blooming ahead through the blackness.

Chapter Seventy-Two

HEATHER FOLLOWED the silhouette at the end of the long, shadowy passageway. She recognized everything about it — and seeing it now, Heather knew she hadn't truly been seeing it for a very long time.

"*Meyer!*" she called.

But the silhouette didn't turn. She could barely see the thing. It had broad shoulders that seemed a bit too pointed, as if part of the shape came from clothing, surely a suit. There was no light in the air. Only a slight retreat of darkness. And except for the slightest hints of movements ahead, Heather saw nothing.

"Wait for me!"

Not Meyer as she'd seen him earlier today.

And not, interestingly, Meyer as she'd seen him before he'd been murdered — which, she felt sure, he most certainly had.

This was Meyer from before. From back when they were married. From when they both lived in LA and New York. When the world had been their oyster. Maybe before Piper, maybe after. But *Meyer*. His walk was impossible to miss. How could she have ever been fooled? Nobody moved like Meyer. Nobody navigated life like the man she'd never stopped loving.

Somehow, the Meyer she'd spoken to earlier wasn't really Meyer. Because he was dead, because Raj had killed him.

But this Meyer was even more real than the man who'd died in her arms. The one who'd bled on her clothes. The one who'd said, with his dying breath (and here, she didn't want to consider that he might have been less than real) that he loved her.

Heather could barely see her footing. She could hear all sorts of conflict surrounding her, but none had entered the strange corridor. It was, visually speaking, just Heather and her ex.

He turned. She couldn't see his face, but she saw the shift of his shoulders, the cocky certainty of his stance.

From far away, he seemed to wave for her to follow. To hurry.

She ran, and the tunnel collapsed behind her, driving her down some unknown throat.

Chapter Seventy-Three

DRAG HER.

Piper heard his voice. She looked up, and he was closer. Though she could barely see him, Piper could feel him just fine. She could sense familiar essence wafting off his body like heat.

Lila was screaming, thrashing. Pure panic. *"They're going to kill her!"*

Piper saw Christopher flinch. His eyes were wide and unfocused. Christopher, Piper decided, was as blind as Lila. She could reach right out and smack his face, and he wouldn't see it coming. Piper could let go of them both then circle the pair in the gloom. It was hard to see much beyond simple shadowy shapes, but she doubted they saw even that.

Lila didn't see her father. Or hear him. The shape and voice was for Piper's eyes only — more connection than reality. More memory than substance.

She doesn't understand, Meyer told her.

Piper looked up at him. She couldn't see any of his

features. He was a mask of nothing. She saw his shape and heard his voice in the recesses of her mind. She wanted to reply. But Lila was frightened enough.

None of them understood. None of them could. Piper had sampled the Astral mind — not with Cameron when they'd passed the double line of monoliths, but when she'd been on the mothership. When she'd stood across the partition from Meyer, untangling a way to save them. When she'd felt his mind in its truest form and felt how it touched the others. How it made them uneasy and forced them to hesitate.

We will dock, the entity that Meyer had called Divinity said.

But then another part of Divinity's voice — one that Meyer's doubt had infected, replied, B*ut we will send you down first.*

Compromise. Uncertainty. The difficulties of a singular mind. She could sense the group mind's bafflement over them both — the way they were nuts with unbroken shells, their thoughts only their own. A million sprites seemed to circle them like an invisible cyclone, trying to puzzle them out, working to believe that two people could survive with nothing between them, each living solely inside their own skull.

Now, watching the shape at the end of the tunnel, Piper understood.

Meyer had never returned. Something else had.

He'd never betrayed them. Without even meaning to, Meyer had always helped them.

"I want Cameron to go with us," she told the shape.

"What?" Christopher said from behind.

But Piper's eyes stayed on the shape in the gloom. Meyer but not Meyer. Him but not him.

The shape nodded.
It understood. Of course it did.
On the wind, Piper heard, *Wait*.

Chapter Seventy-Four

HEATHER'S REACHING hand struck something that felt like dirt or stone. She blinked. She was facing a wall dug out of something; that much was suddenly obvious.

She turned, still in the gloom and able to see almost nothing. But then she saw Meyer — not in front of her as she'd thought, but off to her right, in some sort of chamber. The tunnel through the black was wrong. Now her inability to see made sense. She wasn't mystically blind, with a clear passage through the phenomenon's center. Now she couldn't see because she was in a dark place, like a tomb. Or a crypt.

Meyer flicked on a tiny light. It cut a beam through the darkness, and Heather found herself staring into a starburst that threatened to blind her again.

"Heather?" he said.

But his voice was wrong.

"Who the hell is that?" Heather demanded.

The light flicked toward the holder's face. It was Cameron Bannister. He looked the same as he had two years ago: still just as young, just as untidy in clothing and hair. She had a strange urge to turn away, embarrassed. She'd been so sure he'd been Meyer. Heather felt like her punctured heart was bleeding all over her sleeve.

"How did *you* get here?"

"I could ask you the same question," Cameron replied.

"Not fair that you had a light. I was walking blind."

Cameron seemed as disoriented as she felt. "It didn't work before." He shook his head, shining the penlight through the room. The walls were rock and filth. The air was stale — something Heather now realized she'd been smelling and tasting on the back of her tongue for a while. She'd been walking down. Zigzagging. Where Meyer had led, she'd followed.

Cameron was searching corners. There was a passageway behind her and one behind him. He shone his light into both. There was also a plinth of some sort in the room's center. It looked almost like a fountain, but there was no water. Just a perfectly round, shallow basin.

"What are you looking for?"

"Did anyone pass you just now?" Cameron asked. "Did you feel anyone run by, up that passage?"

"No." In truth, Heather felt like she was shedding a dream and barely trusted her feet. "Why?"

"I …" Cameron paused, probably unsure if he should continue. "I could have sworn there was someone ahead of me. I was following him."

"Who?"

"It was hard to see, but …" A shake of the head. "I thought it was Viceroy Dempsey."

Heather looked up. "Where are we?"

Cameron ran a hand over the rock wall. "I think we're under the Apex." He shone the light around again then located a small stone stage against the far wall, covered in otherworldly glyphs. Cameron had seen it before in a photo with a tablet computer leaning against it, proclaiming *Device missing*.

He moved closer.

"What?" Heather asked.

Cameron stooped. Ran his fingers across the stone. "I've seen this before."

A pebble struck the floor to her left. Heather looked over then back to Cameron. Then there was another small plink, and she looked over again.

Cameron stood, and they approached the plinth. With the small depression in the center, like a fountain without water. A depression with a curious black shadow now sliding from it, its job of attracting their attention duly finished.

"What is it?" Heather asked.

Cameron reached into the satchel at his side.

"I have a guess," he said.

Chapter Seventy-Five

"YOU WERE WRONG ABOUT US, RAJ," the viceroy said.

Raj hurried to catch up. Meyer had a sickening walking pace. Every time Raj tried to reach him, the viceroy walked farther. He did it without precisely moving his legs. He just sort of sped away. Raj was getting tired of not being able to see him in the shadows.

"Wrong how?"

"I accepted you. You didn't realize I did, but I did."

"I know that. I know it, sir." Raj could hear the sycophant slobber in his voice but didn't try to fight it. Something big was obviously happening in Heaven's Veil. First, the network virus, then the Apex powering up, followed by the arrival of another three motherships. Shuttles had been swarming nonstop. The Titans had streamed to the Apex, abandoning all pretense. Only Raj had been smart and loyal enough to hold his post then head toward the action. Only *he* had proved himself.

It was okay to beg a little. Flattery greased the world's wheels. Maybe the universe.

"You were always loyal."

"Of course, sir. Thank you, sir. Can you wait up?" Raj scuffled faster. He could barely see. The tunnel through the ink seemed to be sloping down. Turning. Headed somewhere. Somewhere privileged, probably, for the ceremony of Raj's promotion.

Get your head straight, said an obnoxious, meddling voice inside his head. But Raj ignored it. Meyer had always talked to the Astrals with his mind. There was no question right now that Raj could hear them too. He could sense the alien mood. He could tell how single-minded they were. How agitated. Focused on an outcome that Raj couldn't quite see. Yet. But there would be time for that.

You came here to turn them in, said the voice. *But they've gotten away.*

No, no they hadn't. Raj was quite sure about what had happened. He'd come with his charges; the Astrals had seen it; the blackout had come and … and … well, Raj supposed the Astrals had taken them away. Just as Raj was being taken away under the cover of darkness. For his promotion to viceroy.

Snap out of it!

But Meyer's voice, in Raj's ears, was more compelling.

"You're a good soldier, Raj," Meyer said. "You did whatever you were asked to do."

"Yes, sir."

"And even when you weren't asked, you did what was right. Because you have superb instincts."

"Thank you, viceroy."

"Shooting me, for instance."

Raj waited for more, but the viceroy kept walking, his back turned. There was no irony. Raj believed his sincerity. Why wouldn't he? His head was flying. Ever since the fog's descent, Raj had felt so much better about everything. He'd heard others fighting, but Raj didn't feel like fighting.

He felt like making peace. He felt like he'd finally done right in the eyes of those that mattered.

"You sicced the Reptars on Piper. I didn't like that. But it showed your mettle."

"Sure."

"You were always part of the machine, Raj. Always loyal, well past the point of logic."

Raj squinted. That didn't sound right. But then again, he still felt good. Ever since the fog had entered his lungs. "Thanks?" he said.

"Goddamn *right*, thanks," Meyer replied.

Meyer stopped. Raj came closer. He still couldn't see the viceroy's features well enough to read them, but he closed half the distance. Felt Meyer's approval radiating like a furnace.

"To start a fire, you need a spark. You know that, Raj."

"Of course."

"You can lay out all the kindling and dry leaves and grass in the world, but the fire won't start until the right spark is applied. That was you. You were the spark."

"I was?"

"I have to thank you."

"Okay. You're welcome." But Raj didn't understand. *Sparks? Fire?* He was here for a promotion. He was here to be lauded, praised, lifted up.

"If you hadn't shot me, I might not have been forced to reconsider my priorities. If you hadn't shot me, Raj, there might never even have been a Pall. It was your selfless intervention that forced me to reconsider. You were the spark. Reinvention is good for the soul, so to speak. And when I learned about Trevor? Well, I could accept it."

"Trevor?"

Meyer nodded. Put his hand on Raj's shoulder.

"I need you to do something for me, Raj. You're the only one I trust. The only one loyal enough to do it."

"What's that?"

"Nothing much," Meyer said. "Just watch a man turn a key."

Chapter Seventy-Six

AT FIRST, Christopher thought it was dusk. It was the middle of the day, but it had been dark for so long that he felt his equilibrium slip, the way waking to afternoon light upsets an early riser.

Piper was somewhere ahead, and for what felt like hours (but was probably on the order of minutes), she'd been leading them forward. As far as Christopher could tell, Lila was as blind as he was. But judging by Piper's tone and the confidence of her touch, she could see. Maybe not well, but definitely better than him.

By the time Christopher saw the first light, it was like the closing of a day that had never arrived. There were a mile deep shadows. Black and white shapes that he couldn't make out. There seemed to be an eye of light in the distance, dim and barely there. They walked toward it, and as they did Christopher could see Piper's shape in the lead. Lila's gait picked up; her frame rose from its beaten posture. It was as if they were emerging from an impossible midnight, and even Lila's worry abated as it lifted.

After a while, there seemed to be something farther ahead, near the scant light. Another shape. Maybe *several* other shapes. It took forever to reach them, but they finally did.

The night fled. And fled. And fled. Slowly, Christopher found he could see daylight overhead. Could see the land around him in patches. And looking back, he could see the spherical shadows of four motherships above Heaven's Veil, now hundreds of yards distant.

In the light, there was a long shape, like a building.

A small girl ran forward. Lila recognized her before Christopher did; the girl leaped into her arms. Lila purred and cooed, filling the air with embarrassing noises of comfort. Watching her, Christopher felt the last of the fog subside. In seconds, it was gone, and they were in the bright light of midday, the fog a memory Christopher wasn't sure he'd had.

He looked up. A man with serious bug eyes was looking at him through glasses. Beside him was a teenage girl, her black hair in a ponytail.

"Who are you?" the man demanded.

Christopher, feeling asleep, shook his head and looked to Lila, who showed no signs of recognition. Her focus was on Clara, whom she still held like the little girl she was.

Piper hugged the bug-eyed man. He made no acknowledgement. They were all standing outside some sort of a bus-sized RV, and it looked like those who'd been here had been for a while. There were chairs along one side, and the awning was down for shade that Christopher, until just recently, couldn't possibly imagine ever needing again.

Piper stepped back from the man, who looked at her as if she was crazy, but he was willing to oblige if he must.

Christopher looked at Piper for an introduction, but it

was Clara, in Lila's arms, who did the honors. "This is Uncle Charlie. He's the one who told Uncle Cameron what to do with the key."

Charlie looked at Clara then at Piper.

"I did what?" he said.

Chapter Seventy-Seven

CAMERON'S HANDS FROZE. He held the circular stone — the starter for Thor's Hammer, supposedly, but apparently one key fit many locks — perfectly still. He'd been about to lay it in the plinth's matching depression now that the last of the blackness had fled, but something made him stop with a sense like danger.

In his mind, he saw cartoon images of sprung booby traps: snares snatched from the ground, heavy rocks falling on a trigger, poison darts shot and walls beginning to squeeze inward. All were only symbols, but the meaning came through clearly, along with words as obvious as if they'd arrived in a letter.

Clara's voice, as he'd heard it in his dream. As he'd heard it when they'd shared minds in the cell. It had all made sense back then; *Clara* was what they'd returned to Heaven's Veil to find. She wasn't Thor's Hammer, but the girl knew his mind well enough to help him pinpoint its hiding spot, where Benjamin, a lifetime ago, had buried the knowledge in Cameron's young cortex.

A historical joke. A doozy.

Obvious, Cameron felt certain, once Clara helped him find the memories.

Charlie says that Benjamin thought turning the key would call them. That once it's turned, you'll be trapped.

Cameron wasn't sure how to respond. The communication seemed to be one way. Whatever in the fog had led him and Heather to this chamber, it had done so for a reason. Each of them had a purpose. Cameron had seen the stone's depression and assumed this was his, as carrier of the key. It would start some sort of machinery. It might destroy the Apex.

But it would call them. They would come, and take the key.

Charlie says the same key does both things, and that you will need it again. You can't let them catch you or they'll take it. You can't let them find you here after you turn it.

How do you know this? Cameron tried to ask.

I ran out to ask, silly.

Cameron stared at Heather. He felt his mouth hanging open, his eyes wide. He thought she'd tell him to get on with it. She didn't seem to have any more of an idea how they'd reached the sub-Apex chamber than Cameron, and she was probably in a hurry to flee.

"I heard her too," she said.

"I thought——"

"Live with Clara long enough, and you stop asking questions."

Cameron's head perked up. Something had moved beyond Heather's shoulder, down the passageway. Someone was coming. The sounds were faint, but Cameron could swear he heard someone talking. To himself, maybe.

"What do we——" Heather said.

Cameron realized who was coming.

He dropped the stone key into the depression. Putting both hands atop the thing and pressing down, he turned it to engage the tabs on its sides, the way it seemed suddenly obvious that the thing must work.

The chamber's light had been dim. Now, the Apex strobing above seemed to percolate down the passages, sending blue into the chamber, flashing off the stone walls like a sapphire disco.

As if the energy hadn't ramped down, but *up*.

As if the key, turned in the plinth, had shoved the giant antenna station into overdrive.

Chapter Seventy-Eight

NATHAN STOPPED when the mostly opaque mist began to throb in a sickly blue light. His guide had disappeared; he'd been leading Coffey and whoever else was following down a corridor that felt increasingly like a trap. He'd lost his bearings entirely. At first, it had seemed like he was headed toward the Apex, but he'd gone too far. He'd gone down, up, sideways, then down and up again. It felt like circles, and for a while Nathan thought he might have been following a loop — around the edge of amassed Titans to a more advantageous location above. But now it didn't seem that way at all.

He turned and realized he could see Coffey behind him. Either the fog was beginning to lift, or the light was managing to penetrate what sunlight couldn't.

"It the Apex," Coffey said. Nathan couldn't see much of her face but saw enough to know his usually staunch lieutenant was terrified. There were shapes behind her; the rest of the soldiers must have followed. But if any of them thought they were in charge right now, they surely had another thing coming. They were fish in a barrel. Soon, the unseen force would start shooting.

"Where is it?" Nathan looked forward, backward, to each side. The passage walls were still mostly opaque. Muted blue flashes were coming mainly from each end and above. There was no way to tell the source, diffusing through the mist like light and concealing its origin.

"We were headed toward it," Coffey said.

"We've walked too far. My sense of direction is fucked." He looked backward, suddenly sure it was behind him. But he'd been turned in a maze; he was entirely uncertain. "It could be back there or straight ahead. I don't know in this soup. All I know is it either got a lot brighter just now, or this shit's finally breaking up." He looked around. "Heather. Where did Heather go?"

"Lost her right away. I thought she'd be ahead."

"I could hear her mouth."

"I don't know, Nathan."

Another blue flash. And another. Goddamn if the things didn't look stronger by the round. It reminded Nathan of an overheated coal, glowing bright as bellows blew oxygen across it.

"It's that way." He pointed.

"I'd be happy just to get out."

"That's noble of you."

"We stopped having any control over what came next a while ago. We're being led. Frankly, we don't have much of a choice. If something wants to fuck us, then we're fucked. *Sir.*"

"So your weak will is something thrust upon you, not something—"

Another blue flash, this one clearly from behind. The mist was thinning, no doubt. Nathan could see shapes moving around him: probably Reptars and Titans, somehow held at bay, soon to be visible — and the Andreus clan visible to them.

"It's this way."

"Nathan, I think we were being led *away* from—"

But Nathan could see it now.

The pyramid's gleaming blue glass, now a few blocks behind.

And nothing else outside its front door.

Chapter Seventy-Nine

THERE WAS A CIRCULAR, rotating skin of thin stone sliding over the top of the plinth's key. It was closing the thing in, hiding it. Cameron had a moment of panic, but then saw the key's far edge peeking out from the rotating skin's other side. Emerging. But far too slowly.

Cameron pushed at the cover. Dug his fingernails into the groove between key and plinth. But he couldn't get the thing out until whatever needed to be done was finished.

Heather's head perked up at a sound. Cameron followed it with his eyes. It was coming from the other passage: approaching voices now hitting them from two directions at once.

"Feet," he said.

"Lots of feet. That guy Nathan Andreus. He's outside with a bunch of soldiers. Maybe they've come to—"

Cameron shook his head, holding up a finger for quiet. The stone machinery whirred behind him, grit grinding like heavy sandpaper. He wanted silence, but his action betrayed the chamber's quiet.

"It's not Andreus," he whispered.

"How do you know?"

"Clara said it would call them. Listen. Too steady. No rush." He swallowed. "It's Astrals. Titans."

"So what?" Her face changed. Cameron didn't think anyone had told Heather about the Titans' shape-shifting trick, but she knew. He could see it in her sudden pallor, sharply visible in the flashlight's glow.

"The light. Turn out the light."

Heather had been holding the thing. She didn't hesitate. She clicked it off, and it was as if the black cloud had returned. Scant light bled from both passageways: the one where the Astrals were making their casual, no hurry way down, and the one from which Cameron could still hear Raj talking to … to *someone* who wasn't replying.

The stone continued to grind.

"We have to get the key and go. We need it."

"For what?"

"It's a long story."

Cameron couldn't see Heather in the darkness but could sense her stare.

"Cameron," she whispered.

"Shh."

"You and Piper came back. Nathan told me about his daughter and someone named Charlie Cook. He talked a lot about your father's research, in a way that makes me think he might have died. In the rebel raid we heard about from a few days ago."

"Shh. They'll hear us."

Even more quietly, seeming to move closer, Heather said, "Where is Trevor? Where is my son?"

Cameron felt his skin crawl. Something had led her to this place, just as something had led him. He hadn't spent much time with Heather before he'd taken Piper from the Axis Mundi, but he knew she was vastly different. Life had changed her. And there was more to it; he'd heard Heather updates from Piper, too. This was a changed woman. Just as Cameron's guides had told him things he wouldn't have known otherwise, maybe Heather's had indicated certain unpleasant truths to her as well.

"He's fine."

"Then where is he?"

Cameron could sense a serious, strangely mature gaze that the darkness forbade him to see. Heather was inches away, her voice barely audible. If he'd seen her, Cameron supposed he would have seen the mask that crumbles when a person stops lying — to themselves, most of all.

"He's gone, isn't he?"

"Shh. He's ... okay. I'll explain later." The lies were awful, but she'd chosen the worst possible time to ask. The indigo light was still intermittently flashing, filling the room, leaving only Heather and Cameron, behind the stone plinth, in unbroken shadow. Something was on a countdown, and the slowly revolving disk above was hailing enemies like a clarion call. They couldn't get out with the key unless they could remain undetected. And she'd cry if Cameron told her the truth. She'd yell. She'd throw one of her famous tantrums. Then they'd be dead.

"Meyer isn't Meyer. There's something wrong with him. Do you understand me?"

"What?" Had she bought it? It seemed impossible to believe.

"But whoever he is, he'll turn. He turned last time, and he'll turn again. I'd bet on it."

"What are you—"

Hands grasped both of Cameron's cheeks, palm to skin. He felt himself pulled forward, smelling the fresh scent of rich woman's soap. Heather pressed her lips into his, far more insistent than sensual.

"What was that for?"

"If you ever find him, give him that for me."

Cameron was about to ask more, but Heather stood and ran up the first corridor, toward Raj Gupta's echoing voice.

Chapter Eighty

RAJ BLINKED. Meyer was gone.

In his place was someone with long black hair. Someone he definitely didn't want to talk to. Now or ever. But his head felt foggy, and as he blinked around Raj saw the strange dark pall had cleared. He was at the end of a downward-sloping stone passageway. Somewhere underground? It was so hard to remember how he'd got here, let alone how he'd found himself face to face with Heather Hawthorne.

She grabbed the front of his shirt. Dragged him farther down, toward where Meyer had been leading him. Although Raj was no longer sure about any of that. Had the viceroy really been here? It all seemed like a dream. There was something he was supposed to do. Something that would let him prove himself to Meyer.

They spilled into a dark chamber. In the intermittent blue light leaking down from above, Raj could see that there was some sort of a stone cradle in one corner. There was an altar or something similar in the middle, emitting a slow racket. The grinding stopped. Raj could see a circular depression in its top, with a round thing sitting inside it. Something seemed to move behind the altar, but he'd been jumping at shadows enough. It was a trick of the light, just like Meyer had been.

"You're looking for me," Heather said.

But Raj didn't think so. Now that his head was clearing, he didn't think he was after Heather Hawthorne at all anymore. He'd tried to arrest her once, and no one had cared. Nobody ever cared. Meyer certainly hadn't because the viceroy had been in on it with her. Meyer had turned on them all and recently beaten the shit out of Raj.

He didn't owe Meyer a thing.

The Astrals. That's whom he'd come here to talk to. And he could hear them coming, down the opposite corridor.

Raj moved toward the disk set atop the altar. Heather pushed him back. In the azure flashes, he watched her smile.

"Get out of my way."

"No way. We're finally alone. I've been looking forward to this for two years."

Again, something seemed to move behind the stone altar in the room's center. Raj tried to steal another look, but Heather spun him again. This time, she was against the wall.

"I surrender," she said.

He tried to shake her away. She held fast. The feet were coming closer, their echo through the stone corridors making them sound closer than they were, coming nearer still.

"Come on, Raj. You knocked up my daughter. Don't you want to find out where Lila learned all she knows? Hit me with your licorice stick."

Raj pushed Heather away. She held him tight, holding his hands. The blue flash came. Vanished. Came again.

They were wrapped in black between flashes. During the blue interludes, he could see her face, as obnoxiously hectoring as always.

Raj pushed. This time, Heather gripped much, much harder. She'd been playing, but she had more in her than he'd have suspected now that she was trying. The light went out, and Heather dragged him back. It came on, and he found her staring hard into his eyes, almost through his head. He became aware of the chamber's silence. Other than the slow trod of approaching Astral feet, there was nothing at all.

The lights went out. The lights came on.

"Fuck me, Raj. Come on. Prove that you're a man."

"Get away from me, Heather."

She gripped Raj's crotch. Too hard. He cringed.

"Sorry. I like it rough. I figured you liked it rough, too. Like linear algebra."

He pushed again. This time, Heather pushed back so hard that his skull struck stone, bringing a dull throb of pain. Something skittered past in the shadows, like a rat.

"I'm not leaving until you teach me the secrets of your spicy recipe."

"What the hell are you—"

"Come on, Raj." Her eyes flicked away from him, toward the room's center, and a small smile touched the corners of her lips. She stepped back. "Fuck me like you fucked humanity."

He stared hard. Heather didn't flinch. Her sarcastic smile widened.

"Fuck me like you fucked Meyer. Like you tried to fuck Piper, before she and Cameron fucked you right back." Heather moved back to the stone altar, leaned against it like a diva. She made her voice throaty, like gravel. "Oh,

Raj. Fuck me like Terrence and Christopher and Lila have been fucking you for years."

Raj's eyebrows drew together. He was getting déjà vu. How many times had Heather messed with him over the years? He knew a distraction when he saw it. The last time, she'd been trying to let Terrence into the network center to plant the virus. But he'd seen through her then and could see through her now. He'd been led here under decidedly strange circumstances, but maybe this was why: to catch Heather trying to pull more of her usual bullshit.

He yanked her hard, and she staggered away from the altar.

The thing had stopped moving. Stopped grinding. Stopped turning.

And the stone disk, whatever it had been, was gone.

Raj heard sound from the far corridor: footsteps, running. Decidedly human, in a rush, getting away.

He scampered to follow whoever was escaping, but Heather was holding him back. With much, *much* more force than he would ever have thought possible.

Raj jerked his shoulder to free himself, but after one failed attempt, the footsteps from the other corridor finally arrived. He looked up, still held fast by Heather's grip, and watched dozens of Titans spill into the chamber.

"Oh, thank God," Raj said, puffing his chest as best he could with Heather pinning his arm. "I need to talk to whichever of you is in charge."

The lead Titan looked at Raj for one semi-puzzled second. A few final wisps of the earlier fog seemed to have followed them into the chamber and was circling their waists like a stink. The Titan exhaled, and some of the stuff seemed to puff out like smoke from a cigarette. The big white man was somehow different than Raj had seen

357

Titans before. His eyes were lit with emotion, almost like a human.

The Titan put a strong hand on Raj's free shoulder and pushed him aside without any effort. The blue flashing overhead began to throb, its tempo and intensity increasing as something continued to come undone.

"I've located Cameron Bannister and several of his cohorts and—"

Raj stopped when the Titan looked down onto the stone altar. He touched the empty space where the stone disk had been. He looked up, and Raj saw disappointment. Irritation. Maybe anger. He inhaled. Exhaled. A stubborn tendril of black smoke went in and out with every breath.

Raj backed away. Toward the far passage. Still, Heather held his arm.

"You're wasting your time," Raj said, almost laughing at the absurdity. "After all, they're only Titans."

Heather smiled wider.

One of the white beings moved to block each of the passageways. Then there was a guttural sound like a Reptar's purr, even though there were none in the room.

Raj tried again to flee, suddenly becoming decidedly nervous.

"Fuck me," Heather whispered, holding him fast, "like you fucked Trevor."

Chapter Eighty-One

"FIVE MINUTES," Nathan said. "Then we go."

Coffey looked around. The courtyard was empty. The Titans had either dispersed into the city when the fog had been subsuming them, or they'd all — every single one of them — entered the Apex. Their absence was eerie. Not one of the waiting soldiers was calm. All were fiddling, watching the sky, looking up at the four motherships and the still-circling shuttles. The black fog had entirely vanished to reveal a perfectly powder-blue Colorado sky. The Apex was throbbing in the now-intense daylight like a bomb, an electric hum now audible beneath every cycle.

"We should go now. While we can."

Nathan shook his head. "It led us here."

"Not directly."

"Maybe it was allowing time. Letting the Titans have what they needed to clear the square and go ..." Nathan trailed off. There was no obvious place to end that sentence.

Coffey looked at him, sparing Nathan the irritation of voicing the same thought. She looked up at the Apex.

"Shouldn't we go inside?"

Nathan shook his head. At least some of the Titans had gone inside; he'd seen their white hides retreating into the shafts. The plan had been to somehow destroy the thing — that's what Meyer Dempsey had implied last night, though he'd never specifically said it. At the time, his suggestion had seemed obvious: Go to the fence, let your people in, then go to the Apex and destroy it before it can make whatever broadcast it's about to make. When he'd run into Heather Hawthorne, who'd come his way to breach the fence, the coincidence had seemed even thicker, and Nathan had become even more certain that this was his mission — again, as endorsed by the viceroy.

But Dempsey never mentioned the blackout. Or the strange dark fog. It was as if he'd had no idea after all. He'd implied that Nathan had his support. But how? Why? The details were missing. Nathan was used to following his gut, but now it said nothing. They were the opposite of trapped. Nobody was around to intervene, as if nothing mattered. And maybe, judging by what he was seeing, the Apex was having its fits just fine without him. Unless this was the buildup to broadcast that he was supposed to stop? There wasn't any obvious answer.

He looked around. The area remained soundless and empty.

"Fine. We go in."

A thrashing, wailing noise screamed from inside the Apex. To Nathan, it sounded like a man drawn and quartered — a phenomenon, interestingly enough, that he'd witnessed.

The sounds of running, rushing feet followed the screams.

Coffey's hand settled on his shoulder. He looked over to

see her profile, eyes wide, staring at something to their rear.

When he turned again, Nathan saw a pair of shuttles hovering inches from the ground behind them. Waiting. Silently floating like giant ball bearings.

Chapter Eighty-Two

CAMERON ENTERED the harsh daylight at a run then skidded to a stop as he found the two silver shuttles greeting him like a dour welcoming committee. His arms went wide as he paused, heart pounding. He could hear the Titans and Reptars coming up the passage behind him. The sensations were so overwhelming, he barely saw Andreus even though he was practically standing in Cameron's way.

"What?" Andreus demanded. "What's going on?"

"We have to run! *Go!*"

The shuttles moved forward. Pinching them in. Narrowing the small space between the small contingent of soldiers who, Cameron was amused to see, had brought black motorcycles. Every one of them looked terrified and useless. All eyes wide.

Instead of running, Cameron backed up. He heard the comings behind him and stepped forward again. There was only one reachable way into the Apex — the huge, open-mouthed, downward-sloping tunnel behind him. Cameron could hear the Reptars purring. The patient plodding of Titan feet. He didn't know if they were the same Astrals who'd entered the room as he'd been leaving with the stone key — that he'd seen, peeking around the corner, when they'd entered to surround Heather and Raj. After that, Cameron hadn't hesitated. Maybe running made him a coward, but there were no heroes in that situation. Survivors ran. They'd learned that lesson at Cottonwood.

Behind Andreus, Jeanine Coffey attempted to flank right. The shuttle followed, barring her way. A tall man on the other side tried to go around, but the second in the pair moved to intercept.

"Run through them. Run past them."

Coffey threw Cameron a loathsome look. But he'd had enough. Cameron had watched his father die; he'd watched kids die; he'd just run away from another two deaths because he'd wanted to live — and, if he wanted to give himself a tiny slice of credit, to keep the stone key whole and hidden. But what good would it do now? Staying alive was exhausting. The emotions hard to endure. Piper was probably dead. Same for Terrence, Christopher, Lila, and everyone else. Only Clara was for-sure alive; Cameron could feel her. Could sense her searching his mind, optimistic like stupid kids were as they turned their backs on the world's truths. She would find Thor's Hammer for him. But a fat load of good it would do anyone, now that he was about to die. Again.

"*Do it!*" Cameron shouted at the shuttles.

Andreus turned to look at him sideways. So did Coffey. So did all of the others — who retreated toward the group's mushy middle, where they might be safe as Cameron drew the spheres' fire.

"*DO IT!*" Cameron repeated, stepping forward.

The shuttles didn't move. And Cameron didn't skirt.

He walked right up to them and, knowing how irrational, stupid, and end-of-his-rope ridiculous he was being, shoved the one on the left like he'd push a stubborn person. The chrome-seeming skin was slick without being oily. It didn't budge, and Cameron's hands slipped across its surface, nearly slamming his chin and chest into its belly.

"Do it! Do it, you motherfuckers!" He turned, now seeing the shapes of Titans marching up the tunnel from behind. *"You want to kill us, just fucking kill us!"* He grabbed his satchel with both hands, feeling like the heavy thing was covered with blood: his father's, Trevor's, Danika's, Ivan's, and countless others. Cameron had been spared so the useless disk could survive. He wanted to pull it out now and smash it. To surrender in the loudest possible way. To show them he was *through*, that they could take their victory over Earth and shove it up their alien asses.

The giant chrome shuttle dropped three inches to the stone ground, leaving a crack.

Cameron stepped back.

It began to roll. Not naturally downhill, which would have been backward. But forward, with purpose.

Toward the Apex. Toward the tunnel's mouth and into its guts.

The second shuttle rose a dozen feet into the air, shaking in a way that Cameron had never seen, as if it was trying to tell them something.

Then, as the Andreus soldiers scampered back, the first shuttle rolled down the passage, toward the approaching Astrals, down the pyramid's gaping throat.

Chapter Eighty-Three

Terrence watched it happen.

The first shuttle spun toward the pyramid's entrance — seemingly meaning to steamroll Andreus, Coffey, and a new arrival that looked like Cameron Bannister, but taking no notice when they dodged its approach, leaving it to roll under the Apex like a coin slipping into a slot.

The second shuttle rose into the air and began to flit about, somehow spastic.

Then the humans ran. Toward the street's entrance a block down from where Terrence had bunkered with Malcolm Jons, apparently oblivious to the fact that they were running toward murder.

"They don't know," said Jons, watching over his shoulder. They were in an alcove, surrounded by construction detritus. They'd lost their vision when the strange fog had rolled in, and they'd taken each other's hands without shame. They'd stumbled in the only direction they knew to go: *away*. They'd found this place when the day had finally returned. Citizens kept peeking out, seeing them but saying nothing. Humanity was one now, all wary of the Reptars and Titans swarming at the rear.

He could see an old man at his window, watching Terrence as if hoping to score a vicarious victory. Heaven's Veil had, despite the appearances of freedom and self-determination, lived under a boot for two years. Terrence noted the same silent terror in the eyes of all he'd seen today. They were all staying where they were meant to, obediently holing up in their homes and shops. Not making waves. They'd stay under the whip until they died without lifting a finger.

"They'll come this way. It's more sensible."

Jons shook his big, bald head. "They're headed into Astral central. We gotta get them."

Terrence did the only thing he could think of — picked up a rock and hurled it hard at the group of retreating people. It struck a woman with green hair as she mounted one of the motorcycles and fired its engine. The thing coughed to life with a roar. From their hiding place, Terrence and Jons both watched the group of waiting Astrals turn their heads.

The woman, in her panic, wrenched the bike's throttle before she was seated. It spun out, making a half circle, and pinned her leg to the stone. A man from Andreus's group stopped to free her, but the others all ran. More bikes fired. The army dispersed, "all for one" abandoned in panic's crimson haze.

"Hell, Terrence. Look."

He turned. The Apex was still pulsing, now with smoke pluming from the entrance, and a sound like thunder.

Nothing mattered. Terrence cupped his hands around his mouth and yelled, not caring who heard. The jig was up either way. At least they could die together.

"Over here!"

The melee was too thick. The Astrals barely noticed his shout over the roaring bikes and the rushing of people hither and yon. They began to turn. To move toward the choked alleyway Andreus and Cameron and the others had been heading for. Then something else started to happen. Something that made Terrence's testicles clench and try to crawl up inside his body.

Titans fell on all fours. Their skin charred from powder white to black scales. And one by one, they turned into Reptars.

"Jesus." Terrence didn't shout again, now feeling his skin chill like ice. He waved his arms, trying to capitalize on his newly earned attention.

They rushed forward, staying low. There was little point. The new Reptars were coming, both from ahead and behind. They saw them. They saw the others running, and were angry.

"Run," Jons said.

"Just a second." Terrence could feel breath in his throat like acid. His head was spinning. He thought he might fall over, pass out.

"Come on." Jons grabbed him with his big meaty paw, dragging, urging.

"They're almost here."

"RUN!"

Reptars swarmed. Shuttles buzzed like angry bees above them. Cameron, Andreus, Coffey, and maybe half of the soldiers arrived, breathless, into their futile cluster. Titans marched from above and behind, pinning them in. Motorcycles purred then stalled.

They turned to go, found themselves facing teeth and strong arms.

Then the Apex detonated behind them as the shuttle in its gut blew like a bomb.

Chapter Eighty-Four

PIPER SPUN toward the sound of an explosion in the city's interior. She didn't see it happen. She was near the RV, shielded from the Heaven's Veil skyline by a cluster of trees. By the time she sprang around them and looked toward the sound, she couldn't place what had changed. Then she gasped. The Apex, which had become the city's iconic middle, was gone.

"They did it."

Charlie came up beside Piper, his face more annoyed than victorious. "They were supposed to overload it."

"I guess it overloaded too far."

Piper didn't flinch. She looked toward Clara, no longer reluctant to ask the small girl questions she couldn't possibly answer. Lila had gripped her hand hard enough to bleach the skin, but the girl showed no signs of complaint.

"Are they okay, Clara?"

Clara nodded.

"They did it. They did what you said."

"They just weakened it."

"Then what blew it up?"

Christopher was holding Lila around the shoulders, trying to seem calm and definitely failing. His eyes were giant marbles. As were everyone's in the group, except for Clara's. "Was it Thor's Hammer? Is it over?"

Clara shook her head. "No. Mr. Cameron knows where that is now, though. And he has the key."

"Where is it? Where is Thor's Hammer?"

"It's at Mr. Benjamin's favorite. The place they love, from when Mr. Cameron was little."

"Where, Clara?"

But Clara yawned, unimpressed by it all. "I'm sleepy."

"Where?" Lila demanded, a bit too rough.

"I don't know the place name. He does."

"Cameron does."

"At least Cameron." Before Piper could ask what that meant, the girl went on. "It's a mountain. In a faraway place, across the ocean."

And Charlie, hearing this, said, "Super. I guess we'll grab a rowboat."

Lila squatted in front of Clara, her manner urgent as if she'd just remembered something. "Clara, honey? You said earlier that they were trying to turn on a 'spotlight.' The Astrals, I mean. Is that over? Did they stop it?"

Charlie looked down at Lila then to Piper, who was watching him back. He asked, "What spotlight?"

"To help them find the chest without our help," Clara answered. "So they don't have to keep following us."

Or let us live so they can see where we go, Piper thought.

"But Cameron and the others stopped it. They stopped the Astrals from turning on their spotlight and finding the … the chest." Lila's eyes went to Christopher. Piper saw an unspoken message flit between them: *Or from doing whatever other insidious things might have been afoot for as long as the Apex stood.*

Lila looked toward the city, toward the absent Apex and its missing glow, toward the landing area it was no longer projecting, the signal it was no longer sending through its antenna. No matter what happened next — if Cameron and the rest made it out of Heaven's Veil or not, at least that much had been done. And with prodding, even though she claimed not to know the name of the place she saw inside Cameron's mind, Clara could find the mountain that had once been Cameron and Benjamin's favorite, across the uncrossable sea. So all was as well as it could be, considering.

"They stopped it for a while," Clara said.

"Because of the other Apexes," Charlie said. "I told you this was a fool's errand. They can just do to the others what they were doing with this one. We sure can't destroy them all."

But Clara was pointing at the city. At the hovering motherships, which even in the daylight Piper could see were now starting to glow.

"They don't *need* to turn on the spotlight," Clara said, "if they can make the chest call out for them to hear it."

Lila was still stooping, her skin now paper white. "Clara, honey? What does that mean?"

Clara was still pointing at the glowing motherships.

"We should pack," she said.

Chapter Eighty-Five

CAMERON TRIED TO STAND, but something heavy was on him. His peripheral vision displayed nothing but bodies. Something had blown up. He could barely hear. Sounds were muted, ringing like a distant alarm. Astral bodies surrounded him to complement the humans: all of them equal in the reaper's eyes.

"Get off of me," he said to the person who'd been blown into him. He remembered a feeling like a concussion. Someone had seemed to tackle him. Then, a split second later, something had blown.

He blinked. His head hurt. The inability to hear was disorienting. He could see people rising, or running. Malcolm Jons and Terrence were ahead, but it hurt Cameron to lift his neck and look. He should be dead. Most of the bodies around him, save the few getting up and crawling away, had been sliced and diced by blue glass ... or whatever it was the Apex had belched out when it went down swinging.

The Apex is gone.

The fact was only vaguely interesting. Cameron knew

he'd been trying to undermine it somehow, but the notion that the Apex would have come equipped with a handy self-destruct mechanism had seemed pretty damn convenient. He'd distinctly thought that when he'd been running from Heather and Raj, failing them like he'd failed his father, Trevor, and everyone else. Today had been every man for himself, and Cameron had been no exception. You fled or died. The only catch was the guilt that followed survival.

Cameron turned his head, vacantly aware that someone was yelling at him. Maybe Jeanine Coffey. He remembered seeing her get up a few seconds ago and head toward Terrence, or maybe not. He looked up. It was Coffey, all right, but something was wrong with her. She seemed to be shouting, but barely any sound was leaving her lips. It was funny. He thought about laughing.

Coffey turned and vanished — somewhere out of his line of sight. Cameron couldn't see her, but he seemed to feel her. And it hurt too much to turn his head. Though slowly, his hearing was leaking back. Not much. Mostly, he still heard the whine of that distant alarm — real or in his ears, he hadn't a clue. A teapot's whistle, now mingling with the slightest of shouts.

(Hurry!)

He sensed the word more than heard it. From Police Chief Jons, who looked like he might have taken a hunk of shrapnel to his arm. Red gunk was dripping down his meaty limb, drizzling from his fingers.

Above him, still very faint, Jeanine Coffey said, *"Get up. We have to go."*

And indeed they did. More shuttles were coming. Cameron could see them. More Titans and Reptars spilled from between the buildings, from somewhere behind the smoking pile of debris and rock that was once the pyramid.

The last of the weight left Cameron's back. He wasn't dead. He might not even be cut. His head was clearing, the situation's weight and reality settling on him like a lead cloak.

Coffey helped Cameron to his knees then pulled him to his feet. His satchel had been slung around his back. Coffey pulled it forward, feeling around inside. The key must still have been whole because she visibly relaxed then took the satchel for herself. Still too quiet amid all the ringing, she said, *"He squeezed it between you. It's safe."*

"Who?" Cameron's voice sounded odd to his ears.

As Coffey dragged him forward, Cameron looked back and saw Nathan's motionless body.

Chapter Eighty-Six

THERE HAD BEEN A TICKING sound before the Apex had blown. Nathan must have heard it and intuited its meaning because he'd dived for Cameron's back, toward the key, and what might be the planet's most important object. Jeanine had heard it too. But instead of leaping to protect her general, she'd ducked. She'd covered. She'd shoved her fingers in her ears. And when the dust had cleared, she'd remained mostly whole, with merely a glancing cut across one shoulder.

It's for the best. Everything happens for a reason.

She'd once believed such things. Grandma had said them when things went awry and when Jeanine had been a teenage girl with problems that had seemed so dire at the time, she'd tried hard to accept Grandma's words. It had worked, to an extent. But it wasn't working now. And yet it had to because Nathan was dead regardless. They were fucked up the butt, and the stone key for Thor's Hammer — wherever *that* might be — was only safe for as long as they refused to mourn and kept running.

Jeanine told herself that she'd looked out for number

one because someone needed to lead this group the hell out of … well … out of Hell. Nathan was gone, and the police chief, large though he was, was already flagging. Cameron was dazed, but he'd been weak since he'd watched his father die. It was Jeanine or nobody. And maybe that, in the end, made her saving herself commendable.

But only if she didn't dawdle. Only if she did what needed doing, without hesitation.

The demolished Apex was like a hive of furious hornets. The shuttle had blown its roof off, but it was either an upward-only blast, or the stone floors in the temple below were sturdier than she'd have thought. Looking back as she pulled Cameron toward Jons and Terrence, Jeanine felt as if they must have been spawned down there — as if the Apex, not the motherships, was where Astrals were born.

They boiled out in waves. There were no Titans. Only Reptars.

They came fast. She couldn't just take the key and run; Cameron's brain, if anything, held Thor's Hammer's location. He had to survive — another reason, perhaps, that Nathan had given him a second back when the Apex had blown. Now it was Jeanine's job to get him out.

But they were too quick. They came. She moved, but not enough.

Before Jeanine could think to curl up with Cameron and wait to die — there wasn't enough time to give him the satchel back and die *for* him — there was a hot thump and a sizzle. She felt a hot draft and looked up to see the shuttle from earlier incinerating Reptars in a sweeping wave, firing a solid beam into the pyramid's remains. A scent like cooking pork assaulted her nostrils.

The shuttle seemed to spin; it was hard to tell given its

uniform shape. It lanced out with another beam. The building past Terrence, Jons, and the few remaining soldiers blew backward, crumbling to rubble. There were more Titans beyond, each one already most of its way to Reptar. Another beam, and they were gone.

"What's it doing?" Jons asked, aghast, his voice audible but muffled in her ringing ears.

It was a stupid question. Help was help. The first shuttle had brought down the Apex, and this one had fried their pursuers. It didn't matter what or why. It only mattered that the way, for a while at least, was clear.

Jeanine ran as fast as Cameron could go. She left the others. They didn't matter, and Cameron was slowly returning, his eyes clearing, injuries — if he had any — far from mortal.

A block later, she saw Terrence and Jons. Several of Nathan's summoned soldiers were on her other side, running for their own lives as much as anyone else's.

The shuttle followed. Others came up behind it and fired, Astral to Astral. The lead shuttle seemed to anticipate the blow; it veered to one side and plowed through a building that was either an apartment or a business. It returned fire, but the shuttle merely bounced when struck, undamaged. Then the shuttle in the rear — now joined by three others — fired on the first. The friendly shuttle bounced like a ping-pong ball between blasts then zoomed straight up and was gone. The others pursued, energy beams lancing the newly vacant sky.

They were on their own.

Jeanine dove down, catching her breath and allowing Cameron to catch his. Jons fell into line beside them, alone. Terrence and the others were gone. She looked back. There were no obvious bodies, but it seemed more likely that they'd caught spare fire than deciding to go some-where better.

"We have to look for them," Cameron said, his voice still balled in cotton. "They may be trapped."

"They're dead!"

"You don't know that!"

Jeanine started forward. Cameron pulled her in the opposite direction, straining.

It was maddening. The gate was ahead, practically within sight. The lead shuttle had blown them a path; the gate was as gone as the Apex. They could make it.

Except for the shuttles.

Which, she suddenly realized as Cameron pulled against her, had vanished from the sky. It should have been a relief. Instead, it felt ominous.

Jeanine looked up. The shuttles were gone. Every single one. And there were no more Astrals active on the ground. She, Jons, and Cameron had a straight shot. She could even see some of the shuttles retreating, climbing into the motherships' bellies above.

"We have to go back for them!" Cameron shouted, leaning against her with all of his weight.

But Jeanine was still looking up. At the four mother-ships. And the way they were glowing.

Her eyes flashed toward Cameron. All at once, she surrendered to his pull. She dove with him, keeping hold but letting his momentum hurl him to the ground in a crash.

When he recovered, Jeanine pulled him upright and hit him hard in the throat. Then she handed Cameron to Captain Jons, who tossed him over a shoulder. Then they ran from the city before it killed them.

Chapter Eighty-Seven

LILA WASN'T sure whether she should look down at her daughter, who seemed unimpressed by all that was happening, or the two people she could now see running from the city across the parched open sprawl that the Astrals had cleared when Vail's land had been razed for Heaven's streets to be built.

The people were an odd pair. There was a thin, athletic-looking woman with brown hair and a bald, enormous black man who looked to be made only of muscle. The latter, who had to be Police Chief Jons, was carrying a third person: a stirring form that was probably Cameron Bannister. Or so thought Piper, who kept trying to run forward only to be rebuffed by Charlie and Christopher.

Clara was watching it all. Observing the pair approach with no obvious concern for their safety, or surprise to see them. She was watching the four motherships, which were doing something that spanned all four: a kind of glowing, shared cloud of energy gathered and sparked between them. Lila had no idea what might be happening, but she had an excellent guess that it wasn't good. And yet Clara didn't flinch.

"Clara, honey, let's go inside."

"Going inside won't help, Mommy."

Lila thought it would help plenty. Judging by what had just happened with the Apex, it seemed likely that the motherships were about to blow up some human shit of their own: the police station, a few apartments, whatever it took to keep everyone in line. Maybe her father would turn on the Astrals when he discovered everyone gone, but even if he did they'd find someone willing to subdue a voluntarily conquered populace. Hell, Raj would be fantastic for that job.

Explosions were better under cover. And this particular interior had wheels and an engine. Lila wondered if the Astrals would let them go, but they were sort of hidden back here. They could stick to the trees. Maybe run on foot once farther away, like they'd done all those years ago.

Still, Lila couldn't help but feel a tug. The viceroy's office would survive, and her father was still a chosen one — not just one of nine who'd gone above the ships and returned as media gods, but known by the entire planet. He'd be fine. But she didn't want to leave him behind.

"Come on," Lila told her. "Let's play a game."

Clara gave her a look that said, *Are you kidding me?* and Lila let it go.

The new members of their party arrived. Jons offloaded his cargo, which did, in fact, turn out to be an extremely irate Cameron Bannister. But his anger evaporated when he saw Piper, and they embraced — as friends, not lovers. Lila, who had her suspicions especially after having her own dalliances, took comfort in seeing it.

Clara was watching her.

"Do you miss him?" she asked. "I miss him, Mommy."

"We'll see him again," Lila lied. Although she realized, as she said it, that she had no idea who Clara was talking about.

Cameron disengaged from Piper and squatted in front of Clara. It was strange, the way the man and the girl who should by all rights still be in diapers faced one another as equals.

"I know where it is," he said.

Clara nodded.

"But there's no way to get there."

All heads turned from Cameron as the ships glowed and the energy beneath them began to accumulate. Clara was right: going inside wouldn't make any difference at all.

"What are they doing?" Cameron asked no one in particular.

Clara, still at his side, said, "They're going to make the chest scream loud enough to find it."

Chapter Eighty-Eight

"Get inside."

Christopher looked up, already used to the idea of taking orders from Cameron again after the years lost between them. The old gang was back, if you ignored the truth that it was just the two of them left. No Vincent, Dan, or Terrence. Just Cameron and Chris, investigating Meyer Dempsey on Benjamin's orders ... except that Benjamin, of course, was also gone.

But it wasn't Cameron issuing orders, rushing around the RV and pushing each of the small group inside, taking no shit of any kind while motherships powered up behind them. It wasn't even Charlie (who might have made sense as Benjamin's successor) or Jeanine Coffey (who was military-seeming enough to pull it off). It was Piper. But she wasn't the meek flower she'd once been. Her eyes were hard; she seemed, in Christopher's uninformed opinion, to have a bigger clue about what was happening than anyone other than Clara.

"Where are we going?"

Piper didn't answer. Neither did anyone else. Charlie

had Lila by the shoulders, steering her numb carcass from the rear into the RV. She was going willingly enough but looked blank-faced. Something must have snapped. Christopher supposed he should help, seeing as he, if anyone, was Lila's right hand. Piper was too no-bullshit. When this was over, if they were still alive, maybe she'd become a mother figure again. But right now, Piper was a general.

"I'll—" Christopher began talking to Charlie.

"Get inside," Charlie barked.

As if Christopher weren't, right now, wearing a guard uniform. He bellowed the same order to Captain Jons, who was still bleeding copiously down one arm and may have lost more blood than Christopher had thought at a glance. Cameron looked woozy from being knocked flat, punched out, and carried. Coffey had already explained as much, just as she'd bluntly expounded that Heather "hadn't made it." Lila wasn't supposed to hear that, but no one was being especially careful.

Christopher found Clara already inside, sitting between the forked legs of Nathan Andreus's daughter. She was smiling, putting a comforting hand on Christopher's leg. Grace, above her, seemed either neutral or lost. Christopher didn't know if anyone had told the girl that her father, too, was dead.

He could feel static in the air. Even Christopher's thick, heavy Italian-Irish mane wanted to stand on end. He could see a hazy halo of flyaways rising from Clara's loose hair across from him, Grace's dark ponytail fraying at the end.

He didn't know where Lila had gone. Everything was moving too fast.

Then he saw her just down the long padded bench running along the RV's side. She was upright and alert, her own hair also rising away from her head. But something was off. Something about Lila's face, her posture, the set of her shoulders was different.

Christopher moved down. But before he could put an arm around her, Lila spoke.

"She said they want to make it scream."

"We don't know what that means."

"Clara knows. So does Piper."

Christopher glanced toward the front, toward Piper. Coffey had taken the passenger seat. The girls were at the head of this ship, no doubt. The men had squandered their turn. Meyer had become an alien figurehead and assisted planetary takeover; Benjamin had managed to get himself killed in a mission gone wrong; Andreus had found a similar fate; Cameron had the key to a machine he didn't know how to find. Except that he might. Maybe that was over, and they'd die without reaching something they knew rather than dying without knowing what they were after.

"My mother is dead."

Christopher didn't know what to say. Her brother was dead, too. And, if the implications were correct, her father might be, too.

"My husband is dead."

Christopher's eyes flicked toward Clara. The girl either didn't know or (and this sounded terrible; it couldn't be true) didn't care. Raj had still been Daddy to her. One of them, anyway.

But Clara, out of all of them, looked the least concerned. The least upset. She looked like she was excited to be going on a road trip. And why not? The girl had never left the city.

Christopher opened his mouth to talk, but only an exhale came out. Before he could try again, the RV's cockpit erupted in shouted orders. His lips stilled and slowly closed, his eyes fixing on something behind Lila's head.

He tried to turn away, but she saw his glance and looked, too. Lila's hair lifted higher, electricity in the air gathering into something furious.

"What?"

But she knew what. So did Grace, Jons, Charlie, and Cameron. Lila slid away from the wall-mounted screen behind her as it sparked and popped, dying a sudden, unexpected death.

"Shit," came a voice from the vehicle's front.

There was a Vellum — just a simple ebook reader — on the shelf back there, too. It popped like popcorn.

The stove's dials, farther back, sprang into small flames. The light above the sink. The lights down the RV's center, snapping to black one by one.

And again from the front: "Shit!"

Cameron rushed forward. He stood between the seats, one hand per headrest. "What is it?"

"It's offline."

"Drive manual!"

"I *am* using manual, Cameron!" Piper's dry voice yelled back. "I'm telling you it's offline!"

"What's offline, if you're using manual?"

"Not working! Offline! I'm sorry if I'm not using the right …" Piper slapped the dashboard with her palm, frustration leaking from every pore. Her hair, along with loose ends from Coffey's own tidy ponytail, was fraying, dancing in the air's mounting static, "the *right term*, Cameron!" She slapped the dash again.

"Let me try."

"I know how to drive!"

"Yes, of course, but there's a—"

The small dashboard clock popped like a wood knot in

a fire. A small rain of sparks sizzled through slots in the dash, around the environmental controls. There was a backup camera screen above the clock. It looked like the Vellum's, as if it had been dropped and someone had poured black dye behind the glass.

Christopher couldn't see anything outside the windows, all of which had been drawn. He couldn't see the city through the windshield from back here either, but he could see the mounting glow outside, turning Piper's, Cameron's, and Coffey's faces bright white. Something happening. Christopher shifted, bringing his hand near the right-side table's edge. A large arc of blue static jumped between his index finger and the metal trim strip, making him jump.

"Get out!" Coffey yelled, turning in her seat. "Get out and run!"

But that was ridiculous. Where could they go? The ships were about to annihilate the city, and at least three or four members of their party seemed convinced it would pack a nuclear punch. They'd seen cities hit before. But this time, there were four motherships. This time, Clara had said they had an intention other than destruction — to elicit a *scream*, whatever that meant. This time would be different.

"Go! Go!"

Coffey stood. She shouted. She waved them out as fast as they would go, practically pushing Christopher to the dirt. But once they were all outside, now on the far side of the RV, the light from … from *whatever* was happening over toward the city … was leaking around the big malfunctioning vehicle's side, and no one knew what to do. The feeling of a mounting charge was so immense, Christopher didn't trust himself to get too close to anyone, let alone touch them. He felt like he could arc untold voltages. Each was a generator in themselves, all hair wanting to stand, the air a soup of rushing electrons dying for ground.

"Run!" Coffey screamed, though they clearly had nowhere to go. They could rush for the shallow ravine where she swung her finger to point, or put heads between their legs to kiss their asses goodbye. They could duck and cover for nothing. At this point, it wasn't about saving anyone. It was degrees of destruction, loss, and pain.

Christopher, all too willing to be led if anyone cared to guide him, turned with the others.

But he couldn't see the ravine because there was a shuttle directly in front of them, hovering in poisonous silence, arcs of blue lightning dancing between the ground and its gleaming chrome surface.

Chapter Eighty-Nine

THE SHUTTLE DIDN'T PRECISELY open. It was more that its front, in a door like arch, fell away and was siphoned back into the edges. The craft settled on the grass. Its aperture was darker than it should seem — about the size of an 18-wheeler's trailer, rounded out. Plenty of room to enter, if she'd been dumb enough to do so.

But Coffey, who'd been leading the charge from the ship, merely lowered her hand. They should go around. They shouldn't change their plans. It wanted to settle and land? Fine. Maybe it was malfunctioning as badly as the RV, and they could still flee.

"We could go inside."

Piper didn't understand why she couldn't *see* inside. It was as if the ship had an invisible curtain. It was large, but not *that* large. The motherships were shining a charged spotlight over everything, including the shuttle's doorway.

"No." She couldn't say why.

Something emerged and took her by the arm: *Meyer.*

"Hurry, Piper," he said. "Get inside."

Piper shook him off. She backed up a step then two. It

was her husband, all right. But she felt upside-down, seeing him here. It was wrong in a precise and jarring way.

Trust me, he said. But this time, he didn't *say* it at all.

Meyer was dressed like always. To the nines. In his fine, bespoke viceroy's suit, dark fabric, starched white shirt underneath, red tie and collar buttoned all the way to his strong neck. His dark hair was neatly combed, his green eyes hard, a ghost of stubble on his strong jaw. His cuffs were even perfect as he reached for her. He was the same man she'd seen every day in the mansion — and, honestly, most days before the Astrals' arrival. But the perfection of his dress, here and now, was in itself a problem.

We've had this talk before, Piper. You know I'd do anything to protect you. To protect all of us.

Coffey looked from Piper to Meyer. She seemed to realize something was happening between them beyond the static-filled silence, but her expression was decisive. The energy behind them continued to swell — enough, Piper thought, that they might all get sunburns. For Coffey, the decision was between fat and fire: the least of evils, if only by a sliver.

"Get the hell inside! Hurry!" Coffey demanded, now shoving.

"No."

Trust me, Piper.

"What are you waiting for? It's going to go off any second!"

Piper shook her head. Cameron came up beside her.

"It's not him, is it?" he asked.

And Meyer sent her images, as he had in her distant memory. She saw Trevor. She saw Lila. She saw something else, more like an emotion than anything real: *him*, not as a self-image but as something worth saving. As if he saw himself from the outside and wanted to protect *that* strange person, too.

I don't have time to explain. You have to trust me. You have to feel me.

"No."

Coffey was looking over with her mouth open. She looked like she wanted to punch them. Each beat of Piper's heart felt like a countdown: one second, two seconds, three seconds closer to destruction. If they stayed here, they'd fry.

But this wasn't Meyer Dempsey.

Coffey tried to move forward. To grab Charlie, who grabbed Lila, who already had hold of Clara. But Meyer continued to block the doorway as seconds disappeared, locking eyes with Piper, trying to convince her of a lie. Or a half lie. It was so hard to tell, so hard to recall.

"Trust me," he repeated.

"No. We'll stay here. I don't trust *you* at all."

"Then trust *me*," said a new voice.

A man with sunken cheeks and a long beard appeared at Meyer's side. In many ways, he was the first man's opposite. Where Meyer was polished, the newcomer was disheveled. Where Meyer looked strong, the new man looked weak. He wore a threadbare white robe, his cheeks sunken, color pale and waxy.

But the eyes. His piercing green eyes were the same.

"Get on the ship, Piper," the newcomer ordered.

He was Meyer Dempsey, too.

Chapter Ninety

MEYER PINCHED HIMSELF OFF.

It was more of an intellectual construct than anything he could precisely recall or even conceive, but he believed the other part of himself (the other Meyer, the *real* Meyer, the *donor*, to use the Astral term) when he said that there had been yet *another* Meyer Dempsey between the two of them. He believed that he, himself, had once held a Titan's white body and had been connected more fully to the Astral collective.

He believed it, but it was hard to feel. Hard to internalize and accept. Because he was Meyer Dempsey, after all. Except that the proof was right in front of him in this frail human man: He wasn't the real Meyer. The man in the robe was the true Meyer, and he — whatever the hell he should call himself, be it Titan or what — was the copy.

"I can hear you," said the real Meyer Dempsey.

The being who intellectually knew he was a copy but was unable to fathom it said, "I'm pinching myself off." He stood taller in the drive circle. He lifted the shuttle, watching the city shrink through the craft's semi-translucent skin.

"I can still hear you."

"Divinity feels we are connected. That means you will probably always hear me."

"Of course we're connected. You've sucked my memories like blood."

They locked eyes. They'd had this argument many times already. The quarrel usually required no speech. They shared the same thoughts up until the moment Divinity had taken the Titan he used to be and bled Meyer Dempsey's essence into him. Since then, they'd lived separate lives, but it had barely been a week. The real Meyer didn't remember meeting with Andreus or squaring off with Heather, who hadn't believed he was back from the dead. He did know about Trevor, and almost certainly about his ex-wife. Conveying those thoughts hadn't required words. It was simply understood. Sorrow, regret, and rage flowed against the usual order, this time backwashing from recipient to donor. They didn't need words to argue, and they shared the same obstinance, that petulant insistence on getting their way. Real Meyer knew it wasn't Fake Meyer's fault that he'd been created. He supposed he'd volunteered, but the Astral collective now struck him as bees in a hive with a singular mind. Now that he was more or less human, he couldn't believe it had once been appealing. Especially given what seemed to be happening in the collective now. Especially since the Pall.

"Never mind," said the man in the robe. And, unspoken: *Maybe it's good that there's two of us. Twice the insistence for the same desires.* And at that, he felt his not-quite-human lips smile.

The shuttle rose. It avoided the motherships, knowing the collective wouldn't follow. The weapon was engaged.

Seeing into Divinity wasn't hard — a classic case of the hunter underestimating its prey. Of course he could still feel part of the collective, even after being pinched off from it. Even Piper seemed to feel it, and Real Meyer had told him that she'd only been on the mothership for one short trip. But once you dipped your toe, the ability seemed to stay with you.

He could sense the others, but they assumed he couldn't. They also seemed to have thought him dead, given the confusing data he'd sent back before freeing his doppelgänger — or progenitor, if he admitted the truth. And with Heaven's Veil soon to be ashes, it hardly mattered. There would be eight capitals. Eight viceroys. Meyer Dempsey could be dead. Both of him could be dead and gone and out of their hair, if they'd had any.

"They don't understand."

Real Meyer looked at the others: Piper, Christopher, Lila, Clara, Cameron Bannister, Malcolm Jons, a man who might be from Moab with a teen girl, plus a strong-looking woman who must be Andreus's lieutenant, in a loose huddle on the shuttle's other side.

"Would *you?*"

He shook his head. "I guess not. But I'm still Meyer Dempsey."

"So am I."

"I look the part."

"Then I guess we're equals."

But looking at the huddle, it was obvious that wasn't true. Neither was precisely Meyer to them. The man steering the shuttle on the circle of light — moving them *away* from danger, Piper's doubts notwithstanding — looked like the Meyer they'd always known, though clearly he wasn't. The frail-seeming human, who would take time to re-feed and recover his strength, looked nothing like Meyer. Nobody won. Not yet.

"Why aren't you driving us away?" Human Meyer asked. "The motherships might see us."

"The motherships are occupied."

"Shuttles then."

He said nothing in reply. The original Meyer Dempsey had part of the collective just as Piper had part of the collective, but he was still human. Right now, the swarm's attention was tuned to the signal. He could buzz around the ships, shooting them from the sky as they'd helped blow a tunnel for Cameron and the others. If they'd had another shuttle, he could plant another bomb. They'd never care. Their alien ears were all waiting for the scream.

"You know where it is. Clara has known for a while now. And Cameron has the name."

"Shh."

"Why are we staying? Why aren't we crossing the ocean?"

The charge reached critical. The beam lanced down, filling the city. From high inside the shuttle, there was almost no sound. When the light dissipated, Heaven's Veil was nothing but splintered remains, felled buildings, and canted utility poles. None had survived, and that was the point.

He was cut off from the collective — discarded, like a useless remainder, now that he'd taken on the dangerous mantle of humanity. But he heard the scream same as them. He heard the device from untold miles distant as the outpouring of human agony streamed from Heaven's Veil, recorded now for the ages.

"Did it go?" asked the human.

"It went."

"Will they be able to home in on it immediately?"

"It will take time to triangulate. Human experience is always being summoned to it. This wave was large enough to pinpoint for sure. But we still have our advantage, even if it's a small one."

Human Meyer shook his head in a very Meyer Dempsey way — a way that the new Meyer recognized from his mirror. A gesture that was both dismissive and irritated, conveying scorn at abject idiocy.

"You're wasting time being here," he said. "Let's go."

After an extra moment, he tilted forward in the drive circle, and the shuttle leaped forward — fast but not too fast, in deference to the fragile human bodies inside.

The first Meyer would never understand why he'd wanted to see the city destroyed, to hear the scream as the wretched agony from tens of thousands in tormented pain passed them on its way to the archive.

Part was curiosity, wanting to see if the thing seemed to call from where they imagined it had been hidden.

The other part was human guilt: a desire to savor the great regret over what he'd helped to cause, just as the others had spawned so much pain (both human and inhuman) to him.

Chapter Ninety-One

LILA SENSED the cessation of motion more than she actually felt it. Being in the shuttle did something to her equilibrium — something about the sense of being high in the air in what looked like a bubble from the inside combined with a force that felt like an invisible seat belt. Her fear was making everything worse.

Her father was alive. Maybe. Kind of. Twice.

Lila didn't know how to feel about that. Mostly, she felt afraid, and assumed it would be that way for a while.

When the shuttle slowed and then began to descend, Lila wondered if they'd reached their destination. Despite the confines and the situation's general oddity, Clara seemed to have already adjusted. She kept assuring her mother that there *was* a destination, that they were on their way, and that there was hope after all. She'd been skipping around the ship. Hugging Grandpa Meyer: the sunken-faced man she'd never met but whom she recognized as kin immediately. And she hugged the apparent obvious Meyer as well: the man who'd shared her home, but who'd never, it seemed, actually been Lila's father. Cameron was the only person to leave their human pile. He was standing by the well-dressed Meyer now, acting like they were in a business meeting.

But there was no mountain where they descended, and Clara and Cameron had both mentioned one. Lila had been spacing out, letting her mind go away whenever it wanted, trying not to consider the losses she could barely accept: Trevor, her mother, even Raj. Her husband hadn't been all bad. She'd loved him, once.

But not now. She couldn't handle any of that now.

They seemed to have been slowly moving away, the two Meyers and Cameron discussing topics unknown. And now here they were, slowly coming down, *not* across the sea, *not* seemingly where Clara had indicated.

"There," Cameron said, pointing through the shuttle's floor near the edge.

Lila looked where he was pointing. She saw a long canyon. A short cliff. And, as they came closer, what looked like a demolished building, like a scattered pile of charred matchsticks when seen from high above.

The steering Meyer moved his hands. Leaned slightly. The shuttle came lower.

"What are we doing?" Lila whispered to Christopher. He shook his head.

"By the cliff?" said standing Meyer.

"The arch. Do you see it?"

"There?"

"They knew it was here. The motherships knew; they came right to it. How can *you* not know there's a money pit on this land?" Cameron looked at the frail human Meyer Dempsey. "And you. You were in the ship that parked here. For months, hanging over my father's lab like a beehive."

"I was in a cell," said the human.

"And I can't see all they can," said the tall Meyer. "Only bits and pieces, like parts of a dream."

"The pit is under the arch," Cameron said, apparently not caring to inquire further.

The ship lowered.

But whatever the healthy-seeming Meyer didn't know or couldn't see about the Astral collective, it didn't extend to the details of connecting their shuttle to a pit in the ground, beneath the stone arch.

They waited, hovering.

The feeling of static returned as the ship seemed to refuel, drawing energy from its underground depot like a car at an old-time gas station from back before the world ended.

Chapter Ninety-Two

THE REFUELING, such as it was, didn't take long. Five minutes, and it seemed to be finished — or done enough, apparently, to fill the tanks or batteries or whatever it was that would get them where they needed to go. Jeanine wanted to ask. She knew there had been a mothership suckling power from that pit for months when the Moab ranch had been whole, and that not long ago they'd watched a second do the same, again for a longer time.

Maybe the batteries were bigger on the motherships, or the tanks were deeper. It made sense. But she couldn't shake the feeling that their short stop was more about safety than anything else. They couldn't use the pit below what was once Heaven's Veil for obvious reasons ... but maybe this pit, too, would soon be occupied by massive ships suckling power. Charging up for whatever was coming, now that they'd be able to find Thor's Hammer, too.

The ship slowly backed away from the arch. Then Piper Dempsey said, "Wait."

The ship ceased. Piper stood. She walked toward the

thing's curved outer wall, placing her hands against what looked like lightly fogged glass. She was facing away from the arch and the money pit, as Cameron called it. On the opposite end of the large ship from the others, looking toward the cliff lab, past the house of debris.

Coffey stood. She crossed the space, skirting wide around the pilot in the middle.

"What?"

"There."

Piper pointed. At nothing.

"*What?*"

"You don't see it?"

The hard, cracked land was bare, nothing but bristly weeds, intermittent and hardy. The particular patch of ground at the end of Piper's finger didn't have a single feature. Yet still, Jeanine felt a chill.

She turned her head slightly.

Defocused her eyes.

And saw the same shadow as before, sitting patiently in the middle of the dry land like a dog awaiting its bone.

"It knew we'd come here to charge," Piper said.

"Good for it." She looked at Meyer — the *standing* Meyer; they'd need a way to tell them apart before the second fattened back up. "Let's go."

"No," said Piper. "Don't."

Coffey watched the thing come closer. The shuttle wasn't far off the ground. If it could leap as well as it could spread across an entire courtyard and fill it with opaque blackness, it could reach them in a single bound. She thought suddenly of the air around them becoming like that again: day turned to night in a blink. Would they be able to fly away? Or could it follow them forever, even off the ground?

"It's waiting for us."

"All the more reason to leave."

"It can't get to us. It's stuck out there."

"Good."

"It's stuck here. In Moab. It ran here. But it has its limits."

"How the hell do *you* know so much?"

Piper looked toward Clara. She gazed back out at the thing, now seemingly able to gaze directly at it, and said, "I can feel it. I can feel how it is. How things are for it now."

She turned to the Meyers.

"Open the door."

Jeanine felt a jolt of panic. She grabbed Piper's wrists as if it were her hands nearing the controls. She looked back at the pilot. Her voice left less sure than she would have liked.

"Go. Fly."

Piper pushed Jeanine away. "It saved us."

"It saved itself."

Piper slowly shook her head, still looking through the shuttle's skin. There were footsteps from the rear as the better-dressed of the Meyers approached on polished loafers.

Jeanine turned to him.

"Don't open the door. It has her mesmerized or something. We can't know what the hell that thing is. We don't have any idea."

Meyer, peering out, said, "I know exactly what it is."

He set his hand to the shuttle's wall beside Piper's. The door boiled away. And the shadow leaped aboard, wafting through the arch like smoke.

Chapter Ninety-Three

THEY SLEPT.

The shuttle didn't move like lightning. It was simple physics, Piper supposed; you put a human in something that accelerates and decelerates in an instant, and the G-forces liquified their skeletons. She had time to watch the land speed by far below, to see the mountains become the plains, reliving their trek from New York in reverse. To watch the breadbasket approach. And as they moved east, she had time to see the sun set in a hurry.

And she had time to sleep, exhausted in spite of it all.

Piper woke when her arm moved seemingly of its own accord — Lila, sliding beside her.

"Hey, kid," Piper said.

"I'm sorry. I just ... I couldn't sleep."

Piper looked around the shuttle. One or both of the Meyers must have been human enough yet to sense the mood and had dimmed the lights. The ship's interior turned out to be as liquid as its doors; after they'd begun moving in earnest something had made walls drip up from the floor to create rooms. There was even a bathroom. It was a hole in the floor that sent waste God knew where, but it worked.

"Where is Clara?"

"I left her with Chris."

"Why aren't *you* with Chris?"

Lila acted like she hadn't heard, and Piper spared her the dignity of asking again. She knew why. Lila had lost half of her family today. Piper was the only mother she had, even though she was an adult herself.

"Has Clara told you where we're going?"

"She's out. Conked. Like a kid, actually. Has Cameron told you?"

Piper shook her head. The air was quiet, America's passage silent below.

"He's out, too. Coffey punched him flat, coming out of the city. Did you know that?"

Lila laughed. The small sound comforted Piper in a way that would have been hard to explain.

"Cameron said Heather also gave him a kiss to give to Meyer, but that he's not planning to deliver it."

Lila looked like she wanted to follow her laugh with a smile, but Piper instantly knew that she shouldn't have said it. Lila sniffed, trying to keep a brave face. But her eyes watered, and she wiped them as if trying to deny her feelings.

After a moment, Lila said, "Piper?"

"Yes?"

"What were you arguing with Jeanine about earlier? At the door? It sounded like you wanted to let something in with us, but she didn't."

"You couldn't see it?"

Lila shook her head against Piper's chest.

"It's like a shadow. It takes an eye trick to see it." She sighed. "I only know that we need it, that it needs us, and that it's been a friend. I don't know what it is. But Meyer does. He calls it a Pall, and it seems to be part of him. Something he brought to the collective that they either didn't expect or didn't know how to deal with. Something, maybe, that they forced out like pus from a wound. At least that's the feeling I get from Meyer."

"*Which* Meyer?"

Piper chuckled. "*Meyer* Meyer. Charlie just calls the other one Anomaly."

"Catchy name."

"Mmm."

"Clara says he wants his own name. Because he's not really my dad, even though he has all his memories. He's … something else."

"What name?"

"Clara says she likes Kindred."

"Hmm, sounds like Clara. But I'm not sure if I can get used to calling him that. But I guess it's better than having two Meyers. Or two husbands."

Piper considered things through a moment of quiet. Even setting aside her past with Cameron, did she now have two husbands? Would she make love to the man Meyer had always been to welcome him tearfully home, or hold allegiance to the copy who didn't seem to realize until recently that he even *was* a copy? The knots felt tangled, apt to snag.

The quiet beat continued. Although Piper was beginning to realize that there was a sound after all. A faint hum, like unearthly engines.

"So we just go? Wherever Cameron says?"

Piper looked down. Brushed a sheaf of dark hair away from her forehead.

"And where Clara says. I think they share something, Cameron and Clara. Cameron thinks she's the reason we went to Heaven's Veil, even though we thought it was for something else. He thinks we were supposed to get Clara. She was calling him, maybe."

"Why?"

"So she could help him find what he needed inside his own head. She helped him figure out where this 'Thor's Hammer' weapon was, anyway."

"It's not a weapon."

Piper and Lila both looked up. Charlie was standing in the doorway, still dressed as if for a day at the unfashionable office.

Piper felt her brow wrinkle. "What?"

"I talked to Meyer. Both of them. I'm not eager to believe anything they say, but what they told me fits Benjamin's data. Things that have been bothering me as I've been trying to puzzle out what he left in Moab. He was definitely onto something, and it's corroborated by a lot of ancient aliens theory. It all fits, now that I've heard what they have to say. And I believe it. Enough to bank on."

Piper looked at Lila. They both looked at Charlie.

"So what is Thor's Hammer if it isn't a weapon?" Piper asked.

"I believe it's the Ark of the Covenant, and I think it contains an archive, designed for our judgment."

What to read next

What they have lost, we must find.

The resistance has nearly been wiped out, its numbers reduced to a scant fraction of what they once were. Meyer has fallen. With hope nearly a memory, something must turn the tide of war.

Start reading Judgment today!

A Quick Favor...

If you enjoyed this book, please take a moment to write a short review on your favorite online bookstore so other readers can enjoy it, too.

Thanks so much!

Johnny and Avery

About the Authors

Avery Blake doesn't want you to know where she lives, or what she does. She travels the world, moving from place to place quickly to ensure she can't be tracked. It's safer that way.

When she's not looking over her shoulder, you can find her in the corner of a cafe, facing the exit, typing as fast as she can.

~

Johnny B. Truant is co-owner of the Sterling & Stone Story Studio, an IP powerhouse focusing on books and adaptations for film and television. It's the best job in the world, and he spends his days creating cool stuff with partners Sean Platt and David W. Wright, as well as more than 20 gifted storytellers.

Johnny is the bestselling author of over 100 books under various pen names, including the Fat Vampire and Invasion series. On the nonfiction side, he's also co-author of the indie publishing mainstay Write. Publish. Repeat. and co-host of the weekly Story Studio Podcast.

Originally from Ohio, Johnny and his family now live in Austin, Texas, where he's finally surrounded by creative types as weird as he is.

Also By Avery Blake

Also By Johnny B. Truant

The Dead World Series

Dead Zero

Dead City

Dead Nation

Dead Planet

Empty Nest

The Fat Vampire Series

Fat Vampire

Fat Vampire 2: Tastes Like Chicken

Fat Vampire 3: All You Can Eat

Fat Vampire 4: Harder, Better, Fatter, Stronger

Fat Vampire 5: Fatpocaplypse

Fat Vampire 6: Survival of the Fattest

The Fat Vampire Chronicles

The Vampire Maurice

Anarchy and Blood

Vampires in the White City

The Beam Series

The Beam Season One

The Beam Season Two

The Beam Season Three

Robot Proletariat Series

En3my

Robot Proletariat

The Infinite Loop

The Hard Reset

Cascade Failure

Reboot

The Invasion Series

Longshot

Invasion

Contact

Colonization

Annihilation

Judgment

Extinction

Resurrection

The Tomorrow Gene Series

Null Identity

The Tomorrow Gene

The Tomorrow Clone

The Eden Experiment

Stand Alone Novels

Pretty Killer

Pattern Black

Burnout

The Target

The Island

Devil May Care